She was up on  She danced around the red earthenware pots, hid coyly behind one, pulled down a frond as a fan, and whispered, "Me? Oh, sir!" And she glided out, curtsied, and let her hand be kissed. *"Enchanté."*

She closed her eyes, swaying with the tide of her music. She brushed against a plant and opened her eyes to see what she'd run into.

And across the terrace saw a man, masked and tall and watching her.

He was standing on one foot, leaning against the low wall in a rakish stance. The smile beneath the black-feathered mask held gentle mockery. Blue eyes glittered within the black frame—storm-burnt midnight blue.

He strode out from the shadowed wall. Caralisa took an involuntary step back. He became ever more striking, an overwhelming presence, tall, possessed of a feral grace. His clothes were fine, almost entirely black even to his shirt and cravat. He wore a cape carelessly over one shoulder, held by a chain.

"Your Grace . . ." Caralisa hesitated.

"I am only a count."

"My lord."

He inclined an acknowledging bow and suddenly took her hand and held it in a firm sure grip. Then slowly he raised it to his lips, his eyes fixed upon hers. His smile caressed like a private touch, forbidden, dangerous, alluring. "I think this is how it goes," he murmured, then drew her into his arms for a dance.

Advance praise for MASQUE OF THE SWAN:

Stunning, provocative and unforgettable. A unique voice that sings in the reader's mind.

—Connie Rinehold, author of *Unspoken Vows*

Breathtaking, startling . . . compelling and brilliant. You will never forget this book!

—Katherine Kingsley, author of *No Sweeter Heaven*

FOR THE VERY BEST IN ROMANCE—
DENISE LITTLE PRESENTS!

AMBER, SING SOFTLY   (0038, $4.99)
by Joan Elliott Pickart

Astonished to find a wounded gun-slinger on her doorstep, Amber Prescott can't decide whether to take him in or put him out of his misery. Since this lonely frontierswoman can't deny her longing to have a man of her own, who nurses him back to health, while savoring the glorious possibilities of the situation. But what Amber doesn't realize is that this strong, handsome man is full of surprises!

A DEEPER MAGIC   (0039, $4.99)
by Jillian Hunter

From the moment wealthy Margaret Rose and struggling physician Ian MacNeill meet, they are swept away in an adventure that takes them from the haunted land of Aberdeen to a primitive, faraway island—and into a world of danger and irresistible desire. Amid the clash of ancient magic and new science Margaret and Ian find themselves falling helplessly in love.

SWEET AMY JANE   (0050, $4.99)
by Anna Eberhardt

Her horoscope warned her she'd be dealing with the wrong sort of man. And private eye Amy Jane Chadwick was used to dealing with the wrong kind of man, due to her profession. But nothing prepared her for the gorgeously handsome Max, a former professional athlete who is being stalked by an obsessive fan. And from the moment they meet, sparks fly and danger follows!

MORE THAN MAGIC   (0049, $4.99)
by Olga Bicos

This classic romance is a thrilling tale of two adventurers who set out for the wilds of the Arizona territory in the year 1878. Seeking treasure, an archaeologist and an astronomer find the greatest prize of all—love.

Available wherever paperbacks are sold, or order direct from the Publisher. Send cover price plus 50¢ per copy for mailing and handling Penguin USA, P.O. Box 999, c/o Dept. 17109, Bergenfield, NJ 07621. Residents of New York and Tennessee must include sales tax. DO NOT SEND CASH.

MASQUE OF THE SWAN

REBECCA ASHE

PINNACLE BOOKS
KENSINGTON PUBLISHING CORP.

PINNACLE BOOKS are published by

Kensington Publishing Corp.
850 Third Avenue
New York, NY 10022

Copyright © 1996 by Rebecca Ashe

All rights reserved. No part of this book may be reproduced
in any form or by any means without the prior written consent
of the Publisher, excepting brief quotes used in reviews.

If you purchased this book without a cover, you should be
aware that this book is stolen property. It was reported as "un-
sold and destroyed" to the Publisher and neither the Author
nor the Publisher has received any payment for this "stripped
book."

Pinnacle and the P logo Reg. U.S. Pat. & TM Off.

First Printing: January, 1996

Printed in the United States of America

Prologue

A man and a maid stole away from their sleeping house-holds and came to stand on opposite banks of the river.

Inky clouds edged in silver lace ghosted across the face of a bright gibbous moon. By its spectral light the young man glimpsed the armored shapes of soldiers on the road.

His father had posted men on all the bridges and at all the ferries, and had forbid all the small boat owners, on pain of death, to give passage to him or to his love.

The river stretched out before him like undulant black green glass, running deep, swollen, and cold with spring melt fed from the high hills, and so wide he could not see his love on the far bank, even though there was a moon. No doubt she was hiding, and he was glad that he could not see her; neither then could his father's men.

This morning would be her wedding day. His father had hired a Rhinish baron to take her to wife; and her father had given his word to it; and she, being no one, had no say in it.

Pale glint of polished iron winked from the bridge's stone arch. Sounds carried with unearthly clarity—a clink of spurs on stone cobbles, the snort and light jingling of a warhorse shaking its headstall.

The young man made his way down the reedy embank-ment. He moved with a self-assured walk that was nearly a swagger even in stealth. He came to the water's edge, and there he stripped. Moonlight bathed his skin in a cool blue wash. His muscles rippled with his motions. His chest bore the track of a sword slash gained in honorable service. He carried the scar like a medal over his heart.

He stowed his pack and his clothing in the tall grass and lifted his head to listen. Late spring breeze ruffled his dark hair. The ends of it grazed his wide shoulders.

He stood naked as a young god, his body smooth and shining, until the first touch of water raised his skin all over like a plucked fowl. He waded into the reeds, and out past them to deep water. Cold wrapped round him like a shroud. He pushed himself away from the shore and swam toward the opposite bank.

The river's current seemed to fold in on itself as the spirits that dwelled below beckoned him down, while the heavy force of the great moving mass swept him resolutely sideways. He kept on swimming as if in a nightmare—stroke and stroke and never seemed to draw nearer to the other side.

After a slow eternity, the far bank loomed as a welcome wall of darkness after the shining field of green glass. Heartened, he felt his strength redoubled, and he lunged for shore. He grasped weeds and mud, and pulled himself up gasping to the shallows.

He climbed out, his teeth clattering in his head loud as hoofbeats. The mild air bit like winter knives on his bare wet skin. He did not know how far off course he'd drifted. He had not been able to see much.

And he could not see *her*.

He squinted, saw nothing at first, then spied a flash of moonlight jouncing on a stray lock of golden hair spilled from a black hood.

And suddenly she was with him, surrounding him with a woolen cloak and her arms, and a kiss. Her lips were made of fire, pressed against his. His must have felt like death, numb and rubbery cold. He felt her shiver.

She had brought a flask filled with tea, still hot, and she

pressed it into his shaking hands. He drank, felt warmth spreading through him.

They scarcely heard the light footfalls—it was more the whisper of hems of long cloaks brushing on the grass—and the two shrank into the reeds and stayed motionless until the patrol passed.

The guardsmen were looking for any small boat that might have been left unattended on the water. They would not be looking for swimmers. No one would be so foolhardy as to try to cross Larissa's river that way.

When the stars had crept across the sky, and the moon was winking in and out, there was no more time to spare. She undressed, her motions furtive and uncertain in modesty.

She turned to him shyly, her hair falling round her like a veil, bright golden as an autumn lea, her cerulean eyes wide and frightened. He led her down into the chill water. As she descended, her hair floated up around her, darkened from the color of sunshine to the drab of the grave. She could not swim. He circled an arm gently round her. She let herself lose contact with the ground, trusting him.

The current felt faster now, and she, the lightest of creatures, weighted his progress like an anchor. The top of her head shone bright as a beacon, but he hadn't the heart to dampen it. She was already trembling almost too hard to hold.

Every stroke seemed only another step sideways. The deep current had hold of her and tugged downward.

The inner bank looked no closer, and he was too spent even to shiver, in the grip of an all-consuming languor that sapped strength and will and life.

He felt her slipping from him, and he fought off the benumbing cloud that was closing round his mind.

In their plans Death had been lightly nodded to, to be accepted if it came. Now it was here, demanding its due, and not to be put off. The young man changed his mind. He would go, but he was not willing to give her over to the dark realm.

He saw her eyes—their whites huge and round circling the irises, their blue nearly eclipsed in black, dilated with fear— saw the world and all that was lovely in it in her eyes.

He called on heaven, and then in desperation, on anyone who could hear, to a guard, to any power, *"Not for me, for my lady!"*

Only the river seemed to hear, clinging fast. Then he turned from God altogether and called on a local spirit, the one who dwelled on the Larissan Heights. The Heights were closer than heaven and perhaps not so cold or deaf.

A sudden blot passed over the moon with the sound of great wings and the splash of a great black swan skidding onto the water.

A dark feathery shape appeared next to the floundering pair, seeming to grow even as it neared, a swan of impossible size, big enough to hold her.

The young man lifted his lady toward it. Her arms clasped round its black glossy neck and he helped her onto its broad back. The swan sank low under the weight, its body nearly submerged, with her riding at the waterline. Its wings arched over her like a coverlet.

With a weary hand the young man grasped a handful of tail feathers and the swan carried them both with powerful strokes to the inner shore.

When mud swirled beneath them, the young man righted himself and climbed up among the reeds. He gathered up his lady into his arms and waded to higher ground. The swan turned away sharply, gave a great splash at the lovers, a discordant honk, and it sailed away, shaking out its ruffled feathers. Moonlight made a silver-green arrowhead of its parting wake. Then with a loud quick beating of wings, it lifted from the water; droplets shimmered down like diamonds. It soared away to the craggy black ruin silhouetted on the night sky, the forbidding lordly Heights.

And deeper into the night the slumbering quiet split to the peal of abbey bells.

* * *

The Old Prince in his palace woke, sat up rigid and quaking. Bells. Bells.

He pulled off his silk night cap, as if that would help him to hear. His sleep-muddled thoughts traveled first from *Who is ringing bells at this hour?* to *Who is ringing those bells at all?*

They were not the cathedral bells that were singing. They were the old *abbey* bells, christened St. Agnes and St. John. Those bells had been silent for thirty years. The bells he had not heard since his wedding day.

Their ringing meant only one thing.

I have been defied.

Who could have aided them? When he had made certain that no power on earth would dare abet them.

He lifted the circle crown from his nightstand. It trembled in his freckled hands. *That I should pass this on with such bitterness.* He felt suddenly very old.

He rose, climbed down the three steps from his high bed, and padded in his nightshirt across the silk carpet. He pushed back the great blue velvet curtains at his tall windows, and looked out into the traitorous night.

From his tower window he could see a light where there should be no light. High. Too high. Above even the cathedral's spire.

The Heights.

There were lamps burning in the deserted Heights.

The curtains shook in his grasp, rattling the rings as if he would tear them down. *Damn you. Damn you—but you are damned already, fiend that you are.*

There was nothing to be done now, for all Larissa had heard the bells.

One

Larissa was built on the foundation of a forgotten people. Some of its stones whispered of great age, and Caralisa had been told that a wise traveler spoke a blessing to the moss-covered granite when she recognized ancient markings on it, and asked permission to pass this way. No one could tell her of anything definite that had befallen one who neglected politeness, but it did not do to trouble the sleep of ancient gods.

She had taken a shortcut, which had turned into the long way around, and found herself on a weed-choked path running along the steep bank under the Rue de Temps. The carved stones of which she had been warned were everywhere here, veiled in layers of lichens and vine root, and Caralisa murmured as she went, "Hello. Hello. May I go this way?"

The day was sunny and there was nothing menacing about them now, the old stones. The place seemed only wild and enchanted and secret. And behind a screen of weeds clogged with ivy and thyme, she actually found a door, a wooden one with a black encrusted iron keyhole and black ring. She gave the ring an ineffectual tug. Nothing happened, and because it seemed to lead only into the solid rock face, she let it be. She gathered in her skirts against the brambles, and wandered on in search of the end of her shortcut.

The early folk had been clever engineers. To them belonged the dam, the stone bridges, and the canals of Larissa.

Only later, in recorded history, had come the grand structures of the builder kings. To them belonged Larissa's landmarks, the opera house, the colleges of the université, and all the summer palaces of the many crowned heads of the several kingdoms which had at one time or another claimed Larissa as their own, for the city lay on the crossroads to everywhere. The builder kings had given Larissa its mosaic of styles and its four languages.

When the tiny principality of Montagne asserted its self-sovereignty, naming its single city Larissa as its capital, then was built the cathedral and the royal residence of Montagne's sovereign Prince, whose spires faced the Heights.

One could ride across Montagne in a day—and only that long if one waited for a ferry across the great wide river which looped around the capital city and hugged it to the mountainside.

The town was named Larissa for the citadel, the *larissa,* which had lorded, once upon a time, above the huddled rooftops of the lower city. The high citadel had been erected in the time of the builder kings, but later when the Earth had shrugged and its bottom had fallen away, one could see traces of an earlier hand in the bared foundation stones.

Remnants of the top of the citadel still clung high on the cliff face. Whole rooms persisted up there intact, a strange and ancient bastion, but only birds, bats, angels, and fiends could make their way up there now.

They would have a breathtaking view, probably taking in all of Montagne end to end, with Larissa as the crown jewel on the deep green river which nearly circled it like a neck-lace, or a moat. The town was all alight in the High Season when Larissa was at its most cultured and most cruel. Laris-san festivals dazzled with color and light, and its masques were infamous. Larissa was a place where fashionable people the world over came to get away from who they were, to experience the scent of danger and spice of fear, to flirt with darkness and dishonor and then go home. As it was said:

Larissa doesn't tell. The ribald masques centered around the oldest and most elegant and most dangerous quarter—the plaza underneath the inaccessible Heights. Only fitting, said the church, as that place was closer to the powers of hell.

Larissa, a town that took its sin as seriously as its devotion, had honed hypocrisy to a fine art and boasted the tallest, most magnificent cathedral of all the lands around. The cathedral was the highest building in Larissa unless you counted the ruins on the Heights.

From time to time men had tried to bring down what remained of the citadel—before it could fall down of its own accord onto the busy plaza—but attempts met with failure every time—simple failure at best, more often with tragedy, and the Heights came to be known as haunted.

Doing away with the Heights was not as easy as the speaking of it. No one could be hired now even to try. The church kept up its efforts on its own, until the Young Prince, Maximillian, upon coming to the throne, called off all attempts altogether.

Caralisa's shortcut brought her directly under the citadel, and abruptly ended, the path steeply banked on all sides. Finding herself boxed in, she looked straight up into the high ruin's torn underside, dangling over her like roots of a great elm which had been torn up in a storm, the gnarled tangle of its underpinnings still gripping clods of earth from where it had lost its hold. But instead of the tree falling here, the earth had fallen. Caralisa shaded her eyes from the sunshine and squinted into the dim shadowed recesses. Starlings quarreled and chattered in the overhangs.

From here there was nowhere for Caralisa to go except back the way she had come, or to climb up over the embankment.

Caralisa, who never liked to backtrack, lifted her skirts and picked her way through the brambles and thistles, up the steep bluff to the woven stones of a civilized path.

Caralisa had never been to this place but knew on first

sight where she was—a wide open square busy with many people, street performers, and vendors, amid a kaleidoscope of bright globes on the dormant gaslights, red and ochre cobbles, intricate mosaic roofs, and red and white awnings over open air tables where men and women sat drinking. Seven monumental arches gave access from seven wide avenues, the enameled bricks a different hue on each arch: Gold, Amber, Emerald, Black, Red, Royal, and White. The palace's tower soared high behind the Royal Arch on one side, squared off against the Heights looming on the other.

She was in the plaza. This was definitely out of bounds. Before this moment she could pretend that she did not know where she was—she had not been *exactly* on the Rue de Temps. But she knew where she was now, and this place was categorically off-limits, and she ran as if the sin of it would settle on her out of the air and cling like perfume, for the plaza was enormously wicked.

Sophisticated eyes followed the dash of the common girl across the painted stones, guessing she had stolen something. No one was in pursuit, so she must have got away with it. Either that or she'd had a roll in the grass, for there were burrs on her skirts and she was, for all her lack of decent clothes, a much-needed coif, or any makeup, rather pretty—remarkably pretty in fact if one looked past the shabby attire.

She wore a plain frock of faded pink, high-waisted with full skirts hemmed just above her ankles, giving glimpses of a plain white chemise underneath edged with one poor row of tatting. It left her shapely calves bare, thorn-scratched as a peasant. Her low-heeled slippers were gray and worn. She clutched round her a paisley shawl when anyone with any fashion sense wore a long wide scarf, and it did not match her bonnet in any case.

Even so, she was a beautiful girl, nearly a woman. Caralisa was graced with a sweet face and wide lovely eyes of clear hyacinthine blue. Creamy skin held a comely pink blush. Her cheeks rounded over high bones, and together with a delicately rounded brow and dainty chin, gave her an innocent allure. Her lips were very full with a luscious pouting wanton shape and demure color of pale shell pink. And then there was her hair, a shockingly glorious tumble of brilliant red.

But then all that, and her budding figure's youthful curves, were only a common girl's fleeting glimmer of raw beauty. Those who paid for their looks could temper their envy in knowing that such wild beauties never flowered but withered straight from the exquisite bud.

Caralisa did not stop running until she came to the familiar territory of the pond behind the museum. Petulant students of the université lolled in the spring sweet grass to sleep in the sunlight or to pursue art or dalliance. Weeping willows trailed long fronds in the water. Frogs sang, light-toned spring peepers in chorus with the deep basso *currok!* of the bullfrogs.

Caralisa leaned over to look into the water, saw reflected back her angelic face framed in the loose tresses of her red hair, bright as copper but a richer hue and gossamer fine.

She had gathered some wild roses under the Rue de Temps and she tossed their petals onto the water, pink ships upon the pond's ocean, which ran aground in the shoals of waxy petaled water lilies.

He loves me. He loves me not, she thought, not sure to whom she referred. Young and sheltered, Caralisa hadn't experience enough even to form a decent dream. Her phantom lover was a blur.

She became aware of splashes nearing her. A monk was throwing stones, trying to drive a black swan toward a snare.

She tiptoed toward him. He sighted her and directed her with a jabbing stubby finger and hushed scratchy voice, "Over there. Over there and wave your arms."

Caralisa held on to her flowers with both hands. "What are you doing?"

"Trying to catch it."

Caralisa glanced at the swan. It was black, with a red beak and wary red eye.

"What for?"

"To kill it." The monk huffed and puffed, hiked up his plain brown robes, and tucked up his rosary into his hemp belt. His bared stocky legs were pallid, the dark hairs stark on blue-white skin. His face was red and his shaved dome glistened with exertion above a wreath of dark hair. "It's a demon."

"Oh! But it's so pretty."

"Looks like an angel of light. Don't they say so!" He grunted, held out the noose so far he seemed about to tip over.

"You couldn't be mistaken?" her voice wobbled.

"No." He grunted. "He uses it, you know. It flies around and sees everything."

"Who does?"

"Him. It's a witch's familiar. Monsignor saw it on the rectory spying on him. What's a swan got business perched on a rectory? Devil's work. Ah!"

A sudden violent splashing erupted from the water. The taut trap wire broke the surface, the swan slapping madly with its black wings. The friar pitched in with a huge wave. Both swan and monk disappeared under the churning brown, kicking up water lilies, root end first. Amid the thrashing, the monk's head rose up, his sparse wreath of hair plastered down. He sputtered and gasped, clinging to his pole. The swan pummeled him with strong wingbeats. The monk pulled it in, hand over hand on the pole, till he got hold of its neck, but that was like trying to grip a serpent. Wings dealt him wild frantic blows. Black feathers flew. Talons of its black webbed feet scratched. Its red angry beak struck and drew blood from the monk's bald pate. The monk wrung the neck that twisted and coiled with his wrenching. Then, at once, a high upturned squawk ended the wild honking.

There was a sudden momentary silence, then the limp splash of the body dropping.

Huffing and beet-faced, the friar dragged the swan by the neck onto the shore. His sodden robes weighed heavily on his stout body so he could barely stand.

He looked over his prize. "Looks like a Christmas goose," he said between breaths. "Can you cook these things?"

Caralisa's face was white, her blue eyes wide and watery. Pink lips fell slack in a horrified stare. She shook her head, dumbly. Wilted lovelocks quivered at her ears.

She clutched her paisley shawl to her, twisting her fingers in it beneath her chin, as she stared at the broken bird, so graceful a moment before. Its feathers canted askew, black feet taking on the rigidity of a dead thing. The red eye stayed open, red beak parted.

"Last of this brute," said the monk. He tried to heave it over his shoulder, misjudged the weight, and it rolled off the other round shoulder and fell back down in front of him. He ended up dragging the bird away.

Caralisa stared at the water, at the remaining beautiful white swans with their necks arched over their reflections to form a broken heart when one touched its own image.

She looked down, her own reflection scattered by the heavy drops of her tears.

Then from under the lilacs moved a shadow that was not a shadow, huge wings held up like sails.

Caralisa lost her grip on her shawl, her hands gone slack.

A giant black swan, solid midnight even to its beak and onyx eyes, slipped into the sunlight. It dwarfed the other swans as they did the little ducks. Broad wings fanned over its back, wide feathertips spreading, petaled like a water lily or an opulent fan, to catch the breezes. It glided majestically across the blue water, a lyrical curve to its long fluid neck, haughty, even with its glossy head bowed. Peacocks were not half so proud, nor a tenth so graceful.

Caralisa glanced in the direction the monk had gone, but

he was well away. And she was not about to call him back
and tell him that he had made a mistake.

Caralisa was back on Elm Tree Close by vespers when
they shut the gates and cloistered the girls. After that she
was permitted outside only as far as the roof garden, a terrace
that had been planted above the first-floor parlor, accessed
by French doors from the second-floor hall—or as Caralisa
often went, through the tall narrow windows of the bedroom
she shared with Viola.

The terrace was planted with ivy and climbing flowers,
and hemmed by a low extension of the wall which rose like
a battlement. Young girls were safe at Madame Gerhold's
house.

Caralisa's parents were gone. Her godparents had never
expected actually to have the child on their hands. Suddenly
faced with the task of raising Caralisa, they had put her in
the girls' boardinghouse in town with their own daughter
Viola.

The first horrid year was behind her. This spring was altogether new, with her waking from a long winter of bitter
desolation and learning to smile again. It was a season of
wonder. Caralisa smoothed her dress close to her chest,
thrilled at the change, so sudden and overdue. If she heard
the story of the ugly duckling one more time, she swore she
would start throwing things. Finally. Finally. Her long lost
waistline had appeared and she had breasts, not voluptuously
huge and lush, but rounded and pretty and definitely there.
And her hair, which had always been strawberry blond, had
turned absolutely and irrevocably red and fine as spun silk.
She felt gloriously pretty. And the others thought so, too.
They would look, double take, and say, "Look at you!"

She was seventeen.

It was past vespers and she was up on the belvedere singing to the cool evening air. Caralisa was always singing, even
without her knowing it, and would have been annoying had
she not such a bell-like voice and endless repertoire of melo-

dies. She danced around the red earthenware pots planted with apricot and rubber trees. She hid coyly behind one, pulled down a frond as a fan, and whispered to a phantom, "Me? Oh, sir!" And she glided out, curtsied, and let her hand be kissed. *"Enchanté,"* she said. And danced with a spectre.

She closed her eyes, swaying with the tide of her music. She brushed against a plant and opened her eyes to see what she'd run into.

And across the terrace saw a man, masked and tall and watching her.

"Oh!" She gathered in her shawl, blushing. "How long have you been there?"

He was standing on one foot, leaning against the low wall in a rakish stance. The smile beneath the black feathered mask held gentle mockery. "I don't know," he said, his voice an intimate masculine baritone that reached deep inside her and resonated within. She felt herself vibrating like a plucked string. "I got rather lost."

He strode out from the shadowed wall. Caralisa took an involuntary step back. He became ever more striking, an overwhelming presence, tall, possessed of a strong feral grace. His clothes were fine, almost entirely in black even to his shirt and cravat. He wore a cape carelessly over one shoulder, held by a chain which ran under his sword arm, leaving it free. His hair, brushed back in short unconfined waves in the fashion of the Young Prince, was utterly black like the mask. Blue eyes glittered within the black frame—storm-burnt midnight blue, blue of a sky in which one might expect lightning. He had high-boned elegantly carved cheeks and a straight handsome nose, if the mask did not lie. The part of his face she could see was very handsome, a strong manly chin without dimples or dents, a firm jaw, and mouth both soft and strong, his lips beautifully full and masculine.

He was dressed in formal habit, black on black, with black satin breeches close fitting and buttoned below the knee, and black riding boots. He looked dynamic standing there, the

sky behind his head the profound blue of new dark before
the stars have become fixed.

The cape came off with a wide sweep, in a motion that
took her breath away. She could see now his taut and slender
form, the width of his shoulders, the breadth of his manly
chest. The satin breeches fit close to his narrow hips and
revealed the bulge of masculine sinew interlaced in his thighs
like woven cable.

He tossed the cape aside for the potted bushes to hold for
him, and extended a black-gloved hand.

"Your Grace . . ." Caralisa hesitated.

"Mademoiselle, I am only a count."

Caralisa mumbled, "My lord."

He inclined an acknowledging bow and suddenly he took
her hand and held it in a firm sure grip. Then slowly he
raised it toward his lips, his eyes fixed upon hers, "I think
this is how it goes," he murmured and lightly grazed his lips
upon the backs of her fingers, then drew her into his arms
for a dance. The way he turned her made her arms fall into
natural position, for she was suddenly there without trying,
one hand in his, the other resting lightly on his strong upper
arm. The sensation of his lips pressed to her fingers lingered,
dizzied her. *Dance.* They were poised to dance. She confessed, "I don't know how, really."

"You have most of it. When you're ready, mademoiselle."

She fumbled for voice, realizing she had just been commanded to sing. All the notes scattered every which way like
chickens back home in the country. She kept looking up at
his face. His lips were soft and seductive and hard and determined. The look in his eyes, the eyes themselves, captivated. Such a startling deep indigo they were nearly violet.
And within them darker etched lines radiated from the center,
changing color toward the smoky rim of the iris. Subtle, com-
plex, beautiful . . . and she realized she'd been gazing into
them for quite some time and he had not moved. Till a brow
arched behind the mask, which fit so close that the mask

stretched and moved with it, and he said, "Well?" She pulled back with a start like a sleepwalker awakened. "I—I got rather lost."

His smile caressed like a private touch, forbidden, dangerous, alluring.

She sang.

And he led her in the dance. She moved stiffly, trying too hard. He murmured in a deep voice, "Mind the toes, mademoiselle. Not that there's enough of you to cause any damage even if you tried, but it's inelegant."

She blushed, stopped singing. "How did you get up here?"

"I climbed the wall."

"Whatever for?"

"I heard angel voices. Voice, rather. It was singular."

"For me? You climbed that wall for me? You must be terribly disappointed."

"You are not what I was looking for."

Caralisa blushed furiously. "Where are you from?"

"Samothrace."

She did not know where that was. It sounded far away. A wistful sigh welled up and escaped, "I should like to see outside the wall. At night."

"Whatever for?"

"I want to see magic. I want to see the dark and secret side of Larissa."

"Do you. Do you really." It was less a question than a comment. He still held her. "Don't fight me." He lifted his chin like an upbeat and she commenced to sing again. He drew her with him and she relaxed enough to let him lead her. She was getting the hang of it and soon was gliding across the roof until she could not sing because she was laughing. The notes tumbled into peals of laughter.

He let go her hand and held both arms around her. She touched his chest. She could feel his heartbeat in her fingertips. Their eyes met and she stopped laughing. His eyes were seeing through her, threatening to engulf her and devour her whole.

A bolt of fear reminded her that she did not know him. She was alone in the dark with a stranger. It was fully night by now. The stars shone in earnest.

Silence had fallen around them and he was not letting her go. She felt the heat of his body close to hers. The breaths deepened in his chest with a virile hunger. She was about to panic and call for help when he released her and drew back into a courtly bow. She curtsied like a wooden puppet.

She glanced in toward the house. A shadow moved on the gently blowing white gauze curtains. Viola. Caralisa whispered, "My lord——" She turned but he was gone. "Wait!"

She met with silence except for singing crickets and the other night voices. She roamed the roof garden. He was not there. She whispered plaintively over the wall into the abyss of night, "I don't know your name . . ."

Caralisa climbed back through the window to her room. Viola looked up; her gray eyes widened and she broke into a grin. She hugged up a pillow and fell across her bed with a conspiratorial growl, "You—are—*glowing!*"

Caralisa swept up her sweaty hair with her forearm behind her neck and piled it on top of her head in an unconsciously sultry moment. "I had a glorious evening."

"What *happened!*"

"Magic. That's all." She pirouetted. "A dangerous man taught me to dance. And he kissed my hand. This hand. *This* hand."

Viola snatched it, gave it a quick inspection for supernatural properties, and let it go. "I shall have it bronzed for you." She crawled over the bed to stand before Caralisa and touched her cheek. "You shall leave a bloody track of hearts behind you. What are you using on your skin?"

"Why? What does it look like?"

"Like satin. What did you use to get rid of those things?"

Caralisa had been plagued with blemishes. Too gradually
to notice when, they had stopped appearing. She gave a quiz-
zical guess, "Age?"

"When did this happen?" said Viola.

"I don't know. Do you think I'm pretty?"

"I shall alert the Greek armada. Will a thousand ships be
enough, do you think?"

Caralisa gave Viola a playful shove. "One dinghy will
more than suffice!"

Viola was, to Caralisa's mind, the most beautiful girl who
had ever lived. Caralisa considered Viola her guardian angel.
Her eyes were beautifully shaped and extraordinarily clear
gray, except when she wore blue; then they were slate. There
was about her an air of subdued merriment, and she always
seemed about to smile at a gentle joke. Her features were so
smooth and refined that she ought to have been a titled lady.
She had a straight aristocratic nose—with a ghost of freckles
across it which she merrily detested. Her hair was an unre-
markable shade of ash brown, which was only fair, for it was
luxuriantly thick, and the color brought out the lightness of
her wonderful eyes.

Caralisa let her own hair tumble down around her arms in
a red cascade and laughed for pure joy. Viola squealed and
fell back on the bed to hug her pillow.

A blond head leaned in the doorway. It was Laurel, attracted by the laughter. "Caralisa? Cara*lisa!*" She advanced
like a lean little cat scenting scandal. "You've a lover, Caralisa!"

"No, no, I swear."

Laurel sang, "You were *with* someone."

"Yes, but—"

"You must tell me or I shall make it up." Laurel plopped
onto Viola's bed and patted out a place for Caralisa to sit.
"Come now," she commanded with her sharp thin voice.
"Every detail."

By then Delia was peering in, her head mostly hidden in a voluminous bonnet, her dark hair boyishly short in the aftermath of a coloring attempt that had gone very wrong. "What's up?"

"Caralisa's young man, I suspect," said Laurel wickedly.

"Caralisa has a young man?" Delia cried.

"Noooo," Caralisa moaned.

"Who were you with, Caralisa?" Laurel asked as Brynna and Megan came in and quickly took seats on Caralisa's bed.

"Caralisa was with someone?" said Brynna.

"Who?" said Megan.

"A count," said Caralisa.

"Ooooo," they chorused

"Who?" each demanded. "Who?"

"Where?" said Delia, more to the point.

"He came over the wall," said Caralisa.

There was a minor stampede toward the garden door. Caralisa called after them, "He's gone now." But they all rushed out nonetheless to make absolutely certain. When they came back in, Megan fell into a sit, plump little hands folded in her skirts between wide thighs. "I don't see how."

"I don't either," said Caralisa.

Megan had been a chubby girl turned buxom. She was a merchant's daughter but she had a figure like a tavern wench, round and ample. She considered the others, with the possible exception of Delia, frightfully skinny, and Laurel a veritable stick. Megan called herself a true redhead. Hers was a ginger frizz which became wild in damp weather, and she had freckles on palest white skin. She had green eyes. When Caralisa's hair had darkened from blond to impudent red, Megan stroked it and said, "No one will believe that's a natural color. Is it?"

Megan was sitting in a troubled pout, glancing out the window where Caralisa's visitor had supposedly come. She repeated, "I don't see how."

"Who *is* he?" Delia pressed.

"I don't have a name," said Caralisa. "He's a count and he's from Samothrace."

Laurel unaccountably laughed. "Samothrace?" she repeated with a lilt, a devilish glint in her blue eyes, mockery on her lips. "The Count of Samothrace?"

"Well, yes, I suppose. Why?"

"There is no such man," said Laurel. "The Count of Samothrace is the name of our local *ghost,* you silly goose. Someone is having you on."

"Yes," Megan added hastily. "He is definitely having you on. If he were of honorable intent, he would have left a card at the door."

"He had no intent at all," said Caralisa. "He heard me singing and he came to look. And we danced."

Delia stifled a shriek.

"You don't know how to dance," said Megan.

"I know," said Caralisa ruefully. "He does."

"Whoever *he* is."

"There *is* a real Count of Samothrace," said Viola uncertainly. "I've heard of him."

"Yes, but no one who could show up on the roof garden!" said Megan. "The count used to live on the Heights. Haunts it now. He's been there for ages."

"What are you calling ages?" Viola challenged.

"A thousand years?" Megan estimated.

"Oh. I guess that qualifies as ages," Viola backed down. "Well, wouldn't this be the *young* Count of Samothrace?"

"I've never heard of any kin. There's only the warlock."

"There's no warlock," said Laurel.

"There certainly is," said Megan. "He always wears a mask because he's quite hideous—"

"Beautiful," Delia broke in. "He wears it because he is too beautiful to behold. Like a siren. He breaks the hearts of young women on the rocks. That's the version I heard."

"How would you know?"

"How would anyone know?"

"What's the difference? Either way you drop dead."

Yes, they all agreed it was lethal to look upon him.

Caralisa offered timidly, "He *was* wearing a mask. It was made of black feathers."

"He could hardly pretend to be the Count of Samothrace without one," said Megan.

"Why was he necessarily pretending?" said Viola. "Why couldn't Caralisa have danced with the Count of Samothrace?"

Laurel was shaking her blond ringlets, her thin lips pressed into wry tolerance, so imperiously that Megan snapped at her, "Oh stop. I know Caralisa didn't dance with the Count of Samothrace, but that doesn't mean there isn't one. Remember when Lord Snowbridge hanged himself? Everyone knows he didn't. It was the count. And when Lady Blaindon drowned? That wasn't an accident and everyone knows it."

Laurel gave a superior smile with a slow wag of her head. "Ghost stories. Lord Snowbridge died of his own hand. The police report, if anyone bothered to read it, says nothing of diabolical agents. My father is an inspector and he has nothing but contempt for such rumors." And so, she let it be known by the haughty set of her pointed chin, had she.

"But everyone's seen him at carnival."

"Oh. No *doubt,*" Laurel said liquidly. "A masked man is terribly easy to spot at carnival!"

The others laughed.

"Brynna?" Laurel turned to her for comment.

Brynna never offered an opinion until she saw which way the wind was blowing. When cornered, she offered something dizzy and far afield with a blink of her brown eyes. She fidgeted with a loose strand of her thick auburn hair and gave a little tisk which signaled she was about to speak. "I don't think a man ought to wear feathers."

After an unbalanced pause, Laurel said, "Brynna, it was just a mask."

"Well, then, how do you kiss him without sneezing?"

Delia turned back to Caralisa. "I know who you really saw."

"You do?" said Caralisa.

"I mean, I know who you mean," said Delia. "I don't *know* him. No one does."

"Who is he?"

"You saw the Count of Samothrace."

"O Delia," Laurel scolded. "Don't delude the child."

"I mean—of course there's no such real man or beast or war-witch, -lock, whatever. At least not one who's lived in the last thousand years. What I mean is that there is a man nowadays who regularly goes by that alias. Don't you read the papers?"

"Not that column."

"It's the only part worth reading," said Delia. "How do you expect to get anywhere if you don't know who is worth knowing?"

Gossip was Larissa's chief export. And Delia was an ardent consumer.

Larissa was a land in which to lose one's self. Aliases were more common than names. Legal business could be conducted under an alias. There was no need of a name in Larissa. Some of the aliases were legitimate sounding and meant to deceive. This one was an obvious phony meant to be spotted as such.

"He's a wealthy man if not a truly titled one," said Delia. "He has a line of credit at the bank of Montagne. Even they don't know his name but his seal is good for limitless funds."

The girls paused, daunted. Few even of the nobility were so wealthy.

"His seal must have given him the idea for the alias. His signet is a swan carved in jet."

The warlock on the Heights was closely associated with the spectre of a black swan.

"Well, that would make it easy to remember," said Laurel.

"Especially if he has a lot of aliases. 'If this is Larissa, I must be the Count of Samothrace.' "

"Is this who I saw?" said Caralisa.

"What did he look like?" said Delia.

Caralisa inhaled to steady herself for the task. "All right. He was tall. This tall." She stood up and raised her arm straight up. The girls gave an appreciative moan. "He was very lean—"

"Skinny?" Megan said with a curled lip which dragged her freckles unpleasantly across her pasty face.

"No. Strong and slender and dynamic. His hair was midnight black. If his face underneath the mask is all that the mask implies, he is wonderfully handsome. The mask seemed to fit closer than a glove—as if it had been put on like an actor puts on a beard with spirit gum. It seemed to fit right next to his skin, but who knows how deep it is." She wondered if the illusion of thinness might not cover some boneless hollow of unspeakable hideousness. She shuddered.

"Masks are meant to obscure, not to reveal," Viola warned gently.

"Never mind that," said Laurel. "Just tell me, could you bruise yourself on his ass?"

Laurel, ever pragmatic, hard, abrupt, and direct to the point, did not believe in love. She believed strongly, however, in lust.

Caralisa flushed. She had tried not to look, but in truth she had. She remembered his buttocks' sinuous flow of hard muscle. "Uh . . . probably."

"Concave cheeks, or convex?"

"Um, let's see, the mask came down to here—"

"Not *those* cheeks." Laurel swatted her. "Round like a girl or dimpled in like a stallion."

Caralisa's face burned. Her city friends talked so scandalously in their private rooms. She was not yet used to it. "In, a little."

Delia joined in this line of inquisition, "How big was his . . . you know."

"Cock," said Laurel.

"I didn't look," said Caralisa.

"You had to."

"I didn't. I couldn't let a man catch me looking at his . . . at him." Heat radiated off her face so she could feel it against her eyes.

"Why not? How else will he know what you want?"

"But I don't!"

"Oh," Laurel said in two descending tones.

"Look how red she is!" said Brynna.

"Your face is clashing with your hair," said Megan.

"She wants him," said Laurel.

"I don't." Caralisa was not even sure what it was they were talking about. She had never seen a naked man, and the precise mechanism of the forbidden act was still a bit unclear. She had seen enough farm animals coupling but surely something was missing there. They couldn't be talking about *that*.

"She's still very young," Delia said aside to Laurel.

Caralisa was no more than a year younger than the oldest of them, who was Viola. Caralisa had merely been the last to bloom.

"How old was he?" said Laurel.

"I don't know."

"Guess."

"Older," said Caralisa.

"When Caralisa says older, she means he's not a boy," Laurel commented to Delia. Then to Caralisa. "Over twenty?"

"Yes."

"Over thirty?"

"Maybe."

"Over forty?"

"I would say not. He was not old, but he seemed very, I don't know, *knowing*."

"Ow," said Laurel with a throaty growl that did not express pain. "Time to move over and let a woman handle this."

"Give him up, Laurel, he doesn't exist, remember?"
Megan chided.

"The man with the big bank account does!" said Laurel.

"What color were his eyes?" Delia asked.

"Blue," said Caralisa. "Extraordinary blue."

"That really might have been who you saw," said Delia.
"No one's seen his face but most everyone agrees about the
eyes. Blue. Blue. Blue. And what do they say? Intense. Mag-
netic. Mesmerizing."

"All of those," said Caralisa.

"What a coup for you," said Delia guardedly.

Megan said, "And what would such a man want with a
dance with our Caralisa?"

"The truly powerful can afford to be kind," said Delia.

"What of the real count?" said Caralisa. "Won't he be
angry with someone using his title? Especially if he is a
warlock."

Laurel gave a cluck of impatience. "You haven't heard a
word. There is no real Count of Samothrace. He's a mythical
mountain built on a semihistorical molehill. How can you
take any of this twaddle seriously?"

"I saw a monk kill a black swan today," said Caralisa.
"He said it was a demon from the Heights. The church is
taking it very seriously."

"It's the church's job to maintain mystery and belief in
things that are not."

Gasps surrounded her. "Laurel! How you blaspheme."

They all stared. Laurel had really overstepped this time
and her confederates were no longer with her, even in jest.

Laurel tossed her head with a laugh and brushed her blond
ringlets behind her angular shoulders. "Go ahead, you little
sheep. The church is a paternalistic institution that makes up
its own rules to keep us under heel. I for one—and maybe
the only—am too smart to put my head in that noose."

She rose and went back to her room, blond ringlets flounc-
ing behind her.

Brynna tisked. "I'm lost. How many men are we talking about?"

"Three," said Delia. "The historical Count of Samothrace, the mythical warlock Samothrace, and the man who uses the alias now."

"Oh," said Brynna, then, "Which did Caralisa dance with?"

"Bryn!" Delia giggled.

"None," said Megan. "She made it up."

"Megan, would you return my green shawl, please?" said Viola.

"In a bit. It's downstairs."

"I would like it now, if you please," said Viola.

"I know what you're doing!" Green eyes narrowed within pale lashes.

"I am cold," said Viola.

Megan got up with a huff and stalked out.

Delia, Viola, and Brynna huddled around Caralisa demanding details. They made her retell the dance over and over.

If she just closed her eyes, she could see the moon and smell the garden flowers again, feel the warmth of his body moving close to hers, his strong arm holding her, his guiding hand firm on her back. The two were dancing under the stars to her music. She nearly began to sing with the memory. She trembled at the sense of power she felt from him, his seductive draw. He had taken her by the hand and let her step out of herself into a world of magic, dark mystery, and intimate possibility.

"Are you in love?"

At that, Caralisa opened her eyes. It had all been a sweet dream from which she must wake. She gave a bittersweet sigh as she returned to earth. "He is altogether the wrong sort," said Caralisa. "And I am not what he was looking for. He said so."

Two

Caralisa wore a new dress to Sovereign's Day mass. She had needed a new dress badly but her godparents had been slow in providing one. Viola told them she would not make her debut if they were so badly off that Caralisa must look like a grisette. Three dresses arrived at the boardinghouse immediately—two nice frocks for Caralisa and one ball gown for Viola.

One of the frocks was a dusty pink, which complemented Caralisa's hair. Megan commented, "Real redheads can't wear pink."

Caralisa's hair, though a quite uncommon hue, could be called nothing but red, and the dusty pink looked splendid on her.

Her godparents had even sent matching hats and shoes and Caralisa felt very pretty in church. She could not even feel too badly for the moment about not going to the ball that evening with the other girls.

She was a little surprised that Monsignor even brought it up after mass. "I imagine you're feeling a little left out, child."

"Father?"

"Your friends debut tonight."

Monsignor Fortenot was an imposing man with silvered temples and a resounding voice. He spoke in sonorous round tones, and the girls called him Shakespeare behind his back. All the old dowagers of the parish thought him a dramatically handsome man, and he was very charming to them, especially to the richest and oldest of them. To the rest of the parish he was a very stern shepherd. Caralisa had seen him as a distant and craggy figure when she'd first come to Larissa the previous year. She'd thought him cold and aloof. She must have misjudged him, for him to have noticed her insignificant trouble.

"Yes, a little," Caralisa admitted, blushing and not sure why. He made her nervous. She lowered her eyes and moved her fingers over the white kid cover of her missal. "It's not important. It's kind of you to think of me."

With his Bible tucked under one arm, the other arm securely around Caralisa's shoulders, Monsignor Fortenot directed her out to the church garden. Caralisa clung to her missal with both hands.

"You have been through a trying time, Caralisa. I hope you have found a home here in Larissa." There was a questioning upturn in his voice, and he gave her shoulders a shake and a squeeze. His familiarity surprised her. She guessed that was why she was supposed to call him "Father." But before now she hadn't known that he even knew her name. Last year he'd seemed to look past her, through her, around her, as if she were furniture. That should teach her to pass judgment on a man of God.

"Yes, Monsignor. I remember once visiting town when I was a little girl. That makes it familiar somehow, and it feels like coming home in a way. Because it's an old memory, I suppose. It doesn't look so strange. I remember the Sky Cathedral."

"Our cathedral is grand." Monsignor stepped back, opened his arms slightly, his craggy face uplifted to gaze up at the soaring baroque spire, its ornate stone filigree mapped against the morning sky.

"No, well," Caralisa amended. "Sky Cathedral is what I called the building upon the Heights."

"That!" Monsignor took his arm from around her to cross

himself. He opened his Bible. "My dear child, it is a profane place!"

Caralisa hastily explained, "When I was little, it just seemed so strange and beautiful up there. I only saw how high and majestic and close to God it was—"

The Bible slammed shut with an angry crack that made her jump.

"I'm sorry." She blinked wide hyacinthine eyes. "Have I said something?"

Monsignor Fortenot's black brows met upon the flat shelf of his brow. "Nearness to God is not a spacial thing. And its *height,* its height is of *no importance at all!*" he said with such vehemence that it could be nothing but important.

Caralisa squeaked, "Yes, Monsignor."

Monsignor softened and touched her hair. "But you are a naive child. How could you know more than what you see. This is why I am here. To show you what you cannot see. To sort out the grain from the chaff of your limited knowledge. You should come more often. I haven't seen you in an age. Have you been to confession this week?"

"I have nothing to confess."

"How can a girl look like you and have nothing to confess?"

"Really, I haven't."

"No thoughts? You delude yourself if you imagine yourself pure."

Caralisa was becoming upset. Yes, that had been arrogant of her to suppose she could be perfect. "Give me a minute. Maybe I can think of something."

"Look at you, child. You have become a woman." He seized her hand. She nearly bobbled her missal as he did so. "Feel the touch of human flesh and tell me no burning yearnings of Eve's legacy enter your mind? Your flesh?"

His hand was hot and damp and uncomfortable. Burning yearnings of Eve? "I did eat an apple. Was that not all right?"

"Nothing dark and hot within that innocent exterior?" He

touched the side of her head, caught a strand of her hair between his fingers, and caressed her creamy cheek with it. Rose blush flooded her fair skin.

She was having an untoward thought, but she was not about to confess it. She thought there was something wrong with this priest.

His face was too close. She could see moisture shining on his hard narrow lips. There was a strange liquidity to his amber eyes. She could see every fine line netted in his skin from the stealthy advance of age usually belied by his vigor—and distance. She held her breath so as not to inhale his, which came in hot blasts through his flaring nostrils.

"I'll think of something," said Caralisa and pulled away to go inside.

He was suddenly blocking her way, and she recoiled from the barrier of censed august robes. He gestured like an actor with a wide strong hand. "I press you because you are more than the other girls. I see . . ." His eyes shone, his hands shook as if about to reveal something wondrous. "I see the *calling* in you." His voice arched in a crescendo and vibrated on the word *calling*. "You are to become a woman of God!" he announced as if presenting a magnificent gift.

Caralisa's jaw dropped in disappointment and shock. She cried quite suddenly and without volition, "A *nun!*"

The lines of the monsignor's face altered into lax surprise then into the sharp angles of wrath. Black brows raised then dove, pinched over his high-bridged nose. "It is the highest calling any woman can receive! Try to look joyful! The calling is a gift!"

"I—I don't hear it," she stammered, confused but so relieved that she couldn't hear it that she almost smiled. "I don't hear it."

"Go join the others. Perhaps the Spirit has not yet deigned to make plain to you what is so apparent to me. When the others are out tonight pursuing the things of the flesh and the rituals of common man, know that you have been set aside for a higher purpose."

He spun away with a swirl of his great robes. She was left alone in the garden, sorrowing inwardly. *But I want to go to the ball, and I want a young man to dance with me and kiss my hand.*

Realistically, given her station, there was every probability that Caralisa would never wed. But unexpected things were wont to happen in Larissa. After all, Princess Albertina had been born a commoner. In Larissa how could a young girl *not* dream?

Unless she were fated to become a nun. To give herself to the church would be to renounce dreaming.

The oppressive weight of despair rode heavily on her heart and constricted its ardent beating.

When Caralisa rejoined the others, her lower lip was quivering. Viola said, "You look like you're about to cry."

And with her saying so, Caralisa did.

"I'm so sorry you can't come with us tonight," Viola said. "Please don't cry. I won't go if you cry."

Caralisa shook her head, unable to speak. She waved her hand and her missal, a whimper clogged in her throat, trying to tell her that wasn't it at all.

"Oh darling, what's wrong?" Viola pleaded. Laurel, Delia, Megan, and Brynna gathered round.

"I don't want to be a nun!" Caralisa cried.

The others, even Viola, sputtered into surprised laughter. Viola said laughingly, "Then *don't* be!"

She put an arm around Caralisa and said, "Papa and Mama won't make you, even if you weren't to find a husband, but that just isn't going to happen either. So enough of this."

Megan said, "If she doesn't find a husband, what's the difference? She may as well be a nun."

Caralisa cried, "If I don't find a husband, I have my parents' farm. I can run it myself. I think. But can the church *make* me become a nun?"

"What, like a press gang!" Brynna blurted.

"Yes!" Delia joined in. "The immaculate press gang! Instead of trap doors in taverns to shanghai the drunks to sea, they have trap doors in the pews. You fall asleep in church, the trap opens, and whooops, there you go, Sister!"

"No, no," said Laurel. "The trap door is in the confessional. If you're too pure, they grab you."

"That's it!" said Caralisa. It was funny now. She sniffled with the last of her tears. "I told Monsignor I had nothing to confess this week. Oh my, I must go out and do something wicked straightaway!"

"What about your dance on the roof?" Delia suggested.

"How could that be sinful? Nothing happened."

"It sounds like too much fun. It must be a sin," said Laurel.

Viola patted Caralisa's back, wiped her cheeks with her fingers. "Better?"

Caralisa nodded.

"Then come on. We have only seven hours and you must help me do something with my face and hair—trading heads comes to mind."

Caralisa giggled.

"There's a girl." She took Caralisa by the hand, and waved the others forward. "Come, ladies. We must dazzle."

The afternoon flew past in a joyful bustle of tying ribbons, steaming satin, starching crinoline, and setting and resetting curlers. Caralisa was dispatched into town in search of a silk rose of a more lavender shade of pink, a wider blue ribbon, resin for the bottoms of new dancing slippers, and peppermint leaves to make their breath sweet. She was so caught up in it, she was almost as excited as if she were going herself.

When Caralisa returned from her last errand, Megan was ironing her hair. Caralisa offered to help.

"No," said Megan. "Brynna, you do it. She'll burn it out of jealousy."

"Just don't let Delia at it," said Laurel.

"Hey!" Delia protested, trying to fit curlers into what was left of her own short tresses. "I think I know what I did wrong."

"Bryn-na!" Megan called.

"I'm busy," said Brynna with a tisk.

"Caralisa, help *me*," demanded Laurel who was trying to make the curls stay in her fine limp hair. They kept falling in loose wilted blond kinks.

Caralisa was hooking up the back of Viola's gown, which was blue violet, cut low, with a natural waist. She looked like a princess. Her young man had sent her flowers, and the others were jealous except Megan, who said, "We could all have flowers if we set our sights low enough."

Viola's sweetheart was a tall and lanky, tow-headed youth with a conspicuous Adam's apple. Joshua had an open face and cheerful smile with big white teeth. He and Viola liked to laugh together and their eyes were full of lights when they looked at each other.

Laurel had two gowns, one from her mother, one from her father.

Her father had sent a sweetheart dress. It was a demure floral print taffeta, too sweet and young, with puffed sleeves and all edged in pink rosebuds.

Mother's offering had just arrived that very afternoon. Laurel opened the box to a chorus of gasps. Inside was an elegant Parisian creation of jewel green velvet with an embroidered white lingerie gown to go underneath it, along with long gloves and a fan with matching green beads and pearls and lace. A beaded collar necklace and rich paisley scarf of jewel green and peacock blue and regal purple came with it.

Laurel lifted it before rapt eyes and pronounced with a hard smile, "Closet curtains."

"What?" the others cried almost in unison.

"It's not my size. It's one of Mother's. She had it made for herself, probably some time ago, and decided not to wear it. She buys these things to decorate her closet is all I can think." Laurel threw the sumptuous gown aside, picked up the puffed sleeve taffeta. "I shall wear this one."

"But Laurel!" They all gawked at her incredible choice.

Laurel's thin lips curled into a wry smile. "Dear Daddy. Off by a few years, but at least it's mine."

Brynna retrieved the discarded velvet from the floor. "Can I wear it?"

"Brynna!" Delia and Megan scolded together.

"What?" Brynna blinked back at their horrified expressions. She checked her auburn hair for spiders.

Megan choked, "You *can't*." Megan was very busty and the high waist would make her look positively fat. She could not make a bid on the dress, but she could not let Brynna wear it. God had created Brynna to wear clothes. The deep green velvet did amazing things to her rich auburn hair and warm brown eyes. If Brynna wore that dress, no one would notice the rest of them at all.

"You *have* a gown," said Megan in desperation.

"I like this one," said Brynna. "Caralisa may wear mine."

There was a sudden awkward silence.

Caralisa was no one. There was no point in presenting her, had she a father alive to do it. All she had to offer was a modest plot of land in the country which would be thoroughly derelict and overgrown by the time she was old enough to take charge of it.

She mumbled, downcast, "Thank you, Brynna. I can't."

Laurel said, "Hold out for the Sovereign's Ball, Caralisa. This is *très bourgeois.*"

Caralisa gave a fragile smile, picked up her coin bank, and shook it. "I don't think I have quite enough to buy a title."

Near vespers, when the girls were usually gated in for the night, a line of carriages queued up to the tenement on Elm

Tree Close. Footmen opened the doors, and dapper fathers
stepped out. The girls crowded at the upper-floor window.
Caralisa clapped her hands together. "Oh!" It looked like a
scene from a fairy tale.

Viola's father greeted his daughter in the parlor with tears
misting his eyes. "My princess." He hugged her, pulled back.
"I am so proud."

He gave Caralisa a hug too, feeling guilty for excluding
her. But she was not his daughter. She was a child he had
been saddled with when she was nearly grown. "Poor little
darling."

"May I go to the plaza to watch the masque?" Caralisa
said brightly. "Just to watch?"

"No, no, no!" her godfather said with both hands raised.
"Out of the question."

"I shall take one of the kitchen girls with me."

"No."

"But Larissa's masques are famous," Caralisa pleaded.
"People come from all over the world."

"But no Larissan lets his daughter out of the house during
a masque, except on his own arm to a private party."

"I am not a Larissan daughter."

"Your father would never forgive me." And he would not
reconsider his answer. "As far as I'm concerned, there is not
even a question. You don't know what you are asking."

It was time to go. The girls bustled down the stairs. Caralisa
blew kisses after them. She watched the carriages from the
second-story window, until they wheeled out of the Close,
and the clopping of hoofbeats diminished in the distance.

Hours later when night had fallen and it was time for bed,
Caralisa lay out her nightgown and took down her hair. She
stood at the window brushing her red tresses, listening to
Larissa awakening for the night. Music trilled from somewhere. The glow of lights shone over the treetops and houses,
and bounced off the bottoms of the clouds. The sporadic
crackle of the first fireworks broke here and there. Some-

times laughter carried from roving revelers on their way to
or from some party.

She leaned against the window jamb, pining, alone. The
world was a carnival without her. She paced, sat, got up,
returned to the window, gazed out to the roof garden. Sound
and light lured from over the wall. She inhaled the scent of
the climbing roses; the air was laden with it. The wind was
warm and the night beckoned.

Where is my someone?

Is there a someone for me?

Surely there was something more in store for her than she
could see. She wished she had a gypsy glass that it might
tell her for certain that the future held more than a cloistered
girls' school and a hard life alone on a little farm. Something
was singing to her from beyond the hedgerow. Magic. There
must be magic. This was a Larissan night on which anything
could happen.

Let something happen to me.

She said to the magical night, "Oh please, take me away!"

The sound of a deep voice to one side of her made her
jump. "If you insist."

She turned with a start. He stood with one foot propped
up on the sill of the other tall window, a dynamic figure, a
winking eye, an ironic smile.

She blinked once. Miraculously he was still there, and she
beheld him with an inundation of emotion, a feeling of ex-
ploding stars and double rainbows, of a bright crystal ball
rolling and glittering with her future in it, of her whole world
balanced upon a pivot.

She knew him though he wore a different mask. In joy
she cried, "My lord!" She flew to the other window. His
hands at her waist lifted her up and over the sill to the roof
garden. Then he took her hand and led her laughingly across
the terrace.

In a moment she thought to ask, "Where are we going?"

Effortlessly as a cat, he not so much leapt as he appeared atop the wall, where he turned and said, "Over the wall."

He disappeared into darkness. Caralisa rushed to the wall and peered over and down. He was there, standing on a stack of crates she had never noticed before—perhaps because they had never been there—and he was reaching up a gloved hand for her to follow.

Gingerly she climbed atop the wall in a kneeling crouch. The wind caressed her face as she poised on the edge. The garden wall had become the brink of her small world. She looked over the edge of it with a rush of fear and doubt, the terror of dream become reality. There was a darkly sensual stranger, ready to take her into the unknown.

Be careful what you ask for, her mother used to say.

She had asked. Here it was.

She glanced back. Her room had never looked so safe and cozy and secure and predictable. All she need do was back down from this wall and go back where she belonged, and all the quavering in her stomach would go away.

She steeled herself. *Go. Don't look back. Go. Remember how you felt a moment ago.*

That nice safe room was not safe at all. It was a way station on a bleak road. Nothing was to be had without taking a chance. How Fortune would scorn one who fainted from a wish granted.

But this was all folly. *It is not for me. It is dangerous.*

She had always done as she was told. It had not kept her safe. It had not kept her parents from dying.

Here was a compelling smile and strong hand reaching up to her to take her on a new path, if she would just cast her fate to the singing wind.

She pushed long strands of her hair behind her, reached her hands to his shoulders, and let him take her waist. "Ready?" he said.

She nodded and, at a pressure from his hands, jumped.

She landed lightly, suddenly close to him, her face to his

chest, her arms clutched round him. She felt his heat. Her
nostrils filled with the faint exotic scent he wore. Her pulse
raced with danger. *I am undeniably over the wall.* Her cheeks
burned. She realized she was holding him and she let go at
once.

He stepped back and offered a gloved hand to guide her
down the stepped levels of crates until they were on the
grassy ground. Then they ran through the wildflowers at the
back end of the property, through an open stand of birches
to a waiting barouche on the road beyond.

The count assisted her up and inside. She sat, breathless
and flushed, laughing to him seated across from her. He
looked grand, not entirely in black this time. His evening
coat, trim fitting to the waist with claw hammer tails behind,
was of deepest green, the same rich jewel green as the Parisian gown Laurel's mother had sent, with a tea rose boutonniere. Lace ruffles from his full white shirt spilled from
the cuffs. His silk waistcoat was shot through with golden
threads. He wore a sword. The mask was of silvery fur, the
nose protruding slightly like an animal's muzzle, black and
winter white with whiskers. Tonight he was a handsome silver fox.

"I wanted to watch the street festival," said Caralisa. "My
godfather wouldn't let me."

"Watch?" he said. "In the street? Wouldn't you care to go
in and dance?"

She inhaled quickly, caught up in the idea, visions of castles and wide glittering ballrooms and salons and orchestras
suddenly awhirl, but then she exhaled, recovering her senses.
"I have nothing to wear."

"No." His eyes traveled up and down her with discounte-
nance, and something else as well, something dark and
heated and hidden, held in check by a stout chain. "You
don't."

Caralisa thought of Brynna's discarded gown, but the carriage was already moving and it was too late to go back.

And anyway, the girls' dresses, with the exception of the one
Laurel's mother had sent, belonged in a schoolgirl's first ball
and would be out of place in the count's company. As Laurel
said, *très bourgeois.*

The carriage moved swiftly, the horses trotting briskly, carrying them she knew not where but it was not in the direction
of the town center.

When the carriage halted, they had come to a quarter
where she had never been, where the buildings crowded
close. No one was in the street, no lights, no homes. The
only sign of life was a gasping laugh and giggle from the
black shadows and a duet of heavy guttural breathing.

The count helped her out of the carriage. The enormous
bulk of a building hunched over the narrow alley. The door
had been shimmed so as not to lock, and the count opened
it. Nightbirds took wing, startled at the creaking. Within was
only darkness.

Caralisa edged forward, nervous. What could they be doing here? Where was here? Why had he brought her here?
Her mouth had gone dry. Anticipation and fear pricked underneath her tongue. A thousand bright butterflies fluttered
within her chest, and she did not know if she was afraid or
eager to pass through that door.

She stepped inside, felt the count's presence behind her,
and the door fell shut. In total blackness she said, "I can't
see."

His gloved hand found hers. "You needn't. I can. Follow
me." She crept after the sure sound of his bootheels on the
wooden floor.

"Steps," he warned, and they began to climb, a long high
slow spiral, up and up. She smelled dust and age. The wooden
steps under her thin soles were worn and smooth. Higher,
she heard doves cooing and rustling in rafters, and she wondered what building could be this tall.

Another door creaked open and the count's hand on the
small of her back ushered her in.

For a moment she lost contact with him, and she blundered into a gauzy veil, or drapes, or hanging curtains. She could not see. As she tried to step away, she tripped and fell through the curtains and landed on a mattress. The drapery came with her, wrapping around her. Suddenly scared, she began thrashing in the fabric.

The lights came on. She blinked in the dim lampglow, and stared in wonder from the bed as if she had awakened inside a magician's hat. The wide low room with canted ceiling beams like an attic was crammed full with furniture of all eras, racks and racks of clothes, and stacks and stacks of boxes stuffed overfull with anything one could imagine: piles of shoes, swords, armor, wooden shields and spears, fans and togas, altars pagan and Christian, wands and snowflakes and puppets and torches in cressets, and crowns and sedan chairs—

"It's a theatre!"

—and masks. Many masks.

And set apart, draped over a red velvet chair, was a gown of moon and starlight, shimmering in the dim glow of the gas lamp. It sent prisms of color dancing on the crowded racks. It was white with subtle blues and lavenders like shadows in the snow. The bodice was lined in lace like the flower called Queen Anne's. A headdress of white snowy false hair like spun candy fit onto a white feathered mask. Over the chair's arm draped lingerie, white shimmering stockings clocked with silver, a sequined fan, and a silver necklace with a pendant of blue stone.

"Take off your clothes." Caralisa heard the deep command followed by the brusque shutting of the door.

Caralisa spun, backing away, her heart hammering in fear. But he was not there. The door was shut and she was alone.

She turned a full circle, awkward and self-conscious, feeling very small in the cavernous, laden attic. *What should I do?*

She gathered the fine clothes off the chair and crept in between two racks of costumes and took off her dress.

Should she leave on her underclothes, she wondered. She considered the dress. Its neckline plunged. Her chemise would never never work. Off it came. She held the shimmering skirt against her own drab leggings and then picked up one of the shimmering stockings. Off came her cotton tights.

Nearly naked now, she shivered though it was stuffy and warm in the attic, sheltered among the heavy racks of garments. Something made her sneeze.

The stockings forced her to put on the bustier, a scandalous-looking garment she had to inhale to hook. It pushed up her breasts but did not cover them. Demicups teased round the undersides.

She kept on only her cotton pantelets. No one would see those. Anyway there was nothing here to put on in their place. Every little decision loomed to monumental proportions. What she should be doing ought to be so obvious and it just wasn't! She inhaled and forged ahead. The metallic threads in the shimmering stockings felt strange and scratchy. She found the ribbon garters from the bustier and fixed the clasps at her thighs, feeling wicked. The touch of lace and satin was a new sensation. She felt herself becoming a different being as she changed plumage.

As she pulled the dress on, her heart seized in a moment of panic. *Oh no.* It was too small. The plunging bodice, so far from covering her breasts, barely reached over her nipples. Only a row of lace kept her from scandal. And the sleeves, for all their frothy tiers of puffs and layers of lace and ribbons, did not reach her shoulders.

But the skirts cinched her waist and flared out angelically. The overskirt of silk brocade was tied back like curtains with ribbon sashes, opening to a satin underskirt. The hem floated just above the floor. Perhaps she could put something over the top and still make use of the skirts. She crept out and found a mirror.

Oh!

The dress was not small. This was the way it was meant to look. From her nipped waist she was pinched and pushed up to the dangerously low décolletage, her creamy shoulders and white expanse of her bosom left bare. Her small breasts were pushed up to look large and round and ripe, two smooth white mounds thrust up and surrounded in lace as delicacies being presented for tasting.

The door latch clicked.

Caralisa shrank away, pulling her long hair around her to cover the vast nakedness of her chest and shoulders.

The count strode in and pulled her out by her wrist from between the racks of costumes. She felt his gaze fall upon her with stabbing directness. The emotions playing in his eyes clashed and jangled with all the battling cacophony of an orchestra tuning. None of it came out in his voice.

"Well, that was fortunate," he said appraisingly. He seemed to see nothing shocking or amiss.

Suddenly his hands were in her hair, smoothing it all behind her bare shoulders. He moved behind her, twisted her hair and cinched it with a band. Then he settled the headdress onto her head.

It was heavy and the false cloud of hair fell round her shoulders in a comforting veil of silver white tresses shot with pearls and Queen Anne's lace and white ribbons. On top was a Juliet cap and, at the crown, a crest like a white peacock's.

The mask tipped down over her eyes. She blinked through the holes to find the mirror. Staring back was a wondrous creature, blue eyes framed in white feathers and pearls, with blue-black beads giving exotic outlines to her eyes and brows. She had become an elegant and tempting peacock queen. She was someone else and that saucy neckline belonged to someone else.

"Back straight," the count directed.

"I don't dare."

"Find out now," he advised.

She tentatively drew herself up to regal height. The lace edging moved with her. "There," she said.

He gave her the scented fan of painted tulle, and the necklace. She handed the necklace back. "I need help with this."

He placed it around her from behind. She felt his gloved hands slip under her hair against the nape of her neck as the cool blue stone of the pendant settled into her cleavage. The stone's caress was like him touching her there. It slipped into the nest of lace and closely pressed flesh. The count looked over her shoulder to check the mirror, then he shortened the chain so that the stone lay higher, the bottom tip of the pendant stealing into the forbidden place.

Caralisa wondered, how *did* he manage that with gloves on, and why didn't he take them off?

"What do you think, mademoiselle?"

"Goodness!" said Caralisa, astounded by the vision in the mirror, an exquisite lady with a silver fox looking over her shoulder. "All I need now are glass slippers!"

"Not on my toes you don't," said the count. He gave her white ballet slippers edged with pearls.

She laced the ribbons around her ankles and tied the bows behind them. She retrieved her fan and took the count's offered arm.

He carried a candle to light their way down and down the spiral of stairs. As they left the theatre, he replaced the shim in the door.

"You don't have a key?" said Caralisa.

"I have," said the count.

"Then why did you do that?"

"It's a courtesy. This is the crew entrance. They become jolly tired waiting for someone with a key anytime they want to stitch a costume or paint a flat."

He opened the carriage door for her. She glanced up at the driver before she climbed in. As expected, but altogether jarring nonetheless, the coachman wore the mask of a rat.

· "Does this turn into a pumpkin at midnight?" she asked giddily inside the carriage as it began to roll.

"No, I don't think so," said the count. "It is nearly midnight now."

"And what will become of me?" said Caralisa.

The silver fox leaned in. "That is what you came over the wall to find out now, isn't it?"

Three

The street gave way to the wide plaza so thick with people
that the carriage could not pass. The driver's rat face leaned
down in the window. "My lord?"

"I suppose we could run them down, but let's not," said
the count and opened the door. He dismounted and gave his
hand to Caralisa. She stepped down into wonderland.

Faces went by in a blur of bizarre masks, beautiful and
grotesque. The plaza was a dizzy crushed whirl of color in
a kaleidoscope of people. A host of gas lamps blazed as if
all the stars of heaven had bent low to visit the revel. And
all around the spired skyline fireworks shot starward and
exploded in bright orbs, wreathing all the castles of Larissa
in spectacular red, blue, green, and phosphorescent white.
Their smoke censed the air.

A flutter of colored buntings festooned all the high buildings and the seven arches framing the plaza, flags of Montagne, Larissa, and of the royal house with its signature
swallow in light blue on a white ground. They were even
flown from the cliff face of the Heights, which rose over
everything like a dark titan in a stone mask.

Popping balloons brought down a glittering rain of confetti. A scatter of it settled in bright flecks in Caralisa's snowy
wig.

Amid the varicolored cobbles underfoot, Caralisa noticed
thick round translucent glass *yeux-de-boeuf* set in the pavement. This was only her second time to the plaza. The first

time she had been in so much haste to get away from it that she hadn't noticed such a thing. "Why are there windows in the ground?" she asked.

"There are chambers below," said the count offhandedly, as if underground chambers were the most natural thing in the world.

"Truly?" said Caralisa. "Do they give passage to the Heights?"

"Once upon a great long time ago. But the same quake which brought the lower structure down caved in that passageway as well."

Caralisa stopped over one of the round windows. The thick glass was a milky green blur. She could see nothing through it. "What is down there now?"

"Nothing but a lot of water, timber, and bracing to shore up the plaza lest the next quake bring it down, too. The engineers add a brick, add a beam every year."

"How do they get down there?"

"There is a door," he said without saying where. "It is a treacherous place. I shouldn't go," he said disinterestedly and led on through the assembled masses.

A charging train of street urchins barreled through the crowd. "Oh!" Caralisa said in surprise, pushed off balance by a hard little hand as a child banked off her to zag in a different direction. The count caught her and restored her to balance. She was a moment in recovering, not from the push but from the transcendent instant she had met the count's unyielding strength. It left her bemused and yearning to recapture the sensation again. The children caromed on through the crush, alarmed cries marking their wake.

"Pickpockets and cutpurses," said the count.

Caralisa had neither purse nor pockets, nor money to put in them, so she had suffered nothing worse than the indignity.

"Take nothing with you to masque that you cannot afford to lose," the count continued.

"Then it is fortunate I have nothing," said Caralisa.

Intense blue eyes traveled up and down her. "Oh, yes you have."

She could not or would not guess what he could mean.

A common crowd filled the streets in lively rout. Out here it was hard to tell who was who. They were all a great confused flock of colorful fantastic birds. Inside the palaces would be the lords and ladies. Some rabble bluffed its way inside; that was part of the game. Caralisa felt like one of the intruding rabble, except that she was on the arm of someone who belonged here, she thought as they approached the great doors of the Frankish castle.

She had only seen such palaces from the outside, the grand summer homes of foreign kings who had once upon a time ruled Montagne.

Caralisa and the count passed beneath gonfalons of the fleurs-de-lis, leaving the din of the square behind them, moving toward the delicate strains of the harpsichord within.

Suddenly a black and yellow harlequin was blocking Caralisa's way, a flat palm waiting for something.

"What does he want?" Caralisa murmured up over her shoulder to the count.

"Your card."

She looked up at the Count of Samothrace. He knew she did not have a card.

Rather than produce one, the count continued, "But he is so rude, we shall give him nothing."

And he brushed past the harlequin, clearing a way for Caralisa to advance. She gripped her fan for dear life and made her entrance, to be suddenly confronted by dreams.

Light from the chandeliers danced off the crystals and threw colors on the silk brocade walls. All the rich costumes on the dance floor made her feel quite plain. There were birds of paradise, and titled lords pretending to be Renaissance dandies and kings of eras gone by. Ladies were bedizened in gold and gemstones, arrayed in powdered wigs and hoop skirts. In the center of the hall was laid out an intricate sprawling miniature of old Rome, complete with temples and the famous Colosseum.

Upon a massive throne set up on a dais all draped in red velvet and edged in gold, sat a Roman emperor with golden wreath sprouting clusters of amethyst grapes on his head. He wore a very spare toga of gold cloth on his portly frame, and kept a diminutive violin close at hand. Porcine eyes narrowed and he pointed over the heads of the crowd. The jutting finger had singled out the Count of Samothrace, then it turned over and crooked into a beckoning gesture.

Caralisa felt herself go white. The tendons in her knuckles stood out as she clutched her fan. The count guided her through the splendid crowd, up the steps of the raised dais, to Nero's throne.

The emperor leaned down, belched, spoke. "I thought that was you, Samothrace. Try the cask back there. Stay away from the champagne. That's for the pretenders."

"I shall," said the count. He flipped the edge of Nero's toga. "This becomes you."

"In truth you are a cruel man," said Nero.

"I know. I really must complain about the parti-colored Cerberus at your gate."

"René. He's a boor and I should speak to him about it, but he enjoys it so and it does keep out the interlopers."

"And your friends."

"My friends are too boorish to mind. You got in, didn't you?"

"My lady had doubts," said the count.

"The lady would have had no trouble had she not been with you. Such loveliness we would never turn away." He took her hand and kissed it. "Charmed. You have me this time. I haven't a clue." He was studying her masked face as if he should recognize her. "Very young. I haven't seen you before, have I?"

"No, my lord," Caralisa managed to answer.

"Whose daughter is she, Samothrace?"

"We shall keep our secret awhile," said the count and made to move away.

"It's not fair. You have so many. One man should not be so damned good at it."

As they stepped down from the dais, Caralisa murmured, "So many women, or so many secrets?"

The count did not answer.

He moved apart to fetch them something to drink from the recommended cask.

Caralisa felt exposed in her low décolletage. She had thought she looked quite big until she saw the other women here. One looked down at her critically through a lorgnette, as if searching for what there was to see. Herself, the in-specting lady had great white pillows of half-exposed breasts, and Caralisa suddenly felt like a child dressed up in her mother's clothes.

She walked away and sighed to herself, "This dress is not right for me."

A male voice intruded, thickly and carefully articulate. "Dear girl, it is perfect. One could only improve on it by taking it offff—forgive me. I have drunk to much." The sloppy-faced young man navigated away.

When the count returned to her side, Caralisa whispered, "My lord, I don't know how to talk. What does one say? I'm just a country girl."

"When in doubt, say nothing. Your smile is all you will need. Where is it?"

She couldn't manage one. She covered her bosom with her spread fan. The count took it from her, snapped it shut and jammed it into a flowerpot. "You *have* a mask."

"May I have the fan?" she peeped.

"Never carry a weapon you don't know how to use."

"Weapon?"

"You may observe the experts tonight." He gave her a glass. "One approacheth."

A lady was advancing, fan fluttering at intervals to reveal

and conceal the face below the golden mask. A smile glided across the scarlet lips at the fan's waning. She tapped the count with the closed fan. "Who is that behind there?"

"The Count of Samothrace, at your command."

"Yes, I know that, but when am I ever to see your face? They say you're a perfect gorgon. Will I turn to stone?" She tried to edge the fox mask up with her fan for a peek.

Samothrace turned his head and straightened his vulpine nose.

The lady went on, "Either that or you're so beautiful that no woman can resist." She inhaled so that her breasts rose to brush his waistcoat. "Which is it, my lord?"

"Neither. The keeping of the secret is the all of it."

She tisked, whisked open the fan, and half turned her back in a pout. "I am waiting."

The count took up the cue, "Would my lady honor me with this dance."

She met Caralisa's eyes conspiratorially. "Is it safe?"

"I hardly think so," said Caralisa.

"Oh good." She turned back to the count and gave him her hand.

As he guided her out to dance, the lady's friends moved in round Caralisa. They asked, "What *is* behind the mask?"

She heard herself say on impulse, "Heaven."

Without the fan, she had only the glass to grip. She drank from nervousness, but the glass never emptied. Whenever she looked down, it was always full.

She wandered into another ball room, then another. She wondered where the count was, for she was certain she could not find her way back by herself. He could not be far.

She *hoped* he was not far. Left to fend for herself, she began to feel at first uneasy, and then neglected.

Where was he?

With some effort—and some more wine—she convinced herself that she did not need him. Let him dance with all the ladies in the castle for all she cared. She had admirers too.

She had never drunk wine before, and it did not occur to her to connect that action with the invasive pleasant fuzziness that had taken hold of her. She walked as in a shining fog.

She was feeling warm. All the lights looked bright and glistening. Her skin was on fire and she wanted someone to touch her.

Him. She wanted him. But he was nowhere to be seen. She wanted to be kissed on the lips. She closed her eyes and tried to imagine how it would feel to have the count's lips touch hers.

And suddenly she was dancing. She was being led, nearly carried to the sound of music, her body pressed against a scarlet uniform jacket of the Rhinish guard. Wool prickled through the silk and lace of her bodice. A brass button rubbed tormentingly at a nipple. She tried to squirm away but began to suspect he was doing it on purpose. She looked up at the rake and was instantly mesmerized by his face.

He wore the plainest of black masks. A black pencil mustache surmounted soft cruel lips set in a sardonic smile. Black hair was swept back from a flat brow. A wicked scar snaked down from one high sharp-angled cheekbone. It only added to his air of commanding virility. He kept her pressed indecently close against his body. Black satin hussar breeches were very tight. His hand low on her back pushed her against his masculinity. She felt it rise as they danced. As she arched back, trying to put some space between their bodies, the motion presented her bosom to him. Her breasts strained at the very edge of her bodice, a hair's breadth from ruin. He looked down appreciatively, as if being offered a treat.

In a high silken tenor voice with Rhinish accent, he said, "What stone is this?" His fingers slid down between her breasts and, in no great haste, lifted out the blue stone to rest in his hand. The backs of his hot fingers brushed against the bared tops of her breasts as he examined the stone.

"I don't know," Caralisa choked out.

"It's very pretty." He slipped it back slowly, let his fingers tarry and graze her skin as he drew away. Then he slipped his hand behind her neck beneath her hair to draw her in. He nuzzled her neck, nibbled at her earlobe, traced kisses along her collarbone. She felt his hair under her chin. Wet fire tingled and burned inside her. Her thighs ached. She gasped.

"Oh, you glorious tease," he said.

"I'm not a tease," she said.

His head snapped up. "No?" he said with startled joy. He stepped away and took her hand. "Then, let's to it." He led her quickly from the hall to a corridor and down some stairs to another darkened gallery and outside to the stables.

She followed without question. His enthrallment with her intoxicated her, a stronger brew than wine. Common sense, shame, and caution all blunted or crumbled away entirely with the glowing buzz coursing in her veins.

A horse nickered. The air out there was redolent of fresh hay, the mild horsy odor of manure, and the sweet smell of clean-brushed horses and oiled leathers.

Caralisa's eyes adjusted to the dark. She became aware of men and women writhing in the dark corners with moans and sharp gasps of ecstasy.

She had a dim idea where this was leading, but could not credit that it would go as far as *that*. Protest remained lodged in her throat and withered there. She needed to be a sophisticated Larissan, to live up to the bewitching image of her costume, lest this worldly man see straight through her mask for what she was, and laugh and pity her. She needed her moment in the Larissan night. This must be it. She trusted him, rogue that he was. He seemed so very sure of himself; he must know what he was doing. He was so taken with her; he could not mean her harm. Her head was ringing. His hands were hot, his smile knowing. So very knowing.

And I know nothing. I want to know.

She thought, in hurt abandonment, of the count. Leave her

alone, would he? If he would not show her the mysteries of
the night, then this man would.

That would show Samothrace.

But would he even care? He didn't, or he would be here
instead of this man, showing her what she needed to know.

A kiss on the lips. She was sure she would get her kiss
on the lips. And something sufficiently wicked that she could
tell to impress Laurel and Delia.

The guardsman spread his short cape in an empty stall
and lay her down in the hay.

Her nipples' impudent knobs showed straining against the
confines of lace. To her shock, his heated fingertips dragged
down the fabric so that her breasts swelled to freedom, upright and eager before his ravenous eyes. As he cupped the
soft white mounds in his hot hands, Caralisa felt herself melting. He fondled them and squeezed them with surprising
gentleness. He rubbed his palms across her nipples then circled the pink knobs with the tips of his thumbs so that Caralisa nearly shrieked with the sudden blazing torrent of
sensation kindled in her groin and devouring her in a seething
storm. "So young and sweet," he murmured.

Stop. She should stop him, but she could not imagine how,
he was so delighted with her. The part of her mind that was
horrified was locked in a cage and forced to watch helplessly
as she let him do things to her. Sometimes she writhed a
small motion that brushed her against him, fanning the
flames to excruciating heights.

Was this love? The feeling was so relentless, did it not
have to be love?

But a dissonant chord that had been humming an off-tune
baseline since she had begun this dance was blaring in raucous crescendo. What had she got herself into here? No matter how hard she tried to cling to ignorance, she did know
where this road went and she was becoming very frightened.

"Please," she whimpered.

"Oh, yes," he rasped. As his one profane hand stroked her

breasts, searing the flesh with delicious defilement, the other stole under her skirts, groping higher and higher on her leg sheathed in its glittering stocking until he found the bare skin of her thigh. "Ah!" the sound came from his throat as he kneaded his fingers in her softness, and crept still higher.

Suddenly he pulled back and laughed, astonished. "You're overdressed!" He flipped up her skirts.

Caught between blushing and all the blood draining away, Caralisa was mortified. She had left her plain cotton pantelets on. She had not been sure whether to wear them or not, then had kept them on because, after all, no one would see!

She threw her skirts back down hotly, sitting up. "That will be enough of that, sir."

His laugh sounded brassy bright as he pounced on her, forcing her back down in the hay. "You delicious tease!" He grinned and buried his face in her breasts. He kissed them roughly. She felt teeth on her nipples. She grasped his head between her hands and cried out a ragged sound that was indistinguishable between pain and ecstasy.

A deep voice of mockery fell down like a splash of cold water. "Mademoiselle, may I cut in on this dance?" She looked up at the Count of Samothrace towering over them in commanding stance, sardonic twist to his mouth, mastery in his bearing, his voice all disdain. "You *can* do better than that." And with the back of one hand, he swept the young rake away. The guardsman tumbled off her. Caralisa flushed with shame as she tried to pull up her bodice to recapture her impudent breasts, which seemed to have grown.

The rogue scrambled to regain his footing. His mouth was glistening. He drew his sword.

The count, almost lazily, drew his.

Caralisa cried, "Don't I get a say in this?"

"No," said the count. Then to the rogue, "Sheath your sword, sir."

"I tried!"

The count dropped into a fighting stance, poised for a duel, his sword drew patterns in the air between them.

The rogue posed for challenge, wavered, then took a step back, gathering in his bluff. He sheathed his sword, looked down on Caralisa. "Sweet, but not to kill for."

"Not to die for, you mean," said the count.

"That's for you to answer."

"You *would* have to kill me," said the count.

"No fuck is worth a man's life. Not even your life, cheap coin that it is." The guardsman straightened his clothes, pulled his cloak out from under Caralisa, and marched out.

Caralisa rearranged her rumpled clothes. The count remained on guard, glancing round like an eagle on watch. When she was decent again, he reached down a hand and helped her to her feet. He sheathed his sword.

"Well, mademoiselle. Enjoying the ball?"

Shame blazed flaming bright and hot on Caralisa's lovely cheeks. A horrible lump of it weighed in the pit of her stomach. She was too shamed to feel gratitude for her rescue. It was his fault she had come to this.

"How long were you peeping!" she accused.

"Not at all. But I know this man. Not in the way you almost did. Though many girls do." He picked stray lengths of straw from her false hair. "This is a fetching look for you."

"Leave me alone!"

"Dare I for a moment?" he asked sourly.

"What does it matter to you what I do?" she challenged, and held her breath awaiting his answer. He might have said: *It matters the world, for I have fallen in love with you and cannot bear the thought of any other man touching you.*

The set of his mouth turned bitter. "Apparently as much as your honor matters to you."

Caralisa balled her fists at her sides. She stammered in anger, "You . . . you . . . you . . . you . . ."

"Perhaps you should try another letter of the alphabet," the count suggested.

"*You!*" she raged. "You are a cruel, unfeeling, unbearable *beast!*"

He actually flinched at the last word, as if she had slapped him. He countered coolly, "And what, mademoiselle, do they call girls like you?"

Slut, tart, trollop, strumpet all came to mind. Instead she answered boldly, "Too good for you."

"For me? For *me?*" He sounded amazed, aghast, and about to laugh at her. "What gave you the idea to hold yourself up to *me?* As if I wanted you."

Put so coldly, it seemed a remote notion indeed. "Then why ever did you bring me out with you tonight!" she cried.

"You asked."

"And why should you do my bidding, if you care not?"

"Perhaps it amused me to do so." His sensuous lips hardened into a sardonic near smile. "Why? What else did you suppose?"

The mockery in the question sucked all her pride away. Yes, what had she supposed?

A sob convulsed deep underneath her heart. She held it in. Her eyes felt hot. She would show him no tears. "I am no one," she said in proud irony, daring him to believe it. "I suppose nothing. Do not concern yourself. Oh, but you are in no danger of doing so. I may just as well admonish pigs not to fly." With a haughty toss of her clouds of false hair, she turned away from him, quickly so he would not see the heartbroken glistening in her eyes.

He muttered through clenched teeth at her back, "The, *pig,* my dear, shall take wing anytime it jolly well pleases."

He stalked after her, slid his hand under her wig and behind her neck. She felt the caress of his soft-textured glove. "What are you doing?"

He found the blue jewel which had fallen behind her on

its chain; he brought it back forward and settled it curtly between her breasts.

"Come," he said, turning away. "The night is young."

She followed him in sulking silence, wanting to cry, fighting down the thickness in her throat.

She had not been kissed on the lips.

No harlequin guarded the entrance of the next masque. The finding of it was the only key. The count escorted Caralisa through the gates and into the courtyard of a seemingly lifeless castle of long shadows and stretching corridors. They went up stairs through a long dimly lit gallery, the count's bootheels ringing hollowly off the walls. Caralisa tiptoed at a near run to keep up with him.

On her indiscretion he said nothing further, for which she was both grateful and baffled, wishing he would speak but ready to snap at him if he did. She could not even tell if he was angry, his face as unreadable as if it were all a mask. She was feeling terribly confused and ashamed and wantonly reckless. She wished he would react. She had no idea what he thought of her, why she was even out here with him. She concluded that since he was neither hurt nor angry, that he had spoken truly that he did not care for her in the least and it mattered not what she did. She had hoped those words, like hers, had been spoken in spite, meaning nothing.

The night had all the aspects of a dream and she moved within it as if it were nothing more, doing things she would never consider in waking.

They descended a long curving set of stairs and emerged into the brightness of a garden room under a vast dome of glass panes within a net of stone arches. A fountain bubbled in the center and all around it people were dancing to the music of a small orchestra.

The count's cape whirled off and aside into the arms of a waiting servant. The count guided Caralisa down three steps and turned on the dance floor to face her. He gave a courtly bow. In a stumbling moment she realized she was being asked to dance. She bobbed a curtsy and stepped into his waiting arms. She had drunk too much to be stiff or to resist much. She went where he led, not thinking about it at all.

She tilted her head back to see an image floating in all the reflective windows of the skylight ceiling. She did not recognize herself at first, only wondered who was that dazzling lady with that striking man who danced so well, for whom all the less splendid beings gave way. Caralisa thought she ought to get out of the way with the rest of them and leave the beautiful duo the floor.

Then she laughed. *It's me!*

She looked about her. A space was widening for them. On every side was a ring of admiration and envy. Unaware of her own grace, or the way she looked when she smiled, she could only think: It was the dress; it was the count's sure arrogant leading; it was he. He should have been an actor for his ability to hold an audience. Maybe he was an actor.

No matter. This was her fantasy. The music, his strong arm behind her back, the wide floor. Her senses filled with perfume and spice, and the giddy warmth in her head. She smiled ecstatically, bright peals of musical laughter bubbling from her lips.

He was tall and regal, gracefully erect, strong and lordly. She glided with him where he bid her. She hummed to herself a counterline to the music.

She stepped on the count's boot. He gave no indication of noticing, but continued on, making her look as graceful as a swan.

Too soon, the music trembled out on its final chord. The count stepped back and kissed her hand. There were smiles under the ring of masks as the other guests applauded.

Caralisa was flushed, wishing in earnest that she had her fan. The count left her side to find them something to drink.

In that moment a young man grasped her hand and would not let go.

She had noticed him before, as she had come in, among a knot of loud youths, rich, obviously students, thinly disguised. She'd seen them, or a group like them, at the other party and several more in the plaza.

This one had stood out for his quietness and his beauty— gentle eyes and an artistic face of classical perfection. He wore a billowing white shirt and close-fitting trousers buttoned at the ankles, black pumps without heels, and a carrick cape in typical student dress. Students wore their hats indoors, broad-brimmed low-crowned beaver hats when everyone else was in high crowns and small brims. This youth had pulled his off the moment Caralisa had entered the castle.

His black silk cravat was tied in a poet's big floppy bow. His disguise was no more than a plain black mask.

Caralisa gave a slight tug at her captive hand and a small laugh, but he held on, gazing adoringly like a puppy. He blurted, "Madam . . ." and faltered into uncertainty.

"—moiselle," she finished for him.

"Thank God!" he said.

She giggled.

His light brown hair, parted down the middle, fell in layered loose curls, the back tied with a black ribbon, the shorter curls in front falling round his beautiful face, his expression eager and wholly rapt. He had her hand in both of his now. "You must give me this dance or I shall die."

She looked up inquiringly to the count, who had returned to her side with two glasses.

"We can't have young men dying on us," said the count. "The constable will ask questions." He motioned for her to go. She paused thirstily over the two glasses he held. They were different colors, amber and rose. "Which is mine?"

He presented the rose one. She took a swallow and handed it back.

He nodded for her to run along.

The young student was a well-schooled dancer, though not as authoritative as the count. The floor did not clear for them. The youth glanced back at his rival and asked possessively, "Who is he?"

"My father's ghost," said Caralisa.

His whole being gushed relief. "Not your intended?"

"Not on your life."

His smile was full of beautiful even white teeth. "He is too old for you."

"He is an ogre," she said.

Her new partner beamed. Everything about him spoke of aristocracy, his clothes, his cultured voice, his fine white hands that never labored. His hands were soft, smooth, and warm. One could not tell the foreigners by their accents, for Larissa spoke all languages, but something about him, a gentleness, suggested another place.

He was gazing at her, spellbound. He said tentatively, "I have never seen such a lovely creature as you are. I have been following you, I'm afraid. I thought I'd lost you. But here you are—do I offend?"

She had stiffened and changed color. Where had he followed her? But the expression on his face was all reverent concern. She choked out of a cloud, "No, no." She recovered her poise and said calmly, "No."

And she struggled next to believe that she had just heard the words: *I have never seen such a lovely creature as you are.* They had flown past so swiftly. If she could only recapture them and hold them for a moment!

Of course she was masked and her costume was delectable; still she savored the stolen moment of imagined beauty. As if she could captivate a man like this.

He was the combined essence of all the schoolgirls' dreams, a courtly and handsome young aristocrat from another land, who was entranced by her loveliness. He was all she could imagine ever wanting, and suddenly her fantasy lover had a

face—for that little black mask did not obscure it one whit—
and he was beautiful.

He was so sweet and gallant. He held her with great care,
as if she were the most priceless of the world's treasures.
When he glanced down at her bosom, his expression lost
none of its reverence. "That stone," he said. "It is as exquisitely blue as your eyes."

Her eyes. Those were not part of her disguise. He loved
something that was really hers! Her heart fluttered. In barely
a whisper, Caralisa said, "Thank you, sir."

His eyes returned to her face and stayed. "Your costume
becomes you."

"Thank you. I—I'm afraid I can't say much for yours."

"Oh, but I am Dr. Faustus," he said whimsically. Dr. Faustus was a popular choice of any université student. All it
required was the donning of a mask on top of his scholar's
attire. He motioned to his knot of friends across the hall.
"And there are my colleagues, Dr. Faustus, Dr. Faustus, and
oh yes, that one is Dr. Faustus."

"Pleased to make your acquaintances, Drs. Faustus." She
nodded, smiling gaily.

"Of course that makes your companion Mephistopheles,
for you are surely Helen of Troy."

Caralisa's long lashes lowered. "You don't know me."

"I know enough." His touch was tender upon her cheek.

She looked up in joyous wonder. She did not know what
to say to him. She smiled and blushed and dropped her gaze.
He smiled and blushed and glanced away, only to steal back
and exchange glances anew.

He was so warm after the count's unfeeling rebuff, so
courtly and courteous and sweet. His adoration was a sooth-
ing balm to the wounds her heart had suffered at the hands
of that stinging nettle of a man who couldn't know love if
he lived a hundred lifetimes.

Her young admirer held her closer. She detected the light
scent of some powder, for he was not perfumed. His breath

was sweet. She wanted to be with him like this forever. But the shadow of another was everywhere, and she could not see how such a dream could ever be. She bent her head near his chest and whispered, "We must escape."

She glanced up to see a look of incredulous elation on his face, then one of hunted resolve. He led her in the dance away toward the edge of the garden room. When the fountain was between them and the count, the youth took her hand and they ran through an archway down a darkened corridor. They darted into a side room and he turned up the lamps.

Painted icons surrounded them in a circle of niches. A baptismal fount stood in the center of the round chamber.

"Oh no," she whispered. "This is a chapel."

"But I shall do nothing unholy," he said and lifted his mask.

His was the most beautiful face she had ever seen or imagined, young, perhaps twenty-one, poetically manly, smooth and lineless fair. His features were flawless, a straight nose, soft lips, a strong heroic chin with slight cleft, a deep jaw, wide honest forehead, and melting blue eyes, the brows' gentle curve perfectly drawn. His full head of honey brown wavy hair lay about it in loose curls, so thick and soft-looking she longed to touch it.

"My name is Michaeljohn."

She was staring in mesmerized wonder, motionless. His white hands rose to either side of her head, and he lifted off her headdress with its mask.

A bolt of terror wrenched Caralisa out of her dreamworld. Air wafted on her sweaty scalp, and her vision freed of the eyeholes of the mask. Suddenly she was not this other person, this fantasy creature of the mask. This was Caralisa herself and *he was looking at her!*

With a cry she seized back the headdress, jammed it back on, and, looking out through skewed eyeholes, found the door and ran.

She straightened the headdress as she fled up the long

corridor. His plaintive voice pursued her, "No! Please! Come back! *I love you!*"

She found the garden room, ran through the crowded dance floor. She flew to the Count of Samothrace, who caught her up and without question, snapped to the servant for his cloak, and fled with her.

They threaded back through the darkened labyrinth to the plaza. All the way, Caralisa heard Michaeljohn's voice reechoing in the stone halls, crying like a chained ghost, "Come back, my love!"

Caralisa looked back. Her eyes met his far down the hall. His face brightened. "My love!"

She and the count dove into the crowd.

Michaeljohn ardently dogged them through the crush in the plaza. Fireworks soared and crackled overhead. Sparks rained down. Prince Maximillian and Princess Albertina were out on the balcony, so the plaza was overflowing with people pressed body to body, nearly too thick to pass, all come out to catch a glimpse of the reining pair on Sovereign Day. Albertina was tossing baubles to the crowd. The townsfolk lunged and scrambled to gather them up for luck—nothing of value, as was done in an ancient day, when people died vying for them. These were the cheapest of trinkets, their only worth that the princess had tossed them from the balcony on Sovereign's Day.

The count forged a route through the crush. Past the plaza through the Black Arch the way thinned, and Caralisa and the count could run.

As they came to the river, Michaeljohn was still on their trail. The count helped Caralisa onto the single boat and paid the boatman to push off immediately.

The boat glided out onto the water, leaving Michaeljohn hauled up short at the water's edge. He paced the bank back and forth in helpless frustration.

"We are away, mademoiselle."

Caralisa let her shoulders slump in relief. She dabbled her

fingers over the side into the cold water and touched her face. The water smelled of a cool mountain-fed moist breeze. Wavelets slapped at the boatsides.

Then they heard a splash. The Count of Samothrace barked a laugh and looked back.

Michaeljohn had dived into the river! He floundered in the strong current, slapping among the tall reeds like a hooked fish.

Caralisa cried, "Save him! He'll drown!"

"He'll catch cold," the count suggested dryly.

And in a moment a soggy Michaeljohn was dragging himself back up the inner bank, his wide billowing carrick limp and sticking to him.

The Count of Samothrace muttered in eminent disdain, close to bitterness. "Fool. These waters are too swift even for *true* love."

Caralisa bristled. She did not doubt that Michaeljohn loved her, and she was beginning to question the wisdom of her flight. Why *had* she run from him?

I love you!

The words had struck her like a thrown javelin in the back. She had run on blindly, dazed and staggering. It had taken her until now to realize that she had been hit, and the wound, now cooling, began to hurt. She had no one and she had run from love! From perfect love.

She was swiftly becoming furious with herself. She sat brooding in the boat. She could imagine Michaeljohn's smooth warm aristocratic hands caressing her breasts. She could almost feel his reverent kisses.

I love you!

Her eyelids drooped. She envisioned Michaeljohn's dear and beautiful face gazing upon her nakedness with his adoring blue eyes. She imagined *him* lifting her skirts. If he did it, it would not be unholy.

"I had a spaniel puppy once." The count's deep voice intruded and scattered her delicious vision. "It was that devoted and that stupid."

She flashed him an angry glance and crossed her arms, steaming mad and wantonly hot, desire running riot within her. She could even throw herself at that tyrannical beast if he were not such a sneeringly cold brick wall.

What would he know of love?

Of course he was right to scoff—but not at Michaeljohn. At her. How presumptuous of her to weave a whole future from one magical thread spun on a night of pleasing illusion.

Reality returned hard.

The boat ran aground with a jolt. The count stood and offered his hand.

She took it sullenly and rose. He lifted her from the boat and set her onto the land.

She was surprised to see the count's barouche and the rat-masked driver waiting.

She stammered for words. The count said, "One generally ends up leaving a masque chased by *someone* before the night is over. One should always have an escape ready."

He assisted her into the carriage. The driver took up the reins and drove for one of the bridges to take them back into town, back to the glittering masque of Sovereign's Night.

Caralisa had no idea of the hour when the carriage returned them to the theatre. She looked up and saw stars she had never seen in the spring sky. The count opened the door for her and led her up the stairs. He carried a candle this time to light her way.

He left her alone in the attic to change clothes. She was humming now. She shed her splendrous raiment and put on her simple dress.

Her hair was flattened from the weight of the headdress. Her face looked plain and naked without the exotic plumage of the mask. She looked quite ordinary, she thought. The belle who had danced under a glass dome before lords and ladies had returned to simple Cinderella.

She held the lustrous blue stone of the necklace in her palm. She opened the door and looked for the count. "My lord?"

When he reappeared, she asked, "What is this?"

"Paste."

"May I keep it? It matches my eyes."

"No, it doesn't," he said.

She surrendered it, abashed. He tossed it into a jewelry box and slammed the lid. His manner was glacial, his thoughts fiery.

Nothing could match your eyes!

Caralisa wilted into the red velvet chair. "Can I go home now?"

"No."

He pulled her from the chair by her wrist and led her down a curving corridor. "I want something from you."

Despite her weariness, her heart quickened. Was this it? Did he intend to take her? How on earth could she ever hope to stop him? She knew no one would appear to rescue her this time.

If he kissed her tenderly on the lips, would she let him do what he wanted?

No. She was frightened.

No.

No.

She followed his long strides in the dark. The candle had flickered out and the way was perfectly black. He did not need the light and she could do nothing but follow him.

When the next door opened, she sensed space, a great cavernous openness.

When the gas lamps flickered on, she saw that she was on a narrow balcony over the stage—not in the audience, but behind the proscenium arch. They were on the pin rail, thirty feet above the wings, where were tied off on wooden belaying pins the ropes that held up the stage curtains and lamps counterbalanced with sandbags.

There was a piano on the narrow perch. The count sat on the bench and began to play.

"Oh!" Caralisa cried. "Oh!" It was all she could say, in delighted shock. "That's my song!"

She had never heard anything of hers on any instrument but her own voice. Suddenly it sounded *real*. She did not think it worth repeating, but here it was.

He lost the melody line, fumbled on the keys, stopped, and looked up at her with a penetrating gaze. "I want to know what you're singing. Where do those songs come from?"

She really could not answer that. "I—I sing what I hear on the wind," was the best she could give him.

"The wind sings that way for you alone."

She rested her forearms on the piano and leaned over them. "I know that now." Her hair spilled forward of her shoulders. She ran her fingers back to hold it off her brow. Tired and disheveled, without all the finery, she looked terribly young and vulnerable. "I used to think everyone heard melodies. They were like wildflowers on the roadside, and I was simply the only one who bothered to stoop and pick them."

"No. You are the only one who hears them. You are hearing the earth, the angels."

She shrugged uselessly. "I don't know what to do with them."

"I do." He poised his hands—still gloved—over the keys. There truly had to be something wrong with them. She morbidly wondered what, until he began to play. She joined in with a counter melody, something she had never been able to do before, having only one voice with which to sing.

He laughed—it was a surprised and happy chortle—and kept playing until he ran out of melody. He stopped and said, "Can you write that down?"

Her cheeks pinkened. Her gaze plummeted. "I don't know how to read music," she said.

He grasped her wrist. "Sit." And he made her sit beside him. Caught off balance, she landed so hard she squeaked.

"You shall learn," he said. He took her face in his gloved hand, his grip not rough but inescapable. His fingers held her jaw and turned her firmly to face him. "Face."

"Face?"

With a turn of his wrist, she was suddenly facing the piano. He directed with his other hand for her to look at the musical staff. "Face. The four notes in the spaces. F-A-C-E. These." He released her jaw and played F-A-C-E.

Then he commanded, "Sing for me middle C."

She blinked.

He waited. More to himself than to her—as usual—he said, *"Does* she have perfect pitch?"

She puzzled. F-A-C-E. The third note he had played was called C. She sang a tentative note.

"Of course she does," he answered himself. Before she could flush with pride, he said, "But that's not middle C."

"What is it?"

"It's a C, very well. You're an octave high."

Her uncertainty was not in the note itself but from the name of it. The pitch she could find without problem, so long as she understood what was required of her. To her the differences were as clear as red, green, and blue. But no one had ever told her which was red, which was green, and which was blue. "Never fear," he said. "You can be taught."

"Why bother?" she said.

Something shook his perfect satisfied assurance. Concern rippled under the mask. She could see it in his indigo eyes. They turned to her in consternation, and gently mystified he said, "Why ask?"

And she felt a sudden flood of deep affection for him— quite apart from the dark frightening desire that swept her up then shied away like a fickle sea wind. This powerful man held her silly musical noodling in such regard that she heard herself confessing a secret gut-wrenching pain to him. "I—I tried out for conservatoire." She fidgeted with two long locks of her red hair, pulled them straight, and crossed them before her. "I can't afford it. I auditioned anyway. I thought maybe if they liked me . . ." She waved away the foolish thought. It had been absurdly presumptuous. She didn't know what she could have been thinking. Who had she been to think herself worth a fellowship. She blushed now even to have formed the notion. She shadowed her face with her hair. "After a while and I hadn't heard anything, I came to ask about my application. While I was waiting, I overheard someone behind a partition say, 'That thin-voiced redhead is here.' Then a maestro came in and told me I would never make a singer."

"Not in the opera, no," the count conceded. "Yours is not that kind of voice."

"And you know what kind of dancer I am." She'd spent the evening more on his toes than on hers. It was a credit to him that he had made it look elegant.

"But your songs," he said.

She flushed deep red. "I—I did ask . . . about composing." She faltered, twisted her skirts in her lap. She had never lived through such an embarrassed eternal moment. Not even when the count had caught her with the rogue in the stable. It hadn't compared to those musicians staring at her in taut shamed silence, the air splintery with it. The maestro spoke something so obvious it was painful to be forced to speak it, "Your lack of training is apparent. You haven't the slightest grasp of musical theory and you are a case in point why there are, nor can there be, any women composers."

And there had been the laughter behind the door after she'd gone, the unmirthful snapping of horribly embarrassed nervous tension that could not be held in a moment longer.

"It was quite horrible," said Caralisa. Though it seemed the smallest bit less horrible for having told it to someone. Someone who could read music.

"Their mistake," said the count. "Their loss. Sing."

She did not want to sing. She wanted him to take off that mask and gloves and kiss her.

And if he was offensive to see, then turn out the lamps.

Touch me. Touch me.

Her blood was singing a torrid song. It roared in her ears, pulsed throbbing in her groin.

I would let you.

Then suddenly she was filled with doubt.

No. Please don't touch me.

Her thoughts had vacillated back and forth all night long.

"Well?" he said.

She shook her head. She had lost the train of their conversation, lost in her own thoughts and desires. "What is your first name?" she asked.

"My."

"My?" she said. *Myron? Miles? Mycroft?* "What is your last name?"

"Lord."

My lord. "Oh." She blushed. "I am too forward."

A brow lifted behind the silvery furred vulpine mask. She could not see his brows, but could see the motion lift along his hairline. He bent an elbow to lean on the piano in heavy irony. "You?"

She stood up from the bench, blushing furiously, worse the more she tried to stop. She sang a torrid spate of notes, jumbled in magic and confused with conflicting emotions, fear and wanting.

She stopped and said, "My name is Caralisa."

"This I know," said the count.

"How, when I never told you?"

"I make it a point to find out what I want to know. I don't dwell easily in ignorance."

"Neither do I," said Caralisa.

"Then be uneasy," he said, for he was not about to tell her his name.

Caralisa reeled all her warm feelings back in, stung and

resentful. *I would never give myself to you,* she thought furiously. *Never. I was an idiot to think I could. Don't you dare think you could ever have me.*

She sang a haughty sharp little tune. It soon melted back into longing. Instead of singing "la, la, la," she switched to singing over and over "Michaeljohn, Michaeljohn, Michaeljohn."

Finally she was so tired she could not stay awake. She hung on a rope at the pin rail. A sandbag held her up. She let her head fall back, exposing a creamy expanse of throat. Her red hair cascaded behind her. "Please, please, I want to go to bed."

"Then I shall take you to bed," he said, rising briskly.

He moved to grasp the rope she hung on. He stood before her, over her, looking down hard, their faces close, breath to breath. His eyes were deep as the sky, storm-burnt blue, the look in them caught between passion and menace. Her full pouting lips parted, hungry to be kissed, quivering in fear, seeming so near to what she had thought she wanted moments ago. *No.* He was too . . . overwhelming, the unknown behind the mask too frightening.

She drew back, daunted.

He still gripped the rope she had abandoned.

He leapt to stand on the pin rail, balanced on it, thirty feet above the stage. And jumped.

Her own scream filled her ears, but even as she was screaming, Caralisa saw he was falling in slow motion, like a bird, his black cape fluttering as he descended. His boots struck the stage with a solid rap and he looked up at her. He let go the rope and it whizzed through the wooden block overhead until the sandbag counterweight landed with a thumping bang.

Caralisa screeched, "Don't you ever do that to me again!"

The count called up from the stage, "Mademoiselle, I didn't know you cared."

She gave a wordless growling cry, pounding small fists on the pin rail.

"Come down. The stairs, if you please. If you try the rope, you will just dangle there."

"Oh?" said Caralisa. Just to be contrary she tried the rope. When she put all her weight on it, the sandbag did not budge. She called down, "How much do you weigh?"

"Mademoiselle?" he said indignantly.

Colors chased across her face. "Oh. I've done it again." *Splendid manners, Caralisa!* "It's 'How much do you weigh, *my lord,'* isn't it?"

He chuckled. "Come down."

She found the stairs, a tight steep metal spiral, and she clattered down.

When he returned her home and lifted her over the wall onto the roof garden, it was five o'clock. Caralisa had never seen five o'clock. The house was asleep. No one had missed her.

He said good night on the terrace.

She had lost any anger she held for him. "I had a glorious time," she said. She could not find words to thank him.

"Here." He handed her something. "I caught it in the plaza."

It was one of the baubles Albertina had dropped from the balcony during the Sovereign's Night celebration, a spiral bracelet of amber paste beads.

"It's for luck," he said. "If you want it."

Her blue eyes were alight. "Oh yes!" The trinket itself was worth nothing, but it was from a princess's hand on an enchanted night, and Caralisa believed in luck and magic. She clutched it to her chest. "Yes, I want it." She looked up, smiling radiantly. She gazed into the eyes behind the mask. She couldn't read them, enigmatic indigo blue, speculative, gentle, aloof, hiding something like anger, something like want. There was too much in them to sort apart. She said, "Are you in love with me? Is that why you've done all this?"

"Why, you conceited little wench," he said genially. "How could I possibly be in love with you?"

She shrugged. Yes, it had been a silly thought. And he was not even kissing her hand in parting. She'd really done it this time. She danced to the door, turned. "Good night."

"Good night."

She went in, drew the door softly to.

The Count of Samothrace leaned back against the ivied wall, his hands behind him, bracing himself so he would not slide down, his face thrown back to the heavens.

"How could you do this to me, God? How can I possibly be in love with her?"

I was happy, a worm dwelling in darkness, eating mud and not caring because I knew no else. Until one day my head broke surface and I saw beneath a wide expanse of blue a wide wide world of scents and wonders and sights and sunlight. I never knew there was such a thing as light. Now I am looking up from the slime in which I must live, aware for the first time that my mouth is full of dirt, and my aspect is not fit for this world.

God forgive me for resenting the light when she descends to me and carelessly asks me: Do I love her?

Four

Caralisa found her bedroom door and eased it open. She could make out the silhouette of her bed in the moonlight. The feather duvet was mounded, and for a moment she thought someone was in it. Then she realized why no one had missed her. They all thought she was under the duvet, fast asleep.

She undressed in the hall and stole into her bedroom barefoot.

She turned back her bed covers. At the rustling, Viola sat up and whispered, "Where have you been!" Viola got up and pulled the door in until it snicked, then she lit a candle. Its gentle yellow glow washed a small pool around them. "Look at your *hair!*"

Viola had not been fooled. In fact, Viola had probably arranged the duvet to cover for her.

"Oh." Caralisa touched a hand to her matted hair. "It was mushed down all night." She crawled into her bed, oddly near tears. She drew in the pillow and covers and her mother's quilt around her into a cocoon.

Viola moved in to sit on her bedside. "Are you all right?"

Caralisa sniffled. "Oh, Viola, I've been pretty bad."

"Are you still a virgin?" Viola's voice was unalarmed, undamning.

"Yes. I think so."

Viola smoothed the covers. "Then it sounds like you had a better time than we did, and I shouldn't worry about it."

"Viola."

"Yes?"

Caralisa drew the spiral bracelet of amber paste beads off her wrist and lifted a corner of the blanket to give Viola a peek.

Viola stifled a squeal and seized it up for a closer look. She held it like a jewel. Princess Albertina was the most fortunate woman in the world. One had to believe she had luck to spare and never doubt she could toss it from the balcony on Sovereign's Night.

Viola gave a voiceless screech and a whispered, "You were in the plaza!"

"More than that, I'm afraid."

"What did you wear?"

Caralisa turned onto her back, her arms folded over the covers. She was feeling better, home and safe. She recounted like a dream, "I borrowed a gown from a theatre. It was rather incredible. I wish you could have seen it. I swear it was haunted, the dress. I became someone else entirely. Or maybe it was the mask. Perhaps the church is right about masks. I wasn't me."

"Did you go to a *real* ball?"

Caralisa nodded, eyes sparkling, and she almost laughed. "Several."

Viola stifled another squeal. "Good for you." She put a hand over Caralisa's and gave it a joggle. "Good for you. Take me next time."

"Wasn't the ball fun?"

Viola gave a wry elfin pout. "Don't dignify it by calling it a ball. It was a dance like all the others, only we walked down the stairs on our fathers' arms into a safe corral of hand-selected nice boys. Though, of course, there's no such thing as a nice boy, and first thing one comes up to Delia and stares at her chest and says, 'They want out.' It was that kind of evening. Mostly a tame, staid little dance, the only excitement of the juvenile sort. Chaperoned as usual. It ended hours ago. Midnight. Delia was a smash. I never knew boys were so crazy about a few inches of cotton wool. Some-one licked my shoulder."

"Isn't Joshua a nice boy?"

"No, but I love him." Her gray eyes shone merrily.

"Is he the one who licked your shoulder?"

"No. Josh took that one outside and hit him."

Caralisa fell to brooding, realizing that something similar had happened to her, but oh dear God, it hadn't been her shoulder. And the man who'd defended her wasn't even her love.

"Did you dance with a man?" Viola asked.

Caralisa nodded.

"Was he handsome?"

"One was beautiful—"

"One was! You mean there was more than one!"

Caralisa nodded. "One, well, he was the third one, he was beautiful. And he called me 'my love.' "

"Oh my. What was *that* like?"

"It is not an acquired taste. You like it immediately."

Viola giggled. "And what of the first and the second?"

"One was, um, not beautiful, but . . . captivating. He was very very wicked." She writhed in remembrance. "And then there was the Count of Samothrace, who kept dragging me away from everything."

"Oh ho. Him. I should have guessed he was behind this."

"My guardian devil."

"Is *he* handsome?"

"Who knows. Nice chin."

"You mean you still haven't seen his face?"

Caralisa shook her head.

"What is he like?"

"I hardly know. Neither gentleman nor rogue. Or both. I couldn't say. Arrogant. Arrogant. Arrogant."

"Is he arrogant, by any chance?"

"Now that you mention it, I would say he is arrogant."

"What did he want?"

"I don't know. I think I amuse him. I'm afraid I got rather angry at him. I don't think he will be calling again. Oh Viola, I was pretty bad." Droplets stole from the corners of her eyes and trickled back toward her ears.

"Sleep," said Viola, wiping the younger girl's tears. "That's exhaustion coming out of your eyes. Maybe it's for the best you don't see him again. You had your fling, now you're home and all is well." She kissed her brow and blew out the candle. "Good night."

The feeble light of false dawn paled the black windows of the Frankish castle. The ballroom floor was strewn with crushed flowers, wilted wreaths, and discarded masks. The silk covered walls were smudged with floating ash. In the center of the hall was a blackened pit of embers. In the alcoves, couples lay together, sides rising and falling with long breaths. The hardy souls were on their way up to the castle battlements where breakfast was served with a red drink called "dog's hair."

Golden wreath askew on his head, Nero was negotiating the red-carpeted steps down from his elevated dais. He was watching his sandaled feet when he walked into a living black wall. With a start, he looked up into a masked face.

"Ye gods, Samothrace!" he breathed, hand to his chest.

The count stood aside to make way for the unsteady emperor of the masque.

Never accessible, the mysterious Samothrace seemed more reserved that ever, without animation, hollow and distant.

Nero gestured with his violin to the black wallow of ash in the center of the hall where earlier the elaborate miniature of old Rome had stood. "You missed it. I gave the concert of my life. Infernal model wouldn't catch. We had to splash cognac on it."

"You need to be fatter to be Nero," said the count expressionlessly.

"Eh?"

"Nero was fatter. And he did not play while Rome burned."

Nero scoffed. He took Samothrace's arm, leaned on it heavily, and with his violin bow pointed in the direction he wanted to go. "As if you were there."

"And what if I was?" said the count.

"Were, Samothrace," Nero corrected liked a peevish don. "What if you *were.* Devil take you foreigners. Larissa has four languages, why don't you use one you know? A contrary to fact statement requires the use of the subjunctive. 'What if I was' means you really were there!"

"I know."

It took several moments for the import to penetrate Nero's sotted mind. He gave a nervous laugh. "You devil! You make me believe you when you talk like that, you know. But if I *were* to tell anyone, I should look a perfect imbecile."

"Not a perfect one, surely."

"Why have you come back to torment me?"

"I am in search of mindlessness," said the count.

"And you knew you could find it here in abundance. Come, we're up on the battlements."

They had come to the stone staircase. Nero set himself to huffing and puffing the long hike up. The count followed without effort.

"You did not even bring the picturesque nymph," Nero complained. "Where is your charming companion this morning?"

Samothrace spoke—far away inside himself—as if realizing the truth in the words as he pronounced them, "I believe I have lost her."

"You *lost* her? How careless of you, Samothrace. Keep her on a shorter leash."

"I have never known a woman worth keeping who could be held by a tether of any sort," said the count.

"Aye, more's the pity," Nero rued. He stepped on the hem of his toga. Grumbling, he reeled up the draping fabric and continued up the stairs. "They are inscrutable. If one cannot leash them to hold them, then how *is* it to be done?"

"I wish I knew," said the count. The wistfulness in it was a revelation.

"Ah!" Nero crowed. He turned on the stairs, triumphant. "Ha! Ah ha! Ah ha! Ah ha!" he cried out, trying out a different stress every time, unbridled glee in his porcine eyes. He had stumbled upon a prize—the chink in the unassailable Samothrace's seamless armor. "The girl! The girl! The little girl!"

The count's deep voice dropped lower still to become an ominous rumble. "You suppose you may taunt me with impunity?"

"Why yes and why not," said Nero blithely. "I know you are dangerous, *monsieur le comte*. But murder of a gadfly for merely annoying you is beyond even you."

"You more than annoy," said the count softly. A change came over his eyes.

A *change*.

Nero dropped his violin. It clattered down the stairs. "Jesus, Mary, and Joseph!" Nero tore his glance away, not to look upon what should not be seen. He wrung his plump hands, gazed after his violin. He muttered upon a safe prosaic subject, "Look what you've done. I rather liked that fiddle, you know." When he looked again, the count's eyes were merely frightening.

Nero took his wreath from his head, spoke straightforwardly, "Leave the child alone. You she doesn't need."

"You think I don't know that?" said the count. "She does not need me and I as sure as *hell* do not need her."

"What makes you think you don't?" said Nero, reconsidering his advice. "Love has reclaimed more than one incorrigible wretch."

Because she does not need me. And . . . "I have no wish to watch her die."

Nero shuddered. The way he'd said it. As if it were inevitable he see her die if he love her. Nero argued, "She is less than half your age."

"Much less," Samothrace agreed.

"Then it is unlikely she precede you."

"It is a certainty."

Nero paused. He fingered his gold wreath. Quietly he asked, "Are you cursed?"

"One of us is. I am not sure which. The end is the same." He turned on the stairs to go down. "Your pardon, Excellency. The mindlessness I seek is not here."

He went outside into the gray dawn.

There was no escaping her. She was everywhere.

Everything I want. The last thing I need.

In the light of dawn, whatever had possessed Caralisa the night before released its grip and left her astonished. Where there had been raging desire she could only feel shame and disbelief.

I let him do WHAT? Who was he!

Her heart thudded in panic at the thought that she was ruined.

She was overcome with a flutter in her midriff and prickling at the edges of her tongue with sourness, a wobble in her throat, and sickness down deep. Oh no. Oh no. At the thought of discovery, quills of dread broke out all over her skin. Oh no.

What had got into her?

It wasn't me.

It wasn't me.

And in sudden tentative relief she realized that it had not been she! Not that anyone would recognize.

She had been in disguise and no one would know her if they saw her again! Except for the Count of Samothrace and the beautiful Michaeljohn, who had taken no liberties with her and thought nothing ill of her. He had said he loved her.

Caralisa was easy to disguise because no one knew who she was in the first place. She was no one.

Not ruined. Not ruined. Her shameful secret would remain a secret.

The Count of Samothrace, she felt certain, would not betray her. He was so terribly good at keeping secrets. It had to be secrets, not women, that Nero had accused him of having so many of.

But the rake! That palace guardsman with the Rhinish accent. Thank heavens she had not removed her mask for him!

Who was he!

She could ask the count. The count had said, "I know this man." But she would never see the count again after the way she behaved. And how could she possibly bring herself to ask, "Who was the man whom I let . . . uh . . . you know . . . in the stable?"

She could picture the count waiting and ever so politely saying, "Whom you let do what, mademoiselle?"

No, she couldn't ask. And she didn't want to know.

She wanted to forget it happened.

She felt incredible relief that the Count of Samothrace had not tried anything with her. She might have let him. Depending on which moment he asked.

She had been as a yowling cat. She remembered her vacillation. If he'd have wanted at the wrong time, she would have let him . . . anything. Everything.

She remembered back home on her parents' farm she had a young bitch puppy in her first heat. She had howled and whined to get out, while a pack of dogs paced outside her door.

I am no better than a beast.

She could not face Samothrace again if she had—*Oh no.*
She could not face him anyway. He had seen her with the
rake, sprawled on her back, clutching him, her breasts bared.
He had seen her like that.

Her face burned. It had to be as red as her hair this time.

Suddenly the girls burst into her bedroom in a chattering
flock, all talking at once, reliving the triumphs of their debut,
pausing only to say how sorry they were that poor Caralisa
couldn't have been there.

"Caralisa!" Laurel crowed. "What you did with my hair
was marvelous." She was repiling it on her head and jammed
in the comb.

"Laurel's hair fell," Delia said.

"It didn't *fall,*" said Laurel. "I discovered that men die
when you do this." Laurel pulled out the comb and shook
out her tousled blond tresses. "Just die. My, but yours looks
shabby this morning. Wash it."

Caralisa gave a few desultory nudges at her flattened hair.
She tried to sound interested in the ball. "Did anyone find
true love last night?"

"I don't know. Ask the belle of the ball." Laurel tossed
Delia's padding up in the air.

Delia retrieved her camouflage in a huff. "It worked, didn't
it?" She met Caralisa's pinched brow. "The child looks
shocked."

"I'm not shocked," Caralisa protested. She regarded Delia's accessories in troublement. "I was just wondering . . .
what happens when you undress . . . in front of a man. Won't
he be . . . disappointed?"

"He would have to put a ring on this finger to unwrap
this package," said Delia. "And by then it'll be too late."

"But he'll think—"

"If that's what he married me for, that's his problem," said
Delia. "Where's the newspaper?"

"I have it," said Megan.

"Here," Delia demanded and snatched it away. She turned to the society page. "Did we get a mention?"

Viola read over her shoulder, "Never mind us. Read to us what we missed when we were at our punch and cookies."

The debut was mentioned factually in one line. No one's name appeared.

Laurel consoled them, "If one is Old Guard, one's name should appear in the paper three times in one's life, at birth, at marriage, and at death."

"Yes, they can say that," said Megan. "But all *their* names are in the paper today!"

Delia read the gossip. Caralisa paled and listened to tales of grand masques, the reporters playing a guessing game, "The waltz of hearts but whose was whose?"

Caralisa froze up at the line: "As usual, most masks were in vain."

Caralisa was going to die. She reminded herself over and over that they could not identify whom they did not know in the first place.

Delia paused in her reading as she hit a passage. She groaned, "Oh lord! To die for! Listen: 'The question all Larissa is asking this morning is who was that mysterious beauty seen in the company, mostly, of the ever-masked C de S, though also reported with M de St. F and even of F von K.'"

Caralisa lost all color. Her heart bobbled in her throat. Could they be talking about her? C de S. Comte de Samothrace? Who were M de St. F and F von K?

And was all Larissa truly trying to find her!

" 'This young lovely captivated Larissa's jaded eye, but truly remarkable is that we—and we know everything—still cannot put a name behind the mask.' " Delia folded the paper. "Oh Jiminy, isn't that a wet dream!"

"Girls don't have wet dreams," said Megan.

"Speak for yourself," said Laurel.

Viola, God bless her, asked ever so casually, "So Delia, who are C de S, M de St. F, and F von K?"

"Don't be silly," said Delia authoritatively. "C de S is Caralisa's faithless Count of Samothrace. M de St. F is the young and gorgeous and very eligible Marquis de St. Florian, and F von K is that scoundrel Freiherr von Keigfeld."

Caralisa trembled. Someone had seen her with that wicked guardsman last night! She had his name now, or at least a title: Freiherr von Keigfeld. She did not want to know any more.

And Marquis de St. Florian! Michaeljohn was a foreign lord! Why, oh why had she run from him?

Caralisa quietly got dressed in her plainest dress and put a shawl over her head.

"Where are you going, Caralisa?" said Brynna.

"Church."

"We just went yesterday."

"I—"

"Caralisa's got the calling," said Delia.

"No, um. I'm going to confession. Monsignor scolded me because I haven't been in over a week."

"Why is Caralisa going to confession?" said Megan. "She's the only one who couldn't have got into trouble last night."

"Neither did we," said Viola.

"Speak for yourself," said Laurel. "*I* was kissed, and not by a mere boy."

"Who?"

"Jillian's stepfather."

"Laurel!"

"He felt my breast."

"Over or under?" Delia challenged quickly.

"Over, silly."

"What did it feel like?" said Brynna.

"Because there was only this much between us"—she

held up her dress—"instead of this"—she tossed up one of
Delia's pads—"it felt like nothing you can imagine."

Megan regarded Laurel's chest and curled a lip. "How did
he *find* it?"

"But Laurel, that's adultery," said Delia very seriously.

"Maybe," said Laurel, her sharp little chin held high. "But
I didn't commit it. It wasn't my vow that was broken. *I* never
promised to love, honor, and obey anyone." She glanced over
where Caralisa was creeping for the door. "Have fun, Caralisa. Confess something for me and beware the immaculate
press gang!"

Daunted by the baroque grandeur of the cathedral, Caralisa
lost heart and kept walking. She would have to circle back
eventually. But at the moment she could not bring herself to
go inside. Inside smelled always of precious incense and
costly perfumes. The massive oak doors with their gilded
carvings dwarfed her, and their opening did not so much
admit the penitent as it yawned and swallowed them. The
elaborately carved stone steeple towering majestically above
that imposing portal soared to heights too lofty for her to
face.

According to the church of Byzantion, the tiny principality
of Montagne was not an independent bishopric, and Larissa's
magnificent cathedral, for all its grandeur, was not the center
of a bishop's see. Monsignor Fortenot desperately wanted to
be a bishop. But Larissa's reputation for the unholy was
known to the ends of the earth, and especially to Byzantion.
The Larissans kept embellishing their cathedral. Someday
Byzantion would have to notice how sumptuous and glorious
and deserving it was.

It was grand indeed, and Caralisa could not go in. She
walked stiffly forward, not knowing where to, oblivious to
Larissa's quaint stone bridges spanning green canals, its
crowded shops and wrought iron balconies of the dwellings

above, their windowboxes spilling bright red blooms. She did not notice when the buildings thinned and avenues broadened to garden lanes shadowed by spreading elms and chestnut trees.

She just walked, trying to gather courage enough to turn around, until she found herself at the abbey.

The abbey was simple, rambling, big in a sprawling bulky way, and old—a place to talk to a carpenter's son. Caralisa passed under the old stone campanile, which housed the bells christened St. Agnes and St. James, the old bells that rang only when royalty married.

The abbey served a common flock, mostly its own brethren. Since the cathedral had been built, most people went there instead. The girls attended mass at the cathedral to see what everyone was wearing.

Caralisa crept through the churchyard, which was actually the abbey yard. Only important personages rested below the cathedral. Many wealthy folk threw money at the cathedral in their twilight days, not to divest so as to be able to pass through the eye of a needle, but to buy a place of esteem under its imported tile floor. The abbey yard accepted no reservations, and one was likely to end up next to *anybody*.

Soft green grass was moist and spongy underfoot as Caralisa moved between the peaceful white limestones coated with moss. The abbey was a place most Larissans came home at last.

The abbey was very old, giving it something the cathedral could not have—an ancient tradition. The prince had to marry at the abbey to make his bride the princess and mother of his heirs. It had to be there and only there. If not, the woman was not the princess of Montagne and her children could never be his heirs.

Caralisa crept inside the minster to scents of rubbed cedar wood and melted beeswax. It was a warm and gentle place. Caralisa wiped her feet on a plainspun hemp mat. This was

Rebecca Ashe

the only place in Larissa that made her think of her home in the country.

A voice, too even and gentle to startle, sounded beside her. "Child? What do you seek?"

"I, um . . ." She mumbled around a good deal, unsure if confessions were even heard here or if she would sound silly asking. Finally he sifted it out. "Confession?" he said, and abruptly he was walking, with her in tow, down a long stark corridor. He said, nearly shouting—shouting, in fact— "Brother Joseph!"

A low rounded door opened upon an old man in a small cell. He looked up smiling, his watery eyes bird-bright crescents set within wreaths of wrinkles. "Brother Joseph will hear your confession."

Brother Joseph stood up, shaking and nodding, smiling. He beckoned a gentle gesture to come, then folded his palsied hands in prayer.

And Caralisa confessed to the simple monk in his bare cell. To her shocking revelations the man reacted not at all. As if he'd already heard everything. Or heard not a thing. He made a quaking sign of the cross over her and whisperingly told her to go and sin no more.

Caralisa came out into sunlight. She turned her face up to the clear blue sky, the sun on her cheeks, and she sang for pure joy. Forgiven. She danced through the gate, quieted long enough to creep diffidently through the yard, then burst into song again in the street, accompanied by the impudent chirping of brown sparrows.

As she passed the cathedral on her way home, Monsignor Fortenot stepped out to waylay her. "Where have you been?"

He wore only the black cassock and biretta, a black one though he'd have given his eye teeth for it to have been purple. He looked quite simple except that the beads of his rosary were polished cherry wood and the links were gold. His biretta was velvet and the cassock was camel hair, custom fit to make him look broad shouldered and trim, concealing the bulge of age in his middle. He presented an ever-striking figure with his silvered temples and craggy face. His resonant voice sounded louder than it ought, as if he were projecting to the last pew—or to the second balcony of the opera house.

"O Monsignor," said Caralisa. "You were right. I don't know how you knew. I am a wicked creature. I don't know what came over me. I hardly knew myself."

"You have fallen," he concluded gravely.

"Yes, Father. I did."

"Did you enjoy your sin?"

"I did then, but I don't now. I felt so dirty and I detest my sins, truly I do."

His voice dropped to a low growling whisper. "Tell me what you did. What did you feel?"

"I just want to forget it now."

"That's the sin talking."

"No, it isn't. I haven't got the sins anymore. I confessed them already. They're behind me."

"How do you know what is good?" the monsignor challenged angrily. "You who don't listen to me when I tell you about yourself. Aren't you the one who just sullied herself even as I warned you?"

"But God forgave me. It's forgotten."

"You are a true daughter of Eve," Monsignor boomed, his arms flung wide, and he looked like a black shadow advancing on her. "A temple of sinful flesh. The sin is part of you."

Caralisa backed away, her lower lip trembling, wide blue eyes puddling with sudden tears. Her musical voice quivered low, "God forgave me."

Michaeljohn the Marquis de St. Florian languished in a room full of books. He spun the globe distractedly, his breakfast on the silver tray untouched. He had been pining for days and his friends wondered if he were not ill.

This was the very fever of love.

He kept to his high-vaulted Gothic chamber in the université, the narrow space between its gray stone walls cluttered with the toys of science and music. The shelves, which were built to the high ceiling, were crammed with books, double stacked with books behind books on top of books—books of politics and philosophy, math and science, art and poetry, and moldering arcane books dabbling in magic. There was a saucer set outside his door for a feral cat that roamed the dormitory halls; it came and went like an inconstant familiar. The milk had dried and smelled a bit. There were sweets laid out on the window ledge for the obese squirrels that came in the morning. Sun streamed in diffused through dirty tinted glass set within the tracery of the high trefoil windows. Around him lay scattered in jumbled heaps all his scholarly toys—an astrolabe and telescope, a hollow globe, a skeleton of a shrew and an elephant tusk, the skull of a man with a candle burning within, a violin he'd forgot how to play, an ancient kithara he'd never known how to string, a flute from which he wrested doleful melodies, boxes of beakers and glass tubing and chemicals from abandoned experiments in chemistry, an abacus, a pentagram and vials of magic potions, a trunk full of clothes, a narrow bed, and no room to move.

A black mask hung on the knob of his straight-backed chair.

In the days since the masque, he had turned the town upside down searching for an angel with hair of red silk.

His friends told him that she did not exist.

"I made her up. She was too perfect," he sighed in concession, but then his heart rebelled. "But oh, she was there. She was *there*."

All his efforts had failed to find her. Since then he had languished. The room was in shambles. The flowers in the many vases had browned and withered in shrunken scum-topped water. His attendant (foreign nobility were limited to one servant and they were not permitted to sit for exams in their masters' stead), Marmarle, had not cleaned, for St. Florian had him out on a vain eternal quest to comb the city for the mysterious red-haired maiden, without so much as a glass slipper to fit to her.

Two of his friends, Bernard and Claude, came to the door, a third through the window. Aristide lived just down the hall but enjoyed the climb along the window ledge teetering above the steep drop where the hill rose abruptly from the river bend. The room afforded a dramatic picturesque view of river and hillside, but Michaeljohn did not notice anymore.

Aristide jumped down from the windowsill. He held a scented handkerchief to his nose, picked up one of the vases loathingly with the tips of his forefinger and thumb, and passed it to his own long-suffering attendant, who had followed him the treacherous path in.

"Roger, *do* something with these," he said. And crossing to Michaeljohn, Aristide lifted a lock of brown hair with equal loathing. "And with this. It's nearly dead. Something animate could make use of this room."

Aristide was an exquisite snob with features to suit. He could look down a long narrow nose, and his small mouth was not wide but full with petal lips that fell naturally into an indolent pout. His long face was drawn down to a point at his chin. He was narrowly built, tall, pale as an arsenic eater, and no one would put it past him to be so. The prospect of poisoning one's guest at tea with no danger of dropping dead oneself was an idea that held great fascination for him. Aristide Lord Avenroe was a true Larissan, with a self-indulgent decadence that never touched St. Florian. It ruffled Aristide's pride that the youth could associate with him and go untouched by his influence.

For all his languorous mannerisms, Aristide had a quick restive mind. He had become thoroughly bored and impatient with his friend's malaise.

"St. Florian, you are a bore."

"I am in love."

"As I said. You are a bore." Aristide made a gingerly tour of the narrow space. He lifted a tortoiseshell in his long-fingered hand. "Love. Never have so many afflicted men dedicated so much rhapsodic delirium to their disease. Now I could go on and on about my bout of pneumonia—"

"You *have* done, Aristide," Bernard inserted.

"But love. Men not only rave at length, they read volumes of raving of someone *else's* affliction. It is the most danger-ous and virulent epidemic in the world today and no one's endeavored to find a cure. I for one shall never succumb to love."

"Except for love of self," said Bernard.

"But that is a rational exception. That way one is always certain that one's intended is receptive to his affections and we don't have to face this—*this* . . ." He presented Michael-john as if he were an exhibit of grotesque morbidity. "Gods below, what to call this."

"She," Michaeljohn sighed.

"It speaks!"

"She is the only one who can relieve my suffering. There is a hole in my existence where she belongs. Right here." Michaeljohn indicated his heart.

"Egad. It's terminal. Friends, he is dying. Can I have your skull?" said Aristide, then he added, pointing to the candle. "That one. Not *yours;* yours is full of noxious mush."

"Can I have his hair?" said Claude, whose hairline had been in rapid retreat ever since he was seventeen. It was nearly to his crown now though he was scarcely twenty-one, while Michaeljohn's curls fell in a thick luxuriant honey-brown mane.

"Only save a lock for the lady who slew him," said Ber-nard.

"If one could but find her!" Michaeljohn cried.

A practical and methodical man, Bernard picked up a newspaper. "What does one know of the lady?"

"Nothing!"

Bernard read for clues, " 'The mysterious beauty in the company mostly with C de S.' That would be the man who calls himself the Count of Samothrace, yes? '. . . and also with M de St. F.' Lord, who could that be, my dear St. Florian? I haven't a clue. 'And with F von K.' " Bernard lowered the paper. "Who is this? F von K?"

Aristide answered, "One earnestly hopes it is not the baron."

"Who is that?" Michaeljohn sat up.

"Richardt Freiherr von Keigfeld. Worse company than myself," said Aristide. "One of the palace honor guard."

The guard were sent by courtesy of the King of the Rhine in accordance with the old pact between Rhine and Montagne dating back to Montagne's battle for independence.

"A despicable sort, even by my measure. A first magnitude opportunist. He is the one whom the Old Prince hired to take Albertina's hand in order to bar her from the throne. Our noble Prince Maximillian saved her from that, married her, and made her princess despite the old goat."

"Oh no!" cried Michaeljohn. His angel had been in vile company indeed.

Bernard scowled perplexedly. "Seven years on the guard? What keeps him here?"

"One assumes he cannot go home. If he was with your lady, St. Florian, woe is she."

"Oh no. Oh no."

"But," Aristide continued blithely, "I shouldn't place any stock in that report. It could easily be a lie. According to the Baron Keigfeld, there's not a virgin left in Larissa and he will tell you that he knows that firsthand."

"But we know for sure that she was with the Count of Samothrace," said Bernard.

"Then this is all too easy," said Aristide. "Find Samothrace."

Michaeljohn brought his hands together in slow ironic claps. "O jolly good. Bravo. Find Samothrace."

Aristide turned to Bernard and Claude. "Can I assume this means the man is elusive?"

"Rather," said Bernard.

"Perhaps he has left town?"

"Perhaps."

"Perhaps so has she," Aristide concluded.

"She must be a foreign princess," said Michaeljohn. "Because she is not in Larissa. I would have found her. But I thought this Samothrace was local."

"More or less," said Aristide.

"Then where in hell is he!"

"Very likely where you said."

"Where is his estate? The only Samothrace I know is a Hellenic island."

"That's the only one I know," said Aristide. Bernard and Claude added their nods in confirmation.

"Then?"

"I don't believe he's landed," said Aristide. "I don't believe he's even titled. I personally believe he's a pirate. He has one devilishly huge bankroll."

"Just who is this man?" said Michaeljohn.

"It's hard to say," said Bernard. "There seem to be two separate beings who share the dubious title and make it confusing."

"Two beings?"

"Once, very long ago, there was a magician who lived up on the Heights. He was said to be immortal. A demon. His familiar was a black swan. They say he would ride on the bird's back and circle the town like a vulture and pluck up virgins and the like."

"If he's immortal, what became of him?" said Michaeljohn.

"People stopped believing in him and he went away like all fairy tales do when one grows up," said Bernard. "Now

there is this masked one who comes to Larissa and calls
himself the Count of Samothrace. Some say he is Larissan.
Some say he is in league with the fiend on the Heights. Some
say he *is* the fiend. One can't see his face, so maybe so. You
never see him without the mask, carnival or no, and it is said
that that is because his face is actually hideous as a gorgon
and it would turn you to stone—or else very beautiful to
seduce maidens and corrupt their virtue forever."

"That fiend has my angel!"

"That's only the part he plays," said Bernard. "That is not
the man he is. There's just a face under there. And to keep
up the facade his signet is a swan carved in jet, and he actually tried to buy the Heights."

"Who owns it now?"

"It's branded wasteland and cannot be sold. It's dangerous
and no one can get up there anyway."

"Wouldn't the banks have an address?"

Aristide shook his head. "His seal is good enough."

"I cannot believe they would do business with a man
whose face they have never seen."

"For him exceptions are made."

Michaeljohn slumped in his high-backed chair. "It's use-
less. I cannot contact him, and even if I did, he would refuse
to surrender my angel."

"Probably."

Michaeljohn lamented, "Azure eyes and ivory skin, hair
of red silk."

Aristide sniffed. "Egad. She sounds like the Frankish
flag."

"The hair was part of her disguise," said Bernard. "No
one has hair the color you describe."

"The hair of her mask was white as snow," Michaeljohn
insisted. "Under her mask her hair was red and real. Can no
one help me?"

The valet Roger spoke. "Put an advertisement in the paper:

Doctor Faustus beseeches the White Peacock Maiden to meet him somewhere at a specified time."

Michaeljohn came to life. He leapt to his feet, seized Roger, and kissed him. "Yes! *Yes!*"

"Don't kiss my valet. I shall become quite jealous," said Aristide. "Here comes your own."

Marmarle came to the door, halting quizzically to see his master's sudden animation.

Michaeljohn had seized up a pen and scratched out the message, so hastily he nearly tore the parchment. He thrust the note at Marmale and sent him back out with a push. "Put this in all the papers. Tell them to run it tomorrow. As you love me, hurry or I shall die of a broken heart!"

Five

Caralisa had picked up fresh peaches and cherries at the market and was on her way home. She had only to stop for a gossipy newspaper for Delia, who did not want to be seen buying it herself. "You do it, Caralisa," Delia had said.

Caralisa paid the vendor and tucked the paper under her arm without looking at it.

Ten days had passed since the masque. The Count of Samothrace must have been thoroughly disgusted with her, because there had been no sign of him. She expected never to see him again.

Until a flower fell across her path at the edge of the market. She stooped to pick it up, a red rose newly opened, shimmering dew drops clinging to its satiny petals. She looked around her to find who had dropped it.

"My lord!"

He stood in the shadows, all in black, at the edge of the lane where the narrowest of alleys threaded between two cramped buildings. He touched the brim of his tall black hat in greeting.

His mask was emerald this time and faceted like a gemstone. It covered the top half of his face and was shaped like a strange visage, like a man carved from a gargantuan jewel might look. Otherwise he was dressed in black. His habit was black to his waistcoat, his breeches; even his shirt and cravat were black.

"Did someone die?" Caralisa blurted.

"No," he said. "A conceit of mine."

She held the rose out to return to him. He held up a re-sisting palm, gloved in black. "That is yours. I am sorry you had to stoop for it."

"Thank you, my lord. One generally picks flowers from the earth."

You shouldn't. You should find them in bushels on your vanity. "I am going on a picnic," he announced. "I would have you with me. I shall show you a secret place."

"I cannot." The answer came out before she could even consider it. And when she did, she began to tremble inside and she could only draw shallow breaths.

"Why?"

She hesitated. She could not go off alone with a man. This man.

And why not? She had done it before and no harm had come to her—not from him.

It was not allowed. It was not proper. But why should she not go if she wanted to?

Did she want to?

Very much.

She fit the rose into the basket, on top of the fruit. She avoided looking at him. His very presence provoked feelings no decent girl should ever have. "I have to take this home. I am expected."

"After that."

"I—"

"Do not answer. I'll tell you where I shall be. The old oak tree by the pond behind the museum. I shall be there. You decide if you will or will not."

"Good day, my lord." Caralisa mumbled, fidgeted with her sun hat, and hurried home, faster than she needed.

She had no intention of meeting him.

The man was an occasion of sin. She would not fall from grace again.

She arranged the fruit in a basket and set it out for the

girls. She sat on her bed and turned a peach over and over
in her hands.

I cannot go.

How her heart had leapt when she saw him! The day had
brightened. He frightened and intrigued. Fascination gripped
her and would not for any reason release her.

What could possibly happen? He did not love her. She
was not what he was looking for. The confused maelstrom
of passion and fear was all on her side. She would be as safe
with him as within the impassive stone wall that sheltered
her up on the roof garden.

Or was that the fear? That she would be perfectly safe.

She feared to fall in love with a stone.

Bleak dead ends she was well acquainted with and wanted
no more of. She cried inside; why would God give her a
beacon in her darkness only to show her the rocks in between
and wave her off saying: *That light was not meant for you.*

She warned herself not to set her heart on that man. He
could not be hers. He did not love her.

Don't think on him.

And for your heart's sake, don't see him again!

As Caralisa sat struggling with her heart, the other girls
had found the fruit and seized up the best pieces. Brynna
complained that Caralisa had brought no apples.

"It's not the season for apples," said Viola.

"As if I am to know that," Brynna tisked. "I am city bred.
When is the time for picking apples—when the cows come
home?"

"The cows come home every evening."

"Then there ought to be plenty of apples, oughtn't there!"
said Brynna.

Delia, who was reading her paper, fell over sideways on
the bed with a groan of envy, holding her midriff as if she'd
been stabbed. *"Why* doesn't this ever happen to *me!"*

"What? What?"

Delia sat up and folded back the paper to read. "Isn't this

romantic? 'Dr. Faustus beseeches the white peacock maiden to meet him under the pagan bell at vespers.' "

"What does that mean?" said Brynna with a tisk.

Delia crumpled the paper into her lap. "They met at the masque! He doesn't know who she is and now he wants to find her!"

"There is no doubt a reason she didn't tell him," said Laurel derisively. "Dr. Faustus is a université cad and she couldn't wait to be rid of him. Why else wouldn't she have tipped her mask?"

"Laurel, you have no romance in your soul," said Delia.

Caralisa had become very still except for her heart, which raced inside her.

Dr. Faustus beseeches the white peacock maiden.

Michaeljohn!

She envisioned his sweet earnest face, so young and handsome, the strong line of his jaw and heroic chin, his luxuriant brown locks, his gentle ardent turquoise eyes. She recalled the sensation of his aristocratic soft white hands, so warm when they held hers. She could hear his clear voice as he cried after her: "I love you!"

The words echoed like a magic spell, lifting her heart and setting it giddily thrumming. Someone beautiful she met on an enchanted night loved her! And he was begging to see her!

At vespers.

Madame Gerhold locked the doors at vespers!

No matter. Caralisa must be under the pagan bell at vespers. There were no choices.

Six hours from now. She had to wait six hours.

She looked at the clock. Looked again. Less than a minute had passed. Time was suddenly moving so very slowly.

She rose and changed into her prettiest dress, the one with the rose ribbons. Her hands trembled as she tied the bow.

When the girls noticed her, it was Laurel's thin voice that stabbed into her racing thoughts. "Where are you going?"

Caralisa knew the question was coming. Better now than later. There would be no way for her to get out of the house were she to wait closer to vespers. She needed to leave now and stay out past curfew.

"To the museum pond," she said, as casually as she could. Her voice sounded high and nervous to her own ears. "To sketch swans."

"In *that?*"

Caralisa looked down at her dress as if just noticing it. She tried to think of a good reason to be putting on her best dress. "Um. Yes. I'm making my debut for the waterfowl."

She managed to sound sulky and jealous, and no questions followed. The girls had talked of little other than their debut for the past ten days. Evidently Caralisa was more envious than she had let on.

She seized her matching sun bonnet and her sketch pad and hastened out the door. She was halfway down the stairs when she heard a rattle behind her.

She turned on the steps. Viola stood at the head of the staircase with Caralisa's pencil box. "Drawing pencils?"

"Oh." Face aflame, Caralisa climbed up to take them. "Thank you."

Viola was sweetly smirking. She trilled lightly, "Don't mention it."

Caralisa stole out the door before Madame Gerhold could see her. Caralisa usually asked permission before going out. But she was going to be in trouble anyway when she broke curfew tonight. No use risking not being allowed to go just to fulfill the form now.

At the end of Elm Tree Close she took a breath. Made it! She swung her hat at her side and walked with a dancing step.

I will see him again! He wants me! This evening. This very evening!

Oh my love!

Six hours. She had six hours to pass.

How to begin was easy enough. A picnic with the Count of Samothrace. That would help the creeping hands move around that brutishly slow clock. No one made time fly faster than did he. She was happy to have been pushed to accept his invitation. She had wanted to so badly.

She tried to gather her shining tresses up into her sun bonnet, but her hair was newly washed, altogether undressed, full of electricity, and it floated up crackling.

As she fussed with it, she worried that the count might be angry with her hesitation and would not show. Worry became fear as she arrived at the museum pond.

The tautness instantly released its grip on her chest as she saw the black-clad figure waiting as promised under the gnarled oak tree. He always made her feel alive—sometimes mortally frightened, but never so intensely alive.

As she drew near, the eyes behind the emerald mask raked up and down her, taking in her fine rose dress and spring bonnet. "You needn't have for me."

Her faced warmed. She was quite overdressed for a picnic. "I didn't for you," she said.

"For whom?"

"For me," said Caralisa shortly. "I felt like it."

He escorted her to his waiting barouche.

He did not say how nice she looked or express any regret that it had not been done for him. Caralisa withdrew her heart further into the remotest recess of her being, where he could not carelessly tread on it. She refused, refused to give way to his infernal attractiveness.

I have a pure love and this unfeeling beast can only hurt me.

Only she could not call him unfeeling. There was something powerful in his gaze when he looked on her, a smoldering hunger of terrifying intensity.

But never, she told herself, never suppose that he loves you just because you want him to.

And sometimes she admitted to herself that she wanted

him to. He had given her no reason to suppose that he did. He had been brutally honest in that regard. *Why, you conceited little wench.* Words came no clearer than that.

Conceited? She straightened her shoulders proudly. The Marquis de St. Florian did not think her so! And it was for him that she had made herself pretty.

The carriage was rolling and she about to ask if they might put the top down when the count said, "I need to blindfold you."

She stiffened in alarm. "Why?"

"So that you cannot see," he said ironically.

She made a cross moue. "I mean, *why?*"

I told you I would show you a secret place. I did not say that I would show you the way to it."

"No. I shan't submit to such a thing."

"It won't be much of a picnic by myself." He rapped to stop the carriage. The driver brought it to a lurching halt, and the count reached for the door.

In horror Caralisa saw all her wonderful plans fading into the air like an insubstantial mist.

Swallowing down her stubbornness, Caralisa stopped him with a tentative touch to his black sleeve. "Oh, all right. But you must swear to safeguard my honor while I am at your mercy."

"Better than you yourself," he said, hand over his heart.

Her eyes flashed sapphire wrath as he covered them.

She had worn blindfolds before at party games. She had counted on there being slits of vision at the bottom of the blind. This one, however, was a thorough one. She could not even distinguish light and dark, and it muted even her hearing as it covered her ears as well.

She started to chatter, afraid of the muffled darkness. She wanted to hear his voice.

"I was very annoyed with you after the masque," she said, louder than she ought, as if raising her voice would somehow make all the other sounds speak up too.

"Oh, now that is very interesting," said the count in such a way that he could only mean that *he* had been very annoyed with *her*.

"Yes, but I have forgiven you since," said Caralisa.

"For what?"

"For acting as if you were so much better than I."

"Mademoiselle, I *am* your better."

"Are you a real count?"

"Why do you ask?"

"Some people say that you are not."

"Why do you suppose they say that?"

"I think they don't know, so they make something up to fill the blank spaces."

"And what do you fill your blank spaces with?"

"I don't," said Caralisa. "That's why I asked. Are you a real count?"

"I am the bastard of a king and queen."

She sat up, then leaned forward to hear better and to speak more quietly, "If they are king and queen, how does that make a bastard?"

"Of different countries."

"Oh!"

"I don't want to read that in the papers."

She cried, wounded, "I shan't tell anyone!"

"Not even Viola."

"How do you know about Viola?" She had a strong impulse to pull off the blindfold.

"Viola Constance, daughter of your godparents, John Christopher and Mary Rosalind Tyrolian, whom you came to live with after Joseph Benjamin and Mayella Rose Springer died in a farming accident during the floods of last spring."

"How do you know that!"

"A little bird told me."

"Then I should be more concerned about your little bird! *I* don't repeat tales!"

"We shall see."

The carriage came to a stop. Caralisa reached for her blind-fold, but the count took both her hands. "We walk now."

He helped her from the carriage. She was sure she heard plaza sounds and was afraid she would look imbecilic wearing a blindfold and letting herself be led. But then his hands were round her waist, lifting her. Her hands instinctively found his shoulders and he lowered her down a steep drop. Her feet landed on plant stems and earth. She was afraid she was trampling someone's garden.

"Pardon, mademoiselle, I fear for your pretty shoes," said the count and suddenly she was lifted in his arms. She gasped lightly with the intoxicating sensation of being swept off her feet, one powerful arm behind her knees, the other round her waist, her body pressed against his strong chest. Her arms clutched in darkness and circled his neck to rest on his regally straight shoulders. He moved smoothly with long assured steps, her weight presenting no burden at all. She felt the warmth of his body through his finely textured clothes. The chance grazing of his hair brushed the back of her hand with softness.

He carried her over whatever was in their path, then too soon he set her down again. Her feet touched soft earth. His arms slipped away from her. She lost contact with him momentarily.

Emotions swirled. She reached for balance, found nothing. "Is anyone looking at me?" she said.

"No one at all."

She heard squeaking, a thumping, the grating of a rusty key in a creaking door.

His gloved hand closed round hers and he led her into a cool stone passage smelling of moss and algae. Shadow gave way quickly to warm sunlight again, but with a subtle change in the air, cooler and sweeter. A balmy zephyr caressed her cheeks, the breeze freshened from passing over water and laden with the rich scents of green growing things, waxy spring blossoms, moist earth, and wet rocks.

The count came to a stop and Caralisa walked into the warm wall of his body. Masculine scent filled her dizzied senses and she reluctantly backed away a step.

"Boat," he explained.

"What kind?"

"Rowboat."

He steadied her as she stepped over the gunwale. Her hands groped blindly over a scratchy woolen blanket folded on the thwart as a cushion for her and she centered herself on it. She heard the splashing of the count's boots in the shallows. The boat moved with the shrill scraping of pebbles and mud underneath. The grating sounds gave way to lapping water, the boat rocking a little as the count climbed in with catlike balance. She heard the clatter of oars in the locks, felt the push of a strong rowing stroke propelling them forward.

"There is a parasol beside you," said the count.

She felt around. Her hand touched ruffles. She found the smooth carved wood handle and lifted it. It was scented. She wondered if it was new, or borrowed, or if someone had left it here from the count's last picnic.

She opened it and shifted it until the sun no longer tingled her cheeks.

The count told her she could uncover her eyes now.

"Ha!" she said, doing so. "I know where I am. This must be the river. Your blindfold is for naught."

She took the cloth from her face. Brightness stabbed her eyes and she blinked.

Sunlight glanced off the wide water with cutting brilliance. The rippling mirror of it stretched away in all directions, the serene color of sky and green trees and of high rock cliffs which hemmed it in on all sides. A glistening silvery thread of a waterfall spun down from a mossy emerald rockface and tumbled into the lake before a wide grotto undercutting the cliff. Everywhere Caralisa looked was wild breathtaking beauty and no sign of civilization. It seemed she and the count had left the city, but they could not have. They had not crossed the river, and crossing the river was the only way out of Larissa. Unless one could scale the Heights and go over the mountain, which was quite impossible.

A flight of white swans came sweeping over the rock palisades *en eschelon* to alight in the water, giving voice in rusty squalls.

"How beautiful!" Caralisa breathed. "Where *are* we?"

"Behind the Heights."

"Behind! How did we get here!"

"That is a secret."

"Oh my!" She turned her head round. Trees braved the steep slopes, cloaking them in a mantle of many greens before surrendering on high to bare rock. Catkins spiraled lazily down from their branches into the sky blue water. Willows dabbled long fronds over the banks. Fat gray-brown squirrels played within a stand of white birches clad in delicate yellow green. The hammering of a woodpecker rang from a hollow elm. Birds of a myriad voices whistled, chirped, laughed, and sang.

"It's so wonderful."

The count brought the boat ashore upon a tiny islet in the center of the secret lake where a picnic was laid out on a woven cotton blanket of blue and white. Caralisa uncovered the basket of bread and fine aged cheese, cured meat, sweet preserves, and fresh fruit as the count reeled in from under a willow's canopy a net in which a bottle of wine had been left to chill in the cold shadowed water.

Letting the parasol fall aside, Caralisa leaned back, propping herself up on her arms, turning her face up sunflower-style to the warm bright rays. This was all too idyllic.

She would love to show this to Michaeljohn.

She sat up and twirled the parasol. It was ruffled with white lace. "Not your color," she said to the count. "May I keep it?"

"It is not mine to give."

"Oh." A shockingly intense spear of jealousy stabbed her. "What is her name?"

"Leda."

"Why do you have Leda's parasol?" Caralisa asked tightly.

"I told her you might not bring one."

"Oh." Envy released its clawed grip on her midriff as she pictured a stout and kindly old aunt.

The bread was still warm, the fruit dripping sweetness, the cheese creamy with delicate richness, but Caralisa could hardly taste any of it. She could not think straight for anticipation. The long sunlit afternoon gave her time to imagine and to worry. This place bred dreams and possibilities.

How many Doctors Faustus were there? Michaeljohn had said that all université students were Doctor Faustus. And how many white peacock maidens? Maybe the costume she had worn was not singular. Perhaps it was one of a chorus, and hers had been the only one left, like *Swan Lake* with all its swans. Perhaps there had been peacocks everywhere at the masque, and this evening she would go to the pagan bell to find a whole troupe of université students trysting with a corps of white peacocks.

Or maybe the message was just for her. But he would find her plain and common outside of her fine peacock plumage.

Color came and left her face. She asked the time every five minutes.

She opened her sketch book.

"What are you writing?" said the count.

"Drawing," said Caralisa. "I said I was sketching swans. I had better have a swan to show for it. I don't see the black one. Does it ever come here?"

"There are several black swans."

"The all-black one. Even to its beak and eyes. And it's enormous and kingly. Do you know the one? I don't see how anyone could mistake it. The monks killed the wrong one."

"You would have preferred they kill the big one?"

"I mean they didn't kill the one they meant to kill." And

because he seemed so offended and it was said that the count of Samothrace was a warlock with a black swan for a familiar, she hazarded, "Is it your pet? The all-black one?"

"It has no lord."

"Does it come here?"

"From time to time."

"What time is it now?"

"Soon after the last time you asked. Why?"

"I must be home before sundown."

"The sun is still in the morning half of the sky."

"I should be a little early really."

"It is very early."

"Why do you wear a mask always?"

"To conceal my face."

"Is it so very fair?"

"No."

Oh. She had imagined that it was.

"Can it be so horrible?" she said.

"Sufficiently afflicted to warrant a mask."

"May I see?"

"You will never see my face unadorned."

"Do you trust me so little?"

"You inquisitive little cat. I trust you not at all."

"Yes you do. You told me your history."

"In vaguest terms, I did. Nothing you can hurt me with."

"Why would I want to hurt you!" she cried.

"It is something you could manage."

"But I wouldn't!"

His eyes narrowed and seemed physically to darken. The look within the green mask held something approaching torment. But how could it, on such a serene summer day? He said nothing for a long time. At last he bid her, "Tell me what is wrong. You have been shivering."

"Nothing. Nothing." She broke a coy smile because she had been thinking of Michaeljohn. "Nothing."

She had been humming, distracted. Her music warbled and trembled, ecstatic and expectant.

The count took away her sketch book and gave her a book of musical staffs instead. They were all blank.

He bid her, "Write it down. You know the names of the notes now, and how to show how long to hold them."

"I don't need to write it down," said Caralisa. "I shall remember."

"So that someone else can read it."

"Why should someone else want to read it?"

"So they may sing it. So they may play it. Do you expect to go onto the stage solo and a capella?"

"Oh no." Her blue eyes grew very round, lashes fringing them in a wide wreath. "I couldn't go on at all!"

"Then write it down so your troupe may."

"My troupe," she muttered below her breath. To humor him, she took the book and began to write. She was still humming as she went. "Do you sing?" she said.

"Like a frog."

"I like your voice. Are you sure you cannot sing?"

"I brought a better voice."

He had a violin, which he drew from its case and began to tighten the horsehair bow.

"Very well, you play this line," she pushed a page at him.

"With how many voices do your voices sing to you?"

"Sometimes one. Sometimes very many. Bunches, in fact."

"Bunches," he echoed, amused. He began to play and she sang with him a different line. She heard a deep bass line resonating far below the soprano duet of herself and the violin. *Heard* it. This wasn't one of her voices.

She stopped at once. "You lied!"

The count wolfed a chord. He lifted his bow from the strings. "Madomoiselle?"

"You said you could not sing!"

"That is not precisely what I said."

She shot him an irritated glance. He had only said that he sang like a frog. The frog had a resonant voice.

She glanced away, forgot what she was angry about. She pointed toward the thin thread of a waterfall spinning down from the high precipice into the grotto. "Can we go over there!"

"There is nowhere to put the boat ashore."

"Then we shall stay in the boat. Can we?"

He tilted his head to the side, conceding. He put on a glove, and for the first time she noticed that he had taken one off, the left one, to play the violin. His hand was covered again before she had even looked at it. Her thoughts were not altogether here.

He helped her into the rowboat, pushed it off, and climbed in. He took up the oars and rowed smoothly, dipping one at a time, toward the waterfall. Caralisa sang a new song. She noticed that the count had put the book of staffs into the boat. Indigo eyes glanced from her then to it and back to her. She stopped singing. Her shoulders drooped. "Must I?"

"Well, I cannot; I'm rowing."

She took up the book. "I wish I were a hydra. Then I might have enough heads to sing my songs as I hear them."

"Write down all your voices one at a time. The hydra can be managed later."

"There are two separate melodies going on here. They're singing to each other."

"Is there a story?" he asked.

"Yes. Um. It's called the 'Masque of Hearts.' Once upon a time there was a girl. And she met a boy at carnival. They were wearing masks so they didn't know who each other was. But they fell in love."

"Without seeing each other's face?" said the count, eyes upon her.

"Yes," said Caralisa, oblivious to his fixed gaze. "You don't think it can be done?"

"No," he said flatly.

"Well, they did," she retorted. "Because they fell in love with their souls. And after the masque they desperately tried to find each other. But her father had arranged a prestigious match for her. She received a message from her beloved and she wanted to fly to him, but her brothers locked her up. That's this song here. Meanwhile he is waiting for his love, and when she doesn't show, he guesses that she doesn't really love him, and he agrees to wed a girl of his father's choosing. His father is a duke. His men march him to the altar and he takes the vows and lifts his bride's veil. He has never seen her face before, but their hearts know. It is his love.

"In this song she's supposed to meet him, but her brothers have her locked up."

"How does she know to meet him, if they don't know who each other is?"

"What do you mean?"

"How does he get a message to her if he does not know where to send it?"

"He . . . uh . . . put a notice in the paper addressed to her disguise," Caralisa said nonchalantly, as if she were making it up on the spot. "She went to the masque as a . . . a . . . a . . . golden bird. And he signed it . . . um, what was he?"

"Dr. Faustus?" the count suggested.

Caralisa dropped her pencil. It bounced under the thwart. She pushed jerkily at a loose strand of her red hair. "No. Why?"

His expression did not change. His eyes were steady upon her. "All université students are Dr. Faustus."

"Well, he's not a student," she snapped, and set herself to fishing under the thwart for her pencil. When she came up, she said flatly, "He went to the masque as a white knight." She bent over her book and furiously recorded notes.

Inside she was dying. He knew. He knew. He was pulling her strings just to watch her dance and twitch.

The count must have seen the advertisement. *Dr. Faustus*

beseeches the white peacock maiden. How difficult was that to figure out?

She pushed on as if oblivious, as if she did not care, as if he were not treading on her open nerves. "This is his part— lower, of course. You have to imagine I'm a tenor."

"Difficult."

"Well, try." She began to sing. She paused only to say, "He first sees her and watches her dance." And she sang, gazing up at the waterfall as it tumbled down the rocks, twisting like crystal smoke, shimmering in the light and sending out a rainbow spray where it kissed the stones.

She wrote down several songs, added parts, and they played them together. They returned to the islet and finished the wine. Caralisa hadn't noticed the time passing. The shadows shifted. Light played different colors as the sun sank below the rock wall. The swans gathered into arrowheads and left. The grotto seemed suddenly chill.

"Oh. I must go home!" Caralisa cried.

"You are in time," said the count. "The sun is still quite high. I shall see you to your door."

"That won't be necessary," said Caralisa. "Take me as far as the market."

"What sort of ill-bred rogue do you take me for?" He gathered up the picnic things and rolled up the blanket. "Your door, mademoiselle."

"I need to pick up some things at the market," Caralisa hedged.

"We shall stop together. What is it you need?"

She was stuck now. She did not want to stop at the market. She wanted to get away from him. "There isn't time," she said.

"Of course there is. You will be home by your curfew."

That would be too late. Her curfew was vespers.

She let him blindfold her again if he promised to make haste. When he let her remove the blindfold, the carriage was in the market. No bright sunlight stabbed her eyes. The sun was sinking visibly toward the painted horizon.

She climbed down from the carriage and burned precious minutes buying a sprig of rosemary she did not need. She insisted she could find her way from here.

"Twilight is not an hour to leave a young woman unescorted," said the count.

"Your escort will alarm my guardians," said Caralisa. "I can't be seen to go home in a carriage!"

"Then we shall walk. I shall be discreet."

And he stayed with her as far as the entrance of Elm Tree Close. He lingered there, hanging back in the broad shadow of an elm, watching her to her very door under a darkling sky.

I can't go in! I'll never get out again!

She turned and waved. He stayed there still. She cracked the door and slipped inside. She closed the door soundlessly after her.

She stood in the stuffy dimness of the vestibule at the base of the stairs. She could hear the others moving about upstairs, the kitchen help rattling the pots and pans downstairs, her own heart hammering in her chest. No one had noticed her come in.

She might have slipped back out again, but he would be there, watching.

Bells from the hall clock chimed.

Vespers!

Caralisa crept from the vestibule, under the staircase, to the kitchen. She ducked down and walked in a crouch behind the butcher block tables, dodging the kitchen help, to the back door. She slipped out the back where the vegetable scraps raised a pungent smell. She tiptoed out the back of the yard, creeping along the high wall that supported the roof garden, then darted the open space to the back of the property, through the trees to the road, and *ran* in the fading light.

The pagan garden was clear across town. Michaeljohn would be there now. Now, this moment.

Slow homebound ox carts from the closing market blocked the narrow bridges over the canals. Caralisa ran through the zigzagged streets. As the last bell of vespers shivered out to evening silence, she had barely begun.

When she arrived, sweaty and breathless, her hair all undone, the pagan garden was dark. The black wrought iron gate creaked mournfully upon opening. A flurry of darker shadows speckled the dusky ground like fluttering leaves as a flock of small birds fled from the tree above her.

In the garden the ancient stones held ghostly traces of the last shreds of twilight.

Caralisa's heart pounded from exertion and expectation. Was Michaeljohn here?

Was she the one he waited for?

She could scarcely breathe. The ancient stelae marked graves of those who had died before the church of Byzantion had brought the true word to the land. The stones themselves were half buried in time. The tops showed, weathered away, some of them carved with incomprehensible script and all too clear pictures of men and women saying goodbye. And there were animals. The pagans had been fond of animals. Stone dogs and horses, a giant bull, sometimes rabbits for a child. They had once been painted but they were worn white now. Their snowy marble took on a spectral quality as the ruddy end of twilight faded to cold moonglow.

Caralisa's steps slowed as she drew near the bell.

On her way there she had conceived a horror that she would see someone else under the bell, locked in an embrace with her beloved. Someone, the real peacock maiden, for whom those passionate words had been meant.

Caralisa stole nearer, her breath inheld.

There was no one at all under the pagan bell.

Taut muscles relaxed past relief to disappointment. She walked under the ancient bronze bell encrusted in green patina.

At her feet the scattered petals of a rose lay all about, not so much plucked as torn and hurled in every direction in a frenzy. Bits of paper lay strewn, torn up into tiny pieces like snow, too shredded to try to piece back together. A note perhaps. She gathered up as many of the tiny tatters as she could see. The night was growing very, very dark, gathering clouds enveloping the stars. She started to sob, tears blurring what little she could see.

Then a black serpentine shape reared over the top of a milky white stele. She blinked away tears and squinted at it, not sure she was even seeing it, until it hissed.

She shrieked and ran for home.

She arrived at the tenement in the dark. Deep spongy clouds opaqued the sky. The heavy oak door was shut and locked fast. Caralisa pulled on the iron ring, but her friendly front door had become a frowning impenetrable barrier and it would not move.

She circled round the back and gave a trembling tug on the back door. It gave with a small creak. Caralisa stole in through the dark kitchen. She sneaked out from under the stairs and turned the corner into the shadowy vestibule.

And met with the great square shape of Madame Gerhold blocking her way, gripping her broom with both hands across the broad expanse of her chest. "Where do you think you're going, you little tramp! No sluts live under my roof!"

Madame Gerhold reached over Caralisa's shoulder and threw back the bolt to the door. The heavy oak swung wide to the night breeze. Madame Gerhold jabbed with the broom's stiff ends, poking and pushing at her prodigal charge. Caralisa backed away, squeaking, trying to fend off the buffets with her arms, out to the front stoop.

At once the blows let up and the door boomed shut in her face.

Caralisa screeched and fell against the door, pounding with her open palm. "Let me in! Please! Please! Please!"

She screamed until her voice came ragged in her raw throat. Her hands beat with feeble slaps on the door. "Please!"

She slid down to sit sobbing on the top step. She huddled into its warmth. The air had lost its mildness, but the stone still held some comfort from the sun.

Somewhere in the Close a dog barked. A breeze rippled the thick elm boughs.

Fear overtook Caralisa slowly. She had been thrown out of the only home she had. It was not even hers. It had been given in charity.

What have I done?

She was homeless like those wretched gap-toothed dirty-faced beggars in the market.

Not *like* them. She was *one* of them. She had nowhere to go.

The first raindrops pattered on the elm leaves, and vanished quickly from the heated stones of the street. They gathered strength and pelted down hard in great drops. Steam rose from the warm bricks, and misty phantoms skirted close to the ground.

The hard drops stung Caralisa's skin. They drenched her hair and streamed down her face with her tears. She beat on the door. "Please! Please! Let me in!"

A clanging of the bolt made Caralisa draw back. The door cracked. Madame Gerhold's big-knuckled hand closed on Caralisa's collar and hauled her in.

Blissful warmth bathed Caralisa's soaked skin. She inhaled fragrant warmth. Then she felt the broom bristles.

"Up! Up with you, you little tramp." Madame Gerhold hied her up the stairs with a stout swat of the broom.

Caralisa went to her room and sank onto the bed, bedraggled and wan. Her shoulders heaved as she silently cried. Tears ran hot on her cheeks.

Viola came to her side, enfolding her in a great fleecy towel. "It's all right. You're home now."

Caralisa tried to stop sobbing long enough to tell her that there was something else. She choked out that she had seen a cobra.

"There are no cobras in Larissa," said Laurel, standing in the doorway, her thin arms crossed. "What'd you really do?"

"It was a snake, a great snake, and—it—reared up—up—to s-stand like a m-man and its head swelled from its body and it h-h-h-hissed."

Caralisa was trembling so that they had to believe her.

"Good heavens. That sounds like a cobra," said Viola. "Where?"

"In the pagan garden."

"What were you doing there?" said Laurel but her question was drowned out by Delia, Megan, and Brynna walking heavily and talking loudly in the hall. "Caralisa's back."

"About time."

They burst into the room.

"Oh, they must have dragged the river. Look at you!" said Megan.

"What is going on here?" said Delia. "Did the count show again?"

"Was the count on the roof again!" said Brynna.

"No," said Laurel. "She saw a cobra."

"A cobra?" said Megan.

"There's a cobra on the roof garden!" Brynna cried.

"Noooo," Caralisa said. "The pagan garden."

Delia, speaking for all of them, demanded, "What are you doing out with a cobra in the pagan garden at this hour?"

Caralisa quickly wove a lie, "It was so pretty and sunny and quiet I just fell asleep in the grass. I woke after dark and there was a serpent."

"I thought you were drawing swans at the museum pond," said Megan.

"Th-They wouldn't stay still so I tried to draw a stone one."

Delia gasped with a sudden thought. "Pagan garden! Vespers! Did you see Dr. Faustus and the peacock maiden?"

"Wh—what?" A bolt passed through Caralisa's heart. She had cornered herself.

Delia quoted excitedly from the paper, " 'Dr. Faustus beseeches the white peacock maiden to meet him under the pagan bell at vespers.' You were there! Did she show? Is Faustus handsome?"

Caralisa hoped Delia would not notice the colors chasing each other across her cheeks, white and red. "I . . . slept through vespers." A tear traced down her cheek. "I didn't see a living soul."

She went to bed, crying.

This was her lot, she thought. Not love, not magic. Just an adopted home given in kindness, and she was a wretch for not being grateful for it. She hugged her pillow. She had risked home, safety, everything, on a stupid girlish idea that a handsome young lord she had met at a masque was really trying to find her.

Viola whispered across in the dark, "What really happened?"

"Nothing." Caralisa sniffled. And that was why she was crying. "Nothing happened."

"How is it with the late Marquis de St. Florian?" asked Bernard.

"I believe I shall get my hair after all," said the balding Claude hopefully.

"Is it dead yet?" Aristide inspected the recumbent figure on the narrow bed, arm draped strengthlessly over the side.

Claude lifted a dangling white hand, let it fall. "I think so," said Claude.

"Good night, sweet prince," said Aristide.

Michaeljohn lamented, "Why did she not come?"

"Shut up, St. Florian, I am not done with my speech," said Aristide.

Michaeljohn turned his eyes toward the window. There was no color in the world. He had waited through vespers until it was nearly too dark to see. Too dark for any lady to be out. The only people who showed were curious gossips

who had seen the advertisement and wanted to see who was
Dr. Faustus and the peacock maiden. Michaeljohn had pretended to be one of those until the sun set and he could not
pretend to be idly curious anymore.

"Why did she not come?"

"My dear St. Florian, she has no interest," said Aristide.

Bernard, more kindly, offered, "She did not see the advertisement."

"She could not come," Claude suggested.

"The onlookers scared her," said Bernard.

"She's married," said Aristide.

"Oh please!" Michaeljohn cried.

"You left a note?" said Bernard.

Michaeljohn nodded in his pillow. "It's gone," he lamented. "But there is no answer. I asked for an answer."

"She loves you not," said Aristide.

"It might not have been she who took it," said Bernard.
"Perhaps she never saw it."

"She is not in Larissa," said Claude. "She is a foreign
princess come to Larissa only for the masque."

Michaeljohn sat up. "This is all likely!"

"It lives!" said Aristide.

"I have talked myself out of my hair," said Claude.

Michaeljohn declared, "I shall advertise in all the papers
of all the great cities on the continent. I will find her. Somehow I will find her."

Caralisa was gated for the rest of the summer and well
into autumn. The seasons stretched one into another. Green
gold gave on to scarlet and harvest amber.

On warm evenings when there was a masque she would
hear music from over the wall, and all she could do was listen
and dream. She had to remind herself over and over that she
was allowed to dream. No matter what life forbade her to
have, she need not put reins on her fantasies. In dreams she

was a lovely lady and Michaeljohn was her lord. Michaeljohn was a true and gentle vision, though grown indistinct with time. She had only talked with him once, danced with him once. There was so much she did not know. She colored in the missing pieces in pastel shades.

The Count of Samothrace was the stronger memory, distinct though she had never seen his face. She could summon up his image clearly at any time, too sharp, scalding even to think on. When she dared take liberty with his image, to dream of being locked in his embrace, giving herself to him in passion, she blinked from the painful brightness of it. She winced from her own imagination, as if he could read her mind and he would turn those piercing eyes upon her. As if his very gaze could make her bleed.

She wrestled with her ambivalence toward him. He filled her with fear, with wanting, and with anger that she could not move him at all while he affected her so deeply. Her feelings were as divided as was the man himself. His duality confounded her. He was fire. He was utter blackness. And her heart was not safe with him even in dreaming.

She retreated to the sweet vague image of gentle Michaeljohn. And one night all the answers came to her in a sunlit flash. She sat up in bed trembling for joy.

I know where Michaeljohn is!

When at last she was allowed outdoors again without a duenna, Caralisa went straight for the université.

Michaeljohn did not know how to find her, but she knew where he was. Why not go to him?

She lost courage before the gates which led on to the cluster of hallowed halls nestled on the hillside and overgrown with dark ivy tinged in crimson. The austere walls, quietly intimidating, breathed dignity, aristocracy, and great learning. Through the gates was a world apart. Students, who appeared at home among the ivied stones, sat beneath trees on idyllic college greens dappled with bistered leaves. They strolled arm in arm, conversing in cultured tones.

Caralisa overheard a pair sitting on a bench taking turns reading from a book. Caralisa was surprised to recognize the passage. It was from the *Odyssey,* where Odysseus sneaks into Troy, and Helen recognizes him.

Caralisa took heart. *I've read that!* she thought with a superior inward smile. Until she realized that the pair were reading from the original Greek, translating as they went.

Caralisa's self-assurance shriveled again.

I don't belong here.

And she fancied that every scholar who saw her was thinking just that.

She wondered if Michaeljohn might be embarrassed to see her here.

Her nerve nearly failed.

She found an administrative building and ventured inside. She wandered, lost, until challenged.

A man wearing an antique white wig called her in from the corridor. He was enthroned behind a desk, high as a bastion. He looked down from the high wall of polished mahogany through pince-nez at the winsome maid come before him. A tremor passed over her full lips, and a rose blush teased her soft rounded cheeks. She gazed up with eyes of wide shining blue. But he was a man for whom beauty incited only resentment. He said in a lordly voice, "What do you want?"

"Please, m'lord," said Caralisa. She bobbed a curtsy. "I'm looking for a student named Michaeljohn. He—he might be the Marquis de St. Florian, but I'm not sure. His name is Michaeljohn. He's a student. Can you help—"

A drawer slid abruptly open. The man took out a book, let it drop with a slap onto the desk before him, then opened it and began to write quickly. He carefully folded back the page and tore it out. "Do you know how to write your name?" he asked.

"Why yes, sir," said Caralisa, too surprised to take offense.

He reached the page down to her. "Then put it in the appropriate blank, go away, and never bring your chance child near these halls or I shall call the constable."

Caralisa blinked at the paper he had handed down to her. It was a cheque drawn on the Bank of Montagne, for more Montagnian francs than she had ever seen at once. Pay to: a blank space.

Understanding speared into her gut. Her eyes flooded shamed tears.

She threw down the cheque and ran, out of the building, across the beautiful greens, and out the iron gates.

She wished that Montagne's restless earth would open wide and swallow her up, never to be seen again.

Caralisa turned her shame and frustration into fury at the Count of Samothrace. He was responsible for all this, for keeping her from Michaeljohn. He had sabotaged her rendezvous. It was only proper that he set it right.

If she only knew how to find him.

She had not seen him since the picnic. At first she was glad, for she was very angry with him. But now she needed him and she was angry that he was not there.

After the first frost, Indian summer visited in full blaze. Sharp tang of autumn leaves scented the woodlands, their trees dressed in brilliant crimson and fire yellow.

Caralisa went in search of the count's secret lake. She knew where it was—more or less. It was behind the Heights. She did not know how to get there.

She remembered sounds of the plaza while she had been blindfolded.

She also remembered asking the count about the thick round milky green glass ox eyes set into the plaza's paving stones. The count had said that there were chambers below, which used to give passage to the Heights.

When she found the entrance which led underneath the plaza, Caralisa was sure she was on the right track, until she

opened the door and a wave of dank fetor rolled out, winter
cold and smelling of rot. That part was not familiar at all.

She crept down into darkness. The passage she remembered was no more than ten paces before she had felt sunlight
on her face again. And she did not remember stairs.

She had to stop halfway down because the rest of the stone
staircase was under water. She crouched down on a moldy
step to see what there was to see. Filtered light through the
translucent ox eyes revealed a subterranean ruin of stone and
fallen timbers and dark water everywhere. It looked and
smelled the way she would imagine a flooded crypt.

She backed up the stairs. This could not possibly be the
way.

She had all but given up when she remembered another
door. An impossible door leading nowhere.

Caralisa sneezed and waved away a cloud of floating milkweed as she hiked through dense weeds and burgeoning cat-
tails which clogged the channel running below the Rue de
Temps. She found the retaining wall which held in the foot
of the Heights, and she followed it. So overgrown was the
track that the first time she passed what she sought, and she
had to retrace her steps and double back yet again before
she found it. A door into solid rock.

She put her ear against the wood, and swore she could
hear falling water.

Rusty squawking calls of geese sounded from above. She
looked up and watched a flock of them fly over the rock cliff
in a spearhead.

She pulled the ivy away from the door. It moved easily,
as if its tenacious roots had already been loosed before. She
took up the black iron ring and pulled. The door stayed shut
fast. It did not even rattle against its lock. She gave it a kick
that did nothing better than hurt her foot and jar her shin.

She searched the weeds for a key, but that was futile.

She lifted her head and faced the sheer rock barrier. There was no way over unless she were a bird.

She ended her quest in anger. The count kept his secrets well. She never wanted to see him again anyway.

At Christmas time snow lay deep in a gentle white cloak over Larissa, icing its tiled rooftops and blanketing the hillsides. Cheery red berries ornamented the dark evergreens which peered from underneath the white mantle. Icy carols pealed from frozen bells; cold metal shivered in the brittle air. Ladies strolled the promenades, showing off furs and velvets of deep rich hue, jewel and peacock greens and violets, incarnadine and cobalt.

The girls of the tenement on Elm Tree Close went home for the holidays. Caralisa went home with Viola. Viola's grandmother cooked a goose for Christmas. The family cleared the great room for dancing with uncles and aunts and cousins and neighbors. Carollers came to the door and they were invited in, too. There were wreaths to be hung and spiced cider to be mulled over the fire. They decked the halls with ivy and pine garlands and bright holly boughs. Viola's young man, tall lanky Joshua, hauled in a barrel of water for the children to bob for apples. Together he and Viola looked like a pair of mischievous squirrels. They did magic tricks for the children, and their eyes sparkled when they danced, when they trimmed the tree, when they kissed under the mistletoe. Caralisa helped put together a gingerbread house. She and Viola and Joshua went out and made snow angels until the children came charging out and threw snow balls at them. Joshua bundled Viola into a sleigh, tucked her snugly under furs and blankets, then sat at her side and took up the jingling reins. "Coming, Caralisa?" Joshua called, his nose and cheeks bitten bright red.

Caralisa smiled, shook her head, and said she was cold. She waved them off into the starlight.

She wasn't cold. She joined the children's snowball fight. Then they went inside and she made them all hot chocolate.

Caralisa felt wistful amid the warmth. It was a bittersweet Christmas, not without joy, but also with a sense of void, surrounded by the love of a marvelous family that was not her own.

She did not let anyone see her cry on Christmas.

New Year's Eve brought Larissa's last big masque before the city went to sleep for the winter.

On the morning of the last day of the year, Viola quietly passed a newspaper to Caralisa, her finger pointing underneath a notice:

> *To the white peacock maiden: My love, I have not forgotten you from Sovereign's Night. If you are in town, meet me at the first moment of the New Year under the Arch, the one that is the color of your glorious hair. Dr. Faustus.*

$\mathcal{S}ix$

Caralisa let herself in through the back door to the theater.
She replaced the shim, and climbed the stairs to the costume
storage loft.

She had just put on a light when she heard a rustling amid
the costumes, and she shrank back with a gasp. A tall figure
rose from the shadows to stand upright.

The Count of Samothrace.

"Oh!" she exhaled with a cry, her hand over her drumming
heart.

She had grown to recognize him not by his face, which
she had never seen, nor his mask which changed every time,
but by his posture and motion, his tall elegant build. He was
difficult to disguise.

There was in his demeanor a volcanic brooding, wounded
and hostile and not in the least pleased to see her there.
Surely she could not incite such wrathful agony as she imagined she saw in his eyes. She'd had a start was all, and she
was conjuring nightmares. And in a blink the look she
thought she'd seen was gone. She steadied herself and said
lightly, "They say it isn't a theatre without a ghost. Are you
it?"

His deep cultured voice reaffirmed who he was. "Don't
be absurd. I am looking for a new mask."

"What's wrong with that one?"

It was the mask in which she had first seen him, the black
feathers that fit very closely to show the structure of bones

in his face. It gave the impression, anyway, of being very thin and close-fitting enough for her to envision what he must look like without it. If that were truly the shape of it, it was a handsome face. Unless there were no bones and it was all mask. She shivered. "I like that one."

"You do?" he said.

"It becomes you."

He touched gloved fingers to it, a twist of irony on his lips, then said, "I have used it too often. I need another. The question is, what are you doing here?"

"Looking for a mask."

"You need more than a mask. You're a ragamuffin pretender without a carriage. Will you hike through the snow without an escort and expect to be let in just anywhere?"

She did not need to get in anywhere. She need only be under the Red Arch at midnight. And she had to look radiant. "Where is the peacock dress?"

"In the shop being altogether redone for a new show."

"Oh *no!*" she wailed. She began to leaf through the dresses on the racks, which were jammed nearly solid with costumes. "You must help me."

"Help you? No."

"Then here, I shall help *you,*" she said. "This one must fit." She pulled out a mask of a hideous gargoyle. "It's you."

"You have a high talent for taking a torch to my balls."

"Ladies are not accustomed to being talked to so."

"Since when do you know anything of ladies or what gentlemen do with them?" said the count.

Bereft of an apt reply, she crossed her arms and glared approximately nowhere.

He continued, "You are a common girl with common morals and common manners." He moved closer. His voice dropped, more gentle. "I am not sure who made up the stack of rules that governs ladies' behavior, but it has made bores and liars of them all. They should mutiny. Be glad you are not one of them."

Caralisa turned, with tears in her eyes. "Better than the stack of rules that governs me, which has no rhyme or reason but I know who made them and I *am* mutinying." She returned to rooting through the costumes. "I am going to the masque, with or without your help."

"Why?"

"Why what?" She flipped through the dresses on the lower of the racks. She could not reach the ones on the top even to look at them much less take them down.

"Why is it so imperative you go to this masque?"

"Because I want to."

A slamming sound from far below made Caralisa cower into the shadows away from the gaslight. She whispered, "Will we be in trouble if we're found up here?"

"You will. I am a patron of this house."

"What is a patron?"

"I am not an artist, not in the creative sense. But I recognize genius when it comes to me begging for money."

Caralisa had backed into a white gown and she brought it out to consider it in the light. The count snatched it away from her. "Wrong color." He pulled out something else and tossed it into her arms. "Something closer to your nature." It was flaming scarlet.

She whisked up the fiery red chiffon and spangles. "It's all none of your concern. It's only a costume and I *shall* wear it. Thank you."

She retreated behind the racks to change.

"Wait," said the count.

She turned and he tossed her a small thing like an ornament. It was five rings tied together with a ribbon. She could not figure out what she was to do with it—take it apart or wear it somehow?

"These are much too small for my fingers," said Caralisa.

"They are for your *toes*."

She took them back with her.

She was horrified when she set about trying to put on the

flimsy creation. It was the costume of an Eastern dancer, and
there was barely anything to it. A skirt of long sheer veils
draped from a sequined brief which rode so shockingly low
that the two dimples of her hip bones were on display behind.
The veils were not seamed together so that she could not
walk without revealing her legs, and there were no stockings.
The bodice, if it could be so called, consisted of two veils
attached to a high jeweled collar, draped down to cross over
her breasts and attach to the skirt band at her hips with two
jeweled pins. Everything else was revealed. The costume left
her back bare from jeweled collar to plunging skirt band.
Instead of a mask, a veil shadowed the lower half of her face
from just beneath her eyes. A *ferroniere* dangled a ruby on
her brow. A headdress of beaded chains interlaced with her
hair. The sleeves were nothing but chiffon sheaths with jeweled bands on either end, one a cuff, the other an armband.
They did not reach up to her shoulders. She did not wax as
wicked girls did and she was conscious of the red tufts under
her arms, so she kept her elbows close to her bare sides. She
tried to coax the sleeves up but the cuffs would not allow it.
All her defiance abandoned her.

She crept out from between the racks, hiding behind a
blanket. She said meekly, "I can't wear this. Could you find
me something else, please?"

"Doesn't it fit?" he said.

"No."

"Let's see."

"No. I . . . I can't do this."

But he strode to her and whisked the blanket away.

"Why, you don't have it all on," he said, shock in his voice.
She burned in embarrassment. "Where's the rest of it?"

He withdrew a ruby from his waistcoat pocket and set it
in her navel. "There."

"Oh. Well. That makes all the difference!" said Caralisa,
bright red. She blushed with her whole body, and he would
be able to see it. She burned hotter.

."Turn," he said.

She did, sheepishly. The curve of her back flirted from behind the veil of her thick red hair glittering with beaded chains. The ends of it brushed at the low skirt band which rode at a tempting depth.

"No," he said. "No. Even I could not protect you if you went out like that."

"It is winter and I should freeze," Caralisa declared.

"Not if you stayed indoors."

She did not intend to stay indoors, but she did not tell him. He gave her a new dress, of frosty white and pale blue and icy violet. It was heavy brocade with fur trim. A fur hat and muff and lined cape went with it. It had a reassuring weight as he bundled it into her arms and set a beaded mask on top. She carried it behind the racks, pausing once to peer back. "Do . . . do you think I'm pretty?"

"No," he said.

"Oh."

She retreated. He glared after her.

Such a feeble word. I would never call anyone as exquisitely radiant and divinely and sinfully beautiful as you such a tepid thing as pretty!

He waited for her to dress. After a while he called through the racks, "Mademoiselle, are you not done?"

"I'm stuck."

"Can I help?"

"Yes."

He threaded back through the garments and found her crouched, still in the Eastern costume, with her hair swept in front of her, snarled in the beaded links of the headdress. He came down on one knee on the wooden floor with her and helped extricate the strands.

His proximity to her near nakedness made her clumsy. She could scarcely hold a strand much less untangle it. She was too aware of his dangerously masculine presence, the scent of him. He crouched next to her on bended knee, the heat from his hard-muscled thigh grazing her bared leg. She brushed against him and fire welled within.

She should have put something else on before letting him come back here—lest he think she was flirting with him. She wasn't. She had no intention of it. Truly.

With her leaning over, her veils gaped and offered glimpses of vast areas of forbidden flesh. She stole glances at him to see if he were not glancing back. He seemed wholly intent on freeing her hair. She thought he would have an easier time of it if he took off his gloves, but this he would not do.

She felt his gloved hands in her hair, his breath on her exposed shoulder. Sometimes his fingers would gently caress her bare back as he moved long tresses out of his way. Her skin warmed under his touch.

His expression was fixed, almost grim, in concentration on the task at hand.

I truly must not be pretty at all, thought Caralisa dismally.

The count growled at an impossible knot. He produced a knife.

"No!" she shrieked as he cut.

A beaded link fell away.

A brow lifted—the supple black mask moved with it—as if to ask sardonically, did she truly think he would cut her hair?

He sawed through several links. In the end the headdress was reduced to short strings of beads. Caralisa's hair survived to be brushed and tucked up into the hat wreathed in white fur.

In the costume she was transformed again, to someone elegant and lovely—and warm.

The count had settled on a mask, a green one.

"Green again?" said Caralisa.

"It suits me."

"It's not your best color."

"I did not say it was."

She pouted. He seemed determined to talk around her and make her feel stupid.

"Mademoiselle, may I escort you to the masque?"

She choked down irritation, curtsied, and said, "Please, my lord." She took his arm and let him take her down to where his carriage waited.

The blue parrot was speaking behind a great yellow beak, "The church wants to ban masks."

A shrill giggle bubbled from behind a white feathered fan. "Do be serious," said the lady in the feather boa.

"I am serious," said the parrot, though it was difficult to take a six-foot-tall parrot with a garish yellow bill seriously. "The holy church of Byzantion wants to ban masks. Can you imagine a law against *this?*"

"There ought to be one against that," a deeper voice joined in. "What happened? Did you lose a bet?"

The parrot turned its great protrusion toward the newcomer. "Ah. Samothrace. You are overcome with envy, yes?" The parrot tapped his beak. "Something this long, this hard, this . . . this . . ."

"Yellow?" Samothrace suggested.

"It is exceptional, is it not?"

"But why is it on your face?"

"I lost a bet; what do you think?" the parrot said crossly. "Who have we here?" He lowered his head to see Caralisa over his prodigious beak. "Snow Queen?"

"Yes. I guess." Caralisa stammered.

"And who are you meant to be tonight, Samothrace?"

"The Count of Samothrace." He lifted his mask to reveal a second mask—the gargoyle—beneath it.

Piercing laughter broke from behind the white fan. "You naughty man!" The lady gave him a feathery slap with her boa.

"Not very well done," said the parrot, unimpressed. "It ought to be a swan face. Here, do you require a beak?"

"I couldn't deprive you," the count protested.

"You are the reason for this ridiculous talk of bans," said the parrot.

"I?" said the count.

The parrot loudly cleared his throat, and reset his blue feathered shoulders to an altogether new posture. He smoothed down the front of his garment with his right hand, his left fist thrust in the small of his back as if posing for a military statue. He spoke in excruciatingly articulate tones in a parody that could only be Monsignor Fortenot—the reason they called him Shakespeare:

"Here is the one who goes about perpetually masked. When men and women go forth with their faces covered, evil walks with them. He walks among us at our own invitation. We know not what he looks like, but know he is with us."

Caralisa hid her smile behind her hands, certain it was blasphemy but she could not help laughing. And when the parrot finished, a circle of revelers applauded, laughing. "Very good! Very good! Bravo!" And they tried for themselves to pronounce *e-ville* the way Monsignor did.

She was astonished, for it could only mean that all these impious people went to church. They went to high mass, for Monsignor only read high mass.

Caralisa felt a light touch on her shoulder, the count leaning his face down close to her ear. He murmured, "Who is he meant to be?"

She was quite startled to be answering a question for him for a change. "Why shame on you, my lord. It's Monsignor Fortenot. You don't go to Sunday mass?"

"No. Does he really say that about me?"

"I have not heard precisely that one. But it sounds very like him. He has much to say about e-ville."

"And that includes me?"

"Does it, my lord?"

He did not answer.

The two had been making the rounds of the fetes from castle to castle. At one, a strange ethereal cat woman in a black spangled sleeveless sheath with long black gloves stalked across the floor straight for the count. She had enormous brown eyes and the look of a jaded waif. She carried her cat mask on a wand and flirted behind it as if it were a fan. She walked up to the count and slowly lowered the mask and stood there gazing up at him as if she knew him and expected something of him. She said nothing, but looked as if he were a longtime lover and should know her mind, almost as if he had wounded her and she was awaiting an apology. She handed him her empty glass as if he should see about refilling it.

"You have mistaken me for someone else," said the count.

"No," she said. "I haven't."

"Who do you suppose I am?"

"I never pretended to know anyone. You are a man in a mask. Why pretend beyond what I can see?"

"Then you truly have mistaken me." He placed her glass back into her hand, turned her around, and physically directed her away.

It rankled Caralisa that the cat woman did not even acknowledge Caralisa's existence, as if she were not with the count, as if she were so disposable as not even to be worthy of notice. Caralisa fought down an impulse to assert her position but reminded herself that she did not *want* to be inextricably bound with him. It would have been better if he had turned his attention to the cat and Caralisa could have stalked away in righteous indignation—and gone to meet Michaeljohn.

A twinge of guilt twisted inside. She reassured herself that she and the count were not together, not really. They had run into each other at the theatre. He had not asked her to this ball. He was not her escort. She was free to leave him.

If she could figure out how.

She could not believe her own audacity in using him this way. He was not a man whom one used! He was formidable, and he was someone she could love if she dared, though a great chasm of experience lay between them. But no. Love was trust, and how—why!—could she trust a man who would not let her see his face!

Michaeljohn told her he loved her.

This man all but laughed when she asked if he did. And he did not even think she was pretty. Her throat tightened as she recalled him saying so.

She had every right to go her own way.

She was trying to plot how to elude him when he suddenly set her free. "Stay in the vicinity of the plaza," he told her, collecting his hat and cloak. "I shall find you." And he left in haste.

Caralisa could have broken into triumphant song. Yes, yes, yes, yes, yes!

The only worry was that it was still quite early, and the count might catch up with her before midnight and ruin her rendezvous yet.

She would simply need to avoid him until then.

Then.

Then!

She clasped her hands to her heart as if it would leap together with her soul out of her body.

Michaeljohn. O my Michaeljohn. I love you too! Tonight at long last she could tell him. *I love you too!*

She could scarcely wait until then.

Michaeljohn the Marquis de St. Florian pushed his way through the milling crowd which choked the plaza, attempting not to lose sight of the retreating caped figure whom he dogged. Claude had sighted him first in a Frankish salon, but by the time he could fetch Michaeljohn, the quarry was gone. Aristide picked up the scent anew at the Rhinish castle, and now St. Florian was in stealthy pursuit for himself. Aristide said that the count had a lady with him. There was no one with him now. Had it been she? What had he done with her? Where was she now?

Michaeljohn could not be sure that his lady love would make their tryst at midnight under the Red Arch. But here was a man who could tell him her name. Michaeljohn struggled to keep pace with him.

The pursuit took him weaving through strings and strings of line dances, ducking in between and breaking through. The count had disappeared through the Royal Arch. St. Florian ran all out, slipping on the frozen cobbles, knocking down revelers, enduring their angered cries, to get to the arch.

Clear of the plaza, Michaeljohn paused, leaning on the blue enameled bricks, drawing in sharp breaths and exhaling great frosty clouds.

He had lost him again. He nearly wept for despair, there were so many routes from here. Then he saw the cape turn the corner up ahead toward the royal mews, and St. Florian took off after him.

He skidded around the corner and paused again in darkness. There were no revelers here. Only the rustle of wings of disturbed falcons, fluttering and keening in their jesses.

Michaeljohn turned round and round. He held his breath to listen.

The folding of wings.

The squeak of a mouse.

Fine dusty snow blowing across frozen ground with icy whispers.

Footsteps. Bootheels on stone.

Michaeljohn ran in their direction. He barreled round the corner into an alley.

Suddenly he was off his feet, seized up by his collar and dragged into shadow, slammed against a stone wall, pinned there by one gloved fist, and staring into the green-masked face of the Count of Samothrace. Malevolent eyes smoldered within the deep wells of the mask with preternatural menace. Michaeljohn remembered them blue, but now they looked nothing but black. The count growled down St. Florian's throat, "I don't like being hunted. You shall tell me why."

His towering shape obscured the sky, and in a strangled moment, Michaeljohn knew that he meant to extinguish him from this earth—and he could not say why he didn't, for there was nothing Michaeljohn could do to break his grip. But slowly, as if under great strain, the hand eased on his throat, and left Michaeljohn to stand before the grand glowering figure of the count known as Samothrace. Michaeljohn felt very small and puppyish in the face of his full-fanged menace. He sensed from him long experience and great age, though the count could not be fifteen years his senior. Michaeljohn stared into eyes that had seen forever.

The count's black cape snapped in the winter wind like an enemy flag. Michaeljohn gasped for air. Soft brown curls kicked over his young brow. He stood up to the count and demanded anxiously, "I am searching for the love of my life. My lady. She was with you at the masque last spring. The peacock maiden. I thought she might be with you now. Surely she is here. I have searched everywhere. Where can I find her? You must tell me who she is."

"I must?" His voice was low and rumbling. "Very well. I shall tell you who she is: She is not for you. Forget her."

"I cannot!" Michaeljohn cried.

"If you were not one whose disappearance would cause more than the blink of an eye, we would not be talking. That will not always stop me. As you value your life, do not try to see her again." The count threw him away from him with a power that was staggering.

"Samothrace!" Michaeljohn called at his back.

The count paused to look over his shoulder.

Michaeljohn uneasily held his ground, gripping empty

fists. His cheeks flushed red in the cold; he was nearly crying. Heavy breaths clouded in the frosty air. "I feel like a bloody fool calling you that," said Michaeljohn angrily. "Who are you really?"

"I could be the death of you."

"Who are you, Samothrace!"

The count strode back to him and, glaring down at him, growled low in whispered thunder, "See for yourself."

Michaeljohn seized the green mask and yanked it away, uncovering the mask beneath the mask. He ripped that one away, and faced another mask. He yanked at the third.

The count snarled in pain. "God *damn!*"

Michaeljohn shrank away in round-eyed horror, his hands shaking. He dropped the two masks and broke into a run. He heard long strides gaining behind him, an uproar of wings and screaming falcons in the mews.

"Help! Constable! Murder! Oh murder!"

How to wait and not look like you were waiting?

Caralisa paced underneath the monumental arch with its enameled red bricks, pretending she was seeking shelter from the snow while waiting with the gathering crowd in the plaza to watch the clock tower figures turn over the calendar to the new year at midnight.

She was early. The wisdom of the tenement required one to make the young man wait in the parlor at the very least ten minutes. Five, if you were in love, but never be on time and never *ever* think about being early.

Snow had been gently falling all evening. The streets were white and the colors of the revelers were muted beneath a dusting of it. The seven grand arches—White, Gold, Royal, Emerald, Black, Amber and Red—were taking on a ghostly sameness.

Caralisa glanced about her as a steady stream of celebrants filed through the Red Arch, laughing, staggering, singing. A herd of boisterous students piled in, and paused to shake snow off their carricks and beaver hats, like one giant wet dog, sending everyone else scurrying out from under the arch. Only Caralisa remained, pulling her cloak across her face.

The students reassembled, linked arms, and went galumphing out to the plaza. Caralisa trembled as she lowered her cloak, expecting to see one who might have stayed behind.

But she was alone under the Red Arch.

Within moments, others made their way through. Caralisa tried not to look as if she were tarrying here particularly.

Unlike the first rendezvous under the pagan bell, the gossip mongers of Larissa would not know under which arch Dr. Faustus and the peacock maiden would be meeting at midnight. There were probably a cluster of the curious under the Gold Arch. Ladies so passionately sought seemed always to be blond like Princess Albertina.

Caralisa's heart thumped as the hour drew near. She heard the first carol of the bells. At the clock's midnight striking, what would she see? Would Michaeljohn appear? Or was the message not for her? Were the real lovers, after all, under the Black Arch, where some ardent student prince was meeting a raven-haired gypsy princess?

Blood rushed in her head. She could barely hear the voice of the crowd roaring like an ocean wave, "Ten, nine, eight—"

She darted from one end of the monumental portal to the other, checked outside and around.

"Seven, six, five, four, three—"

She stood on tiptoe, trying to see over the sea of heads.

"Two, one!"

The plaza broke into a riot of celebration. Balloons and white doves and skyrockets soared to the heavens. The clock figures went through their colorful ritual as the bells carolled in the new year.

Caralisa huddled under the arch as if seeking refuge from the chaos.

Michaeljohn was not here.

How long should she wait? Perhaps Michaeljohn was even now trying to negotiate a path through this tumult. She must give him time.

Minutes grew long. The dizzy whirl of gaiety passed her by. Sometimes someone would glance at her and she would shrink into shadow as if to say *I am not for you.*

Tears stole onto her cheeks, hot, quickly turning icy cold. She lifted her mask and wiped them away.

Am I for anyone?

The crowds dispersed slowly, breaking up to go inside to this or that revel. The street players remained to juggle and play instruments for the people passing by. The snow was falling exuberantly now, and most people still outside were on their way to somewhere inside.

A thin crowd remained in the plaza. Lights in the windows burned with a warm inviting glow. Snowfall erased foot tracks, filled them in softly, blanketing the plaza, blanking out the colorful confetti and shriveling the balloons.

Caralisa brushed white flakes off her fur ruff. She pushed at the snow with her white kid boot. The boots were thin soled and her toes were numb.

She ought to set about finding the Count of Samothrace.

Suspicion crept upon her slowly: Where *was* the count?

She looked round suddenly, expecting to see him smiling sardonically from a dark niche.

Suddenly she was a little girl again, collecting love notes from a "secret admirer." She had soon figured out that it was a cruel trick—not soon enough to prevent a few laughs at her expense.

Who really had placed that second notice in the newspaper, and why had the count been so easy to shake from her side at the appointed hour?

It was all a trap laid to torment her, should she prove so foolish as to step into it. And she had.

Mortification weighted her stomach. She leaned against the arch to catch her breath; she felt dizzy and she swallowed hard.

Then she drew herself up. The night need not end like this.

She stalked off—away from the plaza where the count had bid her stay—to find romance or intrigue. This was Larissa. This was a masque. And Caralisa was not so naive as she had been an hour ago.

The clock chimed a perfunctory four o'clock carol.

Caralisa caught sight of the Count of Samothrace across the snowy plaza. She ran to him and flew into his arms.

"Where's the carriage!" she breathed.

"Ah," his voice was deep and warm as his embrace. "You have wandered into the wrong party."

"Yes I did!" she cried, shaking. "Where have you been! *Stop laughing at me!*"

"I'm not."

"Yes you are!"

"Yes I am," he admitted. He took off his cloak and settled it round her. The cold left him as unaffected as a wild thing. He blinked away the snowflakes that settled on his eyelashes. "The only way to tell you was to let you find out for yourself. Are we being chased again?"

"I don't think so," said Caralisa, clinging to his arm as they walked. She felt iron sinew beneath the sleeve. "Just get me out of here . . . please."

"We are this way," he directed her toward an arch. The Black one.

The barouche was waiting beneath it.

Safe inside and under way, Caralisa took off her beaded mask and said, "I have seen things I cannot believe."

"What did you expect?" the count said evenly. "It's a masque."

"I expected . . . wonders. And there are. But there is so much . . . *else*. They were playing Simon Says. You can't imagine."

"But I can."

"Simon was lewd and preposterous. No, he was obscene and so were those people doing what he said. Oh! It's too disgusting. The world is such a wicked place." She blinked quickly, her face tilted up to contain incipient tears.

"Larissa is not the world," the count said gently. "Wonders are only for fresh eyes. Not many can see true wonder. Hearts here are so callused they have lost all sensitivity and their owners must seek gross sensation to arouse some part of them that has not lost all feeling. It needs be gaudy and garish. For they are so sated, so glutted, their senses so blunted that they cannot see any but the brightest colors. They drink in an excess of splendor, so instead of feeling giddy delight they vomit and stagger, just so they know they have drunk at all. There is no nuance, no subtlety. They cannot tell scarlet from crimson or even care, much less tell that red roses carry a different scent than pink ones."

He passed her a perfect red rose which he'd been carrying, and pulled an icy pink one seemingly from her hair. He caressed her cheek with its petals.

Caralisa took both and passed them under her nose.

"They do smell different!" she said in wonder. Then in sadness, "You knew that. And how to find roses in winter. By the time I know half as much as you do, I shall be an old woman and no one will give me roses."

His indigo eyes flashed with anger. "By the time you are old, maybe you will have learned that love is not the sole province of the young, beautiful, and foolish."

His ire startled her. She had never thought of him as old, merely as older than she, but he reacted as if she had offered him a personal insult.

She looked again. His hands, ever gloved, gave away nothing. His neck, what she could see above the cravat, showed taut supple skin, unlined and unwithered. There was nothing of jowls below the mask, which obscured only the top half of his face. So why was he so defensive of old age?

It was said that the Count of Samothrace was some kind of sorcerer. She remembered that the legendary Dr. Faustus sold his soul to the devil in return for eternal youth, and she wondered: *Have I not met up with Dr. Faustus after all this night!*

The count delivered her once again safely to her door—or rather to her godparents' window, as Caralisa was obliged to sneak into their house. The count bid her adieu peremptorily without so much as a kiss on the hand goodnight.

As she parted from him, Caralisa thought she could hear the song of an anguished heart cracking in two, and she assumed it was her own.

Viola had left the bedroom window latch undone and had waxed the jambs so the window slid up with only a whisper.

Caralisa was very quiet so not to awaken Viola, but was surprised to find Viola up and trudging rather greenly back to her bed. Viola gave Caralisa a feeble wave hello/goodnight.

"Are you ill?" Caralisa whispered.

Viola mumbled that she must have eaten too much. She curled up in her bed and pulled the covers over her head.

Sometime later Caralisa's sniffles made Viola sit up and light a candle.

"Did someone hurt you?" said Viola.

Caralisa shook her head in her pillow. "I will never be loved," she said.

She had been so hopeful, so sure. She had seen all her dreams within reach, just *there,* waiting for her. She had known tonight was the night. This was what she had been dreaming of, what her life was about. It all came crashing down and had only just now hit home. "I am alone now and there is no reason to think I shan't spend the rest of my life alone."

"How silly you sound," said Viola.

It was terribly easy for her to say. She had a large and wonderful family and a doting young man whom she loved and who opened the door for her grandmother to carry in the holiday goose and who carved toy boats for her little brothers and bobbed for apples with her at family Christmas parties.

"What of the Count of Samothrace?" said Viola. "Was he there?"

"We spent the early part of the night together. And he brought me home."

"Well then!"

"He is cruel and he taunts me and makes me crazy and I hate him," said Caralisa. "He turns away love and loves me not."

"Why does he take you to the masques?"

"To pretend that he has something special. Everyone thinks I'm a princess when I'm with him. Oh, he dearly loves his secrets!"

"Michaeljohn wasn't there?"

Caralisa's tears gushed forth anew. "I don't believe the message was even from him, Viola. He wasn't there. He has forgotten."

Viola smoothed back her hair. "There is nothing to be said tonight that will make you believe, but everything will be all right. I promise. Go to sleep now and try not to think."

She put out the light.

Caralisa stared into the darkness, crying.

The swaying of the carriage's uneven rocking lulled its sole passenger, half awake, half sleeping, into a dream state. He let himself be rocked. Carriages always made him drowsy. Until he realized that he was not supposed to be in one. He surfaced from his half sleep with a start. He blinked into the dark, pulled back the curtain.

Brittle night wind blew in. The air was hard and thin, sharp edged. His breath stabbed like icicles. Outside, the crooked black shapes of mountains clawed at the dark horizon and loomed on the high road ahead. The creaking of the carriage and steady clopping of horses' hooves sounded weirdly small in the face of it.

"Where am I!"

Michaeljohn rapped on the roof with his walking stick to bid the carriage stop.

He demanded of the driver to tell him where he was going.

"My lord? To the Chateau St. Florian."

Home! But Chateau St. Florian was across the mountains in the next principality!

"Why are you taking me there!" Michaeljohn demanded. "I want to be in Montagne!"

"The gentleman said you had partaken of too much cheer. That I was to take you home. You are the Marquis de St. Florian, are you not? You have been asleep for hours. The fare is paid, my lord."

"Blast the expense! You have cost me my love!" Michaeljohn cried. He sat back in the seat, agitated. Mountains crouched all round him. "What time is it? Where am I?"

"It is five o clock, my lord. We are near Lionheart Pass."

Good lord. Five hours. My lady. My love. "Turn around and take me back to Larissa!"

"At once, my lord."

St. Florian sat up, fully awake now, glowering out the window, letting the ice wind slap his face.

The fiend. That inhuman unholy fiend. Michaeljohn shuddered and dashed the image from his mind's eye. He shuddered again. He tried to think instead of his love. He could picture her still, her countenance undimmed for all the months intervening, her pure rounded cheeks with delightful blush, her petal pink lips so full and innocently tempting, her eyes of beguiling blue, so large and wide, the sweet curve of her brow. She was altogether young and soft, fragile and untouched. The silken white skin of her throat and smooth shoulders and lovely breasts held a virginal allure. He remembered holding her delicate hands. Why had he ever let go? He knew she was his one perfect love.

The sweet image blinked clear, and St. Florian saw what was before his eyes, the angry crags of the night-cloaked mountains—and saw in them a persistent image burned in his mind of the inhuman visage of the Count of Samothrace.

How shall I ever find her when all hell stands between us?

Seven

Viola was to marry, quite soon, in no one's idea of a dream ceremony. Though the girls all lived in terror of turning twenty-one unwed—and the sooner claimed the better—they realized that an event of this magnitude took quite some time to prepare. If it were to be done properly. Both Viola's wedding and the reception would be small simple affairs at her parents' home, this very month.

"January?" Megan scrunched all her freckles together. "Who marries in January?"

"The ancient Greeks considered it lucky," said Viola. "They called it Gamelion. That means wedding month."

"Well for the Greeks," said Delia. "This is the modern world. Nobody marries in January. Jiminy! At least wait until Saint Valentine's Day!"

"Yes, wait. You're making the rest of us look old," said Megan.

But everything was already set.

Viola took Caralisa aside to ask her to be her maid of honor.

Caralisa's eyes shone vivid blue. "Yes, of course! That would be wonderful."

"We're going to live in the country on a farm," said Viola. "You must come visit us and the children."

"You will have children straightaway then?" said Caralisa. There were ways of putting it off, any Larissan girl knew.

Caralisa was not sure how one managed that, but knew that it was done.

"Straightaway," Viola said with a droll twist to her mouth. "Truth is, Cara, I have to marry him. But I want to, so it's all right, don't you think?"

Caralisa sputtered, startled, scandalized, then she blurted, "Yes, of course!" Viola had not turned into a harlot before her eyes. She was still beloved sweet Viola, and tall lanky Joshua loved her so.

So there was the reason for haste.

"Oh, Viola, do you mean this is it? What of moonlight dances on the roof with a stranger?"

"This is what I dream of," said Viola. "A home and hearth, a man who loves me and who I can imagine at my side forever. He laughs with me and he is so funny when he plays with children."

"Then it's better than all right," said Caralisa. "It's perfect."

Viola hugged her tight. "Caralisa, I love you so. But who will look after you now?"

"I suppose I shall have to manage for myself," said Caralisa. "I'm not a baby anymore." She paused then amended, "Not too much of one."

Viola sat her down and took her hand. "I have only one last word of advice to offer. If I have ever told you anything of value." She gave a dreamy look out the window at the cold slate sky. Her eyes were bright. "I can't exactly tell you to hold out for marriage, but oh, Caralisa, do hold out for love."

Larissa was situated high, surrounded by mountains. The air was sharp, and its summer skies were glorious blue. The warm months were filled with open air concerts and garden balls. Its crisp autumns brought many masques. But after New Year's, Larissa went utterly dark. Night fell quickly, and when the snow lay deep, access was nearly impossible. Isolated between the mountains and the river, Larissa's only activity in the winter was at the université.

So after Viola's wedding the girls were confined in the tenement, taking afternoon lessons with Madame Gerhold and receiving local gentleman callers in the evening.

A blot fell on the dark season this year. The dead of winter brought a scandal that rocked even jaded Larissa, a series of crimes so unspeakable that even Delia's favorite paper, which relished the sensational, only reported them in the vaguest of terms. A series of fatal attacks upon young women of low virtue began on a Sunday morning, and continued into what became a pattern of one a week, early Sunday morning before daylight, until the eighth Sunday when the only death that day was a man found floating facedown among the reeds in the river. Next Sunday nothing at all happened, but Larissa was a long time believing that the assaults had ceased. Every Sunday afterward, Larissa held its breath until they were assured that no atrocity was to be found that day.

The church blamed the murders on the visitation of diabolical agents, and even the constabulary, who knew they were seeking a mortal man, did not challenge the idea that Satan was moving the assailant's hand, so grotesque was his work. The church named the fiend on the Heights, and renewed its call for bringing down the citadel.

Common wisdom credited the fiend with the end of the grisly spree rather than its beginning. The common folk took jealous pride in their local spirit, who would listen when no one else would. Who else would answer the cry of a whore in peril? No one claimed that the demon on the Heights was not dangerous, but even the fox did not hunt in his own backyard.

There were murmured suggestions in the days to follow that the drowned man had been behind it all and that the demon had put an end to him. The drowned man's hair matched some found on the victims' clothes.

The church dismissed the accusation as slander. The man had no motive. He was a moral, God-fearing man. He had been a lector for twenty years. He had lived with his mother, a devout churchwoman. He kept no vulgar company of the sort the victims were. Why, he even kept covered the legs of his tables and chairs—to avoid having bare legs on display in a Christian home. And he would not look at a woman below her chin. That this man would consort with such creatures as the victims, much less commit such abominations upon them, was beyond belief. As for the police with their witchcraft forensics, even they had to admit that the blood under the dead man's nails matched none of the victims. The police said it was not even human. It was suggested that he drowned while trying to elude the attack of a wild animal, and his death was unrelated to the attacks on the women.

The case was put away unsolved.

The whole affair had touched the girls in Elm Tree Close only peripherally.

Madame Gerhold found the girls reading an account of the crimes and she broomed them all and sent them to bed without supper for so much as thinking about something so ugly. And that was the end of it.

With the terror put to rest, winter's claws retracted and left it a fluffy white cat. There was a bleak beauty in the pearl gray days when the trees in stark dignity spread their elegant bare frames against the glaucous sky. Berries on the withered weeds shrank to desiccated brown, those that had not been long since stripped by birds. All the green foliage had lost color and fallen. Only the oaks clung to their beggars cloaks of brown tatters.

Caralisa left food for the drab winter-colored birds which visited her sill. She gathered shriveled apples from the cellar, the wrinkled mealy ones no one wanted. If she threw them out in the snow among the trees behind the roof garden, the deer would come.

There were many books in Madame Gerhold's library.

Caralisa now had a room of her own. She could curl up in her mother's quilt with a book and a cup of heated cider by herself.

She spent the winter thus hiding beneath the snow.

Until the Count of Samothrace appeared on her garden wall like a bird of spring. He came when the trees were dressed in a yellow-green haze of new leaves, their roots standing in wet pools of melting snow, and the creekbeds and canals were alive with the cheery peeping of frogs. The air was fragrant with wet bark, new moss, and the first brave flowers. Hyacinths bloomed on the roof garden, pink, white, and the deep blue color of Caralisa's eyes.

Caralisa tugged open the winter stiff window. She forgot how furious she was with him, only remembered that any time he was here, magic happened. Her heart stirred as if it, too, had been sleeping this long winter.

Her unlikely robin appeared in uncustomary white, a white billowing shirt, white cravat, and white breeches, with a red sash round his waist. He was masked of course, red. He looked as if he had been away at sea. He would have made a dashing pirate. He moved with the same cocky walk and easy arrogance that she had come to know him by. He came to her window, a large flat box tucked under his arm. Caralisa leaned on the windowsill. "For me?"

He opened the window wider and, uninvited, stepped into her room. She became conscious of the bed and the girlish furnishings. "Lock your door," he said.

She hastened soundlessly across the floor and softly drew the bolt into its sheath. She turned.

He was too much for this room to contain, a marvelous creature of fantasy in this prosaic familiar surrounding. His presence wanted more space and grandeur. He was intoxicatingly and perilously real. Black boots made little sound. Caralisa heard her own breath, could hear his, and the rustle of his clothes. She was keenly aware of the muffled voices downstairs of the other girls and their young gentlemen callers, and of the watchful Madame Gerhold, and of the kitchen servants. The house was full of people. Caralisa trembled in fear of discovery—and in fear, in wish, that he would throw her on the bed and do to her what forbidden delightful things men do with women.

Without jacket or waistcoat, his manly build was too apparent. His white shirt fit loosely with voluminous sleeves, but when he reached, the fabric drew taut across his side and she could see the outline of woven sinew moving hard power.

His hair had grown long. Black and thick, with a slight wave, it brushed his wide shoulders with the unintentional sensuality of a stallion's mane. He smelled of wood and water, musky and sexual.

Caralisa's breath kept catching; she forgot to exhale. She pulled her shawl round her as if cold, to hide her breasts' swelling. Her nipples had become pert and obtrusive within the thin bodice of her housedress, threatening to betray her wayward thoughts. She felt a warm wet ache between her thighs. Heart quavering, Caralisa whispered, "What are you doing here?"

"I came to see you," he said quietly. The deep timbre of his voice gave even his murmurs a rumbling undercurrent.

"What did you bring me?" she nodded at the box.

"It's your dress and your mask. Your premiere is tonight and you must be there."

"My what!" Caralisa shrieked in a whisper.

He continued as if she had not spoken. His casual masterful motions were driving her to distraction. "I don't care if you cannot get past the dragon who guards your garden. You must attend. Prince Maximillian and Princess Albertina will be there and so must you. You've a box in the dress circle."

"I—! My—!" Caralisa tried to speak, tripping over her tongue.

He held up a warning finger—gloved as always—commanding silence. Caralisa returned to a hush. "Premiere of what?"

"Your musical."

"What is a musical and how is it mine?"

"A play with songs," he said and passed her a program. "They will be expecting a man, no doubt."

She looked at the creamy vellum engraved in black and gold letters: *Masque of Hearts,* story and music by C.S.

Masque of Hearts. Masque of Hearts. She had forgotten. *Masque of Hearts* was what she had called her little tale spun on a summer's day on the hidden lake. It came back to her in an instant, an afternoon spent writing out songs. It had been just a game. She did not think she had been seriously *composing* anything. Learned men with decades of education and apprenticeship with an orchestra did that. It took months and years.

"You made a play out of that?" Caralisa stammered.

"You did," said the count.

A story like a patchwork quilt, spun from gossamer daydreams and sunlight and a rooftop dance, a masque, churchbells, and the songs of a field of daisies that only she could hear.

C.S. They would think it was the Count of Samothrace. It was Caralisa Springer.

The parchment quivered in Caralisa's fingers. "Mine? This is truly mine?" Her eyes misted. She ran a fingertip over the raised letters of the fine script as if to confirm their existence. *Masque of Hearts.*

She threw her arms around his wide shoulders and kissed his cheek. She had meant to kiss his mouth but he'd turned his head as if he did not want it, like an uncle accepting a kiss from a child.

She felt her breasts pressed against him, the heat and hardness of his chest.

"Try on your dress," he said.

She drew back and turned to the box. He'd set it on Viola's

old bed. As she shook the lid free, he said, "It is not from the theatre. It was made for you and you may keep it after this night is over."

She set the lid aside and brushed back the tissue to uncover gold cloth. She picked it up at the shoulders, like picking up a waterfall. It cascaded to full length in a shimmering sheath of gold such as a goddess might wear on Olympus. She looked up at the count. He gave no indication that he was about to leave the room. In fact, he had perched himself on the edge of the windowsill, one booted foot propped on an old blanket chest, and he crossed his arms in waiting.

Did he mean for her to undress for him? She moved haltingly closer to him. He could do with her as he willed. She let her shawl slide to the floor. He need only take the ribbon of her bodice between his fingers and pull the bow loose.

"I am only concerned for the length," he said offhandedly. "There is nothing else to fit." And he took the dress from her hands and held it to her shoulders. The hem brushed the tops of her shoes. "Fine." He said.

Disappointed and on fire, Caralisa was about to say something when the sounds of girls' talking outside the room became louder, accompanied by the thumping of footsteps on the stairs. The count's head moved aside, alert, listening.

The voices, the footsteps, came right to her door. The knob wrenched left and right, the bolt rattled in its sheath, followed by a quick rapping and Delia calling, "Caralisa, open up!"

Caralisa froze. She did not even breathe.

The rapping came again. Brynna chorused in this time, "Cara-*li*-sa!"

Caralisa stayed very still.

Then the girls moved from the door—but not back toward the stairs. They were going up the hall toward the door to the roof garden, whose windows gaped open to this room!

The count drew back and flattened himself against the wall between the two windows as if to become part of it. Caralisa threw the dress back into the box, seized the box and the lid, stowed them under the bed, then jumped into her own bed and pulled the covers over her.

Immediately came a quick glassy rapping on the windowpane, with Delia's head poking in.

The count, to Delia's right, was motionless but for his wary eyes.

Caralisa rolled in the bed to attract Delia's curious gaze to herself.

Oblivious to the presence on her right, Delia scolded, "What are you doing? Get up, sleepybones!"

"Leave me alone. I don't feel well," said Caralisa.

"There's an extra young man in the parlor," Delia sang. "We can't handle them all."

"Leave me alone. I'm on the rag."

"Oh. Truly terrible timing, Caralisa."

In horror Caralisa noticed the program lying on the floor. She tore her gaze from it and hugged her stomach as if having a cramp. "Please, Delia, go away and let me die in peace."

Brynna called in over Delia's shoulder, "Do you want some raspberry leaf tea?"

"No, I want to go to sleep."

Brynna tisked in resignation.

"All right," Delia sang like the final offer of a market woman. She withdrew from the window and the two came back inside through the hall door. Their footsteps retreated down the stairs.

Caralisa threw back the blanket and stood up, shaking.

She hissed at the count, "You've cost me a legitimate introduction." The beast had no interest in her for himself, but it seemed he would let no one else court her.

"I saw him. He's an idiot. They want you to keep him occupied." He moved away from the wall, put a foot up on the windowsill. "I shall return for you in three hours. You shall be among royalty tonight. Unless you have something better planned." He ducked under the window sash. He paused, half sitting in the window as if reluctant to leave her.

He dropped the irony and spoke simply, man to woman, "If I know your mind at all—a most hazardous thing to assume, I know—but if I know you in the least, you will enjoy this. Trust me this time, Caralisa."

And he was gone.

His parting echoed in the deepest recesses of her soul. He had called her Caralisa. The earth, moon, stars, sun, the heavens themselves paused to listen to her name on his voice. *Caralisa,* he'd called her Caralisa. A chord, made of all the colors in the sky, sang on the wind, profound as a touch.

Caralisa sank to the floor and clasped her hands to her chest, trying to contain her unsettled heart.

Why was she shaking this way and what lid it mean?

She had not realized how sorely she'd issed him until she had seen him again.

She got up from the floor and collecte her thoughts. She had to get out of here three hours from now. And Lord, she did not want to face Madame Gerhold's broom again!

It disturbed her how quickly she spun a plot. Larissans must drink in intrigue with the water.

Caralisa unlocked her door and shuffled downstairs, trying to look ill. She was shaking, so it was easy. She peered into the parlor and beckoned for Brynna to come.

Brynna slipped through the door and tisked, "Oh, you look awful. You can't show up like this. You'll scare him away."

"No, no," Caralisa said weakly. "I'm going to take a hot bath. Don't call me for dinner. Would you mind very much if I took you up on that offer of tea? I'm going to go to bed very early tonight."

"Of course," said Brynna with a sympathetic tisk. "Do you know, you're not missing anything. He's a horrid bore and he's fallen in love with Delia. If you go upstairs, I shall bring your tea directly."

"Thank you, Bryn."

When Caralisa returned from her bath, she found the tea service waiting in her room. She mixed it sweet. It was all

the dinner she could think about facing. She dusted herself
with the scented powder Viola had left for her.

Her hair was forever in drying. At last it brushed clean
and crackling. Caralisa drew the window drapes to, locked
her door, and stuffed a towel into the crack underneath to
keep the lamplight from spilling into the hallway. She retrieved her gown from hiding and let the gold cloth drape
and flow over her curves like water. It fastened at the shoulders and at intervals down her arms with pins fashioned into
golden bees. The belt crisscrossed around her waist and the
sandal straps crisscrossed up her shapely calves.

The liquid fabric of the gown shimmered with her trembling. *Shall I let him touch me?*

Does he want to?

Perhaps she would see what sort of stone he was made of
once the two of them were alone in his carriage.

She stopped what she was doing, and gripped the edge of
her dresser, shocked at herself.

I couldn't do that!

But I think that I shall.

Against her heart's frightened hoofbeat tattoo she resolved
a solemn vow to kiss him, and she would not settle for his
cheek.

Or maybe she would dare more than that.

She faced the mirror and experimentally pulled out one
shoulder pin. The flowing cloth slithered off her shoulders
and spilled round her elbows, leaving her naked to the waist.
She could choreograph that to look accidental. She crossed
her arms before her, and practiced a shy sultry look for the
mirror, pouting her lips. She lifted up her hair and let it fall
in a tumble around her nakedness. Rich red tresses teased
her pink-tipped white breasts.

She turned from the mirror. She detested her rounded features. She didn't look sultry, she thought. She looked pudgy.
And she hated her infernal blushing! Unaware of her own

sensuality, she had not seen a fetching wanton in the mirror shying away in tempting dishabille.

The count was right. *I'm not pretty.*

She repinned the shoulder. She remembered in frustration that he had already seen this, and he had remained unaffected. Or was he too much of a gentleman to take advantage of her mishaps?

Very well. No accidents. She could unfasten the pin quite deliberately. She would not risk devastation, his calling her a strumpet, or worse still, his silently turning away.

I have to know. She wanted to be touched. Hunger consumed her common sense.

She brushed out her tousled hair. She did not know what to do with the headdress. There seemed to be something missing.

A rustling of drapes and movement at the window made her start as a gloved hand reached in and gave a muted knock on the window sash. Caralisa skimmed the floor and threw open the drapes for the count.

Outside the window, his face in shadow, he was dressed in breathtaking dramatic elegance, a dove gray evening coat and silver waistcoat, black breeches buttoned at the knee in silver, black hose, and black leather shoes. She had never seen him without riding boots. His muscular calves gave a strong symmetry to his legs.

As he doffed his tall gray hat and ducked his head to come in the window, his face moved into the light.

Startled, Caralisa took a step back.

He was not without his mask. As usual it covered the top half of his face. But this one was disturbing in that it was the color of his skin and fashioned like a normal man's visage, with natural eyebrows fit into it. At a distance he would appear unmasked. Up close it was the dead image of an inanimate face, and she had to wonder why he did not just take it off and show his own countenance.

The count stood fully upright inside her room. He met her

troubled stare. "You don't like it," he said. "I think you look quite striking."

In an off-balance moment she realized he was talking about her dress. "Oh. It's very pretty. Thank you. I—I hate your mask."

"That is unfortunate."

"Why can you not just wear your face?"

"Because it's not a mask."

She did not understand and he would not speak further on it. He helped her with the headdress, drawing her hair up through its crown and letting her red tresses flow down her back.

"But it shows my *hair!*" Caralisa gave a hushed cry.

"No one will know that," said the count.

And the beaded crown made it all look like a long wig.

He gave her a mask. It was white porcelain, covering her brow and cheeks, extending down to the tip of her nose. It was blank and classically beautiful as a marble statue of a Greek goddess. She regarded the nymph in the mirror. "Who am I? Someone Greek."

"Your muse," he suggested.

"Not Venus?" she said.

"No."

"Helen of Troy!" she suggested.

"I sincerely hope not."

She thought he was unnecessarily adamant about it. "I know you don't think much of me, but I feel very pretty. So who am I meant to be?"

"There were nine muses. Pick one."

"Well, who is the muse of music?"

"Music is the art of the muses. Their attributes were farmed out later, and none of the later writers could agree who ruled what."

"So who am I?"

"Calliope, I should think."

Caralisa had always pronounced it like the musical instrument, but he accented it Calliohpi—same as Caralisa.

He had brought an evening wrap for her. A wide square of rich fabric like gold and silver and bronze melted together and still molten. He draped it on her, loosely round one hip with both ends crossing atop the opposite shoulder to fall before and behind in shimmering columns.

He stepped through the window and offered his hand. "Come see what you have wrought."

She put out the light and went to him.

The carriage was not his usual barouche, it was bigger, and when he helped her inside, she discovered the need for space. Someone else was already inside it. A woman dressed in the same fashion as she, with the same blankly beautiful white mask, only her gown was silver and the shoulder pins were cicadas instead of bees and she wore a wig of identical color to Caralisa's hair. She was taller than Caralisa, slightly older, a willowy sylph with slighter curves and more regal bearing. Her features were narrow and aristocratic. Her skin was nearly as pale as the porcelain mask. Her long-fingered hands flowed when they moved. Her back was royally straight and supple as a ballerina's. Her head bowed slightly, and for the way she moved, her silent fragile grandeur, she looked ever so much like a swan.

How could betrayal stab so deeply when Caralisa had not even been aware of trust? Possessive, she did not know she was until she saw another beauty at his side.

How dare you call me by name!

Let him try that again and he would hear about it!

How dare you.

Her eyes were stinging.

How dare you.

Caralisa seated herself across from the lady who said nothing. The count climbed in and seated himself next to the stranger.

Caralisa was about to speak when she saw that he had

changed masks. Now he wore a blank white porcelain one like theirs, only in masculine form. "Better?"

"Yes," Caralisa stammered. "Much." The more fanciful aspect was far less unsettling than the near miss at realism.

"For you," he said.

Caralisa was too upset to feel grateful or flattered. She blurted coldly, "Who is she?"

"This is your lyricist, Leda. Leda, may I introduce Mademoiselle Springer."

Long amber blond lashes within the eyeholes swept down over almond-shaped blue eyes and lifted again in a kind of bow.

"My lyricist?" said Caralisa, too confused and jealous to be polite, put out by the sameness of the beautiful dress and how much better it became this pretender with the red wig. *Her* red.

Leda. Leda of the scented parasol. Leda without an honorific. Not Lady Leda. Not Mademoiselle Leda. Why didn't he go one further and say "my Leda"?

"You gave your songs no words," the count reminded her.

"And what words did you give me?" Caralisa asked Leda.

"Ones suitable to your song and story," said the count.

"Cannot Leda speak for herself?" Caralisa snapped.

"Leda cannot speak at all."

Caralisa blanched to the color of her mask, then flushed red. Her breath caught in a knot of shame. The lyricist could not speak?

Leda sat elegantly mute, eyes unchanging, patient, too well bred to ripple with offense.

Caralisa grew angry with her own fumbling, but she could not force herself to retreat. She leaned forward and hissed at the count in pained anger, "How dare she wear that wig! That color is mine!"

"Leda is allowing you to hide in sunlight. The world will see her false hair and assume yours is also false."

But Caralisa would not allow Leda the quality of generosity. The woman had too many other virtues. Beauty, aristocracy, and the Count of Samothrace. Side by side the two looked like a set.

Caralisa felt plain and common as the farm girl she was, young and clumsy and round and puffy with fat stubby fingers, soft and milk fed next to this woman who was sleek as polished alabaster.

He had never wanted her. Caralisa was glad that she had not made a fool of herself by throwing herself at a man who had no interest in her.

She felt faint from the close brush with disaster. Her stomach and heart galloped together. She fixed the pin firmly at her shoulder.

What a crude and stupid stunt that would have been!

She felt her head emptying, her soul sinking past her heart, all wallowing in a puddle in her gut. They looked so right together. The silver of her gown matched his waistcoat. Caralisa alone was gold. And Caralisa had been so deluded as to think he had ever been attracted to her.

A small creamy sheet of scented vellum appeared over her hands, which were clasped tight in her lap. Caralisa lifted her eyes. Leda was passing her a note. She held a fountain pen in one smooth hand; the other offered the note.

Caralisa took it and read: *I am very pleased and honored to meet you. I hope my words do favor to your beautiful melodies.*

The woman who could not speak could pierce Caralisa's mean little heart with gracious words.

Of course the count would choose someone like this. How had Caralisa ever supposed someone like him would settle for a common little snipe like herself? He could—and had— won someone like this.

Caralisa could not look at her. She mumbled thanks and gazed miserably out the window.

Nearing the opera house, she could not maintain a tight

hold on her gloom. Her pulse stepped up with excited nervousness. Her premiere!

She stepped down from the carriage with the count and Leda, tagging with them like their child as grand doors opened for them and richly uniformed gold-corded ushers nodded bows to them and escorted them up the wide red-carpeted stairs where only titled heads could go.

As they ascended the stairs, Caralisa gazed up at the fan tracery of the ornate ceiling; volutes spread and diverged from the corbels into geometric flowers. Her sandals sank into the thick carpeting and they made no sound.

She had been in the opera house before, with Madame Gerhold and the girls, to see the orchestra in the afternoon. They had been tucked into the seats beneath the balcony far on one side where they could not see half the string section. And once when they'd come to see *Othello,* they had gone up the common ramp to the side seats of the second balcony. She remembered seeing these forbidden stairs, leading under the archway crusted in a frame of gold leaf and lacquered flowers. The girls called it the Pearly Gates, and it was everyone's fantasy to ascend those stairs on the arm of a titled lord who had fallen madly in love with her, and to sit in a box, dressed in a splendid gown, to be envy of the admiring crowd below.

Well, she had most of the dream. The madly in love was too much to ask for. But the ushers called her not "mademoiselle," but "my lady," and all eyes in the house turned when the three of them entered their box. Caralisa held her breath—for a moment she could do nothing else—and tried to mimic Leda who was as at ease as if she had been doing this for centuries.

The count murmured only, "It looks like a full house."

They settled into deep red velvet chairs. The orchestra was warming up, running up scales, trying snatches of tunes and melodic riffs. Caralisa found them familiar yet strange—familiar because she had created every one of them, strange because she was hearing them outside of her head. Her nerves vibrated with the strings. Her stomach waffled. *O my lord.* She picked out shreds of her songs all mixed together and at odds with the tuning violins and oboes and flutes. The musical lines were meaningless inseparable noise to everyone else. She knew each one.

She inhaled hugely and let her eyes wander the wide vaulted ceiling painted with angels and birds and cherubs stringing garlands and ribbons over the heads of the elegant crowd. Murmured din wafted up from the packed floor. Her throat constricted.

So many of them!

A blend of perfumes, sweet and heavily spiced, rose with the rustle of programs, and whispers of crisp satin and spring wools, a sporadic cough here and there. Heads turned, sometimes with a surreptitious pointing at Caralisa, who was dying behind her white mask. *Her. She did it.*

She glanced aside at the Count of Samothrace, ever serene, ever smug.

How could you do this to me!

She felt stripped before all the world. All that was Caralisa was about to be laid out in a spectacle on the Larissan stage.

Leda was passing a note to the count. Caralisa looked over his shoulder.

Where is Vickery? Leda asked.

The count answered, "In hiding, having an extended conversation with a chamber pot, no doubt. You know he never makes an opening night." Then, to Caralisa's perplexed stare, he noted, "Your director. Antoine Vickery."

"Ah," said Caralisa, feeling for the man. She was sure someone had released a cage of field mice into her own stomach. "Can I go sit with Antoine?"

Leda silently laughed.

Then she wrote another note: *Who is that rude young lord standing up and staring at us from the box on house left?*

Leda nodded slightly. The count and Caralisa followed her

gaze across the house to the boxes opposite. The count's face changed. His jaw hardened; a muscle along its edge snaked over it and bulged with the clenching of teeth.

Caralisa nearly leapt from her seat.

A beautifully built manly youth, with wide eager eyes of shining blue, a heroic cleft chin, and soft honey-brown curls—he was squinting and staring and moving his head as if trying to see around Leda and the count, or maybe as if he could spiritually move her mask aside. He gestured excitedly to his friends, a long bored aristocratic snob, a square solid soldierly young man, and a balding scholar with a vast intelligent forehead.

The count said tersely, "That is the Marquis de St. Florian."

"Michaeljohn!" said Caralisa.

"Yes, I believe his Christian name is Michaeljohn," the count added dryly.

In a moment an usher appeared at the archway to the count's box, paused there, and cleared his throat. The count lifted a finger to bid him come. The usher advanced and brought a note upon a silver salver to the count. "For the young lady." He lifted a brow in Caralisa's direction, and he withdrew.

Caralisa lifted her hand toward the note but the count produced a match and flamed it. Caralisa flinched away as the paper burned swiftly with a bright blaze. Across the theatre, a stricken look crossed Michaeljohn's face.

"It must have been ardent indeed," said the count, not letting go until the flames were at his gloved fingertips. He dropped the burning paper into a flowerpot, where it guttered out. Caralisa peered after it. Black crinkled tissue-thin remains disintegrated with her breath.

"It was mine," Caralisa cried. "You had no right."

"You are with me," the count said indignantly. "What do I look like? A hired man? He may send you notes on his own time."

"And what do I look like? The understudy?" Her eyes raked toward Leda.

The count's eyes flashed darkly, rankled. "I shall pretend that was not spoken."

Caralisa inhaled to press further, but suddenly the entire theatre had turned around as if to stare at her. But they were not looking quite *at* her, past her rather, to her right. And even the count and Leda, and Michaeljohn himself, had shifted attention to the royal box.

Heralds had stepped out. Caralisa hastened to stand as well.

When the house was respectfully on its feet, Prince Maximillian made his entrance, with Albertina on his arm.

Caralisa had barely glimpsed the sovereigns before. Now they were so close she could see their faces clearly. Albertina was as beautiful as the tales said, with hair of autumn lea and cerulean eyes of a summer sky. She moved with gentle grace on the arm of stalwart Maximillian, the dashing Prince of Montagne. He held himself like an officer on parade, his face angular and sharp featured, his dark eyes fierce and regal yet so very tender when he looked upon his lady. He seated her with such attention that Caralisa melted inside and almost cried. Oh, for a love like that!

A soft touch on her hand brought Caralisa back to herself with a start. It was Leda, passing her a note:

Their story is as wildly romantic as your Masque of Hearts, read Leda's elegant script.

Caralisa was aware that there was a story to the royal couple, something heroic and wonderful, but she had never actually heard it. All Larissans just assumed that everyone already knew it, and they spoke of Maximillian and Albertina as they did Romeo and Juliet, or Anthony and Cleopatra, as if the speaking of the names said it all.

"What is their story?" said Caralisa.

Leda made a handsign, which the count translated to mean: "Later." For the gaslights flickered and were dimming in the frosted globes of the chandeliers. The murmured voices in the house hushed with a slight crescendo of rustling and shifting that abated swiftly to attentive quiet as the darkness became complete.

A crackle of applause greeted the entrance of the conductor. It settled into silence with the raising of the baton and poising of bows. A downbeat.

The overture began. Caralisa clutched at the arms of her seat on hearing the unfamiliar/familiar music. This was how a poet must feel to hear his words spoken aloud by a stranger—the inflections, the stresses altered—hers, yet grown away from her. No. This was how it must feel to see one's child learn to walk.

The tunes wove together and Caralisa remembered the afternoon on the secret lake. At one point the count had asked her what would happen if she bundled up all her songs from that day into one song. And as a joke, she had done it. Here it was. The overture. She was caught between laughing and pummeling him with her fists and sitting spellbound by the sound of her songs come to life on the voices of so many mellifluous instruments.

The brailled curtain drew open in scalloped layers to reveal a fairytale scene, dreamlike blue and watery green edged in gold and ghostly white as the overture arched to a close. There was a warm rush of applause. Then into the dreamscape sounded a woman's high clear coloratura and a single flute.

Caralisa gasped for the loveliness of it. She shut her eyes, the sound too sweet to bear. This was how it was supposed to sound. This was what the angels were trying to tell her.

The two leads were surely heaven sent. She was lyrical. He was golden. They fell in love and everyone fell in love with them.

Caralisa's music filled the air, sounding new and strange, yet familiar and right. Leda's words were simple and poetic, saying what lovers say, only words enough to connect the songs and ballets.

It began with the girl dancing with her mask of a golden bird in her room, intending to steal away to the masque that night when her nurse was asleep. She asked the mask what she would find there in the song "Something Wonderful." The mask warned her that she must be back before her nurse awakened at daybreak.

Lights came on across the stage at the ducal castle. The boy argued with his father, who had arranged a match for him. The boy resisted. The father stormed out. The boy wanted to know "What of Love?" His friends entered in a boisterous gang, kicking up their heels in a rousing virile dance. They brought him a mask and vowed to show him a good time in his last hours as a single man.

The next scene was the masque. The duke's son, wearing the costume of a white knight, made his reluctant entrance. Then he saw the golden bird dancing and he lost his heart at once. He cut into the line of a dance which changed partners turn by turn. When the partner change brought the two into each other's arms, they sang a passionate duet of instant love. Partners changed around them; they stayed together and moved downstage from the crowd. Lights faded on the dancing chorus, leaving the two lovers alone in a pool of light, as if they were the only two people in the world. They danced a lyrical pas de deux.

They were about to remove their masks but at the cock crow she remembered her nurse and the warning, and she ran. He tried to follow her but his friends intercepted his pursuit and took him away back home.

Their morning songs were sung from opposite sides of the stage. "Who Is She?" "Who Is He?" He bade his servants spread the word: *White Knight beseeches Golden Bird to meet him at the fountain on the village square this night.*

In overlapping song, lights came up on the maiden reading the announcement, which segued into her passionate aria, "I

Must Fly." But her nurse had not been sleeping when the maiden returned from the masque. The nurse found her mask and took it to the girl's brothers. Her brothers broke off her song as she was putting on her cloak to go out. They locked her up in her room so she could not make the rendezvous. Her father told her he had made "A Perfect Match," and she would do as he said. She sang a mournful reprise of "I Must Fly" while locked in her room.

In the following scene the boy paced and fretted around a working fountain glittering under dreamily subdued colored lights. He wondered why she did not come, and at last concluded that she did not love him.

Resigned and sad, the boy agreed with his friends that there was no such thing as true love and he told them to tell his father that he would do as his father wished.

The maiden, locked in her room, sat in a wedding dress, resisting her nurse's attempts to put on her veil. The nurse sang a no-nonsense, "He Is Rich, He Is Powerful," as the girl sang a dolorous reprise of her sweetheart's "What of Love?"

For the last scene a curtain painted with cathedral doors parted to reveal a magnificent set of a grand cathedral with great stained glass windows. The congregation was singing a stodgy arrangement of the "Celebration of Love," making a travesty of it. The boy sang his own song in mournful counterpoint, until the chorus overwhelmed him entirely, drowning him out with the entrance of the veiled bride.

Then, in a wondrous moment, she began to sing, a clear sweet coloratura with a single flute.

He joined in joyfully with gathering spirit, rolling and climbing in exhilaration into a wildly rapturous duet, "My Love, My Love!" The song swelled into the chorus's renewed rendition of the "Celebration of Love," its new arrangement setting the notes free to soar, exultant. The groom lifted the bride's veil and they kissed, leaving the chorus the rollicking jubilant wedding dance as confetti spilled from the flies like colored snow.

Caralisa forgot where she was, forgot the houseful of eyes, forgot Michaeljohn. She dove into the story with the young lovers and did not come out again until the curtains closed on their kiss with the last ringing ebullient chord.

Applause thundered at once and from all around her. Tears were streaming from under her mask. Everyone was on their feet, and the count was bidding her stand. She resisted but he said, "No one sits when the prince and princess are standing."

Caralisa came to in shock. The prince was walking out?

No. He was on his feet heartily applauding. Albertina's shoulders were heaving with her sobs.

The ovation stretched on and on. Caralisa's world rocked on the roaring waves of it.

After the curtain calls, an usher appeared in the arch. The card on his silver tray was royal sky.

"Dry your eyes, mesdemoiselles," said the count. Caralisa only then noticed that Leda was crying as well. "You have an audience with the prince."

Caralisa was ushered through a gauntlet of royal guardsmen uniformed in scarlet who let no one past uninvited. As royal doors parted for her, she craned her head back to glimpse Michaeljohn struggling through the crowds that choked the corridor to the royal loge. The guards shut ranks firmly between them.

Pressure at her elbow bid her go forward.

The sovereigns rose in welcome. Albertina was in tears. She lifted luminous eyes that widened in surprise at the sight of Caralisa. The princess gave a murmured cry, with a soft touch aside to the prince's shoulder. "Maximillian, she's a child!" And then to Caralisa, "Oh, but you understand love!"

Caralisa stammered. The royal couple wore little jewelry but both seemed to be quietly glittering. The princess was soft and gracious in flowing silks, the prince tall and stalwart in his black uniform. Caralisa curtsied near to the floor. "Thank you, Your Royal Highness."

A voice sounded from behind with a hiss so low it was nearly subliminal: "Majesty."

"Your Royal Majesty," Caralisa stammered. "Majesty."

Maximillian was an arresting presence, but too gracious to be intimidating. He dispelled her blundering embarrassment with a smile. This was the Young Prince whom all women of Montagne counted as the handsomest of men—to the bewilderment of the men of Montagne. Caralisa recalled now a discussion at a masque, in which the men and women had been firmly divided. The men insisted that Maximillian's was a face like any of theirs. There were lips less thin; thicker hair of more alluring color than the princely raven. There were cheekbones chiseled with strokes less broad than Maximillian's rough-hewn visage. There were brows less severe. What on earth was it that the women saw that made them melt and sigh? The answer was courage and nobility, responsibility, strength, gentle humor, dignity, devotion to Albertina. "You're not talking about his looks!" the men had protested. "Yes we are," the women had insisted. "We are."

Caralisa snapped out of reverie as a courtier read from a card: "The Count of Samothrace, Mademoiselle Leda and Mademoiselle Calliope."

Maximillian made a droll moue. "The muse?"

"In person," said the count for Caralisa.

"I can well believe it. It is an inspired work you have set on our stage, mademoiselle. I am charmed."

And he inclined his head in a bow to *her.*

Caralisa's eyes were level with the prince's wide chest. A noble heart beat behind the black uniform bedecked with ribbons of valor. She dared steal a glance up to his coal dark eyes—eyes set in the face of the handsomest of men.

Caralisa whispered, "Thank you, Your Majesty."

Then Princess Albertina looped an arm round Caralisa's

and stole her off to the side conspiratorially. "Who *are* you, child?"

"Caralisa Springer," she answered baldly.

"And that would be?"

Albertina was waiting for a title.

"I'm not anybody, ma'am. Sire. Majesty."

Albertina winked and wrinkled her aristocratic nose impishly. "Birth isn't everything." She restored Caralisa to the count's side.

Thankfully Caralisa did not need to say anything else. The count and the crowned pair conferred some moments more on art and theatre. Leda added some comments with handsigns, which the count translated for her.

Her long white hands moved with the quickness of a dove's wingbeats. The count read them with the ease of long familiarity.

Caralisa fell to brooding. She noted that the count had not introduced Leda as his wife. *Mesdemoiselles,* he had summoned them. And so he had announced them.

She recalled something a dissolute king of a masque dressed as Nero had once said, and she wondered again which was it that the Count of Samothrace had so many of: *so many secrets or so many women?*

I don't care, she told herself angrily, building a wall of stone between him and her wounded heart. Let him have his lady swan and whomever else he wished. What was it to Caralisa? She had never felt anything for him but fascination, she was certain.

I don't care.

The guardians of the royal presence yielded at last to the excessively insistent and direly needful young nobleman who was begging audience with the sovereigns.

"I come to the theatre to enjoy myself," Maximillian quietly grumbled in his loge.

"Oh, see him," said Albertina. "It sounds as if he is dying at our door."

"The Marquis de St. Florian," the courtier announced, and Maximillian nodded in resignation for him to send the young man forth.

The young suppliant did not so much enter as he burst in, like a man who has been held under water and only now let up for breath. Soft blue eyes were frantic, his luxuriant hair in disarray. He was dressed as a student aristocrat, a welter of snowy lace flapping from his cuffs and cascading down his chest like a young pheasant cock. Smooth hands of a gentleman clutched at the air in distraction. He had been graced with a trim build and a taut waist. Strong legs showed a fine shape under close-fitting trousers, rising to the firm curve of his buttocks and narrow hips. A man of such fair mold could speed many a young heart, but he retained an air of untouched innocent nobility that said he did not indulge in the havoc which he might have upon nubile hearts. He came with a single purpose, approaching obsession. He gazed round himself, lost. To the monarchs' confusion, he *kept* turning round and looking past them, seeing Maximillian and Albertina but not whom he sought.

His companions hung back in the entranceway; Bernard a stolid solid block of chalky stone; Claude pale and wanting to blend into the carpet; and the insouciant jaded aesthete Aristide trying to contain a smirk. In a moment that one would laugh out loud.

The Marquis de St. Florian blurted out, "Where is she!"

Aristide barely held in a snigger. He gave a cough instead into his fist. The stone-faced Bernard became ever more granite, and Claude swayed on his feet, faint.

The earnest young lord from St. Florian remembered in that moment to bow. "Forgive me, Your Majesties, but . . ." He did not know how to tell the prince and princess—after his frantic appeal to obtain an audience with the crowned heads of Montagne—that he did not want them. He wanted *her*.

Fortunately Maximillian was amused. A smile tugged beneath his straight black mustache. He glanced to Aristide, a local nobleman he knew. "My lord Avenroe. Perhaps you could assist the young sir?"

Aristide sobered only long enough to say, "He is trying to find a girl, Majesty."

Albertina gave a bemused near smile, and said with baffled solicitousness, "Can we help you look?"

Claude made a noise like a frog as he swallowed a mortified sob. Bernard bowed his head and frowned as if to pray at a funeral. Aristide crossed his arms, enjoying himself enormously. He cocked his head to St. Florian.

Michaeljohn pressed ahead, "She was just here, Majesty. The young lady who wrote the songs, or the words. One of those two. The red-haired angel."

"They both had red hair," said Maximillian, at a loss.

"The real one," Michaeljohn said urgently. "The beautiful one."

"I'm afraid they were both beautiful," said Maximillian.

"The golden one!"

"Ah," said Maximillian, pleased to have an answer. "The songstress wore gold." St. Florian wanted the shorter, softly curved, cherry cheeked young nymph who blushed so disarmingly. The svelte silver swan called Leda had been the lyricist.

"Her name, Majesty. I beg you please, for the love of God, tell me her name."

"She calls herself Calliope," said Maximillian. He turned to Albertina. "My love? I believe she told you another name?"

Albertina demurred with a slight shrug that was all innocence. "She was introduced to me as Calliope. The muse."

"Where did she go?" Michaeljohn begged.

Maximillian's coal dark eyes glanced toward his own private exit. He thought for a moment that the rash young St. Florian would lunge through it. Bernard and Claude had edged forward a step, poised to grab him and beat him to the floor and carry him out with abject apologies should he try it.

"She left in the company of the Count of Samothrace," said Albertina. "You might ask him."

The youth crumbled before their eyes. Maximillian, truly trying to be helpful, gathered, "Not a good idea?"

"The problem, Majesty," Aristide explained reasonably, "is that he is a demon, you see."

"Oh God!" Claude wept and Bernard the stone cracked. Michaeljohn tried to hush Aristide, who was marvelously entertained and would not be hushed. "What? *No,* is it now, St. Florian? I am astounded. You've reconsidered your claim? Truly, Majesty, last I heard he was a demon."

"I know what he *wants* me to believe," said Michaeljohn hotly. "I don't know what I believe anymore."

"I see," said Aristide. Then his brow pinched above his long, high-bridged nose. "I think."

"It could have been another mask," said Michaeljohn. "I've been made for a fool again."

"Wherefore? You do that so well for yourself, your lordship," said Aristide. "Let us take Her Most Gracious Majesty's suggestion and go ask Samothrace, shall we?"

Michaeljohn made a move toward the royal exit. Aristide took his arm firmly. "Come along. While they still find this vaguely charming."

His friends escorted the forlorn young lover out the way they came.

Maximillian turned to Albertina. "I can see why he pursues her, poor boy. She is a fetching creature."

"Painfully timid," Albertina said.

"Oh now, I remember a lady of august rank who called my butler 'sir' on her arrival at the palace."

Albertina's cheeks warmed. "I was lately a commoner."

"So she is still. I heard her tell you. And why, under heaven, did you not tell young St. Florian her name? He obviously loves her so."

"How blind you are sometimes, Maximillian," Albertina scolded.

"What?" The prince looked back as if he would see something he had missed. He gave a slight shrug of his square shoulders to admit that he did not see at all. "What?"

"So does the count."

"Does he now?" Thick dark brows lifted in surprise. He had not noticed any sign of it. He frowned. "He does?"

Albertina's long lashes swept down once over cerulean eyes full of knowing. "Madly."

Maximillian ran a forefinger across his mustache thoughtfully. In a moment he hazarded, "Beloved, have you met him before?

"The young marquis? No."

"No. I mean the Count of Samothrace."

A crease furled Albertina's perfect brow. At length she said thoughtfully, "No. I'm sure not. That mask is not enough to disguise such a one."

"Extraordinary, is he not?"

"Yes. So much that I would have remembered had I met him before," said Albertina confidently.

"I know," said Maximillian. "And I haven't either. Only I'm not sure. I . . ."

Albertina took his hand in both of hers. "What?" She was becoming aware of an importance behind his musings. She shook her head to tell him that she did not understand.

Maximillian gazed past her, focused hard on some indeterminate point in space. "It feels as if I—as if we—have. An unnerving man."

And there stayed with him a lingering sense of having been in that unnerving presence before.

* * *

Caralisa listened despondently to the hoof falls of the two horses and the juddering of carriage wheels on the lattice-woven paving bricks. The count's carriage had been waiting for them at the royal exit. The count, in his infinite arrogance, had told the driver to meet them there, so sure was he of an audience with the prince.

Caralisa had counted on seeing Michaeljohn on her way out of the royal loge. She rued her lost chance. She should have thrown herself at the princess's feet and told her: *I love that man and this monster is keeping us apart.*

She always thought of these things too late!

The carriage tilted back the slight incline that signaled another bridge over another canal.

Into Caralisa's hands Leda pushed two parchment pages. Caralisa blinked out of a dream. "What is this?"

"It is later," said the count cryptically.

Caralisa looked at the pages of Leda's elegant scroll.

> *In the days of the of the reign of the Old Prince, the royal heir Maximillian fell in love with a common girl from across the river. By all reckoning Albertina was the prettiest girl in the land, but of no family, and the Old Prince forbade the union. That was to be the end of it, but he underestimated Love. He arranged Albertina's betrothal to a foreign baron and barred her from all river crossings into Larissa—for the only place where a prince of Montagne may marry legitimately is in the old abbey of Larissa. It fell to Maximillian to find a way to smuggle Albertina across the river before her wedding to the baron or all would be lost. Without bridges or boats and ever watched, he had only one desperate path left to him. Maximillian was a strong swimmer. He braved the river's ice waters of spring when they were swift and swollen—difficult enough to swim once alone, but to bring a nonswimmer back with him—it really cannot be done.*

Caralisa lifted her eyes from the parchment. "But he did it."

"Yes," said the count flatly. "Love conquers all, does it not."

As he spoke, Leda raised her brows in an expression of curious new understanding. Of course she could not comment on it.

Caralisa read on:

> On the eve of Albertina's wedding to the baron, Maximillian brought her across the river and to the abbey by the light of the moon. An old monk, cloistered and unaware of the ban, too feeble for anyone to bother sending warning, wed the lovers. The two abbey bells, St. Agnes and St. John, peal only for a royal wedding.
> And late in the night the bells of the abbey rang the wedding song.

Eight

In the morning Caralisa took up the daily paper to see if there might be any mention of her play's premiere. She had not far to look—it was all over the papers. Delia's gossipy publication was far kinder to it—calling it delicious—than were the serious columns of the regular news.

No doubt she had taken Larissa by storm. The *Masque of Hearts* was mentioned in the society section, the music reviews, the theatrical notices, and the religion pages. She had stunned the musical and theatrical worlds. The work was neither opera nor tragedy and they did not know what to do with it. So they judged it by the terms they knew and they made the worst of it.

"The compositions show a stunningly total ignorance of musical scholarship. Women should not be allowed to inflict their musical doodles upon a serious audience. That the composer is uncredited except for her initials is not surprising. She is undoubtedly too embarrassed to claim it."

In answer to the discomforting fact that Princess Albertina loved it, the critics stopped just short of saying that Albertina was a commoner. They were at great pains not to drag the monarchs down with the play, and at great pains to excuse their lapse in taste.

"Those who shoulder the titanic weight of Montagne might well indulge—nay, need!—the diversion of such a fluffy romp as this. But for normal mortals, there can be no care so great and pressing as to warrant the total abdication of thought required to enjoy this tripe."

The drama critic added: "The subject, so far from being a matter of weight, is so insubstantial that any attempt to grasp it causes it to crumble and float away like the inconsequential fluff that it is."

The church column called it sacrilegious.

Of all of them, this bothered Caralisa the most.

Almost as a footnote to all of it, the paper reported that the *Masque of Hearts* was sold out for the remainder of its six-week run.

The count came to her that evening. She almost did not see him amid the hanging wisteria. He had reverted to his black habit and feathered mask, and was sitting so still that he might have been a shadow.

He was looking reflective, sitting on the edge of the low wall, his hands clasped round one knee, the other long muscular leg extended straight, his head tilted aside. Caralisa came out to the garden, as peaceful as she had ever felt around him. A breeze ruffled a lock of his black hair. She wanted to run back in to get her sketch book and capture him in this mood. He seemed at one with the birds and flowering vines, worlds away from the awkward suitors down in the parlor who were not sure where to stand or to put their gawky hands. The count appeared to be listening to the windsongs which he claimed he could not hear. As if he were in another private place, like his secret lake, one he could bring with him and fold about himself as a cloak.

Caralisa crossed the roof garden with a dancing step to join him, feeling light.

A cacophonous honking sounded somewhere moving along the twilit horizon. Caralisa could not find them. "Swans," she said.

"Geese," said the count. "Swans sound even worse."

"I like them," said Caralisa. She sat beside him, an arm's length away. There was a fat envelope resting on the wall. "For me?"

"Reviews," he said.

"Oh." She picked up the envelope and pulled out a fistful of clippings. "How are they?"

"Those are mostly horrid," he said offhandedly.

"They all are!" Caralisa wailed.

"Oh, not all," said the count. "The women's publications adore you."

Those lauded her to the sky, calling *Masque of Hearts* wonderfully romantic and starry-eyed, scintillating, uplifting, and heartwarming.

Any serious publication called it drivel.

"You have provoked the envy of the small gods," said the count. "Unrivaled success will do that. Here. This one is your bank statement."

"My—?" She unfolded it. She had never seen one. It recorded, in the name of Calliope, 1000 Montagnian francs. "Oh my goodness! Oh my God!"

"That should make these go down easier," said the count of the stack of reviews. "I know it's not much. It was an expensive production to mount. If the run is extended—and it looks like it will be—there will be much more profit and you will not need to worry about money for a long time to come."

Caralisa was still absorbing the fact that she had come into 1000 Montagnian francs. It was more than she had ever owned.

"Goodness." She gave a shaky laugh. "I should be able to face anything. Give me one of those."

She pulled out a review and read: "No astonishment is warranted that a woman wrote the *Masque of Hearts*. It is a flimsy plot held together by slender threads of such a dazzling hue that one does not notice immediately how slight they are. Hence the enthrallment by last night's uncritical audience. Its sentimental characterization appeals to the lowest common denominator of theatregoers. The whole of it is sound and spectacle without a single thought to be had. Only a woman could have written it."

"Plot, characterization, thought, sound, and spectacle," the count echoed. "So they retreat to Aristotle."

"I've read the *Poetics*," said Caralisa. "I confess it was the farthest thing from my mind when I made up the story."

"The *Poetics,* mademoiselle, was a critical analysis of plays—of *tragedies* specifically—which had already been written quite some time before. Aristotle was not writing a handbook for playwrights, which it has been used for ever since. Why the *Poetics* should remain canon when all his other sawdust idols have fallen, I am not quite sure. It has no more merit than Aristotle's notion that in producing children men provide the seed and women act as little more than warm earth."

Caralisa blushed hotly. Talk of generation with a man—this man—alone in the garden made her squirm. But he had her curious. She squeaked, "How is it really, between men and women?"

"You hold the seed." He pulled over a vine and fluffed her nose with a flower. Yellow pollen dust made her sneeze. "Men give the equivalent of pollen. Aristotle was wrong about a great many things. Go forth and conquer, mademoiselle, and do not lose any sleep over Aristotle, who is the refuge of rigid men unable to think for themselves."

Caralisa remembered walking through the université, how daunting it was to overhear the students read the *Odyssey* from the original. The four languages of Montagne did not include ancient Greek. "Can you read Greek, my lord?"

"The Count of Samothrace?" he said with heavy irony.

"Is that a yes?"

"Yes."

"You don't look Greek."

"What does a Greek look like?"

"I don't know."

"Obviously."

"I wish you would stop snapping at me," said Caralisa. She fell silent, twirling a flower by its stem in her lap, her head bowed down.

The count said rather gently, "For a woman who has just had a monumental triumph, you look singularly unhappy."

Caralisa lifted her head, spoke what had been weighing on her since morning. "The church called it sacrilege." She turned to him in earnest though she knew he had no reason to believe her from what he had seen. "My lord, I am a good girl!"

The count chuckled benignly. "The church has not seen your play."

"Yes they did. They reviewed it."

"I saw that review," said the count. A hard smile played on his lips. "There is nothing in there to say that they saw it and everything to suggest that they did not. They reacted as they guessed they ought. And the filth which they rail against is the product of their own minds, not anything they saw, for there were no clergymen in the audience last night. I do not overlook much." He quoted a phrase from memory, " 'The glorification of an illegitimate liaison should not be tolerated by a God-fearing society.' Is that the one?"

"Yes!" Caralisa wailed. "But there's not an illegitimate liaison! He marries her! I—"

A gloved finger came to rest upon her lips, shocked her to silence. He smiled at her gently. "You protest to the wrong man. I know this. And the critic would have known this had he been in the audience."

He removed his hand. Caralisa inhaled. "But. But, that's bearing false witness."

"Indeed it is. So why are you taking this one to heart?"

"I . . . I shan't," she said. She straightened her shoulders and shook off the pall of guilt. Believing it this time, she said, "I shan't."

"Read this one." He passed her one from the université's student publication, *Owl and Ivy.* "Oh, they shall pillory me," she groaned. She had already read the scathing article of nearly impenetrable scholarship by the dean of the music conservatoire. This would be from his learned students. From such an august institution as the université, this would be a trashing of extraordinary magnitude.

"Read it."

She braced herself and read: " '. . . a premiere of stunning heterodoxy, the *Masque of Hearts* gives a sprightly snub of its charming nose at the stodgy musical canon, breaking fertile virgin ground with fresh melodic lines and unconventional harmonies. C.S. shakes the foundation of the musical world, and the Old Guard is quaking in justifiable terror. The composer, it has been oft repeated, is obviously unschooled. Of this there can be no argument. Schooling would have snuffed out such a vibrant flame as hers. Thank heaven that the genius belongs to a lady. A young man would have had his genius tutored right out of his brain, to be replaced by a parrot brain trained to spew out approved harmonies as a mimical beast without reason behind the voice. Hail Calliope.' " Caralisa tilted the page to the count and she pointed to two words written in Greek script at the very end. *Aeide Thea.* "What does this say?"

The count leaned over to see. "Sing, O Muse."

Caralisa sat, head bowed over the clippings. They trembled slightly in her hands. Her long red hair fell forward of her shoulders to shadow her face. She must have stayed that way for some time, for the count said, "Well?"

She lifted her head. Dusk was turning to dark. She could scarcely see him. "Well what?"

With quiet intensity he said, "Thank me or damn me, only say what you think."

She gathered in the reviews and the bank statement, thought and emotion reeling. She did not know what she thought. To have her daydreams spirited away and set up naked and defenseless before the world for praise and scorn. To have thousands clamoring to see it. To provoke scalding jealousy. To make a princess cry. To bring her into the presence of royalty. To be paid for dreaming, enough to set her free of an uncertain future.

She shook her head. Her pink lips parted, but for a time she could make no sound come forth. Finally she breathed, "No one has ever done anything like this for me. I can't begin . . . I . . . There are no words." She turned luminous blue eyes up to him in the dark. "God in heaven, my lord, you've given me wings."

Madame Gerhold announced over poetry lessons in the parlor that she had obtained tickets for her girls to hear a string quartet in the concert hall. Caralisa was the only one delighted.

"Can we not go see *Masque of Hearts* instead?" Delia piped up. There followed a clatter of teacups and slamming of books as the other girls backed the suggestion enthusiastically. Madame Gerhold frowned, driving deep furrows into her square face. "No."

"Why not?" they pleaded.

Madame Gerhold carefully marked her place in the collection of sonnets with a satin ribbon and closed it, folded her big-boned hands over its cover primly, and explained tightly, "It is low and vulgar with nothing artistic to recommend it."

"You've seen it then," said Laurel.

Lashless lids flew wide, flashing whites around steel gray eyes. "I have not!" said Madame Gerhold staunchly and proud of it.

"How do you know it is so vulgar?" said Laurel sweetly with a thin sharp smile.

"I have read the notices!"

Caralisa bumped the tea tray and sent a sugar cube bouncing to the carpet.

Madame Gerhold forged onward, "I trust in men of learning. That is what reviews exist for, to guide one's choices."

Caralisa fished under the tea table for the errant sugar cube. She surfaced, flushed, and offered timidly, "Are you certain they saw the play before they wrote the reviews?"

"What a thoroughly simpleminded thing to say, Miss Springer," said Madame Gerhold, as the other girls giggled. "And leave whatever stupid mistakes you make on the floor. I am not schooling you to be a servant."

"Yes, ma'am."

Up in their rooms Megan said, "I read about *Masque of Hearts*—"

"Sounds divine," Delia inserted.

Megan continued, "Your Count of Samothrace is not lacking for female companionship, Caralisa. He produced the play and he took two—two!—women to the premiere. He must like redheads. They were both redheads." Megan dabbed at her own fiery coif. "The composer and the lyricist."

Delia's silver-handled makeup brush hit the hardwood floor with a clatter and roll. She retrieved it clumsily and returned it to her dressing table and sat before the mirror like a stone. She hardly noticed Laurel and Brynna banding together in a comic chorus: "And leave whatever stupid mistakes you make on the floor . . ."

Slowly Delia pulled out a review of the play. *Masque of Hearts,* music and story by C.S.

C.S. A redheaded C.S.

Caralisa had left the room. Caralisa was humming again. Caralisa Springer always hummed.

No. It could not be. Delia gave her head a shake. Silly even to think it.

Then why had Brynna these days taken to consulting Caralisa on every hair style and dress and piece of jewelry she tried on? And Laurel, who thought she knew everything, sometimes asked naive little Caralisa for advice?

I am not the only silly one here, thought Delia.

Unspokenness hung deafeningly in the house.

A carriage was passing through the market on the avenue of the flower peddlers, where many bright stalls crowded the narrow way. The iron shoes of the matched set of plumed grays rang off the cobbles at a smart trot until a sudden wrenching on their reins brought them to a rearing pawing halt. The horses bugled, eyes rolling, forehooves lashing, sending merchants scurrying and crouching among their flower baskets.

When the carriage was stopped, the grays still stamping, their pink-white nostrils flaring and snorting, a vocal clamor sounded within the carriage and its door opened from within before the footman, who had been clinging onto the back for dear life, could get to it. The aristocratic occupant kicked out the steps for himself, then leapt down over them in his haste, landing in a crouch, his wide carrick fluttering around him.

He strode up to the flower stall, whipped his wide beaver hat from atop his thick mane of honey-colored curls, and swept it across his heart as he dropped onto one knee amid the jonquils at the red-haired girl's feet. The young Marquis de St. Florian seized the hand of the maiden in the faded pink dress and begged, "You must marry me or I shall die right here at your feet."

Caralisa's sun bonnet had fallen from her head and hung behind by a drab ribbon. Her silken red locks had spilled from their confines in a bright mass. She stared down at Michaeljohn's beautiful face, his pure turquoise eyes gazing back in adoration. She glanced around as if there could be a mistake, saw around her only a profusion of flowers and inquisitive smiling faces of the peddlers. Fortune had shot a bolt from the blue, and Caralisa reeled under the benign blast. Never again would she find such perfect physical beauty, such dogged devotion, altogether with a title, kneeling in adoration at her feet. She had despaired of ever hearing such a profession from the count who, though certainly not old enough to be her father, often treated her like a child and seemed more likely to adopt her than to offer marriage, if, indeed, he loved her at all. Of that she had considerable doubt. Oh, she had proved terribly useful for his theatrical coup, but love her? He said he did not. She could only believe him.

Now, here, in answer to hopeless prayers, knelt handsome, aristocratic, adoring Michaeljohn, any girl's perfect dream. She must needs love him. Of course she did. Wouldn't she be a fool not to? She stammered, "Yes, of course I shall marry you."

The marquis took her hand in both of his and pressed it to his lips as all the market vendors in the street applauded.

Rumor blazed through the town faster than any fire, so that when the marquis's fine carriage, burgeoning with all the flowers it could hold, rolled into Elm Tree Close, Caralisa found her spare belongings already packed up and cast onto the sidewalk. Madame Gerhold lurked behind the bolted door, clutching her broom.

"Oh no!" Caralisa cried.

"She must surrender to you what belongs to you," Michaeljohn declared.

"That is all of it," Caralisa admitted sheepishly and made to get out and collect her meager bundle from beneath the aged elm tree. She was concerned only for her mother's quilt, the spiral bracelet which the count had caught for her on Sovereign's Night, and the bouquet she'd caught at Viola's wedding.

Michaeljohn restrained her and bid the footman to round up her things.

Upper-floor curtains parted. Girls' faces crowded the window with a flutter of waving hands. Caralisa waved back heartily, wishing she could talk to them, to share her astonished joy.

As the carriage rolled away, Delia turned from the window. Her perky smiled vanished. "It's not fair. Why, that two-faced little social climber. Butter wouldn't melt."

Brassy-haired Megan crossed her plump freckled arms and insisted to the end that there had been some mistake. Laurel tossed back her limp blond ringlets and gave a sharp laugh at the outrageous twist of fortune, and Brynna batted thick lashes over fawn eyes and foundered into dizzy non-comment.

"My darling, you're trembling."

Michaeljohn had been gazing at Caralisa as if she were a vision that would vanish if he took his eyes off her for an instant. He kept his stare fastened upon her and memorized every charming detail, ever nuance, every gesture even to the way her small tapered fingers toyed with the frayed ends of her bonnet's pink ribbons. Their neat short nails formed pretty ovals. Her long lashes cast trembling fringed shadows over lovely eyes of vibrant blue and onto exquisitely curved cheeks. Her lips quivered, slightly parted, lusciously full with a voluptuous softness in a generous pouting shape. A fast pulse moved in the hollow of her smooth creamy throat.

"Are you unhappy?"

Caralisa shook her head, blue eyes watery. She could not help shaking. The hideousness of being driven out of her home did not diminish for having someone to turn to. It was nothing that she could explain, nothing that made any intellectual sense. It was only a feeling. "Where shall I go?"

"Never fear," said Michaeljohn gallantly. "It so happens I've had my eye open—in case I ever found you."

He brought her to an idyllic white cottage on a green hillside where apple trees with blossoms of snow shaded a little yard, and goat bells clanked on the hills. The lovely clustered stone halls of the université nestled higher up the steep terraced hill. Within the white fence was an overgrown garden, a well, and a trellis where grapes grew in untended tangles. A little brook trickled over a runnel of brown rocks and danced down to join larger courses to the green river.

Michaeljohn found the key under the woven mat and opened the door. He opened all the shutters to let sunlight stream in and reflect off the soft white walls and warm wood floors of the airy little cottage.

He turned to her worriedly, "Is it too common?"

"No!" Caralisa cried. "It's *wonderful!*"

He smiled, blushing pleased. "Then this will be ours. We shall live here when we are wed until I am done at the université. Then we shall go home to Chateau St. Florian and I shall surround you in the splendor which you were made for." He told her to decorate the cottage to her taste and to hire a staff to serve her needs. He added, apologetically, "My bachelor quarters are not to be beheld by gentle eyes."

"Amen," a male voice seconded.

Caralisa and Michaeljohn turned. A tall pale aesthete stood in the doorway, a wilted rose in his boutonniere. He went on to declare, "She exists. The lady of long search and many sighs." And he swept his arm across himself with a low bow. "And every bit as lovely as our St. Florian claimed. I am surprised and enchanted, my lady. I am your least humble servant, Aristide Lord Avenroe."

"I am Caralisa Springer," said Caralisa, realizing that Michaeljohn did not know her name to introduce her. He had called her only "my darling" and "beloved."

"Is that not a name for an angel!" Michaeljohn cried.

"That would seem to be the case," said Aristide. "For once

he does not exaggerate. Forgive me, my lady, I am stunned, truly stunned. As for you, sir, we are late, truly late."

Michaeljohn produced a gold-encrusted pocket watch from his waistcoat. Caralisa was gazing in delicious fascination at the taut narrow shape of his waist as Michaeljohn regarded his watch face in alarm. "I don't have my notes with me!"

"Copy Claude's," said Aristide cheerfully. "I always do."

Michaeljohn apologized profusely for running off. "But I could not ask you to wed an ignorant uneducated husband. I leave you to feather our nest." He kissed her fingertips and blew more kisses as he backed through the door.

"Ahem." Aristide cleared his throat, not leaving.

Michaeljohn reentered, irked, his exit ruined. "What?"

"How is she to effect that?" said Aristide.

"How is she to effect what?"

Aristide opened a languid hand at the emptiness of the room. Caralisa stood winsomely in the center of it, hands clasped in her faded skirt, an old country quilt rolled up at her feet.

"Oh." Michaeljohn fumbled at his belt for a bag of gold as Aristide explained patiently, "St. Florian thinks things just happen."

Michaeljohn pressed the gold into Caralisa's hands. The little bag hefted a surprising weight. "After tomorrow you can use my name at all the shops in Larissa. This is for this evening."

He met her eyes with a melting gaze, then seized her hands and kissed them until Aristide physically pulled him away.

Caralisa was at a loss in wonderland. She roamed the neat little cottage, taking in its every board and shelf and shutter, touching walls to assure herself of their substance, that they were not all a dream of hers. She sat on the windowseat daydreaming until the sun was low.

Feather their nest? She did not know where to start. In hunger she milked a goat and found some potatoes in the cellar. This was not how marquisas did things, but it was what she knew, and she could not bring herself to languish like a true lady.

When night fell, she spread her mother's quilt outside on the fragrant grass. She felt the air change. Dampness collected with the evening cool. Rich earth exhaled fresh greenness. She could smell the mossy wet stones of the chuckling brook. Crickets and spring frogs trilled and peeped. Overhead, stars eased into view in their thousands, becoming a hundred thousand of points of light, then millions in a milky glow in the glory of heaven.

Caralisa's eyelids drooped. She fell asleep to the low lazy clanking of goatbells.

The announcement of her betrothal appeared in the morning paper. The society columns staggered before the storm front as they always did in the wake of a successful assault on the titled bastion by a commoner. The mysterious princess had been unmasked. Why, she was a little *nothing!* Some proceeded more carefully, not to tread on the toes of the next Marquisa de St. Florian.

Caralisa discovered the titled world of buying without money. She walked into a shop and instantly had everyone's attention. She need only choose what she wanted and it would appear in her cottage. She threw herself into making the cottage a home. When she overheard muttered gossip and realized she was embarrassing Michaeljohn, she engaged a fashionable designer to create a suitable trousseau for her. Caralisa presented a challenge, being an ingenue. The couturier had not thought that there were any left in Larissa.

Caralisa asked Michaeljohn what he thought of her choices. To everything he approved without looking at it. He said anything was wonderful so long as it pleased her.

As Aristide said, Michaeljohn thought things just happened.

Michaeljohn came to see her everyday, but never seemed

to notice what she'd added—a canopied bed, crisp curtains, a white rug bordered in pink rosebuds, a white provincial table with gracefully curved legs and dainty chairs with intricately worked needlepoint cushions to match. He gazed into her eyes and recited poetry to her. He brought her perfume and flowers and some small gift every day. They dreamed of how sweet life would be together.

Caralisa marveled at his face, its strong sweetness, its heroic profile with deep chin and noble brow, his soft expressions. When he came on horseback, she nearly swooned to see him mounted with such easy nobility. There was something sexual in the image of a young gallant on horseback. And there was a promise of sensuality in his gentle touch on the steed's velvet nose when he led the horse in.

She wanted him to hold her, to feel his hard body against hers. She did not know how to tell him of her longings. She could see that he wanted her too, but he was too much of a gentleman to act before it was proper. Did a gentleman's heart, she wondered, beat more purely than a commoner's? Her own lower birth must account for these base desires which goaded her mercilessly. She looked at him and did not hear his poetry, only the tenor of his voice. She gazed at his tongue moving within his white teeth, saw the motion of his soft lips, and she leaned in to be nearer to them.

Michaeljohn had assumed a long engagement, as was usual, but Caralisa would have none of it. It was the only demand she made on him—to wed at the soonest moment. She was not cool-blooded and would not be content long with dreams.

He confessed blushingly that he was glad she pressed for haste.

She met with resistance where she had least expected it—the church.

Monsignor Fortenot summoned her into his official chambers. He was still garbed in the rich vestments of high mass, and at a decent distance he cut a striking figure. His craggy

face was deeply carved in dynamic lines, and his graying
temples had grown into a silver blaze in his black hair.

Caralisa tried to evade him. "I have already been ab-
solved," she said quickly and made to go out, already opening
her parasol.

"I don't want your confession," said the monsignor huskily, and put a hand out to stay her. His palm felt papery on
her wrists. He drew her into his chambers, then closed the
carved doors and turned with his back to them, blocking
them shut. Amber eyes burned beneath heavy black brows.
His barrel chest heaved beneath his gold chasuble. Passionately he said, "I want *you* . . . not I the man, I the cloth."

Caralisa's eyes darted toward all the smaller doors and
high windows. She wished Michaeljohn were here.

Monsignor started toward her. She flinched away.

He stopped where he stood, midway across the rich red
carpet. "What is this?" He gestured at her with a big hard
palm, mortally insulted and shocked. "What is this? You are
making me angry, child!"

There was such hurt in his reproach that she stung from
her own skittish impulse. What really had she thought he
was going to do to her? "I am sorry, Father." She curtsied
and let him draw near.

He moved in face to face, so close she could taste his
breath, feel his heat through his heavy garments, see the fine
lines etched around his thin, nearly lipless mouth. "What is
it you cannot face? Did you confess all?"

She blinked, his breath puffing on her eyes. She saw the
darker beard shadow on his face though it was shaved
smooth. He licked his thin lips, and his tongue looked hard
and small within the small even gray pearls of his teeth.
Caralisa felt her skin crawling in revulsion, as if it would
retreat without her.

Monsignor put a hand to her face, his palm growing moist.
"I beg you, give yourself to the Church, not to this carnal
union."

"There's nothing bad about it," said Caralisa uneasily. "God gave this union to Man. It's a sacrament."

"It is the refuge of weak flesh." A thumb traced across her rounded cheek on the word *flesh*. Caralisa's eyelashes fluttered with a shudder as if in pain, which was indistinguishable from a tremor of desire. She heard a noise in the monsignor's throat and she shuddered again. "It is not bad," he conceded. "But you were meant for so much better."

"No," she said. "I want a man for my husband. Not a church."

"Don't defile yourself with sinful yearning," he begged, crouching still closer. "Your body is a temple. God wants better for you."

"Why did God build his temple of such weak stuff!" In her discomfiture, her voice came out louder than she had intended. It made him draw back. Taking heart, she raised her voice even higher, loud enough to be heard through the closed doors. "If I build a castle of sand, I am not surprised or angry at it if it melts in the rain. Why is God so wroth that my *temple* melts for a man? I have to believe He knows. He made me. The saint said it was better to marry than to burn; and so I am doing with all haste."

Fortenot whispered raspingly, in an effort to bring her back to a hush, "The saint was talking to men when he said that! Ladies have no such perverse natures. Not as God made them. Ladies are pure and good. They are the conscience of man."

"Daughters of Eve?" Caralisa said ironically, breathing easier with the distance.

Thick dark brows leapt like startled caterpillars. "Where is the sweet child I knew! You are possessed!"

"Wiser is all," said Caralisa.

Monsignor Fortenot's voice boomed sonorously in the grand tones that had brought him to be called Shakespeare. "You have eaten of the tree of knowledge!"

"I suppose," said Caralisa. She did feel quite wise.

"Then you must suffer the consequence!"

"Painful childbirth, I think it is," Caralisa nodded. "I want children."

He stared as if she had grown a second head. Or a first one with a brain inside it, which was unnatural enough for a pretty girl. "You *have* eaten of the fruit!"

Knowledge ill becomes me, does it? thought Caralisa. She needed to find the Count of Samothrace. He had been strangely absent these days and she needed to thank him. She owed him so very much.

"I see where springs this obscene talent," Monsignor growled. Amber eyes glowered with tiger ferocity under the black wiry brush of his thick heavy brows. Their natural arch made him look angry even when he wasn't. His narrow nose arched high at the bridge like a hawk's beak, making him appear, as he did in vehement sermon, the embodiment of wrath.

Caralisa's composure slipped. "What obscene talent?"

"You must recant your obscene music!"

"Obs . . . ? I didn't write the words," said Caralisa, not that she found anything obscene in them. But they were, some of them, very ardent.

"It is not the words that are obscene. Those are merely disgusting. It is those—those—*notes* that arouse unnatural passions and quicken the blood in a man. Where does a young girl come by such ungodly sounds?"

Caralisa foundered. Her full tempting lips moved for a moment without words in a maddeningly sultry motion, trying to find speech. "I—I hear them—"

"Voices!" His tone was a pounce. Thin lips spread to bare small perfectly even teeth, slightly spaced, like a string of dull pearls. "You claim to hear voices? I suppose you think yourself a saint!"

"No!" Caralisa cried. "No! The farthest thing from it! There is no commandment: Thou shalt not compose music! I consider it a gift. Now if you please, Monsignor, I am expected." That was a lie. She would need to confess it. To someone else. She marched past him with distress-inspired force. "Good day."

For all her impatience, the day was upon her before Caralisa was ready. Michaeljohn's family had taken anything whatsoever to do with the wedding ceremony—except for the date, over which she had thrown an unseemly common fit—out of her hands. The advantage of having a bride who was no one was that the ceremony could be done to St. Florian taste. Caralisa became as a doll to be dressed up on the day, wound up, and pointed down the aisle.

When the moment came, she felt quite alone. Having had no hand in the planning, she was quite awestruck with it all and she gawked as the grand doors parted to the opulent grandeur of the cathedral and she was staring up the gold-carpeted aisle strewn with rose petals. Flowers in formal sprays proliferated on the altar, and at the end of every pew, and in the bouquets of her maids, who were all de St. Florian. A bishop, a stranger to her, waited at the far end of the gilded carpet.

The rows and rows of pews were filled with elegant strangers. She could not even have Viola with her, for Viola was near her time.

The magnificent strains of the massive pipe organ filled all the niches and raised a sublime resounding noise to heaven.

The bride gripped the arm of her godfather. His was the only friendly face to be found, and a distant one at that. He made for a cold companion, subdued and daunted by the whole business, uncomfortable in his formal habit that was far and away better than anything he could afford for himself. A vague unease hounded him that he had not found anyone for her, and that he had been looking too low, that she had done quite grandly for herself, that he had not done better for his own daughter. He had a lingering sense that Caralisa was doing this just to show up his failing. He told her only that he wished it were not so fast and he wished that she would have *asked*.

Caralisa wondered where the Count of Samothrace could be. She had heard nothing but silence from him and she began to wonder if he was angry. Or did he care? He had vanished and she missed him terribly. She could not even send him an invitation to the wedding when what she really wanted was for him to be *in* it.

She kept unvoiced a wish that the count were there to do this, to give her away. She scanned the faces in the crowd searching for a masked one, in faint hope that he would crash this affair and scold her for not inviting him.

She stood poised in the door, clutching her godfather's arm and her bouquet. The music changed. The organ swelled to a grandiloquent consummation. The congregation stood and turned. Sounds of wonderment greeted her gown.

Caralisa was seeing all through the gauze of her veil. It diffused the candles, giving them glowing haloes and unearthly soft brightness. The rose window dominated up ahead, daylight shining through its great varicolored round of intricate petal tracery with a leaded quatrefoil at the heart.

Underneath it, the long long aisle stretched to eternal length between a gauntlet of staring strangers. Caralisa advanced slowly, her train dragging. Its long heavy white brocade hooked onto her bustle and fanned behind her like a peacock's folded tail.

Straight ahead, the bishop waited, holding his Bible. Near him, Michaeljohn in white tie and tails stood beaming at her. She could not wait until they would be reunited at the altar once again and forever.

Michaeljohn's blue eyes held a soft shine. The bride suddenly smiled, eyes sparkling, radiant.

She lifted her eyes to contain tears of joy. Sunlight streaming in the rosette window dimmed briefly with an advancing shadow—

—just before the midnight spectre of a giant black swan came crashing out of the sunlight in a glittering rain of colored glass.

The pipe organ gave a few faltering blasts of wrong notes. With the sudden cessation of music rose a concerted scream. The congregation lurched and ducked from a shower of shattered ruby and violet shards, and from the beating of giant black wings.

The great black bird swept a banking turn round the nave. Candles toppled with a splash of hot tallow. Guests lunged into each other away from the falling fire. An alabaster box of chrism fell and cracked, spilling scented oil that ignited in a lively blaze. Heavy wingbeats drew up the flames. Incense caught fire, and heavy scented smoke filled the air. Pandemonium became panicked rout. The mass of people crushed into the aisle where Caralisa was fighting against their current to get to the altar. "Michaeljohn!"

Her stepfather pulled on her arm, trying to drag her back to safety. Someone charged between them and broke his hold. He was quickly swept away in the panicked tide.

There came a loud wooden banging and high-pitched screams of sudden pain as a pew clattered over backward onto parishioners in the row behind. Caralisa staggered, unable to move, pinned down by many tramping feet on her wide train. Its length of heavy fabric became caught and tangled under foot and suddenly she was being dragged down with it. A choking sweet cloud of spice burned her nostrils, the air become black with it. Her knee buckled. A foot landed on her calf. She cried out, knocked off balance. She caught herself with her hands. A knee drove into her face. Another foot stepped skewed on her ankle. A hard shoe tramped on her hand. She was drawn underneath the stampede and pinned there by her gown.

Then strong hands closed hard on her rib cage under her

arms. The grip hurt, but it was hauling her upward. She heard a ripping. Her long train came off with a popping of silk roses from her bustle. Her skirts pulled up from under people who were trampling on them, sending them toppling.

An arm like an iron band circled her chest, holding her tight against a hard lean body as she was borne out of the human current, up onto a pew and over to a niche at the side of the tumult through the swirling air. She could no longer hear the swooping wingbeats of the trapped swan; it must have found its way out.

Caralisa held fast to her savior. She could not see through tearing eyes, but she knew him, his powerful lean body, his height, his sure gentle strength, the calm even pounding of his heart, his gloved hand holding her head to his chest. The Count of Samothrace.

She hugged him tighter, feeling suddenly safe even in the choking smoke and screaming riot.

An angry hissing sizzled as someone tried to douse an oil flame with holy water. Smoke billowed up blacker and thicker.

Rays of dirty light fanned jaggedly through the shattered aureole of the rose window.

Caralisa inhaled smoke, coughed deep honking rasps. The count gave her a handkerchief. She held it to her mouth and nose, breathed in a sickly sweet damp scent. Clouds gathered inside her head. Heat and cotton wool packed her forehead, muffled sight, sound. She doubled the handkerchief to screen out the smoke, but passed out nonetheless, falling into the count's embrace.

Nine

Caralisa wiped grit from her eyes with a dirty hand, which made them sting and tear all the worse. She blinked them clear and focused dazedly on her sooty fingers, remembering how they got that way. She thought she must have smudged her face terribly and she started to look for a mirror when she was arrested by wonder. She did not know where she was. She stared, caught between distress—the full tide of which had not yet caught up with her—and enchantment at her strange surroundings.

She was lying across a high bed under a rich canopy of printed silk damask. The walls were polished stone, all of a piece as if the whole chamber had been hewn out of solid rock but braced with richly finished oak beams.

The chamber was fronted by a half wall surmounted with pillars to form an open gallery leading onto a corridor. Full pillars lined the opposite side, which was hung with heavy draperies. Bright sunlight limned the edges where the draperies joined. The heavy fabric stirred with a movement of air, giving Caralisa the sense that nothing solid stood behind them.

The room was lavishly furnished in a mixture of styles, wonderfully livable, yet aristocratic and rare. This had to be the home of a fine old family who passed down its treasures generation to generation. Some pieces were battered and well worn, like the scarred wood blanket chest which had lost its value in a merchant's eye, showing the harrowing of children and family dogs, but kept because it had passed from a loving hand, or because it was known from childhood and had taken on the status of a childhood friend. A priceless urn filled with sprigs of lavender sat in a corner beneath a marble-topped table on a frame of wrought bronze. Precious carpets of colorful silk, the kind most folk hung on their walls, lay scattered on the floor.

A wash basin sat next to the bed, along with a ewer of water, and snowy white towels of luxurious Egyptian cotton adorned with fine linen fringes.

Caralisa rose from the bed and washed her face. Water swirled gray in the white alabaster bowl when she was done. Her hair reeked of smoke and incense. She took out the pins that had once secured her veil, and she brushed out the snarls with a bronze-handled brush.

She ventured out to the pillared corridor. A brisk breeze inhaled through a gap in the draperies. Dead leaves scratched across the stone floor with a scatter of seed husks and catkins.

The sound of footsteps close behind made Caralisa turn. At once she was staring up into brooding indigo eyes within a black-feathered mask.

Caralisa's voice came out smoke hoarsened. "Where am I?"

He said nothing. With a genial motion he lifted aside the heavy drape. Crisp air and light washed in. Caralisa passed through the offered opening, and the count stepped out behind her to a wide balcony.

She met with bracing high air and a view that stopped her breath for a moment. All Larissa lay below her, spread out like a map as far as the green river, and even to the cultivated fields beyond. She gazed from a strange and lordly angle down on the red and gray tiled rooftops of the town crisscrossed with narrow brick streets and lazy green canals dotted with water lilies. The buildings with their iron filigree railings and flowering window boxes appeared quaint and toylike down below. She clutched at the stout stone banister in a dizzy moment. Even the palace tower lay below her. She was on eye level only with a soaring eagle.

"I'm in the Sky Cathedral!"

This was the Heights itself, the *larissa,* the citadel, inaccessible but to swallows. And to the Count of Samothrace, it would seem.

He was regarding her with a curious steadiness. "You are a lovely bride."

Her hands moved self-consciously to her smudged dress. Footprints showed distinctly on the white skirt. The fabric smelled sharply of incense. "It—it used to have a train." She felt her hair, which lay loose around her shoulders, its ends brushing at her hips. "And a veil. It's ruined."

His gaze remained constant. He was not looking at the wretched dress.

For himself, he wore his black habit. Caralisa guessed it was his equivalent of her dusty pink day frock, comfortable and becoming and worn over and over. He was not wearing the cape, his hat, or a sword. The gloves and the mask, however, stayed on.

He leaned back against the rail, one booted foot crossed casually over the other. Old terra-cotta vases sat along the base of the balustrade, and from them potted vines coiled up the pillars, ill kept, some climbing without restraint every which way, some brown and dead. Grapevines ran riot, springing from squat vats. Green clusters of new grapes hung on thick woody purple vines that gripped the balcony with wiry tendrils. They fit in with the wild grandeur of the place. And it all suited him.

"I was so glad to see you," said Caralisa. "Not just because you saved me." She twisted her fingers nervously. "I mean. I wanted you there, do you know?"

"Why?" His voice came very deep.

"Why?" she echoed. It was an absurd question. She did

not bother to answer. The man was sometimes so obtuse. She gave him a wryly irritated glance.

There was a cut on his face, beneath the mask. She touched his cheek.

"Glass," he said.

Caralisa darted a sweeping look over the city. From here she could see the cathedral spire soaring from among the tiled rooftops. A dark jagged hole yawned where the rosette window should have been. "You were hurt!" Caralisa cried. "Why that horrible beast!"

"The swan?" said the count.

"The swan!" She turned from him, looking for a place to pound her fists. She planted them angrily on the stone railing. "How could it! How *could* it!"

"Perhaps it knew you were making a mistake."

"A *mistake?* Did that demon bird hurt anyone else!"

The count gave a shrug aside with his head. "Cuts from shattered glass. A great many sore throats and stinging eyes. The serious injuries to the guests came from each other. The bird caused a panic but it did not attack or stomp on people or turn over pews onto them or push them down and stampede over them. Precious few of your dearly beloved gathered there today were looking out for any but their sweet selves."

"Michaeljohn!" Caralisa cried suddenly.

"Precious Michaeljohn is unhurt," the count assured her dryly. "Though Lord Avenroe has taken to bed with a stubbed toe."

This provoked a smile from her.

A rustle of wings and scaping of claws on wood from above them made Caralisa shrink. "Bats?"

"Birds," said the count.

"The swan!"

"No," he said, and in fact the sound was entirely too small. "Though it does live here."

Caralisa gave a small surprised gasp. "Is it yours?"

"We share a dwelling is all."

"Honestly!" Caralisa exclaimed. At any previous mention one would swear he was barely aware of the beast's existence. Instead of becoming familiar, the man became more fantastical with every encounter. "And you live *here!*" The half-wild majestic Sky Cathedral seemed the only place able to contain him. Here he became an eagle in his aerie. Caralisa stammered, "I am sorry I did not invite you to my wedding. I hardly knew where to send the invitation." She added whimsically, "In any case I don't believe the post delivers here."

"Why didn't you advertise," he said acidly.

She chose to ignore the comment. "I'm glad you were there. Truly. You're like my father."

He pushed away from the railing and drew himself up stiffly to a menacing height. The mask itself seemed to bristle. "I beg your pardon?"

"I didn't mean to say you were old. I mean you look out for me and help me become someone. That is what a father does, is it not? What he should have done. If he had lived. Sometimes I blame them for dying. Can you believe it? As if they could have chosen otherwise. They could have been more careful. Who was thinking of me? Stupid selfish thoughts. Now I think they asked God to send you to me. To make sure I was all right." She raised wide innocent eyes to him in gratitude.

The count, far from being touched, became quite affronted, and very low he said, "No one's parents would ever send me to their daughter."

"Ah, the fiend on the Heights, you mean." She tilted her head and glanced coyly sideways with hyacinthine eyes veiled by long lashes. A smile tugged the corners of her full lips. "You must admit you are not a very fiendish fiend."

"You know me not," he said darkly.

"Why do you haunt the Heights?"

"Because they are mine."

The answer surprised her. She shook her head, grasping for sense. "But . . . the church is trying to tear them down."

"Some small men within the church are jealous. You see, the Heights reach higher than either the cathedral's spire or the prince's tower."

"But they have no right to destroy this place if it is yours!" Caralisa protested.

"They do not know that it belongs to anyone. I haven't legal paper on it."

"Claim it in court then!"

He gave a black smile. "For that I would need to take off my masks. All of them."

Her voice became plaintive. "And would that be so terrible?"

"Enough to win me the eternal fires of hell—or at least the brief but excruciating fires of earth, for I would surely burn at the stake. Mademoiselle, I am not like you."

"Well, *that* I always knew!"

"I have overtaught you. You have become too clever."

"I have been told," she said sadly. She traced her finger along a marbled vein in the stone railing. "Monsignor said something quite the same."

"Yes. I have since looked in on your Shakespeare. Beware of him. The church is a bad enemy."

"I have no quarrel with the church. Only with Monsignor." A chill raised the fine hair along her arms at the thought of his face looming into hers, the breath whistling through his narrow nostrils, that lipless mouth leaning into hers. She crossed her arms and hugged them close to her.

"You will find a quarrel with the church like killing hornets," the count warned. "Hurt one, and you have the whole hive descended around your ears. The world is a more treacherous place than you think."

"You said Larissa is not the world."

"It is the part we are in at this moment."

They strolled slowly along the parapet. On one side the

breathtaking vista of the city stretched away. To the left, within the pillars, many rooms rambled within the mountain.

The breezes were swift and chill at this height. Caralisa ducked under a tapestry and went inside.

The many chambers were all done in the same diverse chaotic style of used elegance. Silk damask cushions were thinned and worn at the corners. The grandeur of the place was not of the touch-me-not kind. Of course. Why have anything just for show when no one but he ever saw it?

"Where is the beautiful Leda?" Caralisa thought aloud. She had not meant to speak.

"Where should she be?" he countered shortly.

Caralisa's heart unaccountably sped up and her throat became tight. "I thought you were in love with her."

"Leda is my cousin. My first cousin. Given our familial traits, in-breeding would not be the wisest thing we have ever done. With our luck the children would have her voice and my face." He added, more softly, "I have always been fond of Leda and she of me. I suppose wisdom would not stop us, were we in love. I have no wish to marry her."

His face. What was so very wrong with his face that it should be perpetually masked, a thing not to wish upon his children?

The demon on the Heights.

Caralisa searched for some hint of horror in him. What she could see were his splendid eyes that could shine in warmth or flash with cruelty, anger, or ecstasy. His lips were both strong and soft. His firm authoritative chin had always been plain to see. His hair looked coarse as raw silk and so black that in strong light the highlights shone blue-white. She contrived to touch it as if by chance. The back of her hand grazed a black lock. Despite its coarse appearance, it was startlingly soft.

His head turned sharply at the light contact, and she jerked back her hand. She twisted a dead leaf stem as if that were what she had been reaching for.

"I want to go home now," she said. "Michaeljohn will be worried sick."

"I shall see you home in time," he said, gazing away.

"I want to go now," she said.

"Then you are free to go." He left the room abruptly. She made to follow him, darting through the door he had taken, only to find herself in a crooked corridor with no trace of him to be seen.

She roamed the citadel. There were several levels of chambers. She kept taking stairs, half flights, a few steps, quarter levels, downward as she found them, until the opening to the lowest level she discovered bricked over. Roots broke through the floor and anemic ivy twisted round the pillars, its leaves holding the pallor of things that never saw the sun. She backtracked a path upward.

She passed through sumptuous chambers draped with heavy brocades offset by the lightness of blond wood and light colored chintz and cutwork lace. The whole of it was oddly livable and gave a sense of comfort. It was masculine, most of it, but not excessively so. Feminine touches showed here and there in the old things. None of it had the stilted museum quality of the aristocratic homes she had seen before.

Wood framed the windows, which were carved out of the rock. There were no panes in any of them, only drapes and shutters. Some of the rock walls and floors were overlaid with wood or stucco or covered with tapestries. The inner rooms were lamplit or illuminated by light wells cut through to the top of the mount. She found the library, a wide chamber walled with bookshelves but for one, which was taken up by a wide wide hearth of glassy blackened stone. Embers within it still gave off warmth, red glints persisting under the heavy layer of gray ash. Caralisa took up a black iron poker and stirred them. She added a log from the stack.

The whole citadel was singing to her in a myriad voices, exotic, far away, and very old. She had never encountered a place filled with so many songs, from the wind in the gallery and sunbeams through the clerestories. The rooms lay in no particular pattern. It was all a labyrinthine irregular warren, more extensive than she had ever supposed. One could easily become lost.

And she could not find the way out.

Until the count chose to let her, she could not leave the Heights.

Claude and Bernard tried in vain to console the distraught Michaeljohn, who wandered the vacant cottage like a forlorn ghost crying, "Where is my love?" He paced from room to room as if the looking would cause her magically to appear where she was supposed to be. Her touch was apparent everywhere, in every flower vase, her copper watering pail, her bonnet hung on a chair knob, the curtains over the kitchen windows. He snatched up a dainty pair of white gloves which had once encased her pretty hands. He held them and carried them with him room to room. "The Count of Samothrace is behind this!" he declared.

"Likely," Bernard admitted gravely.

"I don't know," Claude hedged, trying to be optimistic. "I didn't see him."

"I did," said Bernard.

"I am certain she is well," said Claude.

"No!" Michaeljohn cried. "If she were well, she would be here! If she is not here, it is because she cannot come!"

"You don't seriously believe the count would hold her captive," said Claude.

"Don't I now!" Michaeljohn exploded. "Who *is* he?"

If he had known something about the man, he might have known where to look for Caralisa. She spoke so much of him. Michaeljohn had not paid attention. Now he desperately needed to know something of his adversary. What unholy sway had he over her soul?

Suddenly Aristide burst into the cottage so breathless and wan that Michaeljohn was alarmed for him. "St. Florian, I owe you an apology." Aristide threw himself into a chair. "Give me a cognac this instant."

Bernard produced a flask from his pocket, for Caralisa kept no spirits in the cottage. Aristide took a gulp, closing his eyes as it burned its way down. He pushed the flask back at Bernard. "Substandard," he said deprecatingly, but his voice and hands were shaking, spoiling the insouciant effect.

Michaeljohn was taken aback by the singular sight of Aristide shaken, his nonchalance all unraveled. Finally Aristide looked up without focus and said bewilderedly, "I have discovered who is your Count of Samothrace."

"Who!" Michaeljohn demanded. "Who is he!"

"What is he, my dear St. Florian," Aristide rephrased for him. *"What."*

Michaeljohn seized him up by his lapels. "For the love of God, man, stop stalling and tell me!"

Aristide turned up helpless eyes, so disbelieving as he spoke that it was a kind of despair. "He is the Count of Samothrace."

Michaeljohn foundered in silent confusion.

Bernard strangled out a laugh. "This is a new one for Aristide. You do it astonishingly well."

"It would be an exquisite jest, would it not?" Aristide admitted. "Were it a jest."

Michaeljohn struggled to grasp the import. Then it sank in, difficult to assimilate—and impossible to believe. The Count of Samothrace. The original. The supernatural monster. Not an alias. The fiend could show himself and call it a disguise, because who in his right mind would take seriously a man in a mask who came to Larissa and said, "I am the Count of Samothrace"?

Suddenly Michaeljohn declared, "Rubbish." He stomped around the confines of the dainty parlor. "Utter rubbish."

Claude remonstrated, "Aristide, have you never seen a fire but that you did not fan it? This is rot, Michaeljohn."

"You saw his face, St. Florian," Aristide reminded.

"Yes. I saw its face," said Michaeljohn.

Claude made a noise of disbelief. "Michaeljohn, how can you listen to this? Bernard, talk to him!"

Michaeljohn waved him back. He did not need talking to. "Tricks. All tricks. It cannot be."

In silent argument Aristide lifted a hand and pointed across himself toward the open window.

Michaeljohn turned; his eyes widened. The others followed his gaze in dread.

There were lights within the Heights and smoke rising from the top of the high rock.

The air was close and stuffy inside the confessional. The abbot could hear a solitary organ playing a single melodic line in quiet brooding solemnity. The abbey's organ had not the overpowering pomp of the cathedral's magnificent instrument. The abbey was a simple place, its minster redolent of wax and sandalwood and time.

Whenever the abbot slid open the latticework shutter, he could see nothing behind the gauze-covered screen. He heard only voices and breathing, often sniffles and tears.

It was late. He had waited through the allotted hours. Most of the candles had burned out. The pews were empty, but the abbot thought he had heard one last late penitent take up the kneeler in the box on his left.

The old abbot inhaled for strength. He slid back the shutter and murmured, "Go ahead."

He met with a pause, a stretched silence with a feeling of void, and he wondered if anyone was there after all. Then he heard a shifting, a rustle of clothes. Came a deep voice speaking quietly:

"Bless me, Father. I am the demon on the Heights."

The old abbot dropped his folded hands into his lap in weary irritation. He scolded softly, "You are not the first nor the cleverest to spin lies in my confessional."

The disembodied voice remained changelessly grim. It rasped through the gauze, "I am not."

In the silence to follow, the abbot heard the truth in that. A sense was coming through the veiled partition of anguished power—deadly serious and altogether sane.

He heard his own voice tremble in a murmur, "Why are you here?"

The voice came out harsh. "I am in hell and I don't know what I have done to deserve this except the sin of being born!"

"Original sin is universal."

"For the deathless? Adam's sons die. My mother did not even suffer the way mortal women do. What sin! I would face death as a mortal man if to live as a mortal man."

"I cannot make that trade for you. Sacraments are for mortals." He racked his store of experience, shook his head. "There is nothing in all the volumes of church writings to address the matter of a demon becoming human. I must conclude you are as your false god made you and beyond the pale of this holy office. Heaven was not made for you, so what is the point in seeking redemption?"

"On Judgment Day, I shall need to go *somewhere!*"

"And I am telling you, I don't know where that is! I never heard of a devil repenting!"

"Demon! Please!" the voice objected. "I am not one of His original heirs. I am a lesser creature. I was never *in* heaven to be thrown *out* of it. I am a simple pagan *daimon* born before God."

"Before Christ, I assume you mean," the abbot clarified shakily, crossing himself.

"Yes. Is there no way into the fold?"

"You are as you were made and I cannot absolve God!"

In crumbling anguish the voice said, "God help me, what can I do?"

"Why?" the abbot said, mystified. Would that some voice from above would come to counter this one from below. "For the love of God?"

"For love of one of God's creations."

The abbot felt the gates of hell yawning open on the far side of the slender partition. A palpable wave of despair washed through the gauze and lattice window. He resisted an impulse to slam the shutter on it to stanch the gushing wound. He clutched his crucifix till the edges hurt his palm. He listened with all his heart but heaven was silent.

"Go with God, I cannot help you."

The town dwarfed from a height became a fragile miniature, with tiny souls tucked within its matchstick doors under the pall of ancient night. They diminished. Soaring high, one became as a god.

The moon rose late and small, shriveled to a scant quarter of its full glory.

A shadow descended from the night sky, flickered batlike over the gray stones.

He stood on the narrow ledge, his back pressed against the gray stone wall next to the high gothic arched window of the scholar's dormitory. Leaded panes gaped open to the late summer air.

He was not sure how he got here. There was a dagger in his hand. His wide chest heaved in great breaths. Rage bubbled and boiled over, consuming thought. He had left the minster in the kind of fury only despair could spawn. He had taken off before wrath could resolve into murderous purpose.

Here, balanced on a ledge outside his rival's window, he recognized what it was he'd come to do.

The wind kicked his black hair across his furled brow. Black feathers masking the top half of his face ruffled in the breeze. His eyes glittered blacker than the night, black as his thoughts.

Below him the grassy precipice dropped off steeply. The height did not bother him.

His gloved hands moved against the stone bricks at his back as he edged near to the window. He pulled off one glove and felt the cold wall's uneven rough hardness on his palm with the light scraping of his nails.

He had seen blood spilled countless times—seen more deaths than St. Florian could know even were he to die on the bloodiest battlefield—

Which you shall not, for your time has come now.

He had seen lives end, had hastened some on their way. Did this little man think that he was a tame lap dog or an impotent thing that he need not fear him?

I warned you.

What value was this speck of life that he should not dash it from his eyes when its existence grieved him so? What worth this bright-eyed callow young scholar in there, sleeping amid his books and learned clutter? He could snuff his flame so easily, without a backward glance.

Or would he look back?

His hand was already bloody. Though he had never spent a life without justification. He had killed. He had never before murdered.

To do so would be to give up . . . what? His soul?

If he were soulless, what was to stop him? Why let something like a conscience vex him when he had no soul to go with it?

That prospect was not going down easily. *Am I so rejected as to exist outside of Creation itself?*

He leaned his head back against the stone and took in a shuddering breath.

The starry sky held his gaze, attention fixed upon a constellation. Cygnus the Swan.

Also called the Northern Cross.

At the top of the cross, the bright ruddy star Deneb shone, a bloody crown. He could see the red in it. Most jaded eyes saw only that it was a bright star, white just as they saw all the others. They did not stop and notice the subtle color.

She would be able to see the color. And to hear it singing.

She pulls color from the gloaming. She hears songs in sorrow. She was so absolutely alive. Never a flame burned so brightly, so completely, that there was no smoke, only a flash of brightness of perfect fire. In her wide blue eyes he had rediscovered youth.

She delights in everything. She had an infinite capacity for wonder and joy. She grasped like a child at all the shiny baubles of the world. It was why she had set her heart on this shallow trinket of a pretty little man sleeping within these walls.

She was a child. *Why don't I leave her alone?*

Because I—I—want her. And he *does not deserve her, does not know what he has. He sees only that she is beautiful. She is more beautiful than he can see, than he can conceive.*

Sometimes she made him so angry he could not talk, could not see straight. She was maddening, flighty and erratic as—as, well, a young girl.

Why do I need that in my life?

But I do. I confess. I do.

She had made an utter shambles of his world's perfect order. Earthquakes caused less upheaval.

And she was attracted to a transitory physical beauty.

And why should she not? So was she. Like goes to like.

Leave the girl alone.

No. He wanted her and could think of no reason that he should not take her. What was to stop him?

What indeed. He could not look away from the stars, the constellation burning a fiery cross. He had never seen it as anything but a swan, and he tried to see it as one again now. Those stars had described a swan before they ever had a cross. There was a cygnus before anyone died on Calvary. It was an accident that there was a cross within the sign of the swan.

The stars misted and blurred. He blinked, rubbed his eyes with the hand that did not hold the dagger.

The fury that had brought him here faltered in confusion.

He spoke softly, voice coming out a guttural croak, "Sir, I am trying to understand. And I don't. I don't."

The cross glowed in the heavens that had rejected him. Or had they?

Who was to say that he was soulless? Need he take the word of a fallible old man in a church? What if he were wrong?

The thought both liberated and enslaved.

The burden of a soul connected him to this earth, to this life. It connected him to her. And it barred him from her.

Because then he could not murder this innocent little mortal who would take her from him forever.

He lifted his face once more to the stars. The swan. The cross.

So which is it?

The stars turned in the slow courses across the sky.

The night wind strewed grit with a swirl of leaf litter and bits of twigs along the vacant high stone ledge overlooking the steep grassy slope.

Ten

Caralisa woke to birdsongs and goat bells, a chuckling stream, and the heavy scent of lilacs. She brushed the white eyelet sheet from her face and opened her eyes to her own room in her little cottage. She wondered for a moment if she had not been dreaming. She stirred and realized she was still in her soiled torn wedding dress.

She threw off the sheet and rose. She heard Michaeljohn's voice out in the garden, frightened and angry.

"He was seen at my wedding!"

Aristide's voice followed, "You needn't shout at me, St. Florian, I am entirely convinced."

Michaeljohn rounded on the doubter, "Claude!"

Claude was standing with his arms stubbornly crossed. "Neither of you know that he had anything to do with the young lady's disappearance, and I'm not sure what a lot of smoke on the Heights has to do with anything."

"He was there!" Michaeljohn railed. "That unholy fiend has carried her off, I know it—*Caralisa!*"

Caralisa stepped out sleepily, wiping sand from her eyes. Michaeljohn caught her up in an embrace as if she had returned from the dead. Just as suddenly he released her, afraid he might have profaned her. He stepped back, gazing at her as if beholding something miraculous.

"What are you talking about, sweetheart?" Caralisa asked.

"Where were you!" Michaeljohn cried.

She hesitated. No, it had not been a dream. But maybe it

was a secret. But Michaeljohn was her beloved and there
was nothing she could not tell him. "The Heights."

The young lords exclaimed loudly and murmured among
themselves in consternation.

"They're his," Caralisa explained reasonably.

"Whose!" said Michaeljohn.

"The Count of Samothrace," she said.

A leaden pause ensued.

Aristide broke it to her, "No deed to the citadel has been
issued in the last seven hundred years."

"You must be mistaken," said Caralisa simply.

Michaeljohn turned to Claude, brows lifted. "What more
do you need?"

Caralisa looked from one to the next. She planted her
hands on her hips. "You look like a lot of conspirators. What
is this about?"

Michaeljohn took her hands. "My darling, you are in terrible danger. You must leave Larissa. Now. Tonight after
dark."

She gave a gentle laugh to scatter his hysteria and express
bewilderment at them all. Her voice chimed like bells. "I
am in no danger."

"No one ever goes up there," a grim Bernard joined in.
Horizontal lines marked his high flat brow. His square face
was grave as a block of stone. "Men have died trying to
scale those Heights."

"Well, it is very dangerous unless you know the way,"
said Caralisa lightly.

"Where is the way?" said Michaeljohn.

"I don't precisely know. I don't remember either the going
up or the coming down."

"This is intolerable!" Michaeljohn cried. His pure blue
eyes were very bright as if near tears. "He took you there,
he means to keep you!"

"He took me there because it was safe," Caralisa gently
chided. "He got me out of danger."

"A danger he created!"

"The swan did it, not he!" Caralisa argued. This was becoming tiresome. For scholars, these young men just did not know how to use their heads. She wished they would leave so she could take a bath. "As for keeping me, why am I here? I didn't *fly*. So he must have brought me."

"At what price?"

"No price," she said in a baffled laugh.

"He thinks you belong to him."

"No, no. It is not like that. He is very bossy, yes. It is just his way. He is my friend."

Aristide said soberly, "Dear lady, how can you not see what is before your eyes?"

"Why do you conjure things that are not before yours! You don't understand!"

Aristide said, "I understand too well. When at last you open your eyes, there will be nowhere for you to run."

She laughed at his silly touching concern. It was odd to see Aristide so grim. "Do not be afraid for me." She rose up on tiptoe to place a kiss upon his cheek.

Aristide's small petal lips pulled down into a lugubrious frown. "You drive men mad and know not what you do. Pure intent does not always beget purity." He tipped his hat and left the garden, taking Bernard and Claude with him.

Michaeljohn started in again, "Listen to me, my dearest, the swan and Samothrace are in league with the devil. He is a warlock, a demon, a madman at the very least. And of the black beast, God knows. We must run away. Aristide says we must leave Larissa, maybe leave the Continent. He says he is not sure even the mountains are barrier enough to contain him. Who knows to what lengths he would go!"

"No," said Caralisa. "I am not going anywhere."

"Aristide says—"

"Aristide says! Aristide says! *I* say no!"

"But my darling—"

"I want to marry you here and now," said Caralisa with a stamp of her satin slipper.

In the end, Michaeljohn relented. He bowed his shoulders and considered what must be done to please her. "I am not sure when the cathedral is free—"

"A small wedding in our own home then. Right here." She pictured a charming little ceremony like Viola's. "I don't need the cathedral."

"My family does," Michaeljohn said ruefully. "I shall see to it. If you want to stay here, then here we shall stay. As I live, my darling, no one will harm you."

Caralisa daydreamed as she strolled past the shops along the canal, wishing she could find the Count of Samothrace to put all this nonsense to rest.

Then, as if conjured, there he was, the Count of Samothrace, turning a corner.

She blinked. It was he, she was sure of it, though he was truly in disguise this time with a wide hooded cape and hawkish mask. She knew him by his strong stride and the power of his presence, his fluid motions which carried all the wild grace of a powerful stallion or a great cat.

She stepped up her pace to follow him. Upon turning the corner she saw that it was a blind alley. A strange man was walking away with his back toward her; and the count, also with his back to her, was closing behind him.

She smiled and stepped forward, about to call out for joy but she saw the dagger first. The count veered into the other man. The momentum took both into a doorway. There was a flash of the long knife gripped in a black-gloved hand, then it disappeared in a thrust.

When the count stepped back from the door, the knife was not in his hand and the other man did not emerge, except for a pallid forearm which hinged out strengthlessly from its elbow to drop onto the cobbles, twitch once, and move no more.

Caralisa pulled back from view and stumbled into a run along the canal. She glanced every direction for a place to turn off this walk before the count could emerge from the alley and see her. She had only seconds at most. Finding no escape near enough, she slithered through the railing and dropped into a small boat tied off in the canal. She crouched against the algae-slicked stones of the canalside, trying to contain her shallow breaths and runaway heartbeat. A sour taste stung at the back of her mouth.

In the placid water of the canal, two pairs of ducks angled toward her. Tourist boats were always good for a handout. The ducks moved in, quacking greedily. The arrowheads of their wakes pointed toward her and brought the attention of more ducks.

A shadow crossed her from overhead. The ducks arrowed away.

Caralisa looked up into a menacing hawk mask leaning over the rail.

"Mademoiselle, what are you doing down there?"

With fluttering hands she fumbled with the bowline, untied it from the brass eye. She pushed off the slick wall and drifted across the narrow canal to the other side. She spidered up the opposite wall, leaving the boat to drift.

She eeled between the rails and turned to stand facing the count across the canal, watching warily his every move. She gripped the railing, ready to launch herself into a run left or right should he make for one of the bridges in either direction.

The count glanced back over his shoulder to see what was the cause of this horrified look. He saw only potted trees, a patient old pack pony tethered to the railing, the whitewashed wall of a shop. He turned back toward Caralisa. "To what do I owe this glance?"

She hissed, throwing a whisper across the canal. "Why did you kill that man?"

Mild startlement moved behind the sinister hawk mask. Caralisa saw a question forming. He was going to ask her if she'd seen it, she thought. Instead he said quite loudly, "Which one?"

Two? There were two? Or . . . *"How many were there!"* she shrieked and at once clapped a hand over her mouth.

A few curious heads turned from the bridge and the shop windows. Seeing nothing interesting—only a masked man and a young woman trying to talk across the canal—they turned again to go about their business.

"It is none of your concern," said the count.

She hissed, her voice very quiet, the shape of her words distinct, "I saw you murder a man!"

"Murder?" he said, offended. "How do you know he did not deserve it?"

"Which one!"

"Any of them," he said. He raised a gloved finger in command. "Caralisa, stay there." And he moved toward the bridge to her left.

Caralisa fled right. She careened round the corner and jumped into a carriage, spilled gold at its occupants to please please get out, and she told the driver to take her with all haste to her home.

She held her hands over her drumming chest. Her mouth tasted of bitter fear.

Restored to her cottage, she ran inside and slammed the door. The ball hammers of the door harp bounced out delicate notes as she ran to the windows and bolted the shutters.

Secured for a siege, she cowered in her room, huddling on the floor beside her bed, hugging her knees.

Caralisa. He had called her Caralisa.

The Marquis de St. Florian cooled his heels in the monsignor's sumptuous office, pacing a lighter track into the

deep scarlet carpet. The room was cheerlessly opulent, and
the air smelled more of perfume than of incense.

The waiting was interminable. Michaeljohn was only trying to reschedule his wedding. He had told the brother his
business. He thought his title might command a certain
amount of attention, even from spiritual circles, but he had
been left to wait. For hours he was put off and put off. Then
he was told to come back tomorrow; all may resolve itself
by then.

Michaeljohn threw up his arms with a sputter. Resolve
itself? He just wanted to set a date for his wedding!

He stalked out of the office. He found, waiting without, a
gaggle of Monsignor's doting wealthy dowagers with whom
he usually held court. It was not like Shakespeare to keep
them waiting. Something terrible was afoot. Michaeljohn set
out in search, to find Monsignor wherever he should be.

Michaeljohn bearded his quarry at last in the vestry. Monsignor Fortenot had just put on his purple robes and was
smoothing back his silvered temples. A deacon held his mitre.

The somber color gave Michaeljohn pause. He noticed
clergymen gathering all over the basilica in ritual garb, many
of them in black. "Did someone die?" he asked cautiously.

Monsignor spoke past him, a vague brightness to his amber eyes. "The Lord works in mysterious ways," he intoned
somnolently. "But He does not tell me. *I* don't hear voices.
Did someone die?"

"Now, see here," Michaeljohn bridled. "I came here to
see about my wedding—"

"No," said Monsignor, cutting him off flat.

"No?" Michaeljohn faltered, struggling for sense.

"This union cannot be!" Monsignor announced. "Not
now! Not here! Not ever!"

Michaeljohn worried at the brim of his hat in his hands.
The muscles in his handsome face had gone slack, his mouth

dropped open. He coughed in disbelief. When he found his voice, it came out pleading. "But *why!*"

Monsignor Fortenot's craggy face took on the lordly aspect of a statue of cold frowning stone. He pronounced, his great voice ringing thunder:

"Because she is damned!"

Tortured day bled into endless black night. Caralisa started at every scratch of a branch against the cottage, every crack of settling timber, every hesitation in the crickets' chirping.

She thrashed, sleepless in her bed, tormented echoes ringing in her mind. *Which one? Which one?*

How many were there!

And she had told him that he was not a very fiendish fiend!

She hugged her wet pillow, her eyes wide open. To close them was to see it over again, the blade disappear, the arm unbend lifelessly onto the pavement.

The crickets silenced.

The crack of moonlight between the bolted shutters of her bedroom window widened to a solid line of pale light.

A blade slid with a whispered scraping into the opening, and lifted the latch.

The shutters swung open wide to reveal a figure crouched in the window—booted feet and spurs, a leather jerkin, hair pulled back in a fat braid. A sword in its scabbard.

Caralisa stared with a sense of unreality. Now that it was happening, it felt like a dream. Detail resolved out of the silhouette to show a woman, neither young nor old, a rough lean sort. A thick leather military-style glove encased one hand. She pulled off the other glove with her teeth and held it in her gloved hand.

"I've been sent to kill you. Come with me." She extended her ungloved hand. Caralisa rose from the bed, pulling on her lace robe over her sheer nightgown. She slid her feet into soft ballet slippers and took the woman's hand. Cool thin fingers closed round hers with hard bony strength. The swordswoman helped Caralisa out through the window into the garden.

"Wh-who would want me dead?" Caralisa squeaked.

"I don't know," said the swordswoman, drawing off her other glove with her teeth, muffling her words as she spoke. "Your music wasn't that bad." She tucked the heavy gloves into her belt.

Caralisa had not yet asked if the swordswoman intended to do what she'd been sent for.

"Leave Larissa," the hired woman commanded.

"No!" Caralisa cried.

The woman's gaunt face showed amazement. She had not expected that reply. She repeated her command with more force. Caralisa started back to her window at a stubborn march.

The woman grabbed her long red hair and jerked her back. Caralisa took a higher grip on her long tresses and yanked them out of the swordswoman's grip.

"All right!" The woman put up her hands in surrender. There was no used arguing with a girl who had no sense to be afraid. "But you can't stay here if you like sunrises."

"Pardon?"

The woman rolled her eyes. "You stay here and you have seen your last one!"

"Oh." Caralisa brought both hands to her mouth.

The swordswoman propped her hip against the birdbath, and hooked her thumbs into her belt. "Do you have a safe place to go?"

Caralisa considered. "The abbey!" she said brightly.

"Christ!" That was a veto.

"But who would dare harm me in a church!" Caralisa said.

There came no answer. The swordswoman was shaking her head at the sky, looking there for strength.

The crickets had taken up their song again. The stream trickled low in the late-summer warmth. Caralisa's nightgown trailed in the cool grass. It was difficult to believe that she could be in danger here.

The swordswoman motioned with her head, moonlight glinting on the fat braid of her rusty hair. "Come on," she bid gruffly.

They threaded along the garden wall. Then the swordswoman caught sight of someone and pushed Caralisa down.

Caralisa held her breath, hugging the earth, grass tickling her nose. She turned her head ever so slowly to look.

The graceful figure of the Count of Samothrace stalked with cat stealth along the cottage wall to the open window.

Caralisa's body was overcome with a violent tremor beyond any control. Why does he want me dead!

She knew now that there was something behind the mask that she did not know at all. Michaeljohn was right. Her heart pounded as if to leap out of her. Tears trickled down to the tip of her nose. She did not dare sniffle.

The swordswoman remained very still. Then with a touch to Caralisa's shoulder, she warned her to get ready to move. At her tap, they both rose and ran.

Caralisa followed the woman until a stitch burned poker hot in her side and she had to stop. She braced herself against a doorjamb, gasping for breath.

The swordswoman waited, pacing with a kind of calm nervousness. In a moment she took Caralisa's hand and led her stealthily through the dark town, crouching along the stone rails of the bridges. The only sounds were of water trickling in the canals, the creak of the swordswoman's leathers, sometimes the distant barking of a dog, and the yowl of cats on the rooftops. Moonlight shone watery bright on the bricks, and lacework wrought-iron railings mapped black spiderwebs on the milky glowing sky.

At one point they shrank back as a small barge laden with

fruit made its leisurely way up a canal. They huddled in a
dark alcove, panting shallowly.

Caralisa dared whisper, "Why have you befriended me?"

"I didn't befriend you," the swordswoman said. "I only
came out of curiosity. This commission is beneath me. I think
I was hired only because no one else would touch it either.
No one of any repute. Oh, you could find a thugee to do
anything for a franc, but he'll turn and inform on you for a
quid. Killing the likes of you is not going to advance anyone's
reputation. He thought I'd take the job. I'm just returning the
insult. Come on."

The barge had passed. The swordswoman led her across
the bridge.

The streets were taking on familiarity. Caralisa realized
that they were nearing the plaza.

Heavy wingbeats and a moonshadow fell across the shining bricks in a cruciform. Caralisa shrank against the wall.
The swordswoman tried to tug her onward with a hiss, "It's
just a bird."

"No!" Caralisa said without voice, terror gripping tight at
her chest.

The shadow flickered up the wall, turned, and recrossed,
scouring the city.

The swordswoman tried to pry Caralisa away from the
wall. Caralisa would not budge. Then she glimpsed down
the street the lighted doorway of the cathedral, glowing
bright from the fires of many candles, the great doors thrown
wide. She saw Michaeljohn within, gesticulating wildly at
Monsignor and a knot of formally hooded monks arrayed
for some ritual. Caralisa broke into a run with a cry.

The swordswoman hissed after her, *"No!"* She chased her
halfway up the street, cursing. "Jesus, no!"

She almost caught her but Caralisa flew up the wide steps,
through the monumental doorway, and inside into startled
Michaeljohn's arms.

And all at once many hands were taking hold of her, tearing her from her love. Monsignor's powerful voice droned, "In the name of the Father, and of the Son, and the Holy Spirit. Caralisa, you are charged with blasphemy and consorting with powers most foul and hateful in the sight of Holy Mother Church."

Monks were dragging Michaeljohn away from her. She heard him calling her name.

Caralisa screamed, "Help me!" as the heavy doors slowly shut her away from the street.

The swordswoman had melted away.

Eleven

Monsignor Fortenot, resplendent in somber purple, advanced slowly on Caralisa. She wrenched left and right in the grip of the monks who held her. Monsignor's sonorous voice droned, "We were about to hold your trial without you, but God delivered you here to answer the charges—and appropriately attired as a harlot."

Caralisa wore only her diaphanous nightgown and lacy robe.

It was only catching up with her now that someone had sent an assassin to kill her. And now to be blamed for not dressing before making her escape was really too preposterous.

She did not know which outrage to answer first. "Trial!" she cried. "This is no court!"

"This is no worldly court and these matters have nothing to do with that which is Caesar's," Monsignor countered. He flourished a commanding gesture at the monks.

They dragged Caralisa up to the sanctuary and forced her to kneel. She cried, "With what am I charged!"

The monsignor spoke over her head to the assembled brethren. "She is possessed. She admits her own possession."

"I do not!"

Monsignor rounded on her. "Did you not say these precise words, 'I don't know what got hold of me. I hardly knew myself—' "

Caralisa spluttered on the verge of hysterical laughter. "I didn't mean it like that!"

"How precisely did you mean it?"

"I said that in confession! I think."

The monsignor opened his arms wide to his audience. "See how deep its hold on her. How it lies even in the face of its maker. The Angel of Light never showed so fair a face. She is altogether gone, anything that was our daughter Caralisa. We speak now to the Prince of Lies. Remember how when our daughter first came to us, her hair was the color of sunlight and how changed it is, to the devil's own!"

Caralisa shrieked, "What has my hair to do with it! If my hair offends God, I would cut it off, but why should it offend Him? He made it!"

A concerted gasp circled the sanctuary.

Monsignor's dramatic craggy face showed a grave frown, but amber eyes gleamed with satisfaction. "Slander of the Almighty ill becomes so fair a face. You have sealed your fate, abominable one. It has shown no penitence—"

"I repent!" Caralisa cried in mounting terror, caught in the power of a supreme authority gone mad from which there was no recourse. This could not be happening.

"Repent what?" said Monsignor cagily.

"I don't know. Whatever it is I am accused of."

"You would admit anything?"

"Yes!"

"Yes, you would. Father of Lies, you cannot lie to get out of the Truth."

"What can I say? Jesus!"

"It curses even now."

"That was a prayer! I don't know what I have done!"

"Yet you would admit what you haven't."

"Anything!"

"You are so willing to lie."

"I don't understand! Everything is twisted!"

"That, of all things you have said, is the Truth."

"O God! O God!"

"And your songs! Your diabolic sounds. You say you *heard* them! Who sings to you?"

"I don't know," she wept.

"Was it God?"

She shook her head, sobbing. She could answer neither way but it would damn her. She could only shake her head, tears streaming down her cheeks.

Monsignor filled in the silence. "I asked her if she were a saint. She said herself that she was the 'farthest thing from it'! These sounds come not from God, but from her unholy master!"

"No!"

"And *did not a black demon crash through the window of this very cathedral at the precise moment that this creature approached His altar!*" The nave rang with his voice. Caralisa could scarcely hear him for her shrieking sobs.

He jutted a damning finger down at her. "You shall be cast from the bosom of Holy Mother Church to be of the *vitandi,* those to be shunned, as an abomination before God!"

The ring of monks parted. The church became ablaze with candles and gaslights as more monks came filing in, black hooded as executioners. Monsignor donned his funeral robes.

Caralisa thrashed in the grip of the monks, screaming raw screeching cries for blind terror, her infernally bright red hair tossing. *"Michaeljohn! Michaeljohn!"*

Brynna, Delia, Laurel, and Megan rose from their beds and stood out on the roof garden, watching the glowing lights over the trees become brighter and listening to the distant clamor. Past midnight, Larissa was stirring.

Laurel went to the window overlooking the street and accosted the milkman leading his mulecart. "What is going on? It sounds like a masque."

"I don't know, miss. But the cathedral, it's all lit up like for a high mass. And there's a mob, it's in the plaza, miss."

The girls roused one of the kitchen servants and dispatched her into town to spy. She came back at a run. "It's Miss Caralisa!" she gasped, all undone. "She's been tried for a demon! They mean to cast her out of the church!"

Laurel said grimly, "Anyone cast out of the church is fair game for burning."

Larissans were gathering in the plaza like a monstrous pack of feral dogs scenting blood. There hadn't been a burning in Larissa in a long time.

Brynna winced, incredulous. "Caralisa? What could Caralisa have done?"

"Oh, that little twit never had the sense to come in out of the rain," said Laurel, fetching her coat.

"Where are you going?"

Laurel put on her coat over her nightgown and tied the belt. "I'm going to see if Daddy can help." The police inspector.

"Are you crazy?" said Delia. "It's past hours! It's the middle of the night!"

The new girl, Alicia, cringed. "What of Madame Gerhold?"

Laurel lifted her blond hair free of her coat to lie loose on her thin shoulders. "Madame G tries to broom me, I shall give her the hard end of it up the hard end of Madame G."

"Can your father help?" Delia called after Laurel, who was already hastening down the stairs.

"Probably not," Laurel called back. There did not seem to be much the police could do. "But it's all I can think of."

Madame Gerhold had heard the commotion from the girls' rooms and she was waiting at the front door. Laurel pushed past her, ignoring her command to stop.

Laurel ran to the end of Elm Tree Close and flagged down a hansom. Madame Gerhold, lumbering close behind her, moved in to bat her down from it with her broom, but Laurel turned her head sharply, "You cannot have my cab." Her blue eyes razored over the broom. "But I see you've arranged your own transportation already."

Laurel mounted, and the carriage rolled away leaving Madame Gerhold speechless in the street.

Back in the tenement the remaining girls fretted in confusion, feeling more ineffectual than ever in the wake of Laurel's futile but decisive charge. "We have to do something," Delia declared.

"Why?" said Megan.

"Why?" Delia exclaimed.

Megan sniffed. "She was always too lucky and too smug."

Delia shrieked, *"Too smug! You would see her burn for being smug!"*

Megan gave a slow smile. "Why not?" She flipped her fiery hair for the mirror. "I never thought she was that pretty. I don't believe she is that evil. But she always got more than she deserved. So here. I never shared a moonlight waltz. I shan't cut in on her hot-foot jig!"

Torches collected in the plaza. Crowds thronged outside the cathedral's door in a waiting pack.

Michaeljohn ran through the mob of them to the royal palace and pounded on the outer gate, crying loud enough to wake the prince. Scarlet-uniformed guards with drawn swords commanded him go, but they hadn't quite the provocation to attack an unarmed foreign lord who was doing nothing more aggressive than make a great deal of noise—and it seemed everyone in Larissa was doing that tonight.

At long last the prince rose and bid someone let the suppliant in.

The attendant had barely time to announce, "Michaeljohn, the Marquis de St. Florian," when a familiar youth threw himself on bended knee at Maximillian's feet. "I beg you,

Your Majesty. It's the demon. It's not her fault. You must
save her!"

The prince motioned for someone to come tell him—
calmly—what was happening.

He listened gravely, becoming shaken. Face pale within
the frame of his black hair, he answered slowly, "I am sorry.
One hesitates to befriend whom God loathes lest one become
loathed of God oneself."

"She is not loathed of God!" Michaeljohn insisted.

"And I wish I could help you," said the prince. "I liked
the child."

"You wish! Why can you not!"

"Excommunication is a church affair," the prince explained. "I am a secular power. I have no authority over who
may or may not belong to the church."

"But if they cast her out as a devil, there's nothing to stop
them from burning her!"

"That is so."

"Surely there is something you can do! Don't you know
someone in Byzantion—"

"Sir."

Michaeljohn had overstepped all bounds. He was asking
the earthly authority of Montagne to go over the head of the
religious authority of Montagne. It took him a moment to
bring himself to take it back. "I regret, Your Majesty." He
stumblingly found the doors.

And Maximillian the Brave covered his face in his hands.

Tiers of hooded monks wreathed the sanctuary. Those of
the inner circle held great stout candles before them like
staffs. Monsignor Fortenot began the ceremony of the end.

The droning responsory continued heedless of Caralisa's
pleading cries. They would not look at her, their faces suffused with disgust or with terrified pity. She looked small
and delicate in their heavily garbed midst, her thin gown and

robe revealing her comely shape. Her rich red hair tumbled loosely around her. Her blue eyes shone pleading luminous in her sweet face. Her pink lips quivered, lush, vulnerable, and soft.

Her judges hardened their hearts against her winsome fragility, no one daring make a stand for her within a hateful throng that could easily turn its collective wrath on one of their own as well.

They came to the point where her captors released their grip on her as too loathed to touch.

"We exclude her from the bosom of our Holy Mother Church . . ."

Caralisa ran to the nearest monk, gripped the hem of his robe beseechingly. "No! Oh, no! Stop! Oh, please!"

His sandaled foot pushed her away in disgust.

"And we judge her condemned to eternal fire with Satan and his angels and all the reprobate . . ."

Monsignor Fortenot moved toward the Book on the lectern. Caralisa dropped at his feet, barring his path. "No! No!"

"So long as she will not burst the fetters of the demon, do penance, and satisfy the Church."

"I repent! O God!"

One deep-toned bell tolled slowly. Its percussions resounded through the sanctuary. "O God! O God!"

Monsignor closed the Book. He took up the big candle, spun it end over, and dashed its flame into the floor.

Caralisa opened her mouth to a long anguished screech.

One by one along the inner ring, candles overturned and slammed down to snuff their flame with a spatter of liquefied wax. Caralisa ran from each to each, begging. "No, no, please. Somebody help me! Almighty God!" She clung to their robes, ran from one to the other as the candles inverted and slammed to the floor with damning resound.

The last candle was cast down. Caralisa screamed, *"No!"*

The holy men turned their backs on her and filed out in silence, leaving her weeping on the floor.

When they were all gone, she lifted her head and ran up to hug the altar.

Monsignor's voice boomed, "Remove your unclean hands from that!"

He wrenched her away, seized up a smoking censor, and brandished it like a morning star. Caralisa covered her mouth and nose from the smoking metal ball and crabstepped backward from its swinging. Monsignor drove her down the aisle. "Out of this house, thou abomination incarnate!"

The great doors parted wide enough for her to back through them. She turned and reeled to a halt at the top of the steps, finding herself faced with a mob at the foot of them. A smoky field of yellow torches nodded as far as the eye could see.

She spun around to run back inside the cathedral but the mammoth wooden doors slammed shut with a hollow boom.

She crumbled at the threshold.

The mob crouched round the base of the steps, hovering at an invisible barrier. Finally someone dared dash up the steps and lay hands on the damned one, and with that the barrier broke.

Many hands grasped at her, pulled her down the steps. A river of bodies dragged her to the Rue de Temps, where someone had pulled up bricks from the street and dug a hole into which men were pounding a tall stout stake. Others brought bundles and sticks and logs, a rope.

Soulless and damned on earth, Caralisa existed outside of pity. No murder was involved here. She could expect mercy from no one.

Pushed up the high pile of faggots, she tripped. Her foot broke through a branch, scraping her calf. Her executioners hauled her up, relentless. Men caught her flailing arms and yanked her against the stake. Hands on her shoulders jerked her around and pushed her back flush with the stake. Stinging fingers dug into the soft flesh of her arms. They dragged each of her hands to cross in back of her. Rope burned and scratched, looping and tightening round her wrists. Faces blank with holy hatred glared straight through her, missing her eyes. The glow of holy vengeance shone upon them.

Within a small oasis in the tumult stood a grim figure untouched by the jostling frenzy. Monsignor Fortenot. He advanced to the foot of the high pile of wood, then leaned up and in toward her. His voice penetrated the clamor though speaking very softly in a stage whisper, "You should have taken the sword. You might have been bound for heaven now and not to certain hell."

He took a torch from out of the crowd and dropped it onto the bundled faggots.

The fire caught at once and licked round the base of the high pyre. The crowd drew back a step. Caralisa screamed long and loud for terror, skittering up on tiptoe as if she could shimmy backward up the stake. "O God! O God!" she screamed aloud.

Fire crackled deep underfoot. Smoke snaked up in bitter gray tendrils. The greener branches caught slowly; sap bubbled from their ends and hissed with a lot of smoke.

The outer base of the stack was burning lively now. A waving wall of heated air rippled the images of the crowd, faces morbidly transfixed, swimming in a distorted lens.

"Our Father who art in heaven . . ." Caralisa cried until she was overcome by insensate terror. She could not finish. She could only scream, and the crowd nodded in vindication.

Michaeljohn was trying to rally his friends in the université, but could not pull them from their vantage posts at all the southern windows and rooftops of the dormitories.

"Heigh ho. I think they lit her," someone said.

Michaeljohn pushed him away from the window to see.

Down in the Rue de Temps a greater flame blossomed

within the waving meadow of torches. A piercing scream cut through the uproar.

A sob caught in Michaeljohn's throat as he gripped the window jambs. He yanked at them as if to tear them off.

"Hello," said Aristide and pointed up.

Michaeljohn lifted a tearful face.

The shadow of a swan blotted out the stars in a moving arrow.

"The demon," Michaeljohn croaked.

Aristide leaned against the wall in petulant languor. He spoke philosophically, "Well. If one has exhausted the resources of heaven, I suppose one might give some consideration to the powers of hell."

The foul stench of scorched hair filled Caralisa's nostrils. The outer strands of her rich tresses which lay draped round her like a cloak were shriveling up into singed coils as heat knifed up through the wood stack in searing blades. Perspiration drenched her nightgown and trickled down her sides. The insides of her nostrils scalded as she tried to breathe. The sticks and logs shifted under her feet as the burning stack settled.

The flames leapt higher. Tongues of orange flickered up through the topmost logs just in front of her feet. Already the air was hot enough to burn the soles of her thin slippers.

Suddenly, from out of the hellish smoke and heat, a dark shape was swirling before her. She thought she was blacking out, but she heard a flapping cape, the crackling of boots tramping on snapping wood. She glimpsed the bright flash of firelight on a silvery blade. It disappeared, and her hands pulled abruptly free, dangling frayed ends of rope round either wrist. Able to move her arms, she threw them round the count's neck. At once she was rising up into his arms, carried a few tottering steps, then dropping with him as he leapt from the pyre. He staggered on his feet then, set her down to stand on solid ground. He took her hand and they stumbled out of the thick smoke to the leeward of the stake, where the crowd was thinnest, and charged through the mob before it could think to stop them.

The cry rose from somewhere, "Get them! Get them!"

The crowd surging after them was stalled by the confused smoke-blinded cluster who did not know what was happening.

In moments they all found the direction and took up the cry. All the torches swept after the fleeing pair.

The count led Caralisa through a door, slammed and bolted it, braced it with a chair, and barreled up several flights of stairs. She ran to keep up, coughing and half blinded by smoky tears gushing from stinging eyes. They passed through another door to a roof and the count braced it shut.

Caralisa squinted round with tearing vision and found that they were treed with nowhere to go from here. She clung to his hand, trying to tell him, but her voice was a cracking raw whisper.

His hand slipped from hers. She teetered, slipped on the roof's incline. She dropped to regain her balance on all fours. She called out, "My lord!"

On every side the river of anger pooled at the base of the building. The crashing of a battering ram sounded at the door down below. The flash of a grappling hook came sailing into the air over the roof. Caralisa squealed and ducked.

The hooks came down and bit into the roof. Caralisa scrabbled over to it, tugged, managed to pull it loose, and she heaved it back down. Cries of outrage and squeals erupted from below. She heard the crashing of the door at street level breaking in.

Caralisa gasped and glanced back. "My lord . . ."

She turned full circle, and found that she was alone on the roof. Oh, God, he had fallen off! "My lord!"

The stomping posse rumbled up the stairs in a stampede.

Directly the braced door to the roof was bowing with the thrown weight of them.

Caralisa crouched on the canted rooftop, half standing, backing away from the buckling door.

With a shriek she tripped backward over something that hit her behind the knees. She fell, limbs thrashing with a violent convulsion of fear, certain that she was plunging to her death. Then instantly she silenced, having stumbled instead into something warm and alive which stopped her fall. She sprawled across a broad silky back. Enormous midnight wings fanned out to either side like great black sails. She felt a sudden bunching of powerful muscles beneath her coiling to spring. She felt a dip, a lurch, then a motion that made her clutch and bury her face into its feathers as it carried her—*down!*—plummeting off the edge of the roof, dropping into empty air.

She screamed with the lightning drop, stomach in her throat. Torches careered up to meet her.

Suddenly with a stomach-plunging swoop, her winged mount swung up on the air and climbed aloft, rising with heavy labored wingbeats. The streets and canals of Larissa were shrinking below her. Air whistled in her ears. Dizzy from the buoyancy, she peered down the long long drop.

The mob crashed through the last door and spilled out onto the roof, to find wind, an empty rooftop, and stillness but for the flutter of wings on the night breeze and Caralisa's high diminishing scream.

The swan alighted heavily on the balcony of the Heights. It folded its great wings with difficulty under Caralisa.

She released her death grip and let herself slide off its broad silken back. Her knees buckled and she crumpled to sit on the stone, shaking violently, holding herself up with wildly fluttering hands. The swan started away.

She reached for it, falling forward. "Don't leave me!"

It turned its elegant head on its sinuous neck. Comprehension seemed to gleam in its brilliant onyx eyes. It slowly walked back to her on neat black webbed feet. She threw her arms round its glossy neck and cried in great bawling release. Great tears rolled off its shining midnight feathers. It unfurled a wide wing and enfolded her within its safe harbor until the sobs no longer wracked her.

In time she quieted. She peered at her strange savior through swollen lids. It was exceedingly beautiful, its graceful form a wonderwork of divine creation. Its exquisitely formed head was filled with knowing. Its presence filled her with comfort, so regal and stalwart of bearing. The swan was not a warlike creature, but it was a royal one not to be tread upon. It carried itself like a sovereign. Caralisa noted in horror that the tips of its splendid wings were singed as if it, too, had touched the fire. She entwined her arms around the base of its neck, and lay her cheek against its inky feathers, filled with love for the truest friend she could ever have.

She jolted upright with a start. The count! She had been so absorbed in her own terror that she had thought of nothing else. How could she forget the count!

She turned to the swan. "The count! Oh, please find the count! He's in terrible danger. He f—" Her voice broke on a sob. "He fell off the roof and I'm afraid he's very hurt if not—oh! Please find him!"

The swan moved apart as if understanding everything she said. It spread its spectacular wings, crouched on leathery black legs, and launched itself into the night.

Exhausted and strengthless, Caralisa curled up on the stone balcony where she was and fell instantly asleep.

Twelve

Swimming toward consciousness through a muddy swirl of dreams, Caralisa stirred stiffly on the rock floor. She thought she had been asleep for a long time, but it was still dark and she wondered if she had not slept into the next evening.

She cracked open swollen eyelids that felt huge and fat, and she dragged herself up the stone balustrade to stand. Torches had gathered down below in the plaza.

"They have come to burn you."

She turned, quivering. It was the count.

"Oh!" She ran to him, threw her arms round his waist. She could feel the hard muscularity of his body beneath his black clothes, hear the fast beating of his heart. He was safe and whole, though he smelled of smoke, and his chin was singed. "How did you get away?" she spoke into his chest.

"On the same black wings that carried you."

"Oh, thank God. I *knew* it understood. I am sorry I ever said anything bad about it. It is a wonderful creature."

Then suddenly she pulled away, remembering the count in the alley, and his stalking her in her cottage. He was not wearing the horrid hawk mask—he was wearing his familiar black feathered one—but she could picture him still in murderous guise. She backed against the railing, clutched at it, and glanced down the prodigious drop behind her. "Are—are you in league with the Devil?"

"Are *you?*"

"No!" Her voice failed when she tried to shriek.

"You were the one tied to the stake," he said reasonably. *"You* have a familiar!"

"That is not the Devil," said the count. "I never met the man. I can make the swan go away if it troubles you."

"No! I love it too well," she lamented. "Oh, but it is diabolical. My music is sacrilegious and so are you."

The count gave a flat expression of annoyance, his mouth stretched thin. "According to whom?"

"I am an enemy of God!" Her tears sprang anew. Her eyes closed up entirely but for the leaking tears.

"Not of God and not of Byzantion." His low voice was a consoling rumble. "Only of the small vociferous god of Larissa. Monsignor Fortenot, to be precise."

Caralisa stopped crying. She remembered with a sudden chill what Monsignor had said at the foot of the stake: *You should have taken the sword.* How did Monsignor know that an assassin had come for her that night?

Monsignor Fortenot had hired an assassin.

"Oh, God, why!"

It was not the count who had meant to kill her. How could she ever have thought so?

Because she had seen him kill.

He moved closer. She froze, torn between dread and trust. She could not guess his intent, when off came his cloak. In the next instant its comforting weight settled on her trembling shoulders and held the warmth of him next to her sheerly clad body. He took the edges of the opening and overlapped them in front of her as if bundling up a little girl to go out into the snow. He seemed wholly unaffected by her figure to tuck it away so securely out of sight.

"Why did you kill that man?" she asked in a whisper.

"Which one?" he repeated as if it were his line in a play.

She thought of the swordswoman. "Did someone pay you?"

"No. Never. Only if I see the rightness of it."

"Rightness? What of forgiveness?"

"What of it? To forgive is divine and I am not."

"So who are you to judge?"

"I don't. I cannot turn away from the desperate."

"And what qualifies one as desperate?"

"One must be desperate indeed to call on me."

She stared at him, dumbfounded. "What are you?"

"Mademoiselle?"

"Michaeljohn says you are a warlock, a demon, or a madman."

"And what do you say?"

"You are a perfect brute."

"Oh, that is a *good* one," he said, amusement in his eyes.

"Why did you kill that man?"

"The creatures I have sent to their God are not men. They abdicated the right to the name by committing acts of inhuman savagery so that they cannot even number themselves among God's beasts. For even the beasts have better reason for what they do—and so have I. If those be men, I rank myself gladly with the animals. There are places in this world where the force of law holds sway; it is a great pity that Larissa is not one of them."

He turned from her, crossing his arms over his wide chest. A strong sinew showed in his neck as he bowed his head to cast a dangerous brooding gaze down at the mob. He spoke again.

"Once upon a time there was a man, a foolish man, who dug himself deeply into debt. His creditor was a ruthless sort and sent an assassin to teach him a lesson."

"How does one learn a lesson from being dead?" said Caralisa.

"One doesn't. The assassin was sent after the debtor's son. I have no tolerance for a man who tries to kill children, much less takes money for it."

Caralisa shuddered. "What is to keep the creditor from hiring another assassin?"

"Me. He is now also gone from this earth."

"How did you get into this affair? Why did you help the debtor?"

"Because he asked."

"And who appointed you rescuer of Larissa?"

He gave a wry smile. "There is a certain onus upon being the local demon."

She could never get a simple answer from him. "Brute," she mumbled almost in affection. "Brute."

Someone below had sighted figures on the balcony and raised a cry. Caralisa spilled tears again. "Why do those people want me dead? They don't even know me."

"Don't be absurd, mademoiselle. No one who knows you could want you harmed."

"Monsignor Fortenot does!"

"Monsignor Fortenot does the opposite of what he wants. He is a twisted man, and his love is twisted inside out."

Caralisa shook her head. "Monsignor *loves* me?"

"In his fashion. He is forbidden to love as a man. Passion must find its own way out. Claws tear the heart. Love is the most merciless of gods. Something so powerful will not be stopped, only turned, often to violence. I can almost understand this man. But he is a little man and it is a craven thing he has done."

"Was I a threat to his vows?"

"Oh, he'd have broken the vows quickly enough." His mask crinkled at the corners of his eyes with his smile, ruffling the feathers there. "You did not give him that choice. That is a difficult blow for a small man to take. It is hard to tell which way such a man will lash out." He placed his hands on the rail and leaned, straight-armed, against it, his face turned up toward the sky. "There is an old joke and I cannot remember exactly how it goes. It has to do with what you do if you catch your spouse with a lover. They say you can tell what country you are from by whom you kill: the lover, your spouse, or yourself. And offhand, I cannot remember which is which."

With casual banter her horror of him was fading. She hazarded, "What if you kill all three?"

"Well, then you are definitely from Larissa."

She almost smiled. "What if you are from St. Florian?"

"Then you threaten to die and go home and write poems about it," he said churlishly.

Caralisa broke into tears in an unstoppable torrent.

"It will be all right," he said.

"How!" she wailed. "It can never be right! I can never go back!"

"You are safe up here," he vowed.

"I want to be down *there!*" Her shoulders heaved. She squeaked Michaeljohn's name.

"Stop!" he commanded, almost begging. "I shall see to it. Only stop this!" He took her chin in his gloved hand and made her look into his stormy blue eyes. "You must wait now and trust me."

She quieted enough to return his gaze in wonder. She heard herself speak. "I do."

The prince lay awake, eyes open in the dark, trying not to disturb his wife with his tossing. Guilt weighed heavily upon him. He was glad that someone had saved the girl from the stake, at least for the moment.

It should have been he.

But he had feared for the crown, for himself. He had a wife to think of. He might have tried to influence a higher office. He might have sent to Byzantion. But the church was a formidable enemy should it decide to close ranks. For what should he risk a charge of aiding a demon? And when the girl had been seen to ride off on the back of a great black swan!

Profoundly shaken, the prince wondered, *Does it mean one is damned if one be rescued by a great black swan?*

He stared up at the high dark vaulted ceiling of his royal chamber.

Every time he closed his eyes, he saw the specters of men he had led into battle, who had died for him, come back to call him a coward.

And to think Maximillian used to be a brave man.

He fell into a troubled dream, only to stir a moment later—or was it hours?—to the sound of bells.

Abbey bells, christened St. Agnes and St. John. The bells that had rung at his wedding.

He sat bolt upright. *What?*

The abbey bells. No mistake.

Then a beating of wings.

At the tall window a shadow moved against the starfield, looming larger to eclipse the sky.

The giant shape of a swan, its broad wings spread in braking, filled the window, swept through it.

The flutter of a black cape.

A man standing at the foot of the bed, his cape settling round him, eyes burning within a black mask.

The prince knew him. This was their third meeting.

The Count of Samothrace fixed an onyx gaze on him and in deep voice demanded, "You owe me."

"So it was you," the prince whispered as he wondered in dread, *Have I sold my soul to the devil?*

Albertina sighed in her sleep. Maximillian moved a shielding arm across his lady. Her hair lay in a golden tumble across her pillow. Long lashes shadowed her fair cheeks. For her he would face any bargains he had made with whatever diabolical power stood there. He knew he was in its debt. He would pay anything to save her. He asked in trepidation, "What do you want?"

Smoldering eyes boring into his softened, became lighter even as he watched, melting from infernal black to a human color of blue, and he said plainly, "Not for me. For my lady."

Thirteen

Caralisa peered over the stone railing, her long red hair hanging over the side. Down below, red jackets of the Royal Guard moved through the mob, dispersing it. By noon everyone who would see her burn was gone but for the monks, who continued with holy purpose, beetling into the passage underneath the plaza in search of a path to storm the Heights.

Caralisa wandered the high fortress as she had all day, alone. She found something to wear in the chest at the foot of her bed and stripped off her singed and grimy night things. The dress she tried on was very old-fashioned, very pretty, of soft green crushed velvet. It caressed her curves, close-fitting down to a rich belt that rode low on her hips, below which the skirts flared. Tight sleeves ended in points over the backs of her hands and secured to her middle finger with a loop. She felt like Juliet.

There were no shoes, and her own slippers were sooty and charred, so she went barefoot.

She found food laid out for her on a long heavy table of ancient oak and she dined alone. She found a piano, picked out a few notes, but she could not concentrate. The songs that came to her were none she wanted to play.

She roamed the marvelous labyrinth, and this time discovered an inner corridor which led impossibly toward light and fresh air. She turned a corner. The way widened. She ascended three steps through an arch into a bedroom which had to be his.

She did not know why she thought so, for they all shared the same quirky rich cluttered elegance. She only knew that this was the one he would have chosen.

It was wide, high-ceilinged, airy, and filled with light from a doorway that opened on the side wall which logic told her should have been solid rock. Heavy damask draperies around it of delicate celadon in an Oriental paisley pattern were tied off with tasseled cords. There was a wide wide bed, with mattresses stacked high, framed by four posts with a single crosspiece between the two head posts. An extended length of the richly patterned drapery twisted up and over the crosspiece with careless art. There were shelves filled with antique books, a mammoth heavy armoire, and at the foot of the bed, a cedar chest with iron fittings. Two life-sized bronze grayhounds, one sitting up, one sleeping, attended the small hearth.

Caralisa moved to the wide door and stepped out onto another balcony, this one not overlooking the plaza, for it was entirely in the wrong direction. It opened to the secret lake, affording a wide private vista over the waterfall.

She felt as if she were intruding here, and she retreated from the chamber. It was so intimately his, imbued with his deft sensuality and deep secret past.

But she was drawn back to it again later. Like the man, it was both comforting and disturbing. By invading his private room, she felt as if she had taken off a mask and was looking upon what she should never have seen. Him. He never let her see *him*.

The count reappeared in the evening and found her in his bedroom. "What are you looking for?"

She spun with a start, cringing. "I was . . . ah . . . snooping," she finished baldly. The rawness of her voice surprised her. She could barely talk.

He was in his customary black. He crooked a finger with a wry smile for her to come out of there.

She noticed he did not say how pretty she looked. Of

course the prettiness was all in the dress. Herself, she was a puffy-eyed horror.

She searched for something neutral to say.

"There aren't any windowpanes," she squeaked. "What do you do in the winter?"

He answered equably, stepping aside for her to precede him from the chamber, "After New Year's I am bound for Africa."

"Africa!" Caralisa had never been out of the postage stamp principality of Montagne. Africa seemed like another world.

"Egypt is pleasant in the winter. This place is intolerable."

Caralisa shook her head, feeling provincial. "I picture striped tents and ill-tempered camels."

"My mother has a villa in Canopus she doesn't use. If I can get there before my half brothers, I stay there. Otherwise we fight over it."

"But you're not . . ." Having started she was bound to finish. "Legitimate."

"I may be a bastard but I am oldest. At any rate our fights are amicable as fights go and I usually win. Here we are."

They had arrived at the dining hall. Dinner was laid on the heavy dark oak table. He pulled out a chair for her, then lit the candles and joined her.

His presence took over the chamber and she had trouble swallowing. He made her heart speed and her breath come short.

The room was too intimate. She had never dined with him. The most she had ever done, the most she could ever manage, were a few nibbled canapés at a masque.

His gaze remained fixed upon her, his silence smoldered with heavy passion growing in the quiet. She could not meet his eyes.

"What is wrong?" he said.

She put down her silver fork. She tried to talk, cleared her throat, and tried again. Anything to break the heavy silence. "How did you get all this up here?" She gave a rap to indicate the stout table of blackened oak. It had a heavy mediaeval look to it.

He seemed unperturbed. "It is an unwritten law in my mother's family that we help each other move furniture."

"Onto a cliff?" she said.

"Usually. We have a penchant for high places."

"This is a fortress."

"All the better. We have the ill luck of being called demons and witches."

"Well, if you were not so secretive, that wouldn't happen," Caralisa scolded.

"You think not." He bowed his head to regard her out of the tops of his eyes.

Caralisa, so lately at the stake, dropped her gaze. Her cheeks warmed. "Well."

"It is why my mother abandoned Canopus," he said.

"Is her face . . ." She'd done it again. Started what she should not have. Now she was stuck finding the least offensive word. "Unusual?" Caralisa stared at him searchingly. He simply could not be that horrible. The way his black feathered mask moved with his smiles, crinkling at the corners with a ruffle of feathers, it could only be pasted on—onto a face with a *very* nice shape to it. Really, it only left the possibility of a superficial blemish, a lurid birthmark, a terrible burn, or God forbid a 666 on his brow. Whatever it was, it could only be skin deep.

The count was amused. "Unusual." He gave a sly smile. "You could say that, I suppose. But not like mine. Hers has got her into a hellishly great lot of trouble."

"Poor woman."

"Don't feel sorry for her. No one does."

Caralisa left her dinner mostly untouched. The count rose from the table and pulled out her chair for her. He poured himself a snifter of brandy. To her he gave an earthenware mug filled with a heated infusion, heavy with honey, spices, and a trace of liquor. "For your voice."

She tried to clear her throat.

"Don't do that," he said. "Drink."

He was making her feel like an invalid. She pushed back her hair. "I must look wretched."

"No, you don't."

She glanced round. "Have you seen Lancelot?"

"Lancelot?"

"The swan. The black one. I call him Lancelot."

He bristled. "I suppose it never occurred to you that it might already have a name!" he said, as if personally insulted.

"No," she retorted. "It did not. You are so careless in its regard—to talk to you, one would never know that you knew of the creature, let alone named it. So I gave it a knightly name."

"Laertes," he gave a deep growl. "It is called Laertes. The name is good enough."

They moved to the balcony overlooking the plaza. The monks had brought torches to light their work. They were busy beneath the plaza, clearing rubble. The small access hole crawled like an anthill.

"Is there any danger of them finding the way up here?" Caralisa asked.

The count's snappish temper passed quickly enough as it always did. "Oh, they have found one," he said serenely.

Her face showed all alarm.

"What they have found," the count continued soothingly, "is not the topic for polite conversation. Excuse me a moment, mademoiselle, I have an unpleasant task to tend to. Keep an eye on them for me."

He quit the balcony. She kept watch. In moments the monks came rushing above ground, coughing and gagging, peeling soaked robes away from themselves as if they were abhorrent. The dry monks gave them a wide berth.

Caralisa remembered then, in her earlier prowling of the citadel, finding the chamber pot. In the same room was a capped opening. She had lifted the capstone and looked down a long long stone shaft. Air swept up as from a great depth, smelling foul and cold, and she'd replaced the cap at once. She suddenly realized that it was a drain.

The count returned to her side and looked over the railing with some satisfaction.

"You didn't," said Caralisa.

"Mademoiselle, I confess I did."

Caralisa laughed herself to tears despite herself. She knew she shouldn't, and she was a horrible girl for laughing at the holy men, but the terror of the past days came bubbling out in hysterical mirth.

She started to sink, unable to breathe. The count caught her, and she ended up gasping in his arms. She calmed, arms clasped round him, intermittently bubbling back into giggles. Finally she sighed and wiped away her tears with the backs of her hands. Her poor ravaged eyes would never be right again.

She moved back to the rail and looked down, searching each figure. "Where is Michaeljohn? He'll be trying to find me, you know. I don't see him."

The count abruptly exploded. "Go to your beautiful St. Florian since he loves you so well, and let *him* protect you!" His eyes flashed darkly. A tremor crossed his burnt chin.

"Oh . . . I must sound terribly ungrateful." She went to him and circled her hands around his arm. "I never said how very much I owe you."

He curtly disengaged himself. "You owe me nothing," he said harshly and stalked away.

She did not see him again for days.

A messenger arrived in Larissa from Byzantion, a fancy boy not from any land near there. He was dressed as a page but the borders of his burgundy tunic were spun gold and his belt was studded with it. His boots were of fine leather and his swift little horse was an Arab. He carried a curved ceremonial dagger at his belt, and an opulent jewel-encrusted cross around his neck. He was a mere servant—but Someone's servant.

He strode into the cathedral and informed the brethren within: "Prepare to receive a delegation from Byzantion."

Byzantion? All Larissa was abuzz. What had they done to provoke the interest of holy Byzantion?

The boy looked round at the cathedral's purple trappings, sniffed the perfumed air, muttered something like, "The provinces." He wheeled around, strode out at a jaunty march, vaulted onto his swift Arab, and galloped back the way he'd come.

In no time, Monsignor Fortenot was at the palace gates, demanding to see the prince.

Maximillian was expecting him, and waited for him on his throne, attired in his general's uniform, decorated and crowned, sceptre in hand, sword at his side.

The monsignor approached without bow or salutation. He carried a sceptre of his own. "It has come to our attention that a certain misguided reprobate has sought to circumvent the authority of the Church of Montagne."

"There is no Church of Montagne," said the prince. "There is a parish of Montagne within the Church of Byzantion."

Monsignor's amber eyes narrowed hawkishly below bristly black brows. His insinuation drew closer to accusation. *"Someone* sent to Byzantion."

Maximillian met his gaze directly. He did not try to dodge the stroke, but met it with his own blade. *"I* did."

Monsignor towered to full height, and lifted his hooded lids as if there were power in his eyes and he would strike down anyone possessed of the overweening audacity to defy him. "You shall regret."

"I already do," said Maximillian. "I regret that I did not do it sooner! And I am horrified when I think that I nearly did not do it at all!"

"You are in league with the damned! Then you shall join

the damned! You have never crossed the Church, Maximillian. You shall learn that the Church never betrays its own. How were you ever able to command in battle? You have just sent for reinforcements for the opposing side! I pronounce you, Maximillian, earthly power, excommunicate!"

"Just like that?" said Maximillian, settling back into his throne. There was comfort in watching the man unravel. Maximillian need not win this battle. Fortenot was going to lose it nicely for himself. "Unilaterally?"

"You think that your throne will protect you, *Prince* Maximillian?" Monsignor's voice dripped scorn on his worldly title. "You are a secular power who dared where you should not." His voice found resonance in the acoustics of the prince's audience hall and filled the rafters with sound. *"My* kingdom is not of this world!"

"And who might *you* be?" The thin, aged voice had come from behind.

Monsignor Fortenot turned, and Prince Maximillian stood up. The prince descended from his dais, dropped onto one knee, and bowed his crowned head.

Monsignor Fortenot squinted toward the door, could not see clearly for the bright sunlight behind the dark figures standing in the entranceway, but he knew the outline of the tall mitre of a cardinal.

The delegation had just come from the cathedral, where even now brothers busily righted the candles, and the wind ruffled the pages of the open Book.

When news spread throughout the town that Caralisa had been exonerated, Michaeljohn was overjoyed. The condemnation was annulled. It was safe for Caralisa to come down from the Heights.

The doubt followed hard: *Could* she come down from the Heights?

Michaeljohn returned to the prince to ask him to use his influence to rescue Caralisa from her prison on the Heights.

But the prince would do nothing. "This is a private affair," he said. "I shall not interfere."

"A private affair!" Michaeljohn cried. "She has been abducted!"

The prince lost patience. "To call spiriting a maid from a burning stake and out of the clutches of a bloodthirsty mob at great personal risk *abduction* is an interesting view of the world, St. Florian. Really, if you did not want her up there, you might have tried it yourself. Good day!"

Reeling from the rebuff, Michaeljohn went to the foot of the Heights in hopes of finding a way to rescue his beloved. He craned his neck back, hoping for a glimpse of her up on the fiend's lofty balcony.

One of the scarlet-jacketed soldiers of the prince's honor guard finally marched over to him. Michaeljohn thought the man was coming to tell him that the prince had reconsidered his refusal to help him, as he had last time, but the soldier said with brusque annoyance, "Move away, sir. There's nothing to see. In case you've not heard, there will be no burning. Move along."

"You don't understand," Michaeljohn protested. The soldier had mistaken him for one of the mob. "She is my betrothed."

"You are the Marquis de St. Florian!" The guardsman's face brightened with a smile that was not altogether kind. Dark eyes appraised him up and down.

Michaeljohn, unsettled, groped for recognition. The stranger was hard and lean, old for a guardsman. His bearing was all cocky belligerence far above the merit of his rank. Jet hair was swept back from a flat brow. His looks were more strikingly virile than they were handsome. An angry scar marred one side of his face from high angular cheekbone to jaw. Silken cruelty twisted his soft lips beneath a rakish black pencil mustache. When he had spoken, it was in a high, Rhinish-accented tenor. Michaeljohn was sure he did not know him. "You have me at a disadvantage, sir."

"Richardt, *Freiherr* von Keigfeld!" The guardsman brought his heels together with a rap and a stiff inclination of his body. "I believe we have a mutual acquaintance in the redhead."

St. Florian flushed hotly and frowned. "Her name is not for your speaking."

"Not if I wanted to, for I don't know it!" the baron said cheerfully. "Did *you* know she has the cutest little beauty mark right here. Under the aureole." He gave a quick tap with his riding crop across his body. The motion had been too swift to follow clearly.

"She has a halo on her arm?" Michaeljohn blinked, struggling for comprehension.

"She has a beauty mark, you simple fop. Not on her arm. And what it's near is not what I'd call a halo. I'd call it a tit."

And the *Freiherr* cackled at Michaeljohn's blank uncertain look and slowness to find rebuke.

The baron pressed on merrily, "You mean you don't *know?* You didn't sample the milk before you decided to buy the whole cow?"

St. Florian slapped him. The grin remained on the roguish face as von Keigfeld's cheek reddened from the blow.

Michaeljohn challenged him to a duel.

The *Freiherr* conceded laughingly, hand over his heart, "If you like, sir, I apologize. I lied. I made the whole thing up. I know the lady not."

Michaeljohn shifted uncertainly, as if there ought to be more he could drag out of the rake. He turned and stomped away, leaving von Keigfeld smirking and bidding the troubled young marquis in parting, "Let your wedding night be one of discovery."

* * *

Cathedral bells brought Caralisa to the railing. Down in the streets below, a grand solemn procession of all the priests and monks of Montagne moved through the basilica's great doors. Bells tolled in sacred celebration. It was not a holiday, and Caralisa could not guess what it was about.

She had just washed her hair; electric gossamer strands lifted round her shoulders with a will of their own.

She was dressed in an antique gown from one of the old chests. She had no stockings and no underclothes. For shoes she had only her burned ballet slippers.

She had grown accustomed to being alone. Footsteps behind her made her spin and clutch at the rail.

The count made an abortive reach for her, but she had already steadied herself. She pushed a long shining red lock behind her shoulder, recovering. "My lord," she greeted him.

His expression behind the black feathered mask was changeless as stone. Only the storm blue eyes were suffused with clashing emotions withheld. His voice was deep and steady as he said, "As you wished, so it is."

"I don't understand," said Caralisa. "What is all that?" She pointed over the railing toward the cathedral.

"They are investing the new monsignor," the count explained. "You might have known him as Brother Joseph."

"Oh, that sweet old man!" She remembered a palsied half-deaf fragile man with a benevolent smile and squinting crescent eyes.

"Come," said the count tersely. He had a blindfold in his hand.

"Come where?" said Caralisa.

"I will take you out."

"I cannot go!" Caralisa shrank away. "They'll burn me!"

"Byzantion has made it known that no one shall harm their daughter Caralisa."

Caralisa dropped to her knees. Her skirt flared out around her. She clasped her hands under her bowed chin and gave silent fervent thanks.

The count extended a gloved hand down. "You may rejoin your flock."

She took his offered hand, moved her skirt from underfoot, and let him help her up. She hesitated. "Won't Monsignor Fortenot—"

"You mean *Brother* Ignatius," he interrupted.

"Goodness!" How he had fallen! "Won't he be waiting for me? Oh my Lord, he is going to be so angry with me now!"

"The former monsignor is angry, true enough," the count conceded. "Mad, I should say. But he is far away by now. Somewhere between here and Byzantion."

"Thank God!"

"You may well thank God, but there were some agents in between here and heaven," he said tightly.

"How!" she cried in wonder. "How did this come to pass? Since when does Byzantion look in on a sparrow falling in Larissa?"

"It is what you wanted, is it not?"

"Yes, but—"

"Then that is how it happened."

"How can wishing make a thing happen?" said Caralisa.

Her question was greeted with silence. She supposed he thought her conversation silly. She said, "But I did not wish him any harm. Truly I didn't. I only wanted him away from me."

"He is that."

"How twisted everything became. Love causes so much trouble." She nestled into the count's chest, slipped her hands under his coat to hug him. She heard his heart beating fast. His voice rumbled within the resonant cage of his chest. "Go now. I fear for you."

She lifted her head, moved an errant strand of hair from her face. "How can I be afraid when you are here?"

The silence smoldered.

She moved away to stand at the rail, curled a finger over

her full lips, inadvertently sexual, and coyly begged, "Can you not show me how to come and go?" She glanced sideways, her blue eyes peering from under the long fringe of her lashes.

"I will take you out," he said huskily. He tossed the blindfold to her.

She wound it round her finger and tilted her head in winsome pleading. "Can I not stay here?"

The count held his breath, then spoke as if far away. "Stay?"

"Until I marry."

His eyes flickered within the mask. His voice dropped a register. "Marry whom?"

"Why, Michaeljohn! Who else?" She giggled. "This place is safer than the cottage. Monsignor Fortenot sent a hired sword for me there. She came right through the window."

The look on his face resolved into anger. Eyes darkened to smoky depths. Caralisa could swear she saw lightning within the storm-burnt blue. His voice contained a rumble of thunder. "If you wish to stay here, then very well. Stay. But mind you, this citadel and all in it are mine!" His cloak came off with a swirl. He seized her wrist. It was very small within his commanding grasp.

She lurched toward him, pulled up short in shock. She looked up into his face, her own expression a wide surprised blank. She saw both passion of want and passion of fury. Her speech stalled in a halting cough then she shook her head in denial. "Why! I never knew!"

"I never told you," he growled.

"Why?"

He let go her wrist, stalked a few long angry paces away from her, turned, and said with the softness of repressed violence, "I am not one to stick his neck out; it is a bit of a reach. I was waiting for the smallest sign that you could love me." He paused a breath then finished with a hard pained mockery of a smile. "I never got it."

Caralisa gave a small laughing cry, shaking her head. "I thought you said you could not possibly be in love with me!"

He did not so much speak as he heaved the words out in two separate breaths, "I *lied!*"

"Have you gone mad!"

"If I am not, it is no thanks to you! You have driven me out of my mind! I never know moment to moment what you think! I'd have better luck divining your heart with daisy petals! She loves me, she loves me not. I should be shredding daisies to kingdom come looking for a straight answer—!"

She broke in to declare, "I have always said I loved Michaeljohn!"

"This I know: you say so. But as I live you don't act like a woman in love! Fireflies are more constant than your affections!" He stalked a circle around her. "That man's singular virtue is never being with you long enough to disturb your dream of what you want him to be! You're a splendid match, I must say—you both want what you cannot have, and neither of you sees what is before your eyes, only what you want to be there. Who knows, maybe even I am attractive when I am out of reach, but I can never see that! I am here to see your horror when I say that I love you!"

Rage so transformed him that Caralisa did not know him. His eyes seemed to turn black.

She refused to hear him. This was not happening. She cried, "You can't! You can't!"

He shouted over her, "And who cast me in the role of your father that the thought of my coming to you in passion evokes nothing but loathing! Why am I not allowed to be a man without you shrinking from me as if I have betrayed you? The horror in your eyes is sharper than all the hired knives in Larissa and more brutal. What exactly do you think I am that it is some kind of surprise that I want you? Am I a big guard dog which must be castrated to be allowed to live around you so that I don't hang on your leg, a thing of disgust? Then be disgusted!"

His gloved hand caught her under her chin, tilted her head up, firm and swift without pain but inescapable and against her will. His mouth covered hers with shocking warmth. She squealed against the hot intrusion of his tongue, which unleashed a wellspring of desire and panic at once. Fear was the stronger, together with alarm at her own passionate reaction. His gloved fingers caressed her creamy throat, making her moan without volition into his mouth. His other hand caught both of hers as she tried to push him away. He trapped them against the wall over her head, stretching her body to full-length and turning any motion she made into a writhing caress against his own body.

With a gasp she found her lips suddenly free, swollen and tingling with fevered want. He was kissing her neck. He buried his masked face in her hair. His lips and tongue tormented her tender skin with feathery heat. The power from him was as a solid wall. His strength aroused her but could not eclipse the terror that left her in thrashing panic. Her struggles brushed her against the hardness of his manly form through his clothes, exciting, infuriating, and horrifying her. She started screaming.

The count pulled back in anger. "Madame!"

She made a feeble attempt to restore them to formality, demanding shakily, "What happened to 'mademoiselle'?"

"You are mine. Yes, you may stay here until you marry. Today is your wedding day!"

He lowered her hands, her narrow wrists still caught in the iron vise of his left hand, and he dragged her as if manacled through the labyrinth and up the three wide stairs. He raised a booted foot high and kicked open the doors to his bedroom. He dragged her within and threw her across the wide bed. She scrambled backward, legs entangled in the draping folds of her skirt. He shrugged out of his coat and untied his cravat. He looked tall and striking in his waistcoat and shirtsleeves, an image of enthralling menace. His body tapered quickly to his firm narrow waist; tight breeches showed an unmistakable swelling of masculine excitement. She backed away in ungainly retreat across the bed.

He seized her ankle and dragged her back toward him. Suddenly he was over her and he descended like a falcon, the full of his violent passion, long pent, unleashed upon her.

His mouth joined hers in a devouring kiss, his tongue penetrating and ravaging her soft mouth. His kisses strayed lower and lower until red velvet barred his way, and with a growl he tore her dress. She cried with its rending. He dragged it down around her waist, trapping her arms against her sides. He kissed a trail of fire down the hollow of her neck and her bared shoulders. His gloved hands closed on the soft orbs of her breasts. They looked vulnerable enclosed in his grasp, his touch fiercely gentle, the horror of it in its violation rather than pain.

His mouth came down hungrily, enveloping one traitorously eager nipple with heated roiling wetness, the texture of his tongue dragging across its sensitized nob, with the slight grazing of teeth. She drew in deep breaths sobbing, feeling less a lover than the prey of a great predator. His hands ravished her with rapacious caresses, seeking out every forbidden contour, molding his palms to her curves. His voracious kisses groped lower, seeking the all of her.

He rose up to kneel astride her and with a great wrenching, tore her dress to the hem, dragging it free from her arms. She clutched at the red velvet, trying to cover herself, now completely naked. He dragged the torn dress from beneath her and hurled it into the fireplace. The embers kindled the dry old fabric and it went up in a blaze.

Caralisa covered herself with her long silken hair and her hands, shrinking back across the wide bed. She took up a big pillow as a shield and cowered behind it, sniffling.

He stalked around the bed, gripping the posts as he turned the corners. She scrabbled round, pivoting to remain facing him with the pillow between them. He paused at the foot of the bed, threw open the cedar chest, and pulled out a gown of ivory lace. "Wear this one," he said and threw it at her.

She pushed it away with a crying protest.

"Or don't wear it," he growled. "Only be ready, my bride. You and I were made for each other. You needn't argue. It is already written." He crossed the floor in long powerful strides away toward the doors.

Caralisa drew herself upright, clutching at one bedpost, and she shrieked after him in defiance, "Where is it written!"

He spun, bringing his hand to his chest. "Here. Upon my heart. And if you can't see it, I shall break you open and carve it on yours!"

He stormed out. The doors shut behind him with a resounding boom. She heard a wooden rush and a metallic rap of a bolt sliding to, then the angry rapping of bootheels on stone, retreating in sharp cadence.

Caralisa curled up in a ball, pulled the big pillows around her, and cried. She could still feel where his hands had grasped her. Her arm convulsed with an involuntary lash against his frightening strength. She repudiated the disturbing heat his kisses aroused within her. No. No. No. She would not be one of the *things* furnishing this citadel.

To try the door would be futile. She dragged a heavy celadon cover off the bed to cloak herself and padded to the balcony.

A fresh breeze cooled her wet face. She hugged the bedcover to her breasts. It drooped low in back, leaving bare her white shoulders and gracefully curved back but for the veil of her hair.

The crystal lake stretched out below, heedlessly beautiful, impervious to sorrow and panic. The willows still dabbled their long fronds into their reflections. The waterfall spun down silvery blue. From the birches appeared a turquoise flash of a halcyon, which tucked back its crest to knife the water then rise into the broad plane tree on the far side of the lake.

Caralisa leaned over the railing and looked at the rocks far below. In her dire need to escape, she still could not hurl herself into its unfeeling splendor.

She went back inside to search for another passage. There was none.

She pressed an ear to the doors to listen. She could not hear over her own quivering sobbing breaths and her hammering heartbeats. She had never felt so small and frightened.

She sank to the floor at the side of the bed, waiting for returning footsteps. She wondered if the sound would give her enough panic or courage to sprint out to the balcony and make the leap. It was the only way out.

A shadow flitted over the patch of sunlight on the floor, momentarily dimming the chamber. A heavy flapping sounded from beyond the curtains. Then the sound became quite loud and settled into a folding of great wings.

Heart leaping, Caralisa leaned into the light to see a black shape perched on the balcony railing.

The swan gave a single strident *honk.*

"Lancelot," she breathed.

The swan turned away from her and crouched as if to take flight.

"Laertes! Wait!" She reached out a bare white arm beseechingly.

The swan craned its glossy black head round on its sinuous neck to look at her. It uncrouched, turned on the railing, spread its enormous wings, and dropped lightly down onto the balcony.

Caralisa crawled, dragging the bedcover with her. She laced her arms around the swan's elegant neck and leaned her face into the silken softness of its lustrous black plumage. She tried to speak, but a clot blocked her throat. She cleared it, whispered, "Take me away from here! Please!"

She made a tentative move to climb onto the swan's back. It shrugged her off with an unfurling of wings. It walked with a slow strut on black-webbed feet farther into the room, toward an arras, and poked its black beak at the tapestry.

Caralisa stood, pulling the green damask around her, and followed the swan. She parted the hangings where the swan indicated. Behind them was only a stuccoed wall. She looked down in puzzlement at the beautiful enigmatic bird.

She touched its glossy neck. It jerked away and hissed at her like a snake. Its shadow snaked along the wall. Like a cobra.

Tears sprang in a return flood to Caralisa's eyes. She pulled her hand away. *Not you too.*

The swan reared up proudly, broad wings spread for balance like majestic sails, its beak uplifted upon a gracefully curved neck as if pointing.

Honk!

Caralisa followed the direction of its bill, quizzically. She saw only a cold stucco wall, an empty candle sconce of blackened silver, and nothing more. She held the arras back farther but the swan gave another impatient rusty piped squawk.

She put a palm on the stucco experimentally. "I don't understand." She gripped the candle sconce. She inadvertently dragged down on it as she withdrew her hand.

The wall began to move. Cracks in the stucco widened, gapped. A section the size of a narrow door recessed. An inrush of cool air blew Caralisa's hair back from her wet face and raised her exposed skin in bumps. The curtains over the balcony opening bowed outward with the sudden crosscurrent.

Caralisa fetched a lamp, and lit it in the hearth where her dress lay smoldering. She returned to the dark opening and reached her lamp to illuminate what was hidden therein.

Narrow stairs curved steeply down, disappearing round a hairpin bend.

The swan, Laertes, had already fluttered down a few steps, paused at the turn, craned its neck back, and honked.

"Wait!" she said.

She sprinted back to the bed, and let her cover drop. She seized up the white dress which the count had commanded her to wear. She hesitated before putting it on, then, decisively, she pulled it over her head. Her fingers, clumsy with haste, fastened half the hooks. She pushed her feet back into her smutted and singed ballet slippers.

She glimpsed herself as she flew past the mirror. The ivory gown adored her figure. She shuddered with the horrible notion that that perfect madman had this tailored to fit.

She was furiously embarrassed that he should know her figure so well. She had never stopped to wonder that everything he ever picked out for her fit as if made for her. How closely was he studying her body to be able to do that?

She saw also in the flashed image in the mirror her face swollen from crying, her hair in disarray like the mane of a wild mare.

There was nothing for it. In any moment the count could return and catch her in this dress and suppose she was submitting. At a tiptoed run she made for the passage and slipped through.

She turned to close the secret door, but the swan was getting ahead. Caralisa heard its diminishing honks far below. From behind her she imagined she heard bootheels in the corridor beyond the bolted doors. In frantic haste she dragged the arras closed, lifted her skirt and her lamp, and started down the treacherously steep winding steps.

A stiff updraft ruffled the candleflame within its globe. It leapt into a gray coil of extinguished smoke.

Caralisa froze in the dark, hunched against the wall. "Laertes!" she hissed.

She listened. She could not hear anything except the rush of water from somewhere.

In a moment she began to distinguish faintly the outline

of steps winding down away from her. She set down the lamp and continued cautiously in the dimness, half at a crawl, one hand holding up her skirt, the other guiding her way along the rough stone wall.

The sound of falling water grew ever louder. The way grew lighter until she could see quite clearly in a faint blue light.

The stairs leveled and the passage widened into a rock chamber, cool and damp, its floor slick, misted with a spray of droplets from the wall of water falling in a sheet before her. Sunlight shone through its translucent shimmer from the other side.

There was no other opening in the chamber.

"Oh no." She turned a full circle. There was nowhere to go.

The swan turned its head, almost questioningly. She could not understand.

"Laertes?"

The swan ran, spreading its wings, and in two steps was aloft, blasting through the waterfall. Instantly it was gone.

Caralisa hiked up her skirt, drank in a few heaving breathes, ran after it, and leapt.

She crashed through the heavy beating wall of water, breaking into bright sunlight and open air—to nothing on the other side. She was instantly plunging *down!*

Before she could scream, she had hit surface and was plunging under its shocking wet cold! Her wide skirt billowed up all round her, her hair streaming up like a comet's tail. Her ears filled with an icy muffling inrush which muted the sound of the myriad bright bubbles rising round her.

Her vertiginous descent slowed. She struggled dreamlike, dragging her limbs through the watery density until her direction reversed. Rising, she kicked and clawed at the water, bobbed up, broke surface, and gasped through the wet sheet of her hair plastered to her face.

She slipped back under and bobbed up again. She grasped at the midnight shape which had circled in toward her. As she went under again, she got hold of a leathery foot. She pulled herself up, grabbed a black wing, found the swan's neck, and looped both arms round it and hung on.

The swan gave an uncomfortable squawk, and paddled laboriously to the bank.

In the shallows, Caralisa climbed out of the lake, staggering from the sodden weight of her gown, teetering through a tangle of waterlilies.

The swan sped away, wings beating against the water, until it was airborne. It soared over the lake and alighted on the high rock palisade a quarter of the way round the lake.

Caralisa made her way at a stumbling run around the water's edge to where the swan waited. Weeds poked through her thin wet slippers, which chafed and blistered her feet. She could not afford to stop and rest.

The sun's tingling warmth eased her wet shivering. Her drying hair lifted from its matted mass by the time she hiked from the lake edge to the rock face underneath the swan's perch.

And there Caralisa found the other side of her secret door, the one she had found so long ago under the Rue de Temps.

She pulled on the black iron ring. Nothing gave. She pushed. The door would not move. She turned round, fell back against the door, and let herself slide to sit on the ground. She may as well be locked up in the room.

Hot tears leaked from her eyes as a whine escaped her throat. She turned, pounded on the door, frantic. He would be after her any moment. He would know which way she had gone.

She groped through the moss around the foot of the rock in search of a key. There had to be a key. She whispered in a litany, "Oh please please please please." Dirt caked under her clawing nails. Her vision blurred with tears.

A dark movement made her cower and sob.

But the black flapping was not a cape, just the wings of a swan. The swan swooped down, stepped out of the air, and folded its great wings. It walked up to her and bowed its silky neck, its black beak touching the ground where she knelt. It gave a hiccup; its throat convulsed like a backward swallow. When it lifted its head, it had coughed up a golden key in the moss.

Caralisa lifted the key with trembling fingers and fit it into the black iron lock. It clattered in her shaking hands, and turned, gave a miraculous *click,* and kept turning with the resistance of moving something aside. She pulled out the key and gave a tug on the ring.

The door swung with a disused creak.

Caralisa scampered through the doorway. She blew a kiss to the swan before she slammed the door and locked it behind her. Then she took the key and scaled the embankment to the Rue de Temps.

She ran past the charred cobblestones round the blackened hole in the pavement where the stake had stood. She dashed into the plaza, jumped out in front of a hansom cab, and begged the driver to take her home.

She was not the first runaway bride he had ever picked up, though probably the most bedraggled. This one was dressed in soaked muddy ivory lace, her long hair a damp wild darkened red mass. Still and all there was a beguiling vulnerability to her. The nymph had made a mess of herself, but underneath it one could see she was very pretty, and no doubt the groom would want her back, so the driver cracked the whip at the horses and made all possible haste to be away.

Fourteen

As the carriage drew to a stop at its destination, Caralisa could see lights burning inside the cottage. In fear she nearly told the driver to keep going. Then through the open window she caught a glimpse of Michaeljohn's fair curls. She leapt out of the carriage and flew into his arms. He beheld her with red-shot eyes that had been crying. "Oh my darling!"

Bernard discreetly excused himself and stepped out to settle with the carriage.

Caralisa clung to Michaeljohn and cried wildly, "He'll be after me! I can't let him hurt you! I don't know what he will do!"

Michaeljohn declared, "No one will hurt you as I live!" He stroked her wild tangled hair. She flinched away, ran to the windows, and pulled all the curtains shut.

"We will leave Larissa," Michaeljohn declared, and Caralisa did not argue this time. She huddled by the window and peered through slits between the curtains to keep watch on the road. Every shifting black shadow became a fluttering cape.

Michaeljohn ordered his valet pack. He barked to Bernard to hold the carriage.

Another carriage appeared up the narrow road, and Caralisa almost died of fright, but it was only Aristide and his manservant, Roger. Upon arrival, they were commandeered to help arrange the lovers' flight.

Caralisa went to her room to peel off the wet dress of

ruined lace. She put on something light and flowing, white stockings, and soft kid slippers. She brushed her hair and tied it up with ribbons.

All around she heard running feet, muttered curses, the rattle of locks and slamming of chests.

She wondered where the guards would be coming from and she kept looking for them to appear. Every glance outside showed only tossing tree shadows and windblown leaves tumbling across the grass like swift birds.

The sun was fast setting. Caralisa came out and tossed the ruined wet dress into the hearth.

"Where did that come from?" Michaeljohn's eyes followed the soiled lace.

"I needed something to wear," Caralisa mumbled.

"Where is yours?"

Fear and weariness made her short-tempered. She supposed he did not remember that her disappearance had been many days ago when she had been roused from her bed by an assassin in the middle of the night. She had been tied to the stake in her nightgown. "My clothes were torn," she said.

"Torn how?" said Michaeljohn, alarmed.

"There are sharp thorns on the Heights," she said. She did not want to talk about how she happened to be in or out of which dress. She did not want to recount that awful scene in the count's bedchamber.

Shuddering, she brought her arms around herself and trembled from an inner chill.

Michaeljohn paced to and fro before the hearth in agitation. "I have feared so for your most precious possession at the mercy of that . . . that . . . Did that beast hurt you? If he did, so help me, I'll . . . I'll—"

"You shall do what, my darling?" Caralisa said too faintly for anyone to hear. She wilted into the window seat and stared out through the curtains. She opened them wide and left them wide.

She still saw no guards. No armed men of St. Florian. No

mercenaries. He had mobilized nothing. The man who would
move heaven and earth for her had arranged a pair of carriages and a few of his school friends. She gazed out at the
futility of flight.

How did he think to defend her? With words? Pretty words.
And he believed them. As if the speaking made them so.

But St. Florian thinks things just happen.

Her heart slowed from its frantic pounding to an uneasy
thudding as she gradually realized that the marquis could
not protect her, and more gradually still realized that no one
was pursuing her.

Michaeljohn hovered over her in consternation. "Are you
unharmed? I hesitate to tell you what sort of man he is. He
is no man at all!"

Instead of shock, he saw some understanding cross Caralisa's blue eyes. She got up, wandered out to the garden to
stand in the open and look up at the empty sky.

"I know exactly what he is," she said softly. And suspected
for the first time that her captor had let her go.

She turned her great hyacinthine eyes to Michaeljohn sorrowfully: "And how shall you defend me, my darling?"

"I have!" Michaeljohn declared. "And I shall to my last
breath."

"How?" said Caralisa. "How have you defended me?"

A deep blush ruddied his fair face. He hesitated. "This
very morning there was a man of the royal guard defaming
your sweet virtue. I called him out. I forced an apology from
him and by God he gave it. I shan't let your dear reputation
be sullied by the likes of that scoundrel."

"A man of the royal guard?" said Caralisa. "Baron von
Keigfeld?"

Michaeljohn's heated animation went blank. "You *know*
him then?"

"I met him at a masque." She wove her delicate fingers
together. "I have been told that he talks about me. I could

not say whether his words are true or false, for I have not heard what it is he says. Will you tell me what he said?"

Michaeljohn's handsome face darkened to scarlet. "I cannot say those things to a lady! It pains me when they attack your sweet name."

"Not so much as when the fire was attacking my sweet self," said Caralisa. That dark lurking hurt came rushing out in a spate. "Where were you then!"

"Why!" Michaeljohn exclaimed. "I had the prince send to Byzantion to have you exonerated of that ridiculous charge! And I defended your honor through all of it."

"Yes, you have spoken of my most precious possession," said Caralisa. "What would that be?"

"My darling!" he protested, blushing darker still. The answer went without saying.

"I rather thought my immortal soul counted for something," said Caralisa.

"You know what I mean," said Michaeljohn.

"No. I am quite sure I don't. Am I a piece of goods that loses value because someone else might have handled it? Do you know what I am?"

"You are my angel!"

All her vehemence collapsed into regret. She said sorrowfully, "I am an actress upon whom you have hung a dream. You wrote a part and cast me in it. Well, I have a confession, my darling. I seem to have done the same to you. Look at me." Her gentle hands enfolded his face as he tried to look away. "Look at *me*," she pleaded in earnest, her musical voice plaintive. "Do you love me or what you want me to be?"

He responded instantly. "I love you! I swear by all the stars in heaven, I love you!" he declared, his limpid blue eyes shining. Then he said, "Do you love me?"

She hung her head. "I don't think so."

"My angel! How can you love and suddenly not!" he cried.

"I did." She lifted her head, shook back her ribboned red locks. "I do. I don't know." She searched the starry sky for words. She was more in love with love, with the images he drew for her on the summer air, than she was with him. She wanted to marry more than she wanted the man. A dear man. But not for her. "You love a silly beautiful child. Who will you love when I am no longer silly, beautiful, or a child? And who will I love when you are no longer beautiful and all I have are honeyed words that never were more than the air they were formed of?"

He launched into a fine poetic speech of the depth of his love and what he would not do for her.

She covered her ears. "Stop! Stop! You did not even hear me!"

He grasped for what she wanted. "I could make you a marquisa!"

"It's not enough!" she cried.

"It is more than a countess or a baroness! Or haven't you been offered the titles!"

Without thinking she drew her palm smartly across his face. She heard the slap before she realized she had done it. They both stared in shock.

Then he crumbled into tears. "I am sorry! I am sorry! I did not say that!" He fell on bended knee and kissed the hem of her dress.

She pulled her skirts out of his hands. "I am not your white peacock maiden," she said sadly. "I wish I were. I hope you find the one you seek."

She went to the bedroom and rolled up her mother's quilt. She took the diamond from her finger and left it on the bed. Quilt under her arm, she walked out. She passed the footmen who had hastened to open the doors of their carriages for her.

She hiked up the unpaved road, shoes crunching on the small stones. At the crossroads she turned outbound, toward the bridge that would take her out of Larissa and onto the road to Viola's farm.

* * *.

Caralisa glanced round herself anxiously as she walked, cringing from the wind, the trees, the shadows. She saw things in the blackness that were not there.

As she neared the water, frogs in the riverbed stopped their singing abruptly.

Did I do that?

She had been hearing, or been imagining, bootsteps that started and stopped as she did. She thought at first they were echoes bouncing off the close buildings of town, but as she neared the river and the buildings thinned away, that hardly seemed possible.

She was ruing her proud march past the carriages. She was footsore and weary, with a long way to go and nothing but darkness to shield her.

She had come to the edge of the city. Once over the bridge she would be forced to finish on foot.

A pebble skittered and tripped over the cobbles in her path.

Did I do that?

She quailed before the bridge. A guardsman's horse stood tied up at one end, with no sign of the sentry himself.

A flapping of wings nearly stopped her heart.

She crouched down as a pair of ducks fluttered away from her and waddled quickly down the embankment and dropped into the water with soft splashes. They swam off with muttered disgruntled quacking.

Caralisa swallowed hard, caught her breath. She started forward for the bridge.

A brassy voice pierced the dark. "Hello, *Red!*"

She spun with a gasp.

An angular cocky figure materialized from the night at a jaunty walk, a short cloak slung over one squared shoulder. She should have been relieved to see the scarlet of the palace honor guard. But she turned cold at the sardonic crooked smile. White teeth caught the starlight with a predatory gleam. A straight black mustache stretched over his lip with his widening grin.

The Baron von Keigfeld.

Caralisa drew herself up in propriety. She reminded herself that—despite their appalling intimacy—they had not been introduced. She was wearing the clothes of a cultured lady, so she would act one. She gave a haughty sniff. "Do I know you, sir?"

His smile was an assault, his gaze groping over her body in blatant lust. "You might not remember me. I am probably one of a legion to you. But I? How could I forget that color?" He tugged a ribbon from her hair. He picked up the end of the red tress that fell loose and he ran it between his fingers. He drew a strand lingeringly across his tongue. "I can still taste your sweet lips on mine."

"I beg your pardon!" She started away in an indignant huff. He caught her wrist, drew her in sharply, and smiled crookedly into her wide horrified eyes.

"There is a stable nearby where we can continue that sweet conversation from which we were so rudely interrupted. Or right here is also fine." He whipped his short cape off his shoulders and spread it on the ground at the roadside.

"No," Caralisa protested, trying to twist away.

He laughed, yanked her in toward him. She shielded herself with her bundled quilt. He wrenched it from between them and hurled it back into the road. He pulled her body hard against his and growled, "You coquettish little whore! Two men have drawn on me, willing to kill or to die for you! I want to know what is worth risking death for! You offered once on Sovereign's Night. I am collecting now!"

With that he dropped to one knee, dragging her down with him. Grasping fingers closed on her neckline and ripped downward, then he threw her skirts up over her head. The fabric flapped in her mouth, which opened to scream. His fingers raked her hips, pulling down her lacy silk underthings. She felt the shock of cool air on her suddenly exposed womanhood, then of hot hands groping at her thighs. She tried to kick, restricted by her undergarments bunched around her knees. She managed to throw her skirts down clear of her face in time to see him pulling down his tight breeches. Moonlight shone pale on white skin that seldom saw the sun. A hard bluish rod with glistening head sprouted from a mass of black curls. His chuckle menaced.

Caralisa thrust a spread palm into his smiling face. He lost his balance and sprawled backward. She found her footing clumsily, trying to pull up her underclothes so she could walk as she reeled back into the road. She blundered into her bundled quilt. She siezed it up as if it were her mother herself and ran across the bridge.

In a moment she heard a horse whinny behind her, together with a hard male laugh like a clashing brass. Iron-shod hoofbeats came clanging across the cobbled bridge.

Her own breath tore through her throat in wrenching sobs.

The laughing stopped abruptly mid-cadence, the sound sheared off. The hoofbeats continued their approach, louder and closer. The horse's labored breaths bore down on her at a driving gallop.

She ran off the road, crying. The hoofbeats quickly gained and overtook in a moment of blind white terror.

And passed her.

A riderless horse, its neck stretched out flat, hooves flying in an all-out run as if demons were after it, plunged ahead into the darkness.

Caralisa kept running until she could not breathe.

At last she fell across her bundle, gasping in great sobs, forced to surrender to her pursuer.

But there was nothing else to be seen or heard.

There was only the wind over the fields of fragrant alfalfa and corn grown tall, its feathery tops nodding in waves; a chatter of nighttime animals; and the night swifts winking across the face of the moon.

Of the baron, and whatever horror had overtaken the horse, there was no sign.

Caralisa unrolled her quilt and drew it round her torn dress as a bulky cloak. She trudged on wearily up the road, the soles of her shoes scraping on the grit and grass which tufted the raised center between deep wheel ruts.

At one point she passed a gap in the corn where the panicked horse had bolted off the road. But for the rest of her journey Caralisa was entirely alone.

It was a cottage much like the one she had left that evening. A pair of bulky draft horses, hopeful of sugar, ghosted her approach along the split rail fence.

Caralisa let herself in through the gate. Joshua's yellow dog stood up without a sound and walked to her, wagging its tail. Caralisa patted the dog and rapped on the door.

Viola answered the knock, baby on one breast. The infant was so tiny and new he could not focus his eyes. Neither could his mother. Viola draped her other arm around Caralisa in a hug, more wilting around her than embracing her. She gave a fuzzy smile and bid Caralisa come in.

Viola shuffled into the back bedroom. Caralisa could hear the low undertone of a sleepy male. Then Viola returned to put on a kettle and sit at their rustic breakfast table.

A mottled cat huddled with its feet tucked up under it on the table beneath the window. It deigned to open one eye to assure itself that all was well in its domain, then ignored Caralisa entirely.

"I hear tales," said Viola. "By the time they arrive out here, they are quite fantastical. The last I heard the women of the town were jealous of your beauty so they set you up and gave you to the beast in a high cave."

It should have been funny but it wasn't.

"Now," said Viola. "Out with it. All of it."

Caralisa looked round at the house and hearth, a quilt begun in its frame, the clutter of baby things, a diaper pail, the closed door down the hall behind which sounded masonlike snores, Viola's milk-stained nightgown, her own torn dress of elegant design befitting a marquisa's bride, the kettle ticking with the change in temperature. She started to cry.

Viola's sympathy never wavered, even when Caralisa's actions in the retelling sounded stupid and outrageous to her own ears.

"Oh Viola," Caralisa cried. "I am the world's only virgin whore."

Viola shook her head. "Coquette, you may be. But those men are no gentlemen."

"Michaeljohn is," said Caralisa.

"Yes," Viola conceded unenthusiastically. "Michaeljohn is."

Caralisa twisted a tear-soaked handkerchief round and round. "Was I wrong to throw away a future with him?"

"If you did not love him, there was no future," said Viola.

Caralisa sniffled, spoke haltingly through tears. "He spoke of my 'most precious possession.' He said that more than once. Oh Viola, *is* it? The best I have is to be given once and lost forever? I do want my one perfect love to have it, but is that the best I have to offer? What about *me?*"

Viola nodded. "I would hate to think that I have already spent my best."

"And what of the count?" Her thoughts returned inexorably to him. Images returned in a maelstrom of violence and sensuality, too hot to touch.

"He hurt you. One cannot live with that," said Viola.

"No. Yes. No." She stammered and started over, "He didn't hurt me really."

"Because you were able to fight him off," Viola filled in.

"I fought . . . He let me go. I couldn't fight him off." His strength, his control, had been absolute, intoxicating if not so terrifying. She had experienced that passionate moment as if plunged into a river over her head, not that she did not like water, but there had been suddenly so much, so fast, and in a drowning relentless torrent. She could do nothing but fight it. And he, like a dam bursting, under control too long, broke out in violence and caught back too late. "He made a monstrous mistake. I think he knows it."

"Did he hit you?" Viola asked soberly.

"No." She shook her head within a curtain of her tumbled hair, then lifted her face. "Viola, he let me go."

"Are you in love with him?"

"No." An involuntary shudder racked her. "No, I can't. He's overbearing and pushy and tyrannical—"

"And arrogant?"

"And *arrogant!*"

Viola sighed a significant sigh.

"What?" said Caralisa.

Viola shrugged.

"What?" Caralisa pressed.

Viola sighed again. "He has seen you as you are. You have played no silly flirtation games with him like the girls do in the parlor. You snap at him. You let him have the sharp end of your tongue. You talk with him and tell him exactly what you think instead of holding back for fear he won't like you. And he loves you still. One comes to appreciate a man who loves you when you look like this." She presented her shabby self. The baby spat on her breast. Viola cleaned herself and lifted the tiny bundle to her shoulder and gently patted his little back. "A bit of a beast, but aren't they all? It is a great tragedy you cannot love him."

Add to that, Caralisa thought, he had seen her flat on her back in a stable with another man—an evil evil man—had listened to her make an utter fool of herself over still another, and he loved her regardless of what she had done or who had known her. To the count anyway, there was more to Caralisa than her virginity. His anger that she consorted with others was not that she had sullied herself. It was simple jealous pain.

It was a great tragedy she could not love him.

"He frightens me," said Caralisa.

"Oh," said Viola, voice heavy with import. "*He* does."

"What does that mean?"

"You who hear songs of winds and trees and birds and angels cannot listen to your own heart."

Caralisa wanted to protest that Viola did not know of what she spoke, but she could not argue with one who was in a safe harbor. Viola obviously knew how to navigate these turbid waters.

Caralisa blinked into an all-obscuring fog of her own making. She shook her head, uncomprehending.

She reached for the baby. "Go to bed, Viola. If you have a bottle, I'll take the little one. I shan't be sleeping tonight."

Viola yawned, smiled. She kissed Caralisa and shuffled off gratefully in the direction of the snores.

Caralisa sat up, rocking the tiny baby, singing softly a tender melody.

Listen to my own heart? What is it she hears that I cannot?

Something about the count? He was, like his strength, intoxicating if he were not so terrifying.

Or was it the intoxication itself that terrified?

The baby fell asleep. Caralisa sat up listening to the night wind. Music came to her, the song of a dying swan.

She gazed into the glowing embers burning low in the hearth.

Without meaning to, she whispered softly, "No."

No one really ever died of heartbreak.

Fifteen

For three nights running, Caralisa gazed into the fire and heard the same song. On the morning of the fourth day she told Viola that she must go.

She returned to Larissa on the back of a stout draft mare. At the bridge she slid off its broad back and let it go. The mare turned away and, at a smart trot, made for home.

Crossing into the city, Caralisa had to stop for a funeral procession, a huge one. The mourners wore palace colors overlaid in black.

The deceased was one of the palace honor guard, Richardt *Freiherr* von Keigfeld.

They said he had fallen from his horse and hit his head on the stones. It was such an ironic tragedy. The baron was an excellent horseman.

Caralisa waited for the procession to pass, then hastened on her way.

She took a room at the inn. She had money for it. The *Masque of Hearts* had gone into an extended run and made Caralisa wealthy in her own right.

She found the newspapers of Larissa gloating over her fall from grace and speculating about her broken engagement with the Marquis de St. Florian. Was she holding out for a duke? they asked. Someone ought to tell her that Prince Maximillian was already taken.

Caralisa stopped in town to buy an umbrella. The vendor tried to sell her a parasol, but Caralisa wanted a heavy one, for rain. The man glanced at the blue sky, looked at her queerly. "It's not looking rain," he said.

Caralisa said nothing. She walked down the Rue de Temps carrying her umbrella and wearing round her neck a fine chain from which hung a golden key.

She found the ivy-covered door locked as she had left it, let herself through, and locked the door again on the other side. She buried the key under a clump of moss and set a stone over it, then hiked around the lake to the waterfall.

Mossy slick steps led up the rocks to the falls. Caralisa raised the umbrella and ducked under the falling water.

Inside the rock chamber behind the falls, she shook off the umbrella and left it folded on the floor, then climbed up the winding stairs to the hidden door of the count's room. It hung open the way she had left it when she had fled.

She paused before parting the arras, remembering that this was his bedroom. In trepidation she peered through, saw no one.

She crept inside. The room was the same as she had left it, empty. The bedcovers were still rumpled, the celadon cover on the floor. A pile of ashes with shreds of red velvet lay cold in the hearth. It was all the same, but not the same.

Dried leaves scudded across the rich chinoise carpets. The room showed a careless neglect, as if it had been deserted not for days but for a season. Wild vines curled in the window. Dead twigs and windblown maple keys and bird feathers and milkweed collected in the corners.

The wind still sang the song of a dying swan.

Caralisa tried the doors. That much was not as before. They swung open at a touch.

She wandered room to room. They all showed the same neglect, cluttered with windblown weeds, leaves, and seed husks as if nature had begun to reclaim them.

She broke into a run. She heard panic in her own voice. "My lord? My lord!"

A different sound reached her ears, a crackling. She smelled smoke.

She ran through the crooked corridor, caught sight of the glow of fire up ahead.

She burst into the library.

Low flames guttered in the wide black hearth. And he was there, reclining near the fire, on his side, propped on his elbow, his body curved catlike, with his long legs in black breeches and black boots extended. He wore a full-sleeved white shirt and black waistcoat. His coat and cravat lay tossed over a chair.

He was slow to turn. He did not rise, only leaned back far enough to look over his wide shoulder, too tired and weak to show surprise. She saw a thinner gaunter man, hollows below his high fine cheekbones become deep. The black-feathered mask circled smoky eyes.

He waited for her to explain herself.

She clasped and unclasped her hands in her skirt. "I—I had a dream you were dying."

He shook his head fragilely, then turned back toward the fire. "I am not dying. I wish I were."

She circled to stand next to the hearth so she was not talking at his back. "You killed Baron von Keigfeld."

"You're angry," he said wearily, like a sigh.

She choked out, "No . . . I have difficulty thanking you for killing someone."

Dying tongues of flame reflected in his deep eyes. He spoke into the fire. "Then thank me for saving you."

"Thank you."

Silence fell between them.

Caralisa edged nearer. "Have you nothing better to do than go about rescuing me?"

"I introduced you to that trouble. I am beholden to keep you from its harm. I do what I must. I believe we are quit."

"I broke my engagement to Michaeljohn," she blurted.

"I don't care. Nothing in life interests me anymore. I haven't even strength to be angry with you. What do you want? Take it and get out of my misery."

"Don't you want me here?"

"No. You take up more of my thoughts than I do of yours. I'll not be an afterthought in my own fortress."

"I shan't go," Caralisa declared. "You are going to talk to me. Why did you turn so cruel? You turned from a protector to a tyrannical ogre. You tell me you love me not, then become angry because you say you do. You have been using me. What about *me?*"

He refused to look at her. He frowned into the fire. Some emotion bled into his stoic tone. "My heart is not brave or big. It is not cruel either. It is not strong at all. I keep it within this iron cage for a reason. Breathe on it wrong and I will die."

"Are you dying?"

"No. You may walk out of here without that on your conscience. Just go now. I would rather let you see my face, than my heart."

"I *have* seen your face."

A set of guarded alarm crossed his shoulders. He spoke very low with hushed caution. "When?"

"Now." She crouched beside him at the hearth so that he could do naught but look at her. "This one is you." She touched the black feathers which cloaked his high dramatic cheekbones, his strong flat brow. Then, very carefully, as if reaching to a fanged and cornered beast, soft as a whisper, she leaned in and kissed his cheek. He remained motionless as a stone. She sat back on her heels. "You said you and the swan share a dwelling. I am told my body is a temple. Is yours then a dwelling?"

His silence assented. He did not move, but for his wary eyes which watched her in something like dread.

"Give me your hand, my lord."

He did not move, but let her pick up his hand and pull off a glove to reveal a well-formed hand, manly and strong, the skin very smooth from being always covered. Only the nails were wrong. They were darkened curved talons. They afforded the hands a quality of savage strength.

She enfolded his big hand between her soft white palms, He scarcely dared breathe. Finally he needed to know. "Well?"

She turned his hand over, ran a finger down his palm, turned it over again to touch a dainty fingertip to a dark talon. "Is there more? I don't see what is supposed to be so horrible."

"At the moment, this is it," he said, then as an afterthought, "The other set of nails." He moved a booted foot, like a cat twitching its tail.

Caralisa entertained a strange wish that there were more to it. It was anticlimactic. She had been braced for a ghastly terror and was steeled to accept it no matter what. But it was just him, as he had always been. The mask was that there was no mask. He had hidden in plain sight. And she had become so accustomed to the mask of black feathers, as she might a man's beard, that his face would look quite naked without it, could it have come off.

"And that is all?" she said.

"Swans are not gentle birds," he said. "They do not fare well with domestic fowl. I am a savage man."

"No." Caralisa dismissed him lightly. "It was you. You let me out of your own prison."

He nodded. "That was I."

She smiled suddenly and scolded, "If you wanted to let me out, why didn't you just open the door?"

His gaze dropped from hers, turned to the fire. "I could not face you. I am ashamed of myself. Can you ever forgive?" He could not face her even now.

"There is nothing to forgive. If I cannot understand the wild lashing of a wounded beast blinded by pain, who yet manages to keep its claws from striking me, then turns me loose, the one who hurt it, then I am a hard-hearted creature. If you unlock your heart, I shall unlock mine and never hurt you again."

He paused. A boyish impudent pout stole onto his face with a glimmer of a smile behind his eyes. "You first."

She laughed. "Only if you tell me to whom I am declaring myself, my lord."

"Laertes. I already told you once. My name is not Lancelot. My name is Laertes."

She clasped her hands round his, held his palm to her heart so that he could feel it drumming. She leaned forward. "I love you with all my heart. Take it, ungentle swan. And if you should peck it to pieces, so be it. Do what you will, Laertes, I am yours."

He caught in his breath in a gasplike pain. "O God. There is a God."

In one fluid dramatic motion he stood up. He drew her up to stand with him, then held her as if poised to dance. "When you are ready, madame."

She faltered only a moment. Then she poured out a new song, effortless as a lark but more joyful. Her heart rode up with the sounds' sweet ascension.

They danced by the firelight, growing warmer. Her song became softer, sultrier. Blood heat sizzled. Everything she felt was too much for a single voice to express. He held her closer. The dance slowed. She faltered, too aware of their bodies touching, feeling his heat and hardness through their brushing clothes.

He brought his hand, warm and firm, under her chin, his fingers on her throat and along her jaw. He tilted her face up and bent his head so that his lips were a breath away.

She lost the thread of melody, and his mouth stopped all the notes to drink in a kiss. The song continued without her, a crystal shiver on the vibrant air, with all of nature and the scent of flowers and the crackling of the fire.

Laertes held her head between his hands, his fingers in her luxuriant hair as his lips moved over hers with savoring hunger, and his tongue stole between her teeth, seeking out the sweet textures of her yielding mouth.

They sank to their knees before the hearthfire.

Caralisa basked in his fingertips' hot touch, the light grazing of his nails, as he loosed the ribbons of her bodice and slid her dress from her shoulders to lavish kisses on her creamy skin.

She arched back to present her throat and her bared breasts to him. His mouth surrounded each vulnerable nipple with ravishing warmth. She melted into a delicious languor even as she felt his gathering strength. His muscles bunched and flexed as he stood, sweeping her up into his arms, and he carried her to his bedroom.

He lowered her onto his bed and crouched over her like a magnificent male animal, proud tenderness and urgent desire in his gaze. Moisture gleamed on his parted lips from kissing her, warm and hungry eyes taking in the vision of her in beguiling undress. As she lay on her back, the white rounds of Caralisa's breasts smoothed to the gentlest rise. They rose and fell with her excited breathing. A tremor quivered on her voluptuously full lips, anxious and wanting, her blue eyes fever bright and expectant.

Shyly wanton, she unfastened the buttons of his waistcoat and shirt, and slipped her delicate hands inside to interlace with the crisp dark hair that covered his chest in a handsome spread.

The sight of her and feel of her light tentative touch drove him to distraction. He bent over her and grazed his lips lightly over her full sensuous mouth. She grasped his broad shoulders and pulled him down with her, opening her mouth to recieve his deepest most penetrating kisses, accepting—demanding—the hot intrusion of his tongue. She responded, sliding her own tongue against his sweet invasion, feeling herself flooded with satin fire.

Together they sank beneath a sea of passion so wide and deep it seemed to have no end, a sea to drown gladly in. She was drawn with him under its waves willingly to sensations unknown.

In a moment came the unbearable parting of their bodies as he knelt up to shed his shirt and waistcoat. Almost reverently he undressed her and beheld her in her naked glory, her beautiful graceful limbs, the bright tumble of her red hair, the delicate tufted triangle of darker red round her womanhood. Her hips moved unconsciously in wanting, their movement inflaming and inviting. He pulled off his boots and unlaced his breeches. The masculine nobility of his form was fully revealed, the hard contours of sleek sinew molded in athletic perfection. A savage vestige showed in the talons, but absolutely a man. His manhood stood upright and eager with hard exigency, its head glistening as if weeping from restraint.

He tossed his clothes aside. His black hair brushed his wide shoulders, a forelock kicked over his black mask. A sword scar showed a whiter welt on the tautly knit muscles of his abdomen.

Free of his clothes, he descended on her. She welcomed him in her enfolding arms and legs, glorying in the sensation of naked skin on naked skin the full length of their bodies. The hard sinew of his bare back glided under her palms. She writhed beneath him the more to touch every part of him to every part of her, to feel her soft breasts crushed against his hard manly chest, his damp wiry hair tormenting her hardened nipples. She spread her legs and felt him between her soft thighs. The hard smooth rod of his manhood glided against her and slipped provocatively past the gates of fulfillment.

She moved like a cat against his stroking hands, thrilling to his touch. He kissed her mouth, her face, her shoulders, and buried his face in her hair. She could feel his guttural stirring hot breath on her neck.

Her hips rose up pleading to meet his thrusts as he slid without entering, leaving her in a fiery inferno of want. She reached down to feel iron sinew inside his thigh. She sought and found the shaft which slid against her channel wet with desire. She guided him to her need. With agonizing gentleness he surrendered to their want.

The sky rent open and a veil tore from her soul, and she glimpsed heaven in painful brightness, transported and filled with splendor, ignited from within.

She felt his murmur with his hot breath and movement of his lips against the shell of her ear, "I love you, Caralisa." His ragged voice stole inside and touched the depths of her being.

I am radiant fire. She threw her head back, exultant, caught in the fiery midst of a glowing aureole, joined with him as one, bathed in light and heat and dazzling bliss. She was losing herself, shredding away to become more than she had been. Her spirit soared on wings of angels as her body groaned in luscious seething pleasure and exquisite carnality.

This was what it was to touch all Creation at once, earth and heaven, flesh and spirit, the beast and the divine, he and she. *We are one.*

Vivid perfume of rose and lilac sang in the air, with cedar smoke from the hearth, manly sweat, and sex.

Roaring in her ears was the primitive paean of pounding blood on fire, a great crashing of all the stars of heaven rejoicing at once, and from her throat only the most elemental groans of a woman in the grip of love's most perfect passion—a delirious primeval song.

Her hips ground immodestly against his as she gave herself over to the timeless motion, mounting to an excruciating pinnacle to join the ends of the circle, the base and the glorious, and in a satin moment crash down in a joyous shattering rain of ecstasy, radiating in waves from the core of her being.

His hand caught her head to his chest. He tasted salty with

a damp sheen of exertion. She heard his heart's strong quick hammer and his deep cracking groan.

With a sharp inhalation he coiled his fingers in her hair, his other hand holding her buttocks to his desperate thrusting until a violent shudder sent his transcendent release pulsing within her. She felt his heated flow and convulsive rapture fill her wave on wave. She shut her eyes and heard his deep voice as if coming from within her very soul, "My love. My love."

Sixteen

Caralisa stretched on the fine sheets, a luxurious sated smile on her face. She was alone in the wide bed. She sat up and found Laertes, wearing only his breeches, crouched on one knee by the small hearth. He was putting a log on the fire. She was struck all over again by his raw virility. He was unbearably handsome. Firelight licked the strong definition of the muscles in his back and sides, the molten power in his arms. The ends of his uncombed black hair brushed his bare shoulders. Barefoot, the long curved talons of his toes appeared only slightly strange. They're all beasts, Viola had said. The talons did not startle. A private secret, they were an endearing flaw that proved perfection. There was a vulnerability and trust in the act of having his secrets so casually exposed for her. She gave a resonant shudder of remembered passion, her body still singing from his touch. He turned upon hearing her stir, gave an intimate smile, and spoke low. "Good morning, my sweet."

She gathered a sheet over her bosom and moved to the edge of the wide bed, nearer to him. She felt a twinge, and she winced. She had passed the smallest spot of blood, not even enough to stain the sheet. She had been led to expect torrents. Her brow furled in troublement.

Laertes set down the wood, his expression concerned. "What is it?"

"Honestly, I was a maid," she said emphatically.

"I believe you. And in any case that is very sweet but unnecessary, for I trust I eclipse all past competition."

"Ha!"

"Madame?"

"Yes, I suppose that would be true had I anything to compare, but must you be so overweeningly arrogant about it?"

"Yes. Caralisa, you never have and never shall meet a humble swan."

"Are there more of you?"

"Only a few. We are all half brothers, sisters, and cousins. Children of the swan. We love only the good and the beautiful and not many can love us. Even in ancient times, before the ascendancy of Byzantion, it was never good fortune to be beloved of a god. We all sprang from Leda and the swan."

"*Leda?*" Caralisa's eyes grew perfectly round.

"No, not Leda your lyricist. Your lyricist is one of my kind."

"Oh," said Caralisa with a self-conscious giggle. "That was silly of me."

But then he went on to say, "I meant her grandmother, Leda."

"Grandmother? You mean great-great-great-great-great-great-great-great-grandmother," said Caralisa.

"No. Grandmother."

"But—but that still makes our Leda immeasurably old!"

Laertes amended without excitement, "It is probably measurable, except that we have all lost count. I am older than my cousin Leda."

Doubt and awe in her eyes, Caralisa whispered, "How old are you?"

"I was born during the siege of Troy."

"But that was—!" She did not know when that was. Far in the misty past, it was sometime before written history began.

"Close to three millennia ago, I think," he supplied.

"I am going to faint."

"No, you're not."

Caralisa's cheeks warmed. "My lord," she said hotly, "You are very much a man. If last night did not prove it, then this very much does. How like a man to say, 'By the by, did I not tell you I am immortal?' "

He paused from feeding the fire to rest one arm across his bended knee, a droll thoughtful curve to his mouth. He confessed, "I suppose I have lived with it so long I forgot that it needed mentioning."

She shied a pillow at his head. He caught it. He moved to the foot of the bed and sat on the floor. Caralisa reached down a hand to caress his midnight hair. "I don't understand," she said. "What of heaven and hell if you cannot die?"

"Heaven and hell become rather insignificant. Unless someone kills me, I am not sure I shall ever see either place— unless from time to time heaven bends low and touches the earth." He reached up and touched her face. "For heaven is surely here."

She gazed at him in wonder, breathed, "Where did you come from?"

"It's a long story."

"I am not going anywhere."

He clasped his hands around one knee. Caralisa leaned over the edge, the shining red cascade of her hair trailing over his bare shoulder and down his chest.

He began, "Zeus, king of the gods, came to Leda—your lyricist's grandmother Leda—in the guise of a swan. Actually no one knows if he was king of the gods, but he was a swan and immortal as all swanfolk are. Leda coupled with the swan and produced an egg. From the egg hatched four divinely beautiful children: Castor and Pollux—also called the Gemini twins—and the two girls Clytaemnestra and Helen, who was known as the most beautiful woman in the world.

"Legend says that Clytaemnestra was mortal and Helen was immortal, but we assume Clytaemnestra could have lived forever as well except that she was murdered. Our enchantment shields us from age, not from honed iron.

"Legend does *not* mention how very much the four inherited from the swan, that they could become swans themselves. It took them a while to figure out that it could be done."

"How *is* it done?" said Caralisa.

"For one, it is not to be done without your feet and your feathers." He opened the chest at the foot of the bed and pulled out his familiar black cloak and black riding boots.

She took the cloak in her hands. It felt like wool, cut in the fashion of a modern man's cloak. She shook her head, failing to grasp what he was telling her. "It's just a cloak. What is it? Are you *born* with it?"

"No. Sometime when you are neither child nor man, you wake with these. And because you were hatched from an egg in the first place, you are not overly surprised. And then all those dreams of flight suddenly make sense and you know you've always had wings. With your cloak you can become one of the swans. But not without it. It did not look quite like this at first. Do you know what a chameleon is?"

"Oh please!" Caralisa recoiled. "Do not tell me you are also a lizard!"

He chuckled. "No. I share a small talent with the chameleon is all. To fit in. My cloak has changed slightly over the centuries. Not its color, but its cut. Otherwise I should look rather dated. As it is, I blend in with what other men wear.

"This is a deadly secret I am telling you, Caralisa. I trust you to hold it in faith. And don't think to make me into a normal man by burning it. You would succeed in killing me. It has been tried. But not to me."

She shuddered and returned the cloak into his keeping. "I swear."

"One of the swan's four children, Helen, Queen of Sparta, was carried away by her husband's young Trojan guest Prince

Paris. She had no choice but to go with him. He stole her
cloak. If someone steals your cloak, he has you. Helen went
to Troy, and the Greeks sent a thousand ships in pursuit.
They lay siege to the city for ten years. During it all, Helen
remained as lovely as day one, and it became known that
she was divine.

"During the siege, the Greek hero, wily Odysseus, stole
into Troy disguised as a beggar. Helen recognized the spy at
once but she did not betray him. Under pretense of compas-
sion, she took the unfortunate beggar into her chambers and
gave him a bath. That much is recorded in the *Odyssey*."

"I've read that!" Caralisa chimed in.

"It is the part that Helen told in front of her husband after
the war was over and she was restored to the Spartan throne.
She left part of the story out.

"What she failed to tell her husband was that there was
more communion between Helen and Odysseus than a bath.
And in the morning, Helen was delivered of an egg. She
gave it to Odysseus, who took it out of the city with him.
Soon afterward Odysseus took a ship back to Greece on a
mission of importance. He took the egg with him and, en
route, left it, together with some spoils from plundered cities,
in the sanctuary of Helen's brothers Castor and Pollux, who
were by then revered as divine heroes on the island of
Samothrace. There is a shrine on the island where men come
seeking protection against shipwreck, for we are all magnificent sailors and no one ever drowned under *my* protection. Even today when one swears 'By Jiminy,' he calls upon
my uncles the Gemini.

"The egg hatched on Samothrace, and here I am. At the
time it was common to name a boy child for his father's
father. Odysseus was son of Laertes. So from my paternal
grandfather I have the name. From my maternal grandfather
I have this." He fanned a taloned hand before his feathered
mask. Like Zeus the swan, he was caught halfway between
the bestial and the divine.

Caralisa touched his masked face. "But Helen, Clytaem-nestra, Castor, and Pollux weren't this way."

"And neither are most of their children. Only some of us carry something of the swan with us always. Six of Leda's brothers are perfect and any one of them could be called Adonis. The seventh has a wing that won't change. As a man he wears a cloak over it to hide it. So I suppose I could be worse off than I am. Leda is mute as a swan and as a woman. She has a pretty face so she marries well, but she suffers some flirtation with the stake as well. Associating with en-chanted swans is not always good for your health. Have I frightened you off yet?"

"Are you trying to?"

"I want you to know what you are getting into before I ask you a question."

"What question?"

"I shall get to it. Ask me something else first. What have I not told you?"

"Well," she thought. "I have heard of a fairy tale of seven swans who were seven brothers. But they were under an evil spell. And they had a sister, but in the story the sister was not a swan and it wasn't that she was *unable* to speak, but if she did then she could not break her brothers' en-chantment."

"Oh, yes, the stories do get turned sideways, do they not?" said Laertes. "That tale was woven at a time when Leda would not change into a swan to save her life. It almost cost her, too. She could have flown away, but she did not."

"Why?"

"She was in love, and she would risk anything rather than let her husband see her change shape like a witch. So she locked her cloak away for as long as her husband lived." His voice turned sad. "I will outlive you, my sweet Caralisa. More even than my father, I have been fated to wander. As much as I want to grow old at the side of one beloved. Now that I have found her. One true love. And when it is over,

turn out the light for good. There is something moving behind your eyes. You do not love me."

"No!" she protested then realized what she wanted to say
was, *"Yes!* I do! I . . ." she stammered in confusion. There
was a doubt clawing at her and he had seen it. "Am I going
to . . . What will . . . ? What will our children be like? I
want to carry a baby for nine months. I don't want to wake
up in the morning and . . . I don't want . . ."

"I don't know," he said. "Does anyone? I would hope they
favor you. My mother gave birth to several children in the
way women do. And I have fathered a few children over the
past centuries. My father was a man, and all my children
have been as human as you are and uncommonly beautiful,
if I do say so myself," he noted pridefully. "But there is
another side to that. I tell you it is the hardest thing on this
earth to outlive a child."

"You have married before?"

"No. And my children all called some mortal man 'Father.' "

"Why, you rogue!"

"I have always stayed in the distance. My children always
had a mysterious dark guardian angel lurking nearby. But I
never told them. Can you not understand what a thing of
terror love is for my kind?"

"Are you afraid now?" said Caralisa.

"More than I have ever been." He turned on one knee to
face her. "All my life . . ." He cupped a warm palm round
her face. "I am afraid of a little slip of a girl. I tried to stay
away, but from the moment I saw you, I knew."

She leaned into his hand, gazing at him, seeing all she had
ever wanted. *From the moment I saw you, I knew.* She
reached to him, stopped short of touching, and cried, "Why
didn't I?"

She could feel a fast pulse of fear in his palm as he said,
"Caralisa, love of my life, will you marry me?"

The chamber seemed full of light. A cool breeze danced

through the draperies, scented with flowers and singing with
the sound of bees and the hearthfire's crackle. She hesitated.
"When I am old, will you love me still?"

He held her hand in both of his and vowed, "We shall
walk in the garden, and when you can no longer walk, I shall
bring you roses through that window."

"Can you love an old hag?" she asked worriedly.

"Can you love a big black bird?" he countered.

She wrinkled her nose impishly. "I *adore* big black birds."

"Have a care. In a moment I shall become quite jealous
of myself."

"I shall be careful. You are so charmingly unreasonable
when you are jealous." She gathered in the sheets and
turned on her side. In coquettish challenge she posed her
last question before giving answer. "What is my prettiest
feature?"

His fingertips grazed her blushing cheek, traced under her
firm round little chin, and touched the full lush softness of
her pouting sensual lips. He gazed into her long-lashed wide
eyes of clear hyacinthine blue. The glorious tousled rain of
her lustrous red hair veiled the creamy skin of her lovely
shoulders and spilled over the pillow. Her delicate hands
clutched the sheets to her tender enticing breasts.

He held her face tenderly in his hands and answered, "It
is the squirrel cage behind your blue eyes. Torture me no
more. I need an answer."

She could scarcely find her breath in startled wonder.
"Yes," she said at last. "With all my heart."

Leda was fussing with Caralisa's hair, but Caralisa would
not stand still. She had spent the night alone in the wide bed
without Laertes. It was bad luck for the groom to see the
bride on the morning of their wedding, but she missed him
as she would miss a piece of her own soul.

Caralisa caught sight of a bride in the mirror and for a

moment did not know herself. She gazed, mesmerized. This
was it. This time she knew in her heart it was for real.

She twisted her fingers, fidgeting as Leda tried to fit on
the veil. Caralisa had asked Laertes where he was going to
find a priest to marry them. He answered that he was not
going to.

"But I want Christian vows!" Caralisa had cried.

"And you shall have them," he had said and did not explain
further. That was last night.

Caralisa told her trouble to Leda. Laertes had asked her
to trust him, but she confessed to Leda that did not see how
he was going to pull it off this time, though he had always
given her anything she wished for.

Methodically Leda put down the brush and the hairpins
and the veil, and she beckoned Caralisa to come out with
her to the balcony.

Caralisa lifted her trailing white skirts and passed through
the drapes which Leda held open for her. She stepped out
onto the stone belvedere overlooking the crystal lake.

The water reflected an autumn blaze and brilliant cloudless
sky. Down below she could see the tiny islet where Laertes
had brought her on their first picnic. Now it was being festooned with ribbons and garlands. A great colorful canopy
was erected over many tables, and dinner roasted over a great
firepit.

All the swans in the world had been coming in since the
night before, great snowy birds, their wings cambered for
a long glide over the Heights and down to join their splendid reflections in the water. Caralisa had heard honking in
the middle of the night with the rustle of great wings. The
early arrivals were on the islet making ready for the reception.

Caralisa watched, not comprehending. What had this to
do with having a Christian wedding without a priest?

Leda redirected her gaze, pointing straight down where
men were dragging out of the grotto an ancient ship. It was

long and wide with a single mast. One square painted sail striped gold and rich purple-brown hung braided on a broad yard.

Leda pointed at the ship, then in pantomime, raised her hand in a salute.

"The ship's captain!" said Caralisa.

Leda nodded and, without further ado, pulled Caralisa back inside to fit on her veil.

When the time came, Leda led Caralisa down the rock-hewn stairs to the waterfall. An awning had been arranged to deflect the cascade and leave a narrow dry space through which she could pass.

Down at the water's edge men waited to help her board the ship.

The crusty captain was a stout man, not of the swan folk. He was dressed in deep blue with brass buttons, and sported lately trimmed bushy side whiskers. He welcomed her aboard with a crumbly voice ruined from shouting over gales. He harbored some misgivings over the strange little ship of which he had been given mastery for this day. His crew, who were mortal men, all of them, were also a little wary. They had been told to expect unusual company. The sailors were all wearing amulets of the Gemini.

They received the bride with deference and with no small amount of envy for the groom.

The swans were still arriving, singly and in twos and in spectacular echelons. They skidded down in the water in bright spearheads, then glided, snowy wings billowed like sails, toward the islet where they melted into men in white cloaks and black boots.

At the transformation Caralisa felt comforted to see a sailor cross himself and murmur, "Mother of God!" She was not the only one daunted by this assembly of legends.

The ship was small. On deck were only men enough to

sail her and to conduct the wedding. A sailor sounded a flute
to assemble the wedding party before the captain.

A figure backed in sunlight, moving with familiar grace,
appeared from behind the wide braided sail. When he passed
from out of the face of the sun, Caralisa saw he was dressed
in white, from cravat to sash to breeches. Only his boots
were black. A dashing figure, he looked as if he ought to be
commanding this vessel for his masterful way and for the
respect of the company around him. He took up a position
by the stout bewhiskered captain, his weight on one leg, one
booted foot forward, hands folded loosely before him. His
smile was almost smug. In fact it was smug, as the cat who
ate the canary. His gaze was tender and possessively proud.
At his side attended a beautiful youth with a long white cape
draped self-consciously over his left shoulder as if hiding
something. Caralisa guessed this was the seventh of seven
brothers.

Mute Leda led Caralisa up to face the captain.

The captain's ruined gravelly voice began, "Dearly beloved, we are gathered here today in the sight of God . . ."

Caralisa's vision blurred, happiness leaking out her eyes.
Her flowers quivered in her grasp. A small laughing sob
whimpered in her throat.

She barely heard the captain saying, "Who gives this
woman?"

There was a pause into which Caralisa stammered, "I—I
guess I came of my own accord."

The captain barked, "Then get over here and take his hand."

Caralisa obeyed with a quick side step, releasing one hand
from the deathgrip she had on her bouquet and slipping a
moist palm into Laertes' warm gentle hand. His fingers
closed round hers with a firm touch, skin to skin. He wore
no gloves. She held fast to his hand, which was warm and
steady. She broke into a joyous tearful smile, beaming up at
him. His dramatic face became a misty blur. He gave a tender
glance down and he winked.

They declared their love as the captain bid them. To the line, "Till death us do part," Laertes added, "and I shall love you forever."

The captain, not entirely convinced of the "man" part of it, pronounced them "husband and wife." He closed the book, but noticed something missing from the text. He growled at them, "Well? Kiss her!"

Rising up on tiptoe, Caralisa tossed her flowers back to Leda and circled her arms round Laertes' neck and lost herself in her husband's kiss.

Viola invited her school friends to a late season tea. They sat in the arbor, passing Viola's gurgling baby each to each to be chucked under his chin, cooed at, and dandled.

Laurel had come the farthest. She had been kicked out of school and had started a florist's shop in Paris. Where she got the capital, the others were afraid to ask, and it was more fun to speculate anyway. She came to tea elegantly dressed and smiling secretively as a cat.

Brynna had several offers of marriage. She was in a quandary over which to take. As she never made a decision without support, she consulted the girls. They gave her four different answers, so Brynna wallowed in indecision.

Delia was betrothed and wearing a diamond the size of Montagne. Laurel had brought her a society paper, knowing that Delia, who made a great show of disinterest in public, would want one but would never buy it for herself.

Delia accepted it eagerly. There were two Royal edicts published in the paper. They were not in the gossip column, so Delia almost missed them.

"Listen to this!" she said and recited from the paper: "'The Larissan Heights have been deeded to Caralisa, Countess of Samothrace—'"

"Countess of Samothrace!" Megan cried.

"Is that our Caralisa?" said Brynna.

"Shhh," Laurel hissed to let Delia continue.

" '—on this her wedding day, because they gave her refuge when the city of Larissa sought to commit grievous wrong against her.' "

"That's our Caralisa," said Laurel.

Delia lowered the paper, her mouth dropped open in display of shock. *"Countess* of *Samothrace?"*

Viola smiled, gray eyes sparkling in merriment. "The prince gave her the Sky Cathedral!" She broke into a laugh. "It's what she always wanted!"

"On this her *wedding day?"* said Megan. "I wasn't invited. Were you, Viola?"

Viola produced a creamy sheet of engraved vellum. "I received an announcement. It doesn't say where the ceremony or reception are."

Megan snatched it. Pale-eyed glance clawed over the engraving. "It doesn't say anything. Caralisa Springer and Laertes, Count of Samothrace." She dropped the announcement to her lap. "Laertes. Isn't that the name of the character who killed Hamlet?" She pushed the announcement back at Viola. "And she caught your bouquet at your wedding. Some friend. And you, Laurel, you got yourself kicked out of school on her behalf. Aren't you sorry now?"

"Do I look sorry?" said Laurel, rubies gleaming blood red on her earlobes.

Delia commented distractedly, her nose in the newspaper, "Countess of Samothrace. Have you ever met such a fickle social climber in your life?"

She scanned the second Royal edict, but passed over it because it was of no interest.

It decreed, as of this day, it was now a Crown offense in Montagne, equal in severity with the killing of a man or of a deer, for anyone to kill a swan.

When the feasting was over, the tables were taken away

to make room for dancing. The music was lively. Most of the dances were done in snaking lines.

The musicians played sprightly tunes on a strange collection of instruments. But the first thing they had played, to greet the bride as she had come ashore, was her own "Celebration of Love" from *Masque of Hearts*. Caralisa applauded, laughing and crying at once.

Much later in the evening, when they were lighting the torches against the dark, when the songs were gay and the dancing spirited, someone pointed to the twilight-colored sky and called, "There she is!"

"Herself," someone commented ironically, a kind of gentle irritation in the observation.

"Only six hours late," another said.

"Oh my, she *was* in a hurry, wasn't she."

The swan came gliding in over the cliffs and banked to make a grand sweep of the crystal waters.

The dancing paused and the company assembled to greet *her* arrival.

The graceful snowy swan came ashore and transformed in a blurred shimmer, too smoothly for the eye to follow, into a woman of such extraordinary beauty that Caralisa wanted to burn away to cinder and never be seen again. The newcomer was arrayed in a glorious white dress of exotic design. The guests stepped politely from her path, smiling hello with affectionate veneration.

The mortal sailors of the ship turned to little puddles in her wake, tongues hanging out, eyes rolling loose across the ground.

Her black hair hung below her waist and brushed at her swaying hips as she walked. Her walk was a song. Her dress was from another time, with a white tiered bell-like skirt; its bodice, which cinched at her tiny waist, fit like a skin but left her magnificent breasts bare. They were impossibly perfect round white spheres, their nipples alluring red. The swan folk were unimpressed. The sailors were melting away, leaving only gaping mouths.

The lady was regal and sensual, soft, moving with controlled swan grace. Her eyes of deepest brown were beguiling.

She connected gazes with Laertes and he *ran* to her. She seized his face in her hands and covered it with kisses, skin, feathers, all.

At that, Caralisa decided that she was dying and it was all right because no one would notice.

Laertes greeted the swan queen with such warmth that Caralisa wanted to run and hide.

Then Laertes turned, reached a hand back to her, and called jubilantly, "Caralisa!"

She advanced reluctantly. He still had an arm around the swan queen's waist when he took Caralisa's hand in his. "Caralisa," he said brightly. "This is my mother, Helen."

Caralisa was struck dumb. She choked and stared into the face that had launched a thousand ships.

Helen's white hands surrounded Caralisa's face and she kissed both her cheeks. "Hello, sweet child. What a darling girl." She stroked the red cascade of Caralisa's silken hair with a white hand. "Are you enchanted, child?"

"At the moment I think so, milady," Caralisa blurted.

Helen turned to her son and caressed his black mask with the back of a white hand. "So this is not a face only a mother could love."

"No, milady," Caralisa said assuredly.

Helen begged a moment's pardon. She linked arms with her son and led him aside for a private counsel. She scolded, "Did I not warn you not to fall in love with a pretty face? Tomorrow she will be as changed as an autumn leaf."

He smiled ruefully. He was blissfully stuck. "I love *her,* Mother."

"My son, my son," Helen lamented, a cry in her soft voice. "You are doomed to a broken heart."

"Yes, that is inevitable, no matter what I do now. But today and all the days intervening, I am the happiest man in the world."

"Then go to her while it is still today." Helen disengaged her linked arm and restored him forthwith to his bride. She said to Caralisa, "So there is a way to snare a swan without stealing his cloak, is there? Be good to my son."

The torches burned brightly against the darkling sky. Helen saw her son and his bride to the boat. The couple boarded and the sailors pushed off. The wind was quiet, and the painted sail hung slack over its pretty reflection in the night-colored water. The men took up the oars and sent a gentle rippling behind them as they tugged their way across the glassy lake to the grotto.

Sounds of dancing and music diminished as the rushing of the waterfall hove nearer. The distant rejoicing reechoed off the sheltering cliff walls on all sides with the high thin singing of cicadas in the forested slopes.

Laertes helped Caralisa ashore. He lifted her up and carried her up the steps to the waterfall. He ducked under the awning. Once they were safely inside, the awning fell away with a tug of a cord, shutting the world out with the closing of the watery door.

Sad, doting gaze of beguiling eyes followed them and stayed upon the curtain of water that shielded the way the lovers had gone.

A cousin came to Helen's side, imploring, "You cannot leave it this way. She will die."

Helen's exquisite profile remained smooth and cool as marble. "And so do they all." Her dulcet voice sounded far away. "What would you have me do?"

Her kinsman sputtered without knowing what to ask for. "Give her wings!"

"She has a winged soul," said Helen.

"You know what I mean. Her. The woman. The one your son would spend the rest of his life with."

"And how shall I accomplish this feat?"

"I don't know," he said in desperation. "But may not one mortal born live forever?"

"I have heard the same legends you have," she said faintly.

"Legends? Helen, *we* are legends."

"Just so," she murmured.

"Just so and no more? A love like this comes once in an eternal lifetime."

Long lashes swept low. "This is what I fear. I would she were not so pretty. I wish he were not so in love."

"But he is. You could just watch it end?"

"I could not bear for my son to be so unhappy."

"There is a way!" he grasped at the hint of possibility.

She did not argue, and her cousin insisted, certain of it this time, "There is a way."

"Perhaps." Helen closed her eyes, secretive as a sphinx, to signal she would say no more, a promise in her ageless smile.

She listened to the falling water.

Laertes carried his bride up the stairs to his room—their room—and set her on her feet. "Countess, you are home."

She huddled close to him, shivering. "My home is cold."

"In a moment, madame." He removed his white suit coat and set it round her shoulders. He went to rekindle the fire in the bedroom hearth.

Caralisa hugged the coat around her and stepped out on the balcony overlooking the lake.

A halo of stars had burned into the night sky. Laertes joined her at the rail, and she drew close to him, sharing his warmth in the evening chill.

A raucous raising of voices and metallic clashing arose from the islet along with a strident trumpeting of swans.

Laertes rolled his eyes. "Your in-laws," he said wryly.

"What are they *doing?*" said Caralisa.

"Scaring away bad luck."

"I think they've done it," she said, still in shock.

The world had turned upside-down—and was suddenly as it should be. She had been living topsy-turvy until now. Abruptly set aright, she staggered from the suddenness, but knew in her heart that all was well at last—like crashing through the looking glass and finding that all she had thought was illusion was real and what she had thought reality was a shallow image.

Laertes guided her back inside, where it was growing warm. He parted from her to add fuel to the fire. When it was leaping high and hot, he stood and turned, his striking masculine form outlined in flame. His eyes of twilight storm blue beheld her with profound desire. He extended his hand. She went to him, flowing into his arms' strong embrace as if it was the most natural thing in the world.

He kissed the tears he found on her cheeks. They kept flowing in heated streams. He gave a small questioning murmur. "Can I have made you sad?"

"I'm not," she sniffled. "I have never been so happy. But you."

"What of me?" he asked, baffled.

"This must seem like nothing," she cried. "It is only a moment for you."

"It is only," he said before he stopped all her doubts and protestations with a lingering kiss, "the best part of forever."

**If you liked this book, be sure to look for others
in the *Denise Little Presents* line:**

Available wherever paperbacks are sold, or order direct from the Publisher. Send cover price plus 50¢ per copy for mailing and handling to Penguin USA, P.O. Box 999, c/o Dept. 17109, Bergenfield, NJ 07621. Residents of New York and Tennessee must include sales tax. DO NOT SEND CASH.

*R*OMANCE YOU'LL
ALWAYS REMEMBER...

A NAME YOU'LL
NEVER FORGET!

Receive
$2 REBATE
With the purchase of any two
*D*ENISE *L*ITTLE *P*RESENTS
Romances

To receive your rebate, enclose:
- ✦ Original cash register receipts with book prices circled
- ✦ This certificate with information printed
- ✦ ISBN numbers filled in from book covers

Mail to: DLP Rebate, P.O. Box 1092
         Grand Rapids, MN 55745-1092

Name_____

Address_____

City_____State_____Zip_____

Telephone number (   )_____(OPTIONAL)

COMPLETE ISBN NUMBERS:

0-7860-_____0-7860-_____

This certificate must accompany your request. No duplicates accepted. Void where prohibited, taxed or restricted. Offer available to U.S. & Canadian residents only. Allow 6 weeks for mailing of your refund payable in U.S. funds.

OFFER EXPIRES 5/30/96

PUT SOME FANTASY IN YOUR LIFE—
FANTASTIC ROMANCES FROM PINNACLE

TIME STORM   (728, $4.99)
by Rosalyn Alsobrook

Modern-day Pennsylvanian physician JoAnn Griffin only believed what
she could feel with her five senses. But when, during a freak storm, a
blinding flash of lightning sent her back in time to 1889, JoAnn realized
she had somehow crossed the threshold into another century and was
now gazing into the smoldering eyes of a startlingly handsome stranger.
JoAnn had stumbled through a rip in time . . . and into a love affair so
intense, it carried her to a point of no return!

SEA TREASURE   (790, $4.50)
by Johanna Hailey

When Michael, a dashing sea captain, is rescued from drowning by a
beautiful sea siren—he does not know yet that she's actually a mermaid.
But her breathtaking beauty stirred irresistible yearnings in Michael.
And soon fate would drive them across the treacherous Caribbean, tossing them on surging tides of passion that transcended two worlds!

ONCE UPON FOREVER   (883, $4.99)
by Becky Lee Weyrich

A moonstone necklace and a mysterious diary written over a century
ago were Clair Summerland's only clued to her true identity. Two men
loved her— one, a dashing civil war hero . . . the other, a daring jet
pilot. Now Clair must risk her past and future for a passion that spans
two worlds—and a love that is stronger than time itself.

SHADOWS IN TIME   (892, $4.50)
by Cherlyn Jac

Driving through the sultry New Orleans night, one moment Tori's car
spins our of control; the next she is in a horse-drawn carriage with the
handsomest man she has ever seen—who calls her wife—but whose
eyes blaze with fury. Sent back in time one hundred years, Tori is falling
in love with the man she is apparently trying to kill. Now she must race
against time to change the tragic past and claim her future with the man
she will love through all eternity!

*Available wherever paperbacks are sold, or order direct from the
Publisher. Send cover price plus 50¢ per copy for mailing and
handling to Penguin USA, P.O. Box 999, c/o Dept. 17109, Bergenfield, NJ 07621. Residents of New York and Tennessee must
include sales tax. DO NOT SEND CASH.*

DENISE LITTLE PRESENTS
ROMANCES THAT YOU'LL WANT TO READ
OVER AND OVER AGAIN!

LAWLESS   (0017, $4.99)
by Alexandra Thorne
Determined to save her ranch, Caitlan must confront former lover Co-
manche Killian. But the minute they lock eyes, she longs for his kiss.
Frustrated by her feelings, she exchanges hard-hitting words with the
rugged foreman; but underneath the anger lie two hearts in need of
love. Beset by crooked Texas bankers, dishonest politicians, and greedy
Japanese bankers, they fight for their heritage and each other.

DANGEROUS ILLUSIONS   (0018, $4.99)
by Amanda Scott
After the bloody battle of Waterloo, Lord Gideon Deverill visits Lady
Daintry Tarrett to break the news of the death of her fiance. His duty
to his friend becomes a pleasure when lovely Lady Daintry turns to
him for comfort.

TO SPITE THE DEVIL   (0030, $4.99)
by Paula Jonas
Patience Hendley is having it rough. Her English nobleman husband
has abandoned her after one month of marriage. Her father is a Tory,
her brother is a patriot, and her handsome bondservant Tom, an out-
right rebel! And now she is torn between her loyalist upbringing and
the revolution sweeping the American colonies. Her only salvation is
the forbidden love that she shares with Tom, which frees her from the
shackles of the past!

GLORY   (0031, $4.99)
by Anna Hudson
When Faith, a beautiful "country mouse", goes to St. Louis to claim
her inheritance, she comes face to face with the Seatons, a wealthy
big city family. As Faith tries to turn these stuffed shirts around, the
Seatons are trying to change her as well. Young Jason Seaton is sure
he can civilize Faith, who is a threat to the family fortune. Then after
many hilarious misunderstandings Jason and Faith fall madly in love,
and she manages to thaw even the stuffiest Seaton!

*Available wherever paperbacks are sold, or order direct from the
Publisher. Send cover price plus 50¢ per copy for mailing and
handling to Penguin USA, P.O. Box 999, c/o Dept. 17109, Bergenfield, NJ 07621. Residents of New York and Tennessee must
include sales tax. DO NOT SEND CASH.*

HISTORICAL ROMANCE FROM PINNACLE BOOKS

LOVE'S RAGING TIDE   (381, $4.50)
by Patricia Matthews

Melissa stood on the veranda and looked over the sweeping acres of Great Oaks that had been her family's home for two generations, and her eyes burned with anger and humiliation. Today her home would go beneath the auctioneer's hammer and be lost to her forever. Two men eagerly awaited the auction: Simon Crouse and Luke Devereaux. Both would try to have her, but they would have to contend with the anger and pride of girl turned woman . . .

CASTLE OF DREAMS   (334, $4.50)
by Flora M. Speer

Meredith would never forget the moment she first saw the baron of Afoncaer, with his armor glistening and blue eyes shining honest and true. Though she knew she should hate this Norman intruder, she could only admire the lean strength of his body, the golden hue of his face. And the innocent Welsh maiden realized that she had lost her heart to one she could only call enemy.

LOVE'S DARING DREAM   (372, $4.50)
by Patricia Matthews

Maggie's escape from the poverty of her family's bleak existence gives fire to her dream of happiness in the arms of a true, loving man. But the men she encounters on her tempestuous journey are men of wealth, greed, and lust. To survive in their world she must control her newly awakened desires, as her beautiful body threatens to betray her at every turn.

Available wherever paperbacks are sold, or order direct from the Publisher. Send cover price plus 50¢ per copy for mailing and handling to Penguin USA, P.O. Box 999, c/o Dept. 17109, Bergenfield, NJ 07621. Residents of New York and Tennessee must include sales tax. DO NOT SEND CASH.